# PRAISE FOR
# *STAY AWAY FROM HIM*

"*Stay Away from Him* had me hooked from the first line. The characters are complex in a way that makes it impossible to tell whom to trust."

—Tasha Coryell, author of *Love Letters to a Serial Killer*

"DeYoung masterfully balances narrative tension with razor-sharp insight into the dark corners of the human mind. This is suspense at its most chilling—and most unforgettable."

—Amy Pease, author of *Northwoods*

"I couldn't put this book down! Fast-paced and hauntingly tense, this book will linger with you long after the final page."

—Jaima Fixsen, author of *The Specimen*

# PRAISE FOR *THE DAY*
# *HE NEVER CAME HOME*

"A wonderfully compelling and wildly intelligent exploration of moral corruption. The fateful story of John and Regan Peters is a powerful, cautionary thriller—a reminder that the road to hell is, indeed, a slippery slope. And DeYoung does a fine job of mapping the way."

—William Kent Krueger, *New York Times* bestselling author

"Surprising, smart, and wonderfully original, this page-turner of a thriller is completely entertaining."

—Hank Phillippi Ryan, *USA Today* bestselling author of *One Wrong Word*

"Brimming with suspense and secrets, this top-notch thriller asks vital questions about identity, marriage, and the stories we tell ourselves. Perfect for mystery-loving book clubs!"

—Mindy Mejia, *USA Today* bestselling author of *To Catch a Storm* and *Everything You Want Me to Be*

"DeYoung writes with a smart, calculated urgency that makes the pages fly by. The perfect summer thriller to keep readers on the edge of their seat."

—Nicole Baart, bestselling author of *Everything We Didn't Say*

"The real deal. Andrew DeYoung sets up his characters with a tactful grit that skillfully mirrors real life, even as situations careen out of control."

—Timothy Lane, author of *The Neighbors We Want*

# Stay Away From Him

## ANDREW DEYOUNG

Poisoned Pen
PRESS

Copyright © 2025 by Andrew DeYoung
Cover and internal design © 2025 by Sourcebooks
Cover design by Ploy Siripant
Cover images © Victoria Hunter/Arcangel, Minerva Studio/Shutterstock

Published by Poisoned Pen Press, an imprint of Sourcebooks
P.O. Box 4410, Naperville, Illinois 60567-4410
(630) 961-3900
sourcebooks.com

Cataloging-in-Publication Data is on file with the Library of Congress.

Printed and bound in the United States of America.
LSC 10 9 8 7 6 5 4 3 2 1

# CHAPTER 1

No one bothered telling Melissa that Thomas Danver was an accused murderer. Not until she'd already spent a whole evening flirting with him—bumping elbows, brushing hands, exchanging glances, even giving him her number before they parted at the end of the dinner party. The other guests that evening were all friends of Thomas's, people who'd always believed in his innocence, and perhaps that was why they didn't warn her about who she was talking to: because they thought there was no reason to.

No reason to think Melissa might be in danger.

She'd first noticed him across the room during cocktails. Thomas looked like a movie star from an earlier age: square-jawed, broad-chested, salt-and-pepper hair, piercing gray-blue eyes. They were both stuck in separate conversations, cocktails in hand, but Melissa found herself taking furtive glances at him in between bits of small talk—and then she caught him looking back. Or perhaps *he* was the one who'd caught *her* looking. When he finally peeled away from the person he was talking to and began to cross the room toward her, Melissa's heart leapt in her chest. She fumbled through an awkward apology to the older couple she'd been chatting with, then turned just in time to meet Thomas's gaze.

"It's *you*," he said, as though he knew her already.

Melissa laughed. "Is it?"

"Yes," he said. "The person everyone wants to meet."

"Oh really? Are they talking about me?"

She made a show of glancing around the room, playing along—and was surprised to find that the other guests *did* seem to be stealing glances at her, talking low behind their hands.

"Let me guess," Melissa said, returning her gaze to Thomas. "The sad divorceé living in Lawrence and Toby's basement. Hiding out, fleeing from her evil ex-husband. Is that who I am to everyone here?"

He shook his head. "That's not what I heard."

"What, then?"

"The mysterious, beautiful woman who just moved into the neighborhood."

Melissa shot him a suspicious look. "Liar. That's not what they're saying."

He made a comically confused face. "They aren't? Well, they should."

Melissa was certain that no one had ever thought her *mysterious*, and it had been ages since anyone had called her *beautiful*. Her ex-husband never did—not at the end. "No one would ever describe me that way," she said.

"I would," Thomas said without hesitating. "I *will*. The beautiful woman I met at a dinner party. But, tragically, I didn't get her name."

"Ah," Melissa said. "A Cinderella story. How will you find me tomorrow? A glass slipper?"

"What about this cocktail glass?" he asked, reaching out, touching her—cradling the wrist holding the frosted coupe, studying her fingers wrapped around its stem with wonder, as though he'd never seen a hand before. "It fits you so perfectly. Like it was made for you. I think I could find you just by the way you hold a martini."

"No need for that," Melissa said, pulling her hand back. The feel of his fingers on her wrist lingered. "You can call off the search. My name's Melissa."

"Melissa," he repeated, looking her in the eye and holding her gaze. "I'm Thomas. Thomas Danver."

He paused after finally giving her his name, as though Melissa should know it—but she didn't. Melissa was new to town. She hadn't watched the Twin Cities news three years ago, when Rose Danver went missing, and "Thomas Danver" became a household name. She'd never debated the evidence against him with friends, never took a stance on his guilt or innocence.

At that moment she knew nothing about him at all—nothing aside from the fact that he was one of the most attractive men she'd ever spoken to, and that he seemed to be interested in her.

"It's a pleasure to meet you, Thomas Danver."

# TRANSCRIPT OF RECORDING

*[Exhibit A in the matter of Ramsey County v. Thomas Danver: transcripts taken from recordings of therapy sessions between Thomas Danver and Amelia Harkness, Danver's therapist. The sessions took place over a period of three months following Rose Danver's disappearance.]*

**Thomas:** Wait, are you recording this?

**Amelia:** Excuse me?

**Thomas:** It looked like you were just setting up a recorder in that drawer.

**Amelia:** No, just putting my phone away. You have my undivided attention.

**Thomas:** Because you know, with what's happening in my life right now—the investigation, the news vans parked outside my house… If a recording got out, leaked to the press—

**Amelia:** I already told you, Thomas. I'm not recording. Besides, I've got more reason than you to keep this a secret.

**Thomas:** Why?

**Amelia:** We've talked about this. It's unethical for a therapist to treat someone they've had a prior relationship with. It clouds my judgment. I could lose my license. My reputation.

**Thomas:** There's no law against me talking to a friend about my problems, though. Getting emotional support. Isn't that supposed to be a good thing? It's not my fault that you just happen to be a brilliant psychiatrist.

**Amelia:** I'm not sure others would see it that way.

**Thomas:** I'm sorry. I know it makes you uncomfortable. I just—I need help, Amelia. And I couldn't imagine going to someone else, to walk into a room with some stranger and tell them about my problems. Not with my face plastered all over the news. Who could be objective? What therapist would even agree to see me, with everything that's being said about me?

**Amelia:** I understand. I do. This is an extreme circumstance. That's why I agreed to these…these meetings.

**Thomas:** Besides, I don't see how you have *more* to lose than me. I'm accused of murder. I could go to jail.

**Amelia:** But I thought you didn't have anything to hide. Right? Nothing to say in here that could help the case against you. Unless you persuaded me to do this because you wanted to confess to someone.

[pause]

**Amelia:** Thomas? That was a joke.

**Thomas:** I'm not laughing. I don't have anything to confess. You know that.

**Amelia:** Maybe we should start there, actually. Since that seems to have struck a nerve. You're telling me—

**Thomas:** Amelia, please. You know me. We've been friends since college.

**Amelia:** Still, I think it would be good for you to say it out loud. To say it in here, with nothing to gain or lose.

**Thomas:** I'm not saying it.

**Amelia:** Why not? Wouldn't it feel *good* to say it without cameras, without reporters, without police, without lawyers—just you and me, in the privacy of these four walls?

[pause]

**Thomas:** Not really.

**Amelia:** No? Why not?

**Thomas:** Because saying it is just a reminder that I *have* to say it. That my wife is dead. And that half the people in this town think I killed her.

**Amelia:** *Presumed.*

**Thomas:** What?

**Amelia:** You just said Rose is dead. But she's only *presumed* dead.

[pause]

**Thomas:** I think we both know she's dead.

**Amelia:** Do we? She's missing, from what I know. The police think she's dead—obviously they do, otherwise they wouldn't be charging you with killing her. But do we really know it's true? It's interesting to hear you say she's dead, with so much certainty in your voice. *How* do you know?

[pause]

**Amelia:** Thomas?

**Thomas:** I just know. I can feel it.

**Amelia:** That brings us back to the original question, I suppose. If you *know* Rose is dead, someone might be tempted to wonder—someone who doesn't know you as well as I do, maybe, but still—to wonder whether you, you…

**Thomas:** You're really going to make me say it, aren't you?

**Amelia:** I think it's important. For what we're doing here. To establish, from the outset.

**Thomas:** I didn't kill my wife.

# CHAPTER 2

Melissa and Thomas ended up sitting next to each other at dinner, pulling their chairs close at the far end of the table. Their elbows bumped together as they ate, but neither made any move to scoot their chairs away from each other.

"I feel a little bit like we're in the kids' section down here," Thomas said low in Melissa's ear, close enough that she could feel the warm whisper of his breath on her neck.

She glanced up the length of the long table through the flicker of candlelight, Lawrence and Toby presiding on the other end, pouring wine and leading conversation. The other guests seemed to be talking local politics—Melissa caught a murmur about something being "a public safety issue, really"—and rather than trying to figure out what dull thing they were discussing, she turned back to Thomas, her shoulder tilted up to partially obscure a coy smile.

"I'm sorry," she said. "You wish you were more a part of the grown-up conversation?"

"No, the opposite. I always liked sitting at the kids' table, myself. That's where all the fun is."

"Now I'm feeling some pressure," Melissa said.

"Pressure?"

"To be fun."

"Don't worry," Thomas said. "I'm already having fun. I wouldn't have sat by you if I wasn't."

His hand crossed over to lightly squeeze her forearm in reassurance. She felt the warmth even after he let go.

"So what shall we talk about?" Melissa asked. "What's the conversation at the kids' table?"

"Toys," Thomas said. "Play. Schemes."

"Schemes," Melissa said. "That one. I like that."

"What do you have in mind?"

"You're the one who brought it up. I was hoping you'd have an idea."

"Sneak away?" Thomas suggested. "Run off to the lake? Have a dip?"

Melissa's eyes drifted to the window, where the small lake near Lawrence and Toby's house was a black void in the darkness.

"A dip? I'm not dressed for it. Neither are you."

Thomas nudged her with his elbow, and she could tell it was on purpose this time. "Why should that stop us?"

Melissa giggled—actually *giggled*—as she realized what he was suggesting: skinny-dipping. It was a joke, of course, Thomas playacting the part of an irresponsible teen flirting with the girl next door at the kids' table as the parents talked about more serious adult topics. At least, Melissa *thought* he was playing around. She was scouring her mind for something to say in return when the conversation at the other end of the table intruded again and pulled her attention away.

"I'm afraid to go for a walk with that beast stalking around," said an older woman sitting in the middle of the table. "You know it actually ate our neighbors' dog and left the carcass in their backyard?"

Melissa gulped and set down her fork as the conversation continued, those around the table nodding in sympathetic agreement. She leaned toward Thomas.

"What are they talking about?"

"Oh, just the legendary local coyote," Thomas said, a trace of a smirk in his voice. "Menace to pets and hikers alike for the past year or so."

"*Here?* In the city?"

Thomas shrugged. "Well, the suburbs. And in case you haven't noticed, there's as much nature here as there is developed land."

Melissa accepted the correction with a small nod. Thomas was right. The lake was right there, past the backyard, and Lawrence and Toby's property also adjoined a large wooded area, full of ancient creaking ashes and oaks whose leaves fluttered black against the moonlit night sky. Melissa still didn't know her way around the neighborhood too well, but her understanding was that the Twin Cities' north suburbs alone boasted a handful more lakes, dozens of parks with haphazardly connected trails, and nature centers set between housing subdivisions. Perhaps it wasn't so odd to imagine a coyote threading stealthily between ranch homes, haunting the edges of strip malls, lurking in ditches by freeways.

"It's a little overblown, if you ask me," Thomas said. "People here are so fascinated with the coyote, you'd think we had a serial killer."

"Sounds to me like they're scared of it," Melissa said.

"They're just bored," Thomas said, then turned to someone at Melissa's left, a beautiful redheaded woman dressed all in black, her eyes hidden behind chunky-framed glasses whose lenses caught the yellow glow of the candles. "What do you think, Amelia? Do you have a diagnosis?"

The woman, who until that moment had made no effort to speak to Melissa or Thomas, turned and flashed a wry smile.

"Classic displacement," she murmured, low enough for only them to hear. "Fear of the other, fear of violence, of chaos and social decay—all laid onto the shoulders of a single wild and possibly imaginary canine that's only looking for an occasional meal."

Thomas chortled. "Amelia's a psychiatrist," he explained to Melissa. "And a *savage* judge of character, as you can see."

"*Savage?* Thomas, I'm hurt. You know my purpose is always therapeutic."

"Right. That's why I stopped seeing you. Because you were a little too...*therapeutic.*"

The woman shook her head. "You're terrible," she said, then offered a hand to Melissa over the half-empty plates. "Amelia Harkness."

Melissa accepted the handshake and said her own name, feeling a little lightheaded. Maybe it was the wine on top of the pre-dinner cocktail—but she was also having more than a little trouble keeping up with everything that had just passed between Thomas and Amelia. She felt as though she'd stepped into the middle of something, some complicated dance, that had been going on for a while and had very little to do with her. It seemed as though their words contained secret messages, perhaps a jab or two, an attack and a parry. She couldn't begin to puzzle through it all, but her thoughts snagged on the question of what Thomas had meant when he said *That's why I stopped seeing you.* It was the *seeing you* part that made her pause. Romantically? Or as a psychiatrist?

"I hear you're new to the area," Amelia said to Melissa. "How are you liking it?"

"Oh, fine," Melissa said. "I didn't know anything about a coyote, though. And what was that you were saying about...violence and... and decay?"

Amelia waved her hand. "Oh, Thomas was right—I was just being bad. This is a safe neighborhood."

"Mostly," Thomas said.

"Well, of course, there's *some* crime here, just like anywhere. A recent rash of vandalism—most people think it's kids, teenagers. The usual amount of drug use that happens behind closed doors in affluent communities. Alcoholism, instances of domestic abuse. We're not immune from the problems that happen in any community."

"You're forgetting the big one," Thomas said. "Three years ago? Remember?"

Amelia's mouth tensed, her lips going flat and pale. Then her face softened, her skin wrinkling at the temples. Melissa still couldn't see the other woman's eyes very well behind her glasses, but she felt certain in that moment that there must be sadness in them.

"Oh, Thomas," Amelia said, an ache in her voice. "I'm so sorry."

"What is it?" Melissa asked. She was getting that dizzy feeling again—and not just from the speed at which the night had devolved from harmless flirting to discussing wild predators and local crimes. There was also, just then, the confusion and vague embarrassment of wandering into something she didn't understand, of being the only person who did not have a critical piece of information that the others in the conversation seemed to possess. What were Thomas and Amelia talking about? What had Amelia forgotten—and why was she apologizing to Thomas for it?

Melissa was considering whether to press them on these questions or let the moment pass, when she sensed some movement on the other side of the dining room. Behind Lawrence and Toby at the head of the table, someone stood on the landing at the top of the stairs that led to her basement apartment. It was Bradley, Melissa's five-year-old son, a soft blanket wrapped around his shoulders and his hair mussed up from sleep.

"Shit," Melissa muttered, nudging her chair back. "Thomas, Amelia—I'm really sorry. I have to get this."

She felt everyone's eyes follow her as she walked to Bradley.

"Nothing to see here, folks," she said as she rushed to intercept her son. "Just a bedtime refugee."

A bit of polite laughter bubbled up from the table, and even though she didn't want to feel embarrassed, Melissa's cheeks flamed. The sight of Bradley's pajamas and bedhead felt like a crack in the glamour of the dinner party, a shard of family messiness intruding into the classy ambience Lawrence and Toby, Melissa's hosts and landlords, were trying to strike for the evening.

"Mom, I can't sleep," Bradley whimpered when she reached him.

"It's okay, bud. Let's get you downstairs." Melissa put her hand on the boy's back, between his shoulder blades, and began to guide him toward the steps. She glanced back to silently mouth *I'm sorry* to Lawrence. He shook his head and gave her a dismissive downward wave—*no big deal*. In that same moment, Melissa caught sight of Thomas on the other end of the table, who actually looked sad—no, *bereft*—to see her go.

Then they were down the steps, Bradley and Melissa, away from the chatter of the dinner party and into the quiet of the apartment they'd been living in for the past month, ever since moving to Minnesota. It was a nicer space than the words "basement apartment" might suggest. There was a big main room for the kitchen, dining, and living room, and because Lawrence and Toby's house was built into a hill, they had a walkout to the back, a little patio where Melissa took her coffee in the morning. Past the edge of the yard was the clutch of trees and woods on one side, the lake on the other. The bathroom and bedrooms were down the hall, but Bradley and Melissa stopped in the living room. Melissa sunk to a knee to look her son in the eye.

"Hey, bud," she said. "So what's going on? It's late."

"I want to sleep," Bradley said. "I do. But my body won't let me calm down."

"Hmm. Your body, huh?"

Bradley nodded. He and Melissa talked about *bodies* a lot: what they wanted, how they were feeling, how to trust them, when it was okay for others to touch them and when it wasn't. It was all the talk in preschool and kids' books, and Bradley had picked up on it as a way to get what he wanted, claiming that his body wanted ice cream instead of broccoli or, as he was now, that his body didn't like bedtime.

"Yeah. My body won't let me calm down."

At the top of the stairs, the door clicked open. Thomas poked his head in, looking timid about intruding.

"Hey," he said. "Sorry, I hope this is okay. I just thought, maybe I could...?"

Melissa glanced at her son, checking his reaction. He was shy around new people, especially men, for reasons having to do with her ex-husband that she preferred not to think about. But she was surprised now to see that Bradley was responding well to the sight of Thomas, looking at him with curiosity rather than fear.

"Come on down, Thomas," Melissa said, and his heavy footsteps creaked down the stairs.

"Hey, big guy," Thomas said, walking toward Bradley and sinking to a knee, getting on the boy's level with Melissa. "My name is Thomas. I'm a friend of your mom's. A new friend. What's your name?"

"Bradley," he said. "I'm five."

"*Five*," Thomas said, widening his eyes. "Wow. That's big. Hey, are the grown-ups being too loud up there?"

Bradley nodded. "Yeah," he said, the trace of a whine in his voice. "I can hear voices. And now my body won't calm down."

"Oh, man," Thomas said. "Bodies will do that sometime. I know exactly what that's like."

Something welled up in Melissa, and for a second, she felt like she was about to cry. It had been so long since she'd seen a man be gentle with her son. Her ex-husband wasn't physically abusive, but he could be cruel with his words. He was, Melissa had come to understand, a deeply unhappy man, and when he was upset about something, he wasn't above yelling at Bradley to make himself feel better. In a situation like the one they were in now, Melissa's ex would've told Bradley to shut the hell up and go the fuck to sleep. Melissa had wanted so badly for him to be a good father, for Bradley to *have* a good father, that on some days it was almost a physical ache. Now, seeing a man treat her son in exactly the way he deserved to be treated brought an ache of a different kind.

"Are you maybe a little scared to be downstairs all alone?" Thomas asked.

"A little," Bradley admitted. "Mom says I'm brave. But it's hard sometimes, when it's dark out."

"You *are* brave," Thomas said. "I can tell. But even brave guys need help sometimes. What if we put you back to bed, but your mom and I stayed in the next room for a little bit, until you got to sleep? Would that help?"

Bradley made an exaggerated nod, his eyes huge, his soft, round face so open and vulnerable that Melissa felt the urge to freeze the moment in amber, to remember him forever as he was just then.

"Where's your bed?" Thomas asked.

"Down the hall," Bradley said. "It's a race car."

"A race car!" Thomas said, exaggerating his voice in that way people do with kids, but not so much that Bradley would think he was being made fun of. "That's cool! Can you show me?"

Bradley marched down the hall proudly, with Thomas and Melissa following.

Bradley's room was dark but for a little lamp on the bedside table that cast spots of colored light in the shape of stars and moons and spaceships across the walls and ceiling. Up against the wall was the race car bed, a gift Melissa couldn't afford but bought Bradley anyway, to ease the transition to a new bedroom, a new city, a new life. Thomas lingered by the door while Melissa and Bradley walked in. The boy jumped up onto the bed and pulled the covers up to his chin. Melissa sat on the edge of the bed to smooth down the blankets around her son's body, then gave him a kiss on the forehead.

"Sleep now, okay?"

"You'll stay down here? You're not going back upstairs?"

Melissa nodded. "Just down the hall. You're safe here. Okay?"

"Okay. Good night, Mama. Good night, Thomas."

Melissa almost laughed with surprise at her son's saying good night to Thomas—a man he'd met only minutes ago. She glanced back, where Thomas stood with his shoulder against the doorframe. He smiled.

"Good night, buddy."

Melissa and Thomas walked down the hall, then paused at the edge of the living room. There came an awkward moment when neither of them seemed to know what to do. Thomas lingered by the foot of the stairs, and Melissa stayed close to him.

"I'm sorry I intruded," Thomas said, breaking the silence. "I just thought, if you had to be down here doing parent stuff, you might want some company. I still remember how it could be, stuck with little kids while everyone else gets to have adult interactions."

"Of course," Melissa said. "I'm grateful. You're good with kids. You have your own?"

"I do," Thomas said. "Two girls. They're a lot older than Bradley. Teenagers. I haven't had to put a kid to bed in a long time."

Melissa glanced at his left hand, hanging against his thigh. No ring.

"I'm also a pediatrician," Thomas added. "I've got some practice calming kids down. A lot of them don't like going to the doctor."

Melissa blinked, picturing it: Thomas in a white coat, a stethoscope hanging from his neck. Calmly caring for children, putting them at ease the way he did with Bradley. Charming them—and their mothers too.

"You didn't tell me you were a doctor."

"Kids' table, remember?" Thomas said, flashing a grin. "No work talk."

They lapsed into silence for a few moments. Above their heads, the soft murmur of voices at the dining table erupted into sudden laughter.

"Should we go back up?" Thomas suggested. "Seems pretty quiet in Bradley's room. I imagine he's asleep by now."

"Maybe we should," Melissa said. "Before we do, can I ask you something?"

"Sure, anything."

Melissa paused, trying to decide how to pose her question. "You said you've got girls. Two of them. But you're here alone. No ring on your finger. You're…divorced?"

"No," Thomas said. "Widowed. Or…uh, *widowered?* I've never gotten clear on how that word is used."

Melissa's hand rose to her mouth. "Oh my God. Thomas. I'm so sorry. I didn't know." She was mortified to have dug up something painful. A divorce was one thing, but a dead spouse was something else entirely. And that word, *widower.* Melissa didn't know anything about Thomas's marriage. Maybe it was terrible, like hers had been. But it was hard in that moment not to imagine that he'd loved his wife, that he was crushed when she died, that he still loved her, even now, in death.

Thomas's eyes widened at Melissa's embarrassment. "Melissa, don't apologize. Oh God, you're going to look at me differently now, aren't you? You feel sorry for me? I'm a tragedy case, is that it?"

Melissa didn't say anything. That was exactly what she was thinking.

"It happened a while ago, okay? Three years now. I wish I hadn't mentioned it at all, because I really wanted to—and now…"

"Wanted to what?" Melissa asked.

"Well," he said, his gaze dropping. "I was hoping to ask you for your number."

Melissa spiraled into herself. The truth was that she did want to give Thomas Danver her number, that after their brief flirtation upstairs and his gentleness with Bradley downstairs she couldn't imagine coming to the end of the night with no way of telling when she'd see Thomas Danver again. But she also remembered a promise she'd made to herself, after her divorce. She had decided to be alone for a while. She didn't know if she was ready for a relationship again.

"I'm sorry," Thomas said in response to her silence, pulling up his hands in apology. "I ruined it."

"You didn't," Melissa insisted, stepping closer to him. "I'm glad that's what you wanted. I wanted it too. I was hoping you'd ask."

As Melissa said it, she realized it was true.

———

"So, Thomas Danver, huh?"

Lawrence had a leering grin on his face. The dinner party was over, the guests gone, and Melissa thought he was probably a little drunk—drunk on the cocktails and wine he and Toby had been pushing all night, drunk on the buzz of a successful dinner party. Everyone had gone home happy. Now he and Melissa were sitting in the wreckage, perched on two stools in the kitchen as Toby, Lawrence's partner, worked on the dishes.

"Toby, do you need help?" Melissa asked.

"Don't you change the subject," Lawrence teased. "I was asking you about Thomas Danver. I saw you two canoodling down there at the end of the table."

"We weren't *canoodling.*"

"You absolutely were," Toby said. His arms flexed as he

scrubbed at a stainless steel pot in the island sink. "You were also gone downstairs a *long* time."

"Hey!" Melissa said, feigning insult. "Traitor. And after I offered to help you with the dishes."

"Don't be mad, I'm all for it," Toby said, flashing a smirk. "Lawrence met Thomas years ago at a neighborhood running club, and I swear he's had a crush on him ever since. You'd be doing me a favor by taking him off the market. Then I won't have to worry about this guy leaving me for the hot neighborhood doctor." He flicked Lawrence playfully with the end of his half-wetted dish towel, then swung it back over his shoulder.

"Oh, you're terrible," Melissa said, even as she thought of Thomas in a running club and remembered just how fit he'd looked, his chest and shoulders broad, his stomach trim, his thighs thick as fence posts.

"Come on, just tell us," Lawrence said. "What's the story with you two?"

Melissa shrugged. "There's no story. I just like him."

"And?"

"Well, we didn't have a quickie in the basement, if that's what you're asking." She gazed off to the side, a smile coming to her lips as she thought about what had really happened. "It was sweet, actually. He helped put Bradley to bed. Really put him at ease. He's good with kids. I can tell he must be a good—"

She cut herself off before she said it, but it was too late. Lawrence and Toby knew.

"A good *dad*?" Toby offered. "Oh, honey. You've got it bad."

Melissa covered her face with her hands, shook her head, then cracked her fingers just enough to peer out. "I don't know what the hell I'm doing. I just got out of a horrible marriage. I'm not ready for this."

"There's no law that says you can't flirt with a good-looking guy a little bit."

"It's worse than that, Lawrence. He asked for my number. And I gave it to him."

Lawrence shrugged. "There's no law against that either. Go on a date with him, if that's what's going to make you happy." Lawrence paused, poked at the tines of a fork on the counter. "Though there is one thing you should know, before you hear it from someone else."

An odd note had crept into Lawrence's voice, and suddenly he wasn't meeting Melissa's eye.

"Lawrence. What?"

"It's nothing, really. Thomas is a great guy, he's a friend of ours, a respected pediatrician—everyone who knows him loves him. I swear, Melissa, he's great."

"But?"

Lawrence winced, sucked air through his teeth. "He told you his wife died, right?"

Melissa nodded. "Yes. That doesn't bother me."

"Did he tell you how she died?"

Her mind raced ahead, trying to anticipate what Lawrence could possibly be trying to tell her. Car accident, cancer, brain aneurysm—she couldn't guess how Thomas Danver's wife had died or why it should make any difference.

"He didn't say anything about that. And I didn't pry."

"Rose—that was Thomas's wife's name, Rose. She was murdered."

Her hand came back up to her mouth. "Oh my God," she said.

"There's more," Lawrence said. "Thomas was the one who got charged for it."

"Got charged..." Melissa said, catching on slowly. "You mean—"

"I mean the guy you just gave your number to was accused of murdering his wife."

19

# ROSE

*[Exhibit B in the matter of Ramsey County v. Thomas Danver: journal entries written by Rose Danver. The entries are undated but appear to have been written over a period of six months prior to her disappearance.]*

*My husband is going to kill me.*

*I've never said those words out loud, never even written them out until now. But I've thought them plenty over the years of our marriage.*

*My husband, Thomas Danver, is going to kill me.*

*You know what's ironic? Thomas was the one to suggest this journal. He posed it as an alternative to the therapy he refused to pay for anymore, because he said it wasn't working. (Is that really true, Thomas? Did you really care if my therapy was working or not? Do you actually want me to be well, to get better? Or are you more afraid of me spilling our secrets to a stranger?) He said this could be a way to keep track of my negative thoughts, to record them and interrogate them.*

*See, my husband thinks that most of my thoughts are irrational, and that I'll realize that if I sit with them long enough.*

*I wonder if he knows that my negative thoughts—irrational or otherwise—are mostly about him. Specifically, my fear of him.*

*I wonder if he knows that my first words in the journal he suggested I keep are about how I think he's going to hurt me someday.*

*Maybe he does. Maybe he simply thinks it's safer to have me writing them than to risk me saying them out loud.*

---

*Do I really believe Thomas is going to kill me? I'm honestly not sure. Even when I think it, I don't always mean it literally. No, most of the time it's an exaggeration, a bit of anxious hyperbole that runs through my mind when everything's going sideways. I think it in the way wives think such things when they know their husband is going to be so mad at them, mad enough that words like angry, furious, or livid don't seem to measure up to the reality.*

*When I forget to bring the car in for an oil change for months on end, until smoke starts rising from the hood.*

*When I spend the day in bed instead of going to get groceries and he and the girls come home to an empty fridge.*

*When I knock a vase off the shelves, bump a picture off the wall, break yet another wineglass after a midday drink or two—or five.*

*Oh, Thomas is going to kill me.*

*It is an irrational thought. It has no relationship to reality. Because not only is Thomas not literally going to kill me, most of the time he doesn't even get mad at me—making the thought irrational on a figurative level too. It doesn't matter how big my mistake is. Things don't seem to faze him. Everything just rolls off his back.*

*Last week, for instance, I had another one of my bad days. (They're happening more often lately.) To begin with, I couldn't drag myself out of bed that morning. This happens to me sometimes—more than sometimes, actually, as my depression's been getting worse. Though in the mornings, it* feels like too much, and too little, to call what I feel simple depression. Depression is something that lives in the mind. In the thoughts, the emotions. That's what I always believed. But this—this feels more like something that's settled into my body, a bone-deep wrongness that's bled from my brain into my flesh, invading my cells like a cancer. When it hits, I'll stay in bed, listening to Thomas's and my girls' hushed voices coming from the kitchen, whispering to each other, wondering what's wrong with me. Or worse, not talking about me at all. Not caring about me, just wanting to get away.

That's what happened that morning last week. Thomas asked me if I'd be getting up, and then he stomped out of the room after I turned over without answering (he's going to kill me), he went downstairs and made breakfast for the girls without me (he's going to kill me), and then he was the one to take them to school, even though technically that's my job most days (he's going to kill me). Then the house was silent, and I was alone, negotiating with myself to get my pathetic, worthless, chronic fuckup self out of bed. But I couldn't do it, and couldn't do it, and sometime around noon I had the idea that maybe I could trick myself into getting up by promising myself a treat if I did. Chocolate for breakfast, a pastry on my way to do that day's errands.

No, my brain said, a glass of wine.

So that's what I did. I got out of bed, went downstairs, and poured myself a glass of wine, threw it back in a single gulp.

I'm sure that was great for my sad little brain. A big glass of white wine on an empty stomach, after I was feeling depressed and wrung-out like yesterday's dirty dishcloths. No? Not good? Huh.

Well, good or bad for me, one glass became two, two

became three, and three became the whole bottle—and by the time I was done, there was no way I was getting anything done that day. I went back to bed.

Thomas is going to kill me, I thought as the clock ticked toward the time when he usually came home. I imagined him walking in on me in bed, still in my pajamas and smelling of alcohol. The look on his face as he realized what I'd become. The pathetic thing he married. An anchor, weighing him down, something he was stuck with.

But the thing is, he wasn't even mad.

"Oh, babe," he said when he got home. He sat next to me on the bed, pressed the back of his hand against my forehead. "Are you not feeling well?"

My face was red and tear-streaked, my skin lined all over with the wrinkles of the pillowcase I'd spent most of the afternoon crying against. I must have looked terrible.

"I'll take care of dinner tonight," he said, either not noticing the smell of wine on my breath, or pretending not to notice. "Don't you worry. Just rest."

---

Thomas always takes pity on me. He never seems to get mad, rarely raises his voice, no matter what I've screwed up this time. He's never killed me, metaphorically or literally.

You win, Thomas. This thought is truly irrational. What was it my therapist said, before Thomas made me fire her? Your brain is lying to you.

Except...

Except sometimes there's a cruelty in Thomas's kindness. A deep meanness in how nice he is all the time.

This doesn't make sense, I know. But bear with me.

*Thomas is perfect. So perfect. Everyone says so. He's,* like, the perfect man—*you're so lucky to have him. Lucky—because he's got it all together, while I'm a mess. Everyone knows it. I know it. And he knows it.*

*Not only does he know it, he uses it against me. I swear he does. He loves to be the good one, the together one, the perfect one. The one who makes the meals and brings the girls to school. The one who's great at his job, who makes all the money. The one who contributes. The good doctor, good husband, good father. And I swear, he never loves it more—never loves being perfect more—than when I'm a fuckup.*

———————————

*But also—there was one time when I'm pretty sure he actually wanted to kill me. When the thought wasn't just figurative, wasn't remotely an exaggeration.*

*His voice hissing in the quiet dark of the hotel room. The girls next door, a thin wall separating us, cowering in the dark of the night, wondering what was going to happen next.*

*"It was just an accident," he seethed at me, his voice a quiet roar, just barely held at bay. "An accident. That's all."*

*I blinked, unable to meet his furious gaze. Tears coming hot at the corners of my eyes.*

*"There's something wrong with you," he said. "You're not right. You're crazy."*

*In that moment, I truly did believe he was capable of ending my life. That the next person to have an accident would be me.*

*I've tried not to think about it. Tried my best to forget. But it's colored every interaction we've had since—the day my husband really did want to hurt me.*

*Maybe it's not such an irrational thought, now that I think about it.*

*My husband wants to kill me.*

# CHAPTER 3

*You idiot.*

That was Melissa's first thought when Lawrence told her that Thomas Danver, the man she had been flirting with all night, possibly murdered his wife.

*Nice work, Melissa. You sure know how to pick 'em.*

Her cheeks flamed, and she wanted to sink into the floorboards, let them swallow her whole. Until she realized that she really shouldn't have been beating herself up about this. That she wasn't the only one to blame here.

"Wait a second," she said, shooting a glare at Lawrence. "Are you telling me you invited an *accused murderer* to a dinner party at your house? And that you just sat by and waggled your eyebrows at me while I spent all night basically throwing myself at him?" Her anger gained momentum as she thought about everything that had happened that night, without Lawrence or anyone else saying so much as a word of warning. Sitting next to Thomas at the end of the table, brushing elbows, letting him pour his honeyed words into her ear. Then being alone downstairs with him, letting him meet—

*Oh God.* Bradley. Her *son.* The poor kid had only just escaped the orbit of his emotionally abusive dad. Now she'd introduced him to a literal murderer. She'd brought a killer into Bradley's *bedroom*, let him see her boy in his race car bed frame.

"Lawrence," she said, struggling to speak through the sudden panicked nausea that rose to the back of her throat, "he met *Bradley*. My *son*, Lawrence. Tell me you didn't let a murderer come into the same building as my son. He's all I've got left."

Lawrence grabbed her by the forearm, and she shot him the hardest, sharpest glare she could muster. But he held fast to her and didn't flinch away from her angry gaze.

"Honey, calm down. You know I'd never do that to you, right?"

Melissa pulled away, and Lawrence loosened his grip enough to let her break free. "I don't know. I *thought* so."

"Melissa," Lawrence said. "I'm hurt. When you came to me and told me you had to get out of that marriage, I told you that you could stay here as long as you want. I told you this would be a safe place for you and Bradley, to heal and figure out what comes next. And I meant that. Okay?"

"So how do you explain this?"

"Thomas was only *accused* of killing Rose," Lawrence said. "He didn't do it."

Melissa bit back a bitter laugh. "Oh, what a comfort. Why didn't you tell me earlier? He didn't do it. Perfect. All is forgiven."

Now Lawrence was the one who looked angry, and Melissa felt a little stab of guilt. Maybe she'd gone too far. She was the outsider here, the one who'd just moved to town. Lawrence knew Thomas better than she did—he must have, or he and Toby wouldn't have invited him into their home. Maybe she should try to hear Lawrence out. She took a breath, held it, then blew it through pursed lips.

"I'm serious, Melissa," Lawrence said. "The whole thing was so unfair. Anyone who actually *knows* Thomas can tell you he's not a murderer. He's one of the kindest men, the most *respected* men, in the neighborhood. He's a pediatrician, for God's sake! He dedicates his whole career to helping kids. And they had the audacity to accuse him of murder? Ridiculous."

*Respectable men can be evil too.* The rejoinder was on the tip of Melissa's tongue, but she bit it back. She'd resolved to be quiet, to listen. That didn't mean she couldn't think it, though. *Respectable men can be evil.* Some pastors and priests turned out to be serial sexual abusers; some cops were also killers. Some accountants embezzled money; some investors committed financial fraud. Ted Bundy's neighbors all thought he was a nice, quiet man. There was no limit to what a cloak of respectability could hide. Who was to say an admired pediatrician couldn't also be a wife-killer?

"He's also a great dad, and a great husband," Lawrence said. Then he hesitated, realizing what he'd just said. "Well, he *was* a great husband, I guess. Not that Rose exactly made it easy."

"What does that mean?" Melissa asked. You were supposed to speak well of murder victims, of dead women—not to imply that they were complicated in any way. "How did she not make it easy on Thomas?"

"I loved Rose, I did," Lawrence insisted. "She was beautiful, and wonderful in her own way. But she had problems. She was not a happy person."

*Not a happy person.* Melissa ran the words through her head, trying to decode what they meant. Lawrence seemed to be backing away, speaking in euphemisms. Mental illness? Substance abuse? Suicidal thoughts, maybe even an attempt? She thought about prodding further, but Lawrence had already moved on.

"They had their ups and downs, but Thomas was a saint through the whole thing. He was the rock of that family. Everyone could see it—he was the one who was keeping them from falling apart. So when the police came after him, after all he'd done for Rose, while he and the girls were still *grieving*, and with so little evidence..."

Lawrence trailed off, practically sputtering with anger as he remembered.

"They didn't have much evidence against him?" Melissa asked. She was starting to feel a little better—the more Lawrence told her, the more she began to think that maybe she *wasn't* cursed, *wasn't* a fool after all. Perhaps she wasn't so wrong in seeing something in Thomas that night, not so wrong to flirt with him a little. The picture Lawrence was painting—not of a deceptive person whose outward respectability masked evil, but of a genuinely good man wrongly accused—was appealing to her. She wanted it to be true.

"Melissa, it was ridiculous," Lawrence said. "They didn't even have a body."

Now Melissa actually gasped. She wasn't exactly a legal expert, but she'd consumed enough true crime podcasts, streamed enough murder shows on Netflix, that she knew it was unusual, some might say even *irresponsible*, to pursue a murder prosecution without a corpse. She was beginning to understand Lawrence's anger, to feel it with him on Thomas's behalf, an inner objection to the injustice of it all: accusing a man of murder, ruining his reputation and his life without even being able to prove that a murder had *happened*.

"What originally happened was, Rose just disappeared one day," Lawrence said, snapping his fingers in the air. "Nobody knows where she went, she's not answering her calls, no signs of foul play, she just left. Thomas spends maybe a day or so looking for her, talking to this person or that person, he drives up to this cabin they have up north, but she's not there either, and so he finally breaks down and calls the cops, reports her missing."

"So it's a missing persons case?"

"Yeah, to start. And it goes on the news and everything, her picture's everywhere, they're asking for anyone who's got information that could lead to her discovery to come forward, there's search parties walking through the woods and the fields nearby shouting her name, candlelight vigils. The whole routine that happens when someone goes missing."

"Right."

"But then, it starts to seem like the cops aren't looking for her very hard. They're spending more time looking at Thomas, actually. Searching his house, bringing him in for questioning multiple times. And then eventually they declare Rose dead—*presumed dead*—and charge Thomas with murder."

"What did they have on him?"

Lawrence scoffed, letting out an angry puff of breath. "*Nothing*, Melissa. Just a mess of circumstantial evidence, rumor, conjecture. It was lazy police work. A woman goes missing, you don't have any leads—so just arrest the husband."

"That can't be. There must have been *something*. Otherwise, why would the case have gone to trial? Did anything come out there?"

Lawrence shook his head. "The prosecution never made their case against Thomas. They were in the middle of jury selection when the charges were dropped."

Melissa's mind ran ahead of Lawrence's story. The prosecutor must have found some new evidence—something that exonerated Thomas.

"The cops messed up the investigation big-time," Lawrence said. "It turns out, someone had been stalking Rose, threatening her before her disappearance. Rose had even filed a complaint before she disappeared, but the cops didn't do anything about it—and after she went missing, they didn't follow up on the stalker either. From the beginning, they were totally focused on Thomas as their only suspect."

"Who's the stalker?"

"Nobody knows," Lawrence said. "There was no name in the police report that was filed after Rose reported it. Rose might not have known who was following her. She was a beautiful woman—I always figured it was some lonely, unhinged guy who saw her and became obsessed, started following her around."

Melissa shivered at the chilling plausibility of it. This was one of her own fears—one of the many that women lived with every single day: that a man, any man, could simply see her and decide that her life, her *body*, was his. His to take, his to destroy.

"Thomas's lawyer announced all this to the press. He'd discovered the original police report and everything. It was a huge story, a huge scandal for the sheriff's department and the county attorney. The next day, it was all over. The charges were gone."

"It looked bad," Melissa said, putting it together, looking between Lawrence and Toby. "The cops and the prosecutor—they just wanted it all to go away."

"That's right."

"And then?"

Lawrence shrugged. "And then nothing."

"Nothing? For three years?"

"Nothing. No arrests, no breaks in the case. No hints about who the stalker might have been. Thomas will ask the cops sometimes if there's anything new, any leads. They only say it's an active investigation, they can't share anything. I think technically it's classified as a cold case by now."

"How terrible," Melissa said, thinking of Thomas, wondering what it must have been like to live in limbo like he had for three years. Not knowing whether his wife was dead or alive. Not knowing who was responsible for her being missing. And not being officially exonerated in the eyes of the public, still an object of speculation, of whispers, of theories. Without a break in the case, without a new arrest, people must have wondered whether he was guilty or innocent. Spinning theories with what little they knew. Taking sides.

It was clear which side Lawrence was on. And on the basis of what he'd told her, Melissa was on the same side: the side of Thomas's innocence.

Part of her, though, wondered if Lawrence was telling her everything. There were pieces of the story she still didn't understand, that still didn't make sense. Lawrence's insistence that there was no evidence against Thomas, for instance, nothing to indicate that he might've killed his wife. It simply couldn't be true. Yes, maybe the case had been weak, starting with the lack of a body, the absence of definitive proof that a murder had even been committed. Still, no case made it all the way to jury selection without *some* evidence. No self-respecting prosecutor prepared to bring a case to trial without some slim hope of being able to convince twelve people that a crime had taken place. That their suspect was guilty.

Melissa wanted to believe Lawrence—but she didn't have the luxury of taking his accounting at face value. For her, the stakes were higher. Her divorce was barely a month old; she'd gone through hell to get away from a bad man. She'd made a mistake, marrying her ex-husband, realizing too late what he was. She couldn't afford to do that again. Thomas Danver had already met her son, had already gone home with her number.

She had to know everything.

---

I can't stop thinking about you.

The text buzzed on her phone while she was getting ready for bed. She wore a cream-colored camisole and soft cotton shorts, and she was rubbing lotion on her hands and forearms up to her elbows. There was an intimacy to receiving a message from Thomas just then, as she was preparing to climb beneath the covers of her bed. It was almost as though he'd stepped into the room, and she drew in a breath as she remembered the physical reality of him: his broadness, the sinewy strength running through his arms and shoulders, but also the gentleness she thought she saw in his eyes, in the curve of his mouth, in the delicate movements of his hands.

She glanced at the phone a moment, her hands frozen on her arms. Then she grabbed for it, her thumbs quivering over the screen as she thought about what to say. After a second's pause, she tapped out a reply.

I can't stop thinking about you either.

It was true, even if it didn't tell the whole story. Melissa hadn't thought of anything but Thomas since he left—though a lot of that was the thinking she did with Lawrence, learning who Thomas was, what had happened to his wife, and what he may have had to do with it. Did he kill her, or didn't he? Was he a murderer, or an innocent man unfairly accused in his hour of deepest grief? She'd been continuing to obsess over those questions as she got ready for bed: as she peeled her party clothes away from her skin, as she wiped away her makeup and washed her face, as she brushed her teeth and gazed at her own eyes in the mirror, wondering what it was that she wanted, what she could possibly be thinking, and what she should do next.

Somewhere between the bathroom and her bedroom she decided: She wasn't going to do anything. If Thomas texted, if he called, she'd simply decline to see him again. Politely but firmly. She didn't believe he was a murderer, not really. But she also didn't need stress in her life right now. She didn't need mess. And Thomas—his dead wife, the accusations against him, his whole sordid story with its twists and turns—was both. Stress and mess.

But now he was in her bedroom—his words were, anyway—and she found herself wondering if she'd made the right decision.

I wish you were here with me.

A flush of heat passed through Melissa. It was late; Thomas

must have been getting ready for bed too, or even messaging her while he was *in* his bed. There was only one thing *here with me* could mean. Melissa tapped out a response.

Dr. Danver. We barely know each other.

The reply came quickly.

We wouldn't have to do anything. We could just talk. Or I could hold you.

She breathed out, letting out an involuntary sound of satisfaction.

I'd like that.

Three dots appeared.

I'm not going to be able to sleep tonight. Not until I know.

Know what? Melissa asked.

The three dots again.

When I can see you again.

She held her breath. This was it. The question she'd been struggling with all night. Should she see him, or shouldn't she?

Melissa closed her eyes and searched inside herself. There was a fluttery, nervous feeling in her chest and stomach, and if she was honest with herself, it wasn't so different from fear. She was afraid of Thomas, a little. Afraid of his past, perhaps? Or afraid of how she felt about him? She wasn't sure. The two fears didn't feel so different, she realized. Both were at their core a fear of being hurt—a fear of giving someone the *power* to hurt her. Becoming vulnerable. Falling for someone was always a plunge into danger. A free fall that was exhilarating and terrifying at once.

Maybe, Melissa reflected, it was *herself* she was afraid of. Afraid she couldn't trust herself in a new relationship so soon after her marriage had fallen apart.

But then she pushed down further, beneath the fear, and found something else alongside it. Tangled up with it.

Excitement.

Melissa opened her eyes and responded.

Soon.

Soon? Thomas replied.

Yes, she texted back, soon. I just need more time.

It took a few seconds for his final message to come through. When it did, the back of her neck tingled.

I'll be waiting.

# CHAPTER 4

Melissa might have left things like that with Thomas forever—
might have left him *waiting*—had not the very next day, a Monday,
been so absolutely terrible, making the prior evening's flirtations
take on an idealized glow, seeming a fairy tale in retrospect. A sto-
rybook place Melissa felt desperate to get back to.

There was, to begin with, Bradley's first day at a summer daycare whose tuition Melissa couldn't afford—except you had to
spend money to make money, and if Melissa was going to find a
job and start paying down all her legal debt from the divorce, she
needed to get her son in some childcare first, bridging the gap to
kindergarten in the fall. Bradley was an anxious kid, didn't like new
situations, and as Melissa had feared, he cried and clung to her legs
at drop-off. The staff had to pull him away from her, and then he
screamed as she walked away, practically crying herself.

After that, she botched a job interview that Lawrence had
helped her set up, a bookkeeping job at a carpeting installation
company. The owner interviewed her, fat and imperious behind
his desk in a shabby, cluttered office, and when he demanded to
know why she hadn't had a job in a while, she somehow ended up
telling him the whole sordid story: bad marriage, motherhood,

expensive divorce. At the end of it, the man smirked, sat back, and asked her why she wanted this job. Melissa hated him, knew that he was the kind of boss who belittled his employees, that if she ended up sitting with him in this cramped office, he'd spend the days sniffing around her, finding excuses to put his sweaty hands on her shoulders, her neck, the small of her back. Before she could stop herself, she blurted out the truth.

"I don't *want* it. I *need* it."

---

And so, when Melissa unexpectedly ran into Thomas, she experienced the sight of his face as a welcome relief. She'd come into a coffee shop and ordered the sweetest thing on the menu, an absurd concoction of coffee and milk and caramel, whipped cream and sprinkles, hoping the bomb of sugar on her tongue would somehow erase the events of the morning. The barista shouted her name when she slid the drink across the counter, and it was as Melissa grabbed it that Thomas came up behind her.

"Melissa?"

She turned, and there he was.

"I thought that was you!" he said, gripping her by both elbows in a sort of half-hug. His blue eyes sparkled, an ice-white smile breaking across his face and dimpling his lightly tanned cheeks.

Melissa was so happy to see Thomas that she found herself wanting to fall against his chest, to close the small remaining space between them and let herself be enveloped by his sinewy arms. All that held her back was the hot cup in her hands, the fear of spilling it. But not any fear of *Thomas*, she was surprised to realize—no fear of the things she now knew about him, the things he'd been accused of having done. The events of the morning had brought her face-to-face with the realities of being divorced, of being single, of being alone: the thousand small humiliations and indignities of protecting and providing for her son without anyone to help her. No one strong and soft and kind to stand beside her through it, to comfort her in the face of it. That was precisely what Thomas seemed to be, just then, and in that moment she forgot every reason she had not to want him.

"I can't believe you're here," she blurted, which seemed, as she said it, a colossally dumb thing to say in a way she couldn't quite pinpoint. "I'm a mess."

Thomas squinted at her, cocking his head in what looked like genuine confusion. "What are you talking about? You look lovely. Why so dressed up?"

"Oh," she said, looking down at her interview outfit, a tight black pencil skirt and high heels. "I had a job interview."

"How did it go?"

"Pretty terrible," she admitted.

"Oh, no. I'm sorry to hear that. I'm sure it went better than you think."

"I doubt it," Melissa said.

At her back, the barista shouted out another name, and an annoyed-looking guy in a baseball cap squeezed by Thomas and Melissa to get his drink.

"Hey, would you like to sit with us?" Thomas asked.

"Us?"

Thomas extended a hand toward a table in the corner, where a woman raised her hand and waggled her fingers in an awkward, unsmiling wave. It took Melissa a beat to recognize her from the night before.

"You remember Amelia, right?" Thomas asked.

Melissa followed Thomas to the table. "Amelia. Of course. You were sitting next to us at dinner."

Amelia gave a thin smile. She sat on the other side of the table on a pale wooden bench, which ran across the length of the wall. She'd draped an arm on the back of the bench and sat with one leg folded casually across the other. On the table in front of her was a ceramic cup with the foamy remnants of a cappuccino clinging to the sides. Melissa took the moment to examine Amelia more closely than she could the night before, in the haze of candlelight and wine. She was red-haired; fair-skinned; a dotting of freckles scattered across her nose and the delicate skin of her upper chest, bare above the low V of a tight-fitting black shirt with long sleeves.

She took her hand off the back of the bench and reached across the table. "It's good to see you again. Melissa, right?"

Melissa nodded and clasped her hand, feeling intimidated. Amelia was classy, put together, with a vague air of aloofness about her. Melissa couldn't tell, but she thought Amelia might dislike her a little.

Thomas pulled out a chair for Melissa, then brought another to the table.

"I'm not always so good with names," Amelia said, a small smirk coming to her face. "But I remember yours because you were the talk of the party last night."

"Lawrence and Toby's gorgeous tenant," Thomas added, then nudged Melissa's knee with his under the table. "Didn't I tell you?"

"Lies," Melissa said. "Stop flattering me."

"He's not lying," Amelia said. "That's what people were saying. But then, this is a small neighborhood. We're hard up for gossip. Last night, the talk was about you and Thomas, actually. Practically sitting in each other's laps down there at the end of the table. People asked me about it, you know. After you both disappeared downstairs." She raised a hand, palm forward in the air like she was taking an oath, closed her eyes, feigning innocent ignorance. "I told them I didn't know anything about it."

Heat rose to Melissa's cheeks, but Thomas laughed a booming laugh that filled the coffee shop.

"You jealous, Amelia?"

Amelia only shrugged, giving him a thin and opaque smile, and for a second Melissa thought she *might* be jealous—that that was where the cold vibe Melissa sensed was coming from.

And actually, Melissa might have been feeling a little tug of jealousy too, as she thought of what was happening here, the scene she'd come upon. Thomas, the man she met last night, the man she'd given her number to—albeit reluctantly, and later regretfully—out for coffee with a beautiful woman. A woman wearing a skintight shirt and showing more than a bit of cleavage as she leaned over her empty cappuccino cup and half-eaten pastry, her arm lying on the table and extended toward Thomas like an invitation. There seemed to be something between them, some friction, some heat, and Melissa would have bet every last penny she had to her name that these two had *history*.

"Amelia and I have known each other since college," Thomas said, seeming to read her mind. "We've stayed friends since then. She's my next-door neighbor. We do coffee once a week."

"Every Monday," Amelia said. There was the hint of a brag in her tone, of possessiveness, like she was making a point of communicating how much better she knew Thomas than Melissa did. How much more claim she had to him.

Thomas glanced at his watch. "I need to go, actually. I'm needed at the clinic."

"Saving lives," Amelia said.

"Hardly," Thomas said. "It's mostly bonked heads and strep tests." He turned to Melissa. "We'll talk soon about that date?"

Melissa hesitated. She thought it was a little unfair of Thomas to put her on the spot like that, especially after she had asked for more time the night before. At the moment, though, she was struggling to recall why she was hesitant to say yes to him in the first place. Struggling to recall everything Lawrence had told her: the dead wife, the murder case, the rumors, the news stories. None of that seemed real. Thomas couldn't possibly be a killer. Not the man sitting before her.

"I'd have to get a sitter for Bradley," Melissa said, deflecting. "I don't know anyone in town yet."

"Make Lawrence do it!" Thomas said, then snapped his fingers, getting an idea. "Or my girls! They're responsible, I promise. It would be perfect."

Melissa let out a laugh, delighted at his eagerness. "We'll talk. You go to work."

Thomas glanced at Amelia, then back to Melissa. "You two will be okay alone?"

"We're big girls," Amelia said with a trace of sarcasm in her voice. "I think we can handle ourselves."

Thomas stood, leaned across the table to give Amelia a kiss on the cheek, and then, before Melissa was prepared, he was leaning toward her to do the same. Melissa wasn't used to this—her friends back in Montana weren't the kind to kiss hello and goodbye—and she had a little moment of panic when she wasn't sure what to do. Was she supposed to rise from her chair and meet him halfway? What should she do with her hands? Flustered, she ended up turning toward him just as he was about to kiss her, and he ended up catching the corner of her mouth instead. She blushed, heat rising fast all the way to the crown of her scalp, and was about to apologize, but he was already out the door as though nothing had happened and they didn't just accidentally kiss on the lips. Maybe he didn't even notice.

Melissa took a second to collect herself, and when she looked up, Amelia was looking at her like she knew something Melissa didn't. She realized that she actually *was* a little nervous to be left alone with Amelia. They barely knew each other, and Amelia cut an air of sophistication that made Melissa feel like a pitiable rube by comparison.

"What is it?" Melissa asked. "Do I have something on my face?"

"No," Amelia said. "Only...you two seem to be getting along."

"Getting along?" Melissa asked, a little irritated at the knowing way Amelia was speaking. "We just met yesterday."

"I know," Amelia says. "It's just—he seems to like you. And you obviously like him."

"*Obviously*, huh?" Melissa expected Amelia to shrink at this, to back off—but she didn't. Only went on looking at Melissa, long and unblinking.

"Yes," Amelia said. "Obviously. By the look on your face just now. When he kissed you. And how fluttery you got when he surprised you at the pickup counter."

Melissa glanced away, tucking strands of hair behind her ears with sharp, angry movements. Whether Amelia liked her or not, Melissa was starting to think she might not like *Amelia* very much.

"I'm sorry," Amelia said. "I'm not trying to embarrass you. I'm sure nobody else noticed. Thomas especially. I'm adept at reading people, is all. It's my job, in a way."

Melissa tried to recall if Amelia had shared her job the night before. Another detail lost in the flurry of the dinner party.

"I should remember this. What do you do again?"

Amelia reached into a handbag sitting next to her on the bench, then came out with a business card. She handed it across the table.

"*Dr. Amelia Harkness,*" Melissa read aloud. "*Psychiatrist.*" She looked back up. "That's right, I remember now. *Classic displacement.* You made Thomas laugh last night by psychoanalyzing the whole table."

Amelia gave a small nod, and something clicked into place in Melissa's mind, the woman coming clear to her for the first time.

She could picture Amelia sitting across from a client much like she was sitting across from Melissa right now, hearing them pour out their problems, listening calmly, not giving anything away, gently prodding with questions. Suddenly she seemed a little less mean, a little less aloof, and a little more—what? Dispassionate? Impartial?

"I probably need someone like you," Melissa said.

"Why's that?"

"Lawrence didn't tell you why I moved into his basement? That wasn't part of last night's gossip about me?"

Amelia shook her head. "Nobody said anything to me."

"Divorce," Melissa said. "A bad one."

Amelia's eyebrows raised a little, but she didn't betray much of a reaction, and she didn't press for additional details. *Dispassionate*, Melissa thought. *Impartial.*

"And you think you might need someone to talk to about that?"

"Oh, I don't know," she said. "Maybe. Probably. I don't even know what I need right now."

"That's normal," Amelia says. "I could give you some names, if you wanted."

Melissa cocked her head. "Not you?"

"It's best to see someone you don't know. We've only just met, but…"

A memory from the night before floated into Melissa's head. *That's why I stopped seeing you.* Thomas had said it to Amelia at dinner, and Melissa hadn't known what he meant at the time.

"You don't treat people you know?"

Amelia nodded. "It can get a little hazy sometimes. But yes, ethically, it's best not to. That's called a dual relationship."

"So, you and Thomas—you didn't treat him? Last night, something he said, it made me think… Is that what he meant?"

Something odd passed across Amelia's face. She pressed her lips together, broke her gaze with Melissa.

"Thomas and I—it's complicated. We've known each other forever. And I've never *treated* him, exactly. Never charged him for my services, never took him on as an official patient. But he did come to me for help. When…" She broke off, and her eyes drifted up to Melissa again. "I don't know what you know."

"Everything," Melissa said. "Lawrence told me everything. Last night, after everyone left."

"Then you must understand. Thomas was—he was close to falling apart. His wife was missing. The girls were beside themselves. And he was being accused of killing Rose. I wasn't totally comfortable with it, seeing him like that. Professionally, it brought up…issues. But he didn't trust anyone else. And I could see he was hurting. I don't know. I'm not proud of it. And I'd appreciate it if you didn't tell anyone."

"Of course. Who would I tell?" Melissa was surprised at Amelia's transformation, seemingly brought on by the turn in the conversation. One minute she'd been confident, cultivating an air of superiority, as though she was above it all—above Melissa. But now Amelia had turned nervous, jittery, her hands darting to the plate on the table and ripping the remainder of the pastry into pieces, seemingly just to give her hands something to do. And she was no longer meeting Melissa's gaze for more than a fraction of a second at a time before darting her eyes away again. There must have been more to it than a past breach of professional ethics, but Melissa couldn't possibly guess what. And she had a thousand questions she wanted to ask, but no idea where to start.

"Were you ever—" Melissa began, then cut herself off.

"What?"

Melissa hesitated before finishing the sentence. "Together?"

Amelia laughed. Some measure of her confidence, her aloof calm, seemed to return to her. "You mean romantically? Is that what you're asking?"

"Yes," Melissa said softly.

She smiled, and now she was fully back—aloof Amelia, superior Amelia, distant and dispassionate Amelia. "Oh, whatever was between Thomas and me is ancient history. You don't have to worry about me."

Melissa wanted to believe her, but Amelia's smile hinted at the opposite of her words—hinted that Amelia would have liked there to be something between them, maybe. That Melissa *did* have to worry about her, if it was a relationship with Thomas she wanted.

"Although..." Amelia began.

"What?"

Amelia pressed her lips together, sighed through her nose. "Just that you might want to be careful there. Starting anything with Thomas too quickly."

"Why?" Melissa asked, her stomach suddenly churning. Was this it? Was Amelia about to tell her—or hint, at least—that she thought Thomas really was a murderer? "Is it about...the case? What he was accused of?"

Amelia shook her head—though again, there was something strange and complicated in her eyes. Some hesitation. Some lingering doubt. Not the reflexive dismissal of the accusations that Melissa had expected and hoped to see.

"No," she said carefully. "No, I don't think so."

"You don't *think* so?"

Amelia looked off to the side. "There was a moment. A moment when I believed it might be true. Thomas was acting so strangely, after the accusation. He wasn't himself. And I thought..." She blinked, and some trance seemed to break. "But no. Then everything came out, about the police mishandling the case. And I immediately regretted it. Regretted doubting him. No, I don't think Thomas killed his wife."

"Why, then?" Melissa asked. "Why should I be careful?"

Amelia squinted. "Well, *something* happened there, didn't it? Rose *is* still missing, three years later. And her killer—if she really was killed—is still out there."

The skin on the back of Melissa's neck tingled. She was sure she was imagining it, but she felt for a second as though she was being watched. Followed. Spied on. She glanced around the coffee shop, but nobody seemed to be looking at her. She turned back to Amelia, leaned across the table, spoke low.

"You think Thomas's family is being targeted? That I'd be in danger if I decided to see him?"

"I can't say that," Amelia said. "But *someone* is responsible for whatever happened to Rose. So, who? And why haven't the police found them yet? There's also the fact that Thomas is just *damaged* by what happened. It was a trauma. He's still recovering. The girls too."

"Of course. It must have been terrible."

"And by the sounds of it, you're recovering as well. Your divorce."

Something stabbed in Melissa's chest, and it took her a moment to realize it was anger. She had mentioned her divorce to Amelia, but that didn't mean Amelia could throw it back in her face as a reason she shouldn't see Thomas. They barely knew each other. Amelia hadn't earned the right.

"I care about Thomas," Amelia continued. "And the girls. I'm their godmother, you know. I want the best for them. I want them to heal. And I'm not sure if this is that opportunity." She gestured vaguely toward Melissa.

For a moment, Melissa was speechless. She couldn't be certain she'd actually heard what she heard. Couldn't believe it. Had Amelia just insulted her?

"I'm confused," Melissa said, finally. "Are you trying to protect me? Or him?"

Amelia looked her in the eye, and it was impossible for Melissa to read what she saw there.

"Just be careful."

———————

When Melissa got back into her car, she started the engine but then just sat back, feeling a little dizzy. "What the hell was that?" she muttered to herself under her breath. She couldn't get a handle on the conversation she'd just had with Amelia Harkness—Thomas Danver's next-door neighbor, maybe ex-girlfriend, and unofficial therapist to him in the wake of his wife's disappearance. Melissa felt like she'd been ambushed, though technically, Amelia was never anything less than polite, calmly delivering what only *might* have been veiled insults.

One thing was clear: Amelia wanted Melissa to stay away from Thomas. But why?

Not because she thought he was dangerous, surely. There had been something unsettled in Amelia's eyes when she talked about the time after Rose Danver's disappearance, when charges had been brought against Thomas for her murder—but Amelia ultimately said she believed he was innocent, and she was still friends with him today.

No, if Amelia was trying to keep Melissa away from Thomas, it was for her own reasons. Selfish reasons. The only thing she could think of was that Amelia wanted him for herself. She spoke of him being damaged, of needing to heal. She even implied that she cared deeply for him and his daughters. And it seemed to Melissa that Amelia wanted to be the one to heal him, to move from being his friend to his lover, from his daughters' godmother to their mother. She all but confirmed that she and Thomas dated long ago— perhaps before he met Rose. Maybe she'd always thought of him as the one who got away. And ever since, she'd been biding her time, waiting for him to be ready. Now she wanted to swoop in and claim him as her own—but Melissa was in the way.

It was enough to make Melissa forget all the reasons she'd wanted to wait, to go slow with Thomas. His wife's disappearance, the murder charges against him, even Melissa's own messy divorce—it all fell out of her head, shrunk down to nothing. All she could think of just then was *him*: his body, his smile, his eyes. An admired doctor, a committed father. A good man. And he wanted *her*. What the hell was she waiting for?

Just then, she got a text. She glanced at the screen.

It was Thomas.

How was your chat with Amelia? She's great, isn't she?

Melissa's jaw clenched. Yes, she typed back, pretending enthusiasm. I enjoyed talking with her!

That's great. She's a really important part of my life.

Melissa spent a bit of time typing out her reply, making sure it was just right.

I can tell. And I want to get to know her better. If she's important to you, she's important to me.

She added a heart, then sent the message.

Thank you. That means a lot to me.

That was all Melissa got, and for a second, she feared she'd gone too far, gotten too intimate, made this serious when she should have kept it light.

But then the three dots appeared.

Have you given any thought to that date? I'd love to see you again soon. On purpose, not by accident.

She breathed out.

Yes, she typed back. As soon as possible. When?

When she saw his answer, she gave a little scream of delight.

Why not tonight?

# TRANSCRIPT OF RECORDING

**Amelia:** So why are you coming to *me*, Thomas?

[pause]

**Thomas:** I'm not sure what you're asking.

**Amelia:** What's unclear?

**Thomas:** It's two questions in one.

**Amelia:** Is it?

**Thomas:** Sure it is. Number one, why am I in therapy? Why do I want to talk to someone at all? Number two, why, out of all the therapists I could have gone to, did I choose you? My best friend from college, former girlfriend, next-door neighbor, godmother to my two daughters… Should I go on? Why am I insisting on talking to someone I've got history with?

**Amelia:** Okay. Two questions, then.

**Thomas:** So which one were you asking?

**Amelia:** Both, maybe?

**Thomas:** And which one should I answer first?

**Amelia:** Client's choice.

**Thomas:** Maybe the why-you question is the easier one to answer.

**Amelia:** And?

**Thomas:** I don't know. I guess it's just, I don't really trust anyone else.

**Amelia:** Counselors have a code. Confidentiality. You could see anyone in the whole city, the whole *world*, any therapist, and they'd have to keep whatever you tell them to themselves.

**Thomas:** I know that. But also, would they *really* observe confidentiality? Everybody's gossiping about me. I'm in the papers, in the news. When I step out my door, I've got cameras in my face, people shouting questions at me. I drive around town, and people follow me. In the grocery store, people walk up and tell me that I'm evil—or that they think I'm innocent. Everyone's got an opinion about me. Everyone's talking.

**Amelia:** And? How does that pertain to whether a therapist would keep your sessions confidential?

**Thomas:** You mean to tell me a therapist wouldn't at least be *tempted* to tell someone that they're treating the guy who's been in the news every night for the past three weeks running? Maybe he wouldn't tell the press, but he'd tell his wife. Or a friend, over drinks. The guy he plays racquetball with. Something to brag about—and then the person listening presses him for details. Maybe he protests at first, he can't, he's a professional, like you've been saying. But then he lets something slip. Just to keep his audience interested. And then that person tells a friend, and that friend tells another friend, and maybe *that* friend puts it on social media, and somehow it ends up in the news.

**Amelia:** You really think that would happen?

**Thomas:** Maybe not. But it's what I'm imagining. I can't stop. With anyone else—anyone but you—it would be what I'm thinking about the whole session long. Checking what I say. Holding back. And I can't do that. It's too important, what's happening right now. This trial, preparing for it. It's my whole life on the line. My kids' future. I have to stay sharp right now. I can't fall apart. What we're doing here—I just, I need this. I need to talk to someone if I'm going to keep it together.

**Amelia:** Maybe that brings us to the other half of the question. Why are you in therapy, period?

[pause]

**Thomas:** I don't know if I can…

[pause]

**Amelia:** Thomas? Don't know if you can what?

**Thomas:** [sniffs]

[rustling of tissue paper]

[sound of nose blowing]

[throat clearing]

**Amelia:** Go on. You can tell me.

**Thomas:** I'm just… I'm not doing great, Amelia.

[pause]

**Amelia:** Tell me about "not great." What does that look like? What does it feel like?

**Thomas:** God, I don't even know where to start.

**Amelia:** Start anywhere.

**Thomas:** Well, my wife is dead, for one thing. Maybe. Probably. I don't even know for sure. I haven't seen her body.

**Amelia:** That's called *ambiguous grief*. When a person feels grief, but it's not entirely clear what they should be grieving. Not clear what they've lost. It's incredibly difficult.

**Thomas:** That's right. I'm hollowed out, sad and angry and I can't even *think* sometimes—but also, I have no idea what it's all about. What I'm even feeling all of this *for*. Was Rose murdered? Did she kill herself? Did she go on a walk and fall into the river and drown? Did she leave me, leave *us*? I don't know. And the not knowing—it's as bad as the grieving.

**Amelia:** Okay. This is good. What else?

**Thomas:** Well, in the middle of all this…this *ambiguous grief*, as you call it, the world has decided that I'm to blame. That I killed her.

**Amelia:** Not the whole world, Thomas. Your friends believe in your innocence. Your daughters. Me.

**Thomas:** Sure, but a good portion of the world, they think I'm a killer. You have any idea how that feels? My wife, the woman I love, the girl I fell in love with all those years ago—you remember, don't you, how in love we were? Then we get married, and we make a life together, we have these beautiful girls, and the woman I fell in love with becomes the mother of the children I love more than life itself. Rose, my beautiful Rose, she's gone. She's the one person who I most want to find, the one face in all the billions of faces in the world that I'm completely desperate to see, who I'd be completely *relieved* to see. And some detective, some county prosecutor, some journalists get it into their heads that I killed her? That I snuffed the life out of her? That I'm capable of doing that to someone I love? I can't even put words to it.

**Amelia:** That sounds incredibly difficult.

**Thomas:** And then you add the girls to it. Think of it—two girls, a fourteen-year-old and a twelve-year-old. What they must be going through. Losing a mother, that's trauma enough. But then to also see their father accused of killing her? What's worst of all, what absolutely kills me, is that I can't protect them from any of it. I can't protect them from what people are saying, what they think I did. It's in their heads, even if they don't believe it.

**Amelia:** You're a good dad, Thomas. The girls have exactly what they need in you.

**Thomas:** Do they, though? I swear, sometimes it's all so much, I feel like it's literally going to break me in half. I go to bed some nights thinking this is it, that I'll just die in my sleep—as if a person could die from stress and sadness. And maybe a person could. But then every morning I wake up, still alive, and I have to go through it all over again. It's all just…

[pause]

[muffled crying]

**Thomas:** I don't know how I'm going to get through this. You have to help me.

# ROSE

*My husband is cheating on me with our next-door neighbor.*

*Next up on the irrational thought tour!*

*But is this one really so irrational? Thomas did used to be in a relationship with Amelia. They were together for a couple years in med school, then they broke up not long before Thomas and I met and started dating. From what I can tell, things were pretty serious between them. I don't know much about that time in their lives. They never really talk about it. But from a few things they've said—stray, barbed comments—I've gotten the sense that they weren't so much broken up when Thomas and I met, as taking a break. (Cue* Friends *music and Ross shouting, "We were on a break!") I was Thomas's rebound from Amelia, a fling that wasn't supposed to last. But then we did last, got married, had the girls, bought a house.*

*And Amelia Harkness, for some reason, stayed close by every step of the way. She was Thomas's best friend during the years we were dating, my maid of honor in our wedding, at his insistence. And when we settled in this house by Lake Julia in the northern suburbs of the Twin Cities, she somehow ended up as our next-door neighbor. The girls call her Aunt Amelia.*

*My husband's ex-girlfriend—his beautiful ex-girlfriend—is an honorary member of the family. Thomas loves her. So do the girls.*

*I'm the only one who's not so sure. Who's merely tolerated Amelia's presence for years. Sitting at our table for weekend dinners. Her occasional pop-ins asking for Thomas's help lifting something heavy or doing some work in the yard. Or when I wake up from a midday nap and realize I'm alone in the house, only to find my husband and kids next door with her, playing board games and eating popcorn and laughing. The very picture of a perfect, happy family—with Amelia Harkness playing the role of wife and mother in my place.*

*Sometimes I can't tell if she's the other woman, or if I am. If she and Thomas were meant to be together, and I'm the one who's the usurper.*

*But are they having sex? That's the question.*

*They certainly have before. You don't spend two years in a relationship in your twenties without having lots of sex. And that's bad enough. Not that my husband had prior relationships, prior sexual partners—everyone comes into a marriage with a history. No, what's difficult is constantly being reminded of that history. Plenty of women are married to men with ex-girlfriends in their past. But how many women have to live next door to one of those ex-girlfriends? How many of them have to be constantly reminded of their husband's past love for another woman?*

*It comes to me in flashes. Some of the time, I can put all of this out of my mind, think of Amelia as just another person, a woman living her own life, no threat to me. But then she and Thomas will exchange a glance, a brief gaze that feels charged and private. A smile will come to the corner of Amelia's mouth, a distant and intense look to Thomas's face, and then I'll remember. Amelia and Thomas have been together. They've seen each other naked, can close their eyes and picture it anytime they want to. And I picture it too, not wanting to, but the images come to my mind all the same, Amelia and my husband tangled together in ways that are as intimate and vulnerable as it is possible for two people to be together.*

*No one should have to have these kinds of thoughts. And sometimes I'm furious at Thomas for forcing me to have them, by insisting on keeping Amelia in his life. Shouldn't I be enough for him?*

*Ok, so they have had sex before, and that's bad enough—but are they having sex now? Have they ever had sex while Thomas and I have been together?*

*They've certainly had the opportunity, living so close together. All Thomas would have to do would be to sneak over when nobody was watching, creep through Amelia's back door, go to her in her bed. She'd be waiting for him, I'm sure, in something silky, something she bought with him in mind, meant to slip easily off her body. Then he'd creep back home after they were done, maybe take a shower over there first to wash the smell of her off him before sliding back into bed next to me.*

*This is what I imagine. But has it ever happened? I'm ashamed to admit it, but there've certainly been nights when I've been dead enough to the world—passed out from too much to drink or overmedicated with pills to help me sleep—that he'd easily be able to slip out of bed and come back an hour or two later without my knowing.*

---

*I even mentioned it to Amelia once. We don't often spend time alone, just the two of us, but a week ago she came over and rang our bell in the middle of the day, when Thomas and the girls were gone. She'd gotten a piece of our mail by accident and wanted to return it to us. When I answered the door, she looked surprised to see me, and she explained what had happened with halting words, handed the envelope*

55

to me from a distance, as if afraid to get too close. Her nervousness piqued my curiosity, and I invited her in. Maybe I wanted to torment her. This woman, a family friend, who I'd come to view as a rival.

We sat in the living room. I didn't offer her a glass of water or a cup of tea, even though that would have been the polite thing to do. Instead, I just watched her, observed her hesitation to meet my gaze, fascinated. Amelia was usually so confident, but something about being alone with me unsettled her.

Eventually I just came out with it.

"I think Thomas might be cheating on me." I didn't mention her, didn't make any accusations. I just said it and waited for her reaction. Maybe I was testing her.

Oddly, she seemed to get calm then. Her fidgeting fingers stilled, and her eyes rose to meet mine. She gave no sign of being perturbed. Only blinked, cocked her head with a disinterested look, and asked, "What makes you say that?"

I realized then that I'd made a mistake, given Amelia the upper hand. I'd allowed her to transform into her therapist self, the way she's most comfortable: treating others as specimens to be studied. Now I was the one caught off guard. I couldn't say anything about her, about the fact that she's Thomas's ex-girlfriend and that sometimes I catch them banging each other with their eyes. So I made something up.

"Oh, I don't know," I said. "He seems…distracted. We haven't really been having sex—my fault, mostly, since I'm never in the mood, but I imagine it makes him frustrated. Unsatisfied."

"And you think he's found someone else to meet those needs," Amelia offered.

"Might be cheating. I said might."

"Have you considered talking to him about it?"

I scoffed. "What, asking him if he's cheating? He'd just deny it."

"I was thinking talking to him about the lack of intimacy you're telling me about."

I cringed just thinking about it. "I couldn't."

Amelia was quiet for a bit, thinking. "And the thought of him cheating. What does that do to you?"

"It's torture." I looked her square in the eye. Challenging her to see me, to understand what I was really saying. You're hurting me. Please stop. Please stay away from my family. Please let him—let me—go.

"If the thought hurts you so much," Amelia said, "maybe there's something else you should be thinking about. Something else you should be asking yourself."

"And what's that?" I asked.

"Is your husband the kind of man who would do that?"

———

I thought about it for a long time after she left. Thought about what Amelia was really trying to say to me with the question.

Because Thomas isn't the kind of man who would cheat on me.

Not because he loves me, not because he only has eyes for me, not because I'm as beautiful, as sexy, as the day we first met. Not even because he's faithful, dependable, or good.

No, Thomas wouldn't cheat on me because he's too attached to the idea of himself as a good man. Because he's built up this image of himself—in our family, in the community, in his own mind—as the perfect man. A protector of children. *A supportive friend and neighbor. A good husband. A great dad.*

*And cheating on your wife—well, that's something that bad men do. Not men like him.*

*But what keeps chilling me, what I keep coming back to, is the way Amelia glared at me when she asked it—*Is your husband the kind of man who would do that? *Her eyes an accusation.*

*She knows.*

*Thomas isn't that kind of person. But I am.*

*I'm the one who cheats.*

# CHAPTER 5

Bradley started crying when Melissa pulled her car into Thomas's driveway.

"Are you going to leave me here?" he blubbered from the back seat.

Melissa's heart crumpled in her chest, and she felt herself regretting the decision to go on a date with Thomas so quickly. What was she thinking? Thomas was so convincing with his charm, his persistent texts, his refusal to take no for an answer. His obvious interest in Melissa had prevented her from thinking clearly, but now, sitting in her car outside a near-stranger's house with a scared and crying five-year-old in the back seat, she finally saw the absurdity of Thomas's plan.

Bringing her son to be babysat by a strange man's daughters, while they went on a *date*? It was a terrible idea in about a dozen ways at once, starting with the fact that Melissa and Bradley had only just moved to town, and Bradley was still adjusting to a new place, a new home, a new set of routines. He wasn't remotely ready to be left behind with a sitter. He'd already had one meltdown that day when Melissa tried to drop him off at daycare. What he needed now, in the evening, was some quality time with his mom, his trusted person—with *Melissa*. Not to be dumped with some strangers again.

Add to this the fact that the babysitters in question were the two daughters of a man Melissa was going on a date with, and this bomb of a bad idea became practically nuclear. Leaving aside the question of whether she was ready to be dating at all, her son certainly should not have been meeting Thomas's kids so soon. It would only confuse them all, bring uncomfortable questions that Melissa wasn't ready to answer. What if Bradley came home asking if Thomas was his new dad? If Thomas's girls were his sisters? There was a right way to handle these things, Melissa realized—and this wasn't it.

She spiraled where she sat in the driver's seat, leaving Bradley's question—*Are you going to leave me here?*—unanswered. Thomas's house was located in a cul-de-sac near the same lake that Lawrence and Toby's house sat on a half mile away, and the circle of houses felt like a crowd of faces surrounding Melissa and staring. One of the houses must have been Amelia's, and Melissa wondered if the other woman was standing just inside, watching through the window, wondering if Melissa was going to get out of the car.

"Mama?" Bradley prodded, calming but still with a shaky whisper in his voice. "You're not leaving me here, are you?"

"Just for a little bit," Melissa said, not quite comfortable with the idea herself but too embarrassed to flee, now that she'd come this far. How would she explain it to Thomas later? She turned around in her seat and looked Bradley in the eye, summoned her most comforting smile. "Remember what I say when I have to leave you somewhere for a little while?"

"Mama always comes back," Bradley said. He was pulling it together, his eyes still wide and trembling with tears, but not actively crying anymore. Trying to be brave.

"That's right," Melissa said. "Because I love you. My love's like a rubber band, right? Whenever I go away, it yanks me right back."

Bradley giggled, like he always did when Melissa used the metaphor. "If you went really far, would it boing you back hard enough that you'd fly through the air and land right on top of me?"

"It might. My love is just that strong. I might even come crashing into the house and make a mom-shaped hole in the wall."

Bradley's giggle rose to a cackle. "Okay," he said. "Do you think they have toys?"

"Let's see."

-----

Thomas met them at the door, with a teenage girl standing a few paces behind him in the foyer.

"Bradley!" Thomas said. "How about a high five, bud?"

Thomas reached out a hand, and Bradley smiled and slapped it. Thomas sunk to his knees to speak to him eye to eye. He was ignoring Melissa, but she didn't mind. What she wanted most just then was for someone to help her son feel comfortable, and once again seeing Thomas's ease with kids, his pediatrician's bedside manner, her temporary objections to the evening began to melt away.

Thomas extended an arm behind him. "So, Bradley, this right here is Kendall. She's my daughter. And I was telling her about this really cool kid I met last night, and the awesome race car bed he has in his room, and she told me she wanted to meet you and hang out. Isn't that right, Kendall?"

The girl at Thomas's back gave a little eye roll, but when she answered "Yeah, Dad," her voice was sweet and earnest. Her shoulders were narrow, her limbs thin and lanky, and she had sandy-brown hair reaching past her shoulders.

"Kendall recently completed a babysitting course at the Y,"

Thomas said, addressing his words to Melissa. "She knows the Heimlich, CPR, all sorts of safety stuff."

"*Dad*," Kendall said with another eye roll, though the smile didn't leave her lips.

"What? I'm proud of you. Maybe you'll follow your old man into the medical profession?"

"It's just babysitting, Dad," Kendall said.

Thomas turned back to Melissa. "Kendall's started babysitting for parents around the neighborhood. Some of the kids are just babies. She's doing great."

"Wow," Melissa said, and raised an eyebrow. "Making any money, Kendall?"

"A little bit," the girl said, blushing.

Melissa nodded and left it at that. She remembered what it was like to be that age. The feeling of being not quite at home in her body, in her personality, that could set in around the start of puberty and stick around for a while. The nonspecific embarrassment of being seen, spoken to, questioned by adults at that age. Sometimes it was best to leave them alone.

"Do you want to show Bradley our board games?" Thomas asked. "Do five-year-olds still like Chutes and Ladders? Candy Land? Sorry, I'm out of touch now that my kids are basically grown-ups." He nudged Kendall on the shoulder, which brought another wave of embarrassment.

"Dad, stop," Kendall said. "Come on, Bradley. I'll show you what we've got."

She reached for Bradley's hand, and he took it without hesitation, happily walking alongside her as she led him back into the house. Melissa felt a happy little pang as she watched the two of them walk off together. Bradley looked back once, and she nodded him on.

"Didn't you say you have two girls?" Melissa asked after Kendall and Bradley had gone.

"Rhiannon," Thomas said. "My older daughter. Seventeen. Sulking in her room. You know. *Teenagers.*"

*Sulking.* The word made Melissa wonder. Sulking about what? About *her*?

Thomas moved to the end of a staircase close to the front door and called up.

"Ree! Come out and say hello to Melissa."

Above their heads, a door clicked open, and footsteps creaked down the hall.

Melissa shook her head. "No," she whispered. "She doesn't have to..."

But it was too late. In the darkened hall above, a teenage girl appeared. She looked a lot like Kendall, but older, her face sharpened, angular, and guarded where her sister's had been rounded and open.

"What?" the girl asked from up the stairs.

"Aren't you going to say hi to my friend? This is Melissa."

"Hi," Rhiannon said after a pause, her voice deadened. Then she turned and walked back to her room. The door clicked shut.

---

"I'm sorry about that," Thomas said in the car.

"What?"

"Rhiannon. She was rude."

"It's fine," Melissa said. She thought it was pretty obvious what Rhiannon's coldness was about—and she didn't blame the girl at all. Her dad was going on a date. And she wasn't sure what she thought about it, at best. At worst—she hated it. Hated Melissa.

"She's a great kid, actually," Thomas said. "A great student. Honor roll. Varsity volleyball. She'll be a senior in the fall."

He drove through a tangle of winding suburban streets to a

destination he hadn't yet told her about. Steering and working the blinker with one hand, he draped the other casually on the console between him and Melissa.

"But she's also gotten a little complicated the past few years. She used to be really sweet, like her sister. But now—well, you saw. She's quieter than she used to be. Not as warm. Sullen. Sometimes she gets angry. I don't know, we're working through it."

His voice was tight with pain and worry, and Melissa touched his hand, a light caress with the tips of her fingers.

"Don't apologize," she said. "It's all right. I was Rhiannon's age once. Kendall's too. She's, what?"

"Fifteen," Thomas said.

"I thought so. Something happens to girls around their age, Thomas. They get complicated. Because life gets complicated for *them*."

Thomas sucked air, hissing through his teeth, his eyes pained as they gazed ahead at the road. Melissa knew he was imagining losing Kendall too—his sweet youngest daughter, slipping into the opaque depths of adolescence.

She touched him again, to bring him back to her, but this time she left her hand resting on his, and he gave her a brief look.

"They're still your girls, though," she said. "They'll always be yours. And they'll always love you."

"You think so?"

"You're a good dad. They feel safe with you. I can tell."

Thomas blinked a few times, his lashes whipping up and down furiously, and he heaved a huge breath that seemed to bring him a measure of calm.

"They've had a rough go of it, is the other part," Thomas said. "It's not just their ages. It's also their mother. Losing her. That was hard on everyone. Traumatic."

"I know. I've heard."

Underneath Melissa's palm, Thomas's hand tensed.

"So people have been talking," Thomas said. "Telling you things about me."

Melissa gave his hand a squeeze, willing him to turn it over and lace his fingers in hers.

"All good," she assured him. "The only people I've talked to are people who care about you. Who are on your side. But yes. I've heard some things."

"Then I guess we'll have plenty to talk about."

The car slowed, and Melissa looked up just as Thomas pulled off the road into a parking lot. The building was a gray box with tall windows looking into a sleek, gleaming dining room inside. A pergola of stained wooden beams wound with climbing vines overhung a stone patio with tables and umbrellas, sandy lanes tracked with the paths of scattered bocce balls, an unlit brick firepit sunk into the ground. A few small parties of people sat sipping at glasses of wine under the late afternoon sunshine, flights of reds and whites laid out on paper cards, with charcuterie boards of cheese and prosciutto sweating in the heat. A sign above the door read, simply, *Veritas*, and Melissa felt a shiver, recalling the aphorism: *in vino veritas*. In wine, there is truth.

It felt like a sign of another kind: a manifestation, an omen, a portent. A message from the universe, clear as a fortune cookie or horoscope. Truth. She needed to know the truth.

---

Inside, most of the tables were empty, and a host with a close-shorn beard greeted them a little too eagerly.

"Welcome!" he said, flashing his teeth. "Are you here for our singles event?"

Thomas groaned. "You're kidding."

The host blinked, his smile dimming only slightly. "Every third Monday is singles night."

Melissa laughed, glancing around the dining room and understanding something about the sparse crowd. It was pretty good for a Monday, actually—there were a little more than a dozen people there, and they were all sitting alone at tables or at the bar, carefully eyeing each other.

"You wanted to keep your options open, Thomas?" she asked. "Play the field a bit if we didn't hit it off?"

"I swear, I had no idea," Thomas said. "Do you want to go somewhere else?"

"Hell no. This is hilarious. A first date on singles night? How can we possibly pass that up? Maybe I'd like to keep my options open too."

Thomas smiled grimly. "Oh, I'm sure you would. Very wise."

The host's face brightened again. Maybe he was the owner, desperate for more customers on a quiet evening.

"You'll take a name tag, then?"

"Hell *yes* we'll take name tags," Melissa said, grabbing for the sticker and marker the host slid toward her on the stand. "I'll do his too."

She scribbled out a couple names, then put her name tag on first. Thomas squinted as she pressed it onto her shirt.

"Xena?" he said. "Seriously?"

"That's right. The warrior princess. Ever heard of her?"

She stepped toward him and placed his name tag over his lapel pocket, letting her hands linger on the hard bulge of his chest as she spread it flat. When she withdrew her hand, he glanced down at the name she gave him, took a moment to read it upside down.

"Biff," he said. "Very nice."

The host grabbed some menus, tapped them twice on the stand. "You ready?"

"Biff?" Melissa asked.

He grinned, then bowed and extended his arm. "After you, Xena."

They got seated at a high-top and ordered a couple glasses of wine. Thomas went through the whole ritual when he got his glass of Malbec, swirling the liquid in the glass, holding it sideways to examine it, then sticking his nose in the glass to give it a sniff. Finally, he took a slow, thoughtful sip. As he went through all this, Melissa glanced around the room and took note of the women casting glances toward their table.

"We're being watched," she said.

"The men are looking at you. Waiting for their opening to come chat you up."

"They're not," Melissa protested, though now that he mentioned it, she noticed several of the men looking their way as well. They weren't looking at *her*, though—they, too, were looking at Thomas. Jealous that their prospects, the women they came here to meet, all seemed to be attracted to someone else. It was hard to compare to Thomas, with his beautiful eyes and smile, his perfectly fitting shirt falling straight over his stomach but pulling tight at the shoulders, chest, and arms, hinting at a lean, muscled body beneath. Melissa couldn't help but feel sympathy for all of them, the men and women both, the vulnerable hope embodied in the careful way they'd done up their hair, their makeup, the outfits they'd chosen—nice but not too nice, trying but not too hard. It was hard and scary and embarrassing, looking for love.

"Shall we make it interesting?" Thomas offered. "How much you want to bet that if I left the table and went to the bathroom right now, by the time I came back there'd be at least two men at the table, trying to get your number."

He shifted his weight on his chair and put a foot on the ground like he was about to get up, and Melissa reached forward to seize his hand on the table.

"Don't," she said. "Stay."

The other women in the room might have been staring at Thomas, but he was only looking at Melissa, gazing intently across the table with an expression so warm it might as well have been the sun. Thomas turned his hand over and grabbed at hers, preventing her from pulling it back—but she didn't want to anyway. She let her hand lie there in his, glanced down at it as he ran his thumb lightly up and down her forefinger, her skin tingling at his touch.

"So," Thomas said. "Melissa Burke."

"That's me."

"I finally got you to come out with me."

"Finally?" Melissa asked. "We met each other, what? Barely twenty-four hours ago?"

"An eternity," Thomas said. "That's what it's felt like. Would you believe me if I told you I've basically spent every waking hour since then thinking about you?"

She shrugged. "Why don't you give it a try?"

"I've spent every waking hour since we met thinking about you."

Melissa flashed him a sly grin. "I don't believe you."

Thomas laughed, a surprised and delighted bark. "Well, it's true."

She lifted her hand out of Thomas's but didn't withdraw to her side of the table. Instead, she curled her fingers around Thomas's wrist and ran her hand up to his forearm, tracing the lines of his veins, his bones, the tendons and sinews of muscle.

"I bet you say that to all the women," she said, resting her chin against her other palm and looking him in the eye.

And she couldn't be sure—but there might have been a hitch in his breath, a reaction to the touch of her fingers on his skin, inching under the fabric of the sleeve rolled almost to his elbow.

"What women?" he said softly. "There's been nobody, Melissa. Not since Rose."

*Rose.* The name of his first wife, his *dead* wife, fell out of his lips and dropped on the table like a stone. Melissa had almost forgotten about her—*almost*—in the brief awkwardness of walking in on the wine bar's singles night, and the light banter that ensued. Biff and Xena, arguing about which of them was drawing stares. But the mention of his wife was a reminder of the specter hovering over the table, the unspoken thing shading every touch, every look, every word. Melissa took her hand away and set it in her lap, sat back in her chair.

"Did I ruin something just now?" Thomas asked. "I shouldn't have mentioned her."

Melissa shook her head. "You didn't ruin anything. And you shouldn't avoid mentioning her name. She's part of you."

"And how she died? What about that?"

"That's part of you too. And we can't avoid talking about it forever. We shouldn't."

"Oh, why not?" Thomas sighed. He poked at the table, scratched the nail of his forefinger against a knot of the varnished wood surface, then folded his arms and propped them on the surface. "All right, look. I've been trying to figure out what to say about this since we met yesterday. I figured someone would tell you about—well, about everything that happened. And that you'd have questions. But to be honest, I still haven't figured out what to say. The only thing I can really say is what I've *been* saying all this time. I didn't kill my wife."

Melissa breathed out, a tension she didn't realize she'd been carrying releasing from her body.

It wasn't much. A simple denial. He'd say it even if he was guilty.

"It was so unfair, everything that happened," he said. He was no longer meeting Melissa's eyes, looking instead at the table. "So *terrible*. First, Rose disappears without a trace. That was bad enough. I was sick with worry, actually physically sick. Frenzied with it. But I had to be strong, for Rhiannon and Kendall. They were scared, and so was I—but I had to put on a brave face, tell them everything was going to be all right."

Thomas's fingers fidgeted nervously on the table, and Melissa reached forward to place her hand on his. His eyes cut up toward her with some mixture of surprise and relief.

"That must have been hard," Melissa said.

"It was. I was barely keeping it together."

"You're a good dad."

Thomas sighed and shook his head, dismissing the compliment. "But then the police decided to declare Rose dead, *presumed* dead, and suddenly they started looking at *me* as a suspect, and...I don't know. It broke me, Melissa. Into a million pieces. To be looking for someone, to be as desperate as I was for her to be okay—and then for the world to take it into their heads that I'd killed her? That I was capable of that? I kept on trying to imagine it, to imagine doing what they said I'd done. To...to stab her to death with a kitchen knife. To roll her up in a tarp, my beautiful wife, like she was nothing more than some trash I was hauling away, to take her to a field and—"

Melissa's breath came shallow, listening to Thomas describe it. The specificity of what he was saying—a kitchen knife, a tarp, a field—shocked her. These were things she hadn't heard before, things Lawrence hadn't bothered to tell her. She snatched her hand away from Thomas's like she was touching something hot. How could Thomas even imagine such things, have these things in his head? Unless...

"That's what they accused me of," Thomas said. "That's what

they said I did." He looked at her with eyes large and pleading, and Melissa realized she'd hurt him by pulling back her hand, by breaking contact with him just then, when he was talking about something that caused him pain. She should reach for him again, she knew, reassure him. But she couldn't bring herself to do it.

"I'm sorry," she said. "I'm sorry for bringing it up. You don't have to talk about it."

"No, I do. I want to finish." He took a deep breath, let it out. "It honestly makes me sick to even think about it. To think about doing those things. I couldn't. I'm a doctor. A healer. A protector. Not a killer."

"I believe you," Melissa whispered, as though trying to convince herself. Then she said it again, more loudly: "I believe you. Okay?" Her moment of being unnerved by the specifics of it, the details of the accusations against Thomas, passed. She felt herself moving toward him again, tilting into his gravity, his pain. What she wanted, she realized, was to *fix* Thomas, to heal him, to release him from the overpowering emotions that gripped him as he talked through his plea of innocence. He'd claimed that being accused of his wife's murder broke him into a million pieces. And he was *still* broken, Melissa could see now, still trying to heal, the cracks still showing. His girls were too. The three of them each carried it differently, the trauma they'd endured—but each of them was hurting in their own way.

"Hey," Melissa said, trying to catch his eye. "Look at me. I believe you, all right? You're a good man."

Thomas let out a grim, exhausted chuckle. "I know of some people who'd like to tell you different."

"Well, I don't care what they say. Because I know what I see. I know what I *know*."

"What do you know?"

She smiled and leaned forward, once more running her hand

up Thomas's forearm to the crook of his elbow. "I know that you're handsome. That you have a kind face. That you saw me, and that I saw you, and that there was something undeniable in it. *Is* something undeniable. Something exciting and comforting at the same time. Something that feels like—that feels like it *could be*—home."

"Yes," Thomas said softly.

"And I know that my son is comfortable around you. That you put him at ease. That you're the kind of man he deserves to have in his life."

Thomas sat back and let out a deep sigh. They both spent a long moment in silence.

"Well," Thomas said after the pause, "things got serious at this table, didn't they?"

"They did."

"Where do we go from here?"

"I have no idea," Melissa said. She glanced behind her and spotted a corridor at the other side of the dining room, a sign for the restrooms. "Tell you what. I'm going to the ladies' room. And when I come back, we're going to start over. Keep it light from now on. Deal?"

Thomas nodded. "Deal."

---

In the bathroom, Melissa gave herself a long, hard look in the mirror. Like most people, she must have glanced at her reflection a dozen times a day, brushing her teeth, checking her makeup. But there was something different about the way she looked at herself now. It was one of those times she looked in the mirror and was surprised by the person she saw there. The woman in the mirror was calm, she was collected, she was beautiful. She looked like she knew exactly what she wanted. Glowing with the certainty of it.

There was no one else in the bathroom, so Melissa let herself speak out loud. "That's me." Then she kissed the tip of her finger and planted it on the mirror.

When she got back to the table, there was a woman standing close to Thomas, talking to him. Blond, tan, attractive, the black straps of her bra visible underneath a tank top, shoulders bared and gleaming under the lights.

Thomas glanced at Melissa as she walked up. "Here she is now," he said, as though he was just talking about her.

"Can I help you?" Melissa said to the woman.

"I was just leaving," she said coldly, and then walked away.

Melissa grinned as the woman receded to the bar. "Told you."

"Told me what?" Thomas asked.

"That someone would hit on you if I stepped away from the table."

"It wasn't what it looked like."

"And what if I want it to be what it looked like? I like all the women here being jealous of me."

Thomas sniffed a laugh, shrugged. "All right. It was what it looked like."

Melissa glanced around the room, felt the furtive glances being shot their way.

"What if we *really* give them something to be jealous of?"

"What do you have in mind?" Thomas asked.

She was still standing, her purse in her hands; Thomas was perched on the edge of his tall chair, legs splayed, feet propped on the ground. Melissa set her purse back on the table and stepped toward him, then grabbed at his shirt right under his throat, the fabric bunching up in her hands.

"This," she said, and pulled him toward her. Their mouths opened as they met, and Thomas tasted of the red wine he'd ordered: chocolate, berries, pepper. He pressed into Melissa and let out a little moan. She felt the vibration of it all the way into her chest.

"Want to get out of here?" Melissa said when they parted.

"Yes, please."

# CHAPTER 6

Lawrence and Toby weren't home, but Thomas and Melissa snuck into the house all the same, stealing around the back and creeping through the sliding door to the basement. Thomas was on her right away once they were inside, his hands seemingly everywhere at once on her body, his mouth mashing against hers, opening as though he wanted to devour her whole.

"The bedroom," Melissa managed, her voice low and raspy.

Thomas led her there by the hand, practically tugging her down the hall and through the door. At the foot of the bed he paused, pulled her close, and kissed her again—long, soft, and tender. His hands stole up to Melissa's chest, cupped her breasts through her top. Melissa let herself fall back toward the bed, tried to pull him with her, but he held back, remained standing. She gazed up at him as he unbuttoned his shirt. As it came off, she got her first look at the body she'd only been guessing at under those clothes, as taut and muscled as she'd imagined, every part of him—his shoulders, his arms, his chest, his stomach—having a shape, a contour, a pattern of lines and shadows. He stood there for a moment, then he reached down and began to undo Melissa's pants. She started to help him with the buttons, but he shook his head.

"No," he said, his voice rough. "Let me."

Melissa let her arms fall back, her hands close to her head, and let Thomas peel the clothes away from her body. As he moved her limbs this way and that, she knew there was something about what was happening—what she'd allowed to happen, what she'd made happen—that was foolish, even dangerous. Bringing a man home, taking him into her bed so soon after she'd met him. Both with children waiting for them, wondering where they were, what was taking them so long. Melissa should've been telling Thomas to stop, telling him that they should wait, that this was going too fast. That would have been the smart thing, the responsible thing. But the wrongness of it only brought a dizzying rush, a drunken feeling Melissa wanted to give herself over to.

And when every inch of her skin was bared to the close air of the bedroom and Melissa saw Thomas's eyes drinking her in, every last ounce of resistance left her, like a physical presence suddenly removed and forgotten.

"God," Thomas said, his voice growing tender. "You're beautiful, you know that?"

Melissa reached for him, pulling him toward her, his weight on top of her body, his mouth moving to the soft skin of her neck. As he kissed her, she explored his body with her hands—his arms, his back, his shoulders. Her fingers tracing the shape of him. Her breathing came faster, and she trailed her fingers into his hair, grabbed a fistful and angled his head toward her, his eyes toward hers.

"I've been waiting so long for this," he said.

Melissa let out a small, airy laugh. "We only met yesterday."

"It's been a long time, I mean," Thomas said. "Maybe I've been waiting for *you* a long time."

His voice grew thick, full with emotion, and as Melissa looked at his eyes, she wondered what he saw in her. What she was to him, what she represented. If the sight of her was tangled up with the memory of his missing, presumed-dead wife. The look in his eyes was more than lust—there was grief there too, and hope, maybe.

Melissa put a finger on his lips.

"Quiet now," she said, and let a sly smile rise to her mouth. "Just have your way with me, would you?"

Thomas's answer was his silence, his mouth opening with a sudden sharp breath.

Neither of them spoke again until it was to whisper each other's names, until they were panting *yes* into the close air of the room— and Melissa didn't let go of Thomas until she was done with him.

---

In the silence after, Melissa simply lay back, staring at the ceiling. The room felt as though it was spinning, even though she wasn't drunk, had only had a sip or two of her wine. Some balance in her was shifting, the recklessness that had driven her into bed with Thomas receding, all the hesitations she'd been holding at bay growing large, shouting at her: *This was a mistake. You shouldn't have done this.*

"What is it?" Thomas asked. "You're quiet. Are you okay?"

"Fine," Melissa said.

"Was that all...okay?"

She softened at his sudden timidity, his vulnerability. "Yes. It was good."

"But?"

Melissa wasn't sure what to say. Not sure how to name the disquiet that had come over her, the sudden animal anxiety thrumming in her veins, the feeling of having stepped recklessly into a place where unseen dangers lurked.

But she had to say something. So she opened her mouth.
And started talking about her ex-husband.

---

Melissa met Carter when both of them were in their midtwenties. Trained in accounting, Melissa was the bookkeeper at a small software company where Carter worked as a quiet coder. Melissa still didn't know what it was about his shy, soft-spoken nature that attracted her to him. But something about him gave the impression that he had a secret, a great one that he'd only tell if you really earned it. And she wanted to earn it.

Melissa did know that she thought Carter was beautiful. His gentle doe eyes, his soft brown beard, and his hands—God, his hands. Even now, knowing everything she knew of the shit show that their marriage became, she loved to think of his hands, both strong and delicate at once.

She was the pursuer at first, flirting with Carter at a couple work happy hours. He mostly just smiled and received her attentions quietly. Later, Melissa asked him out, and he said yes.

It wasn't exactly a legendary romance. Carter was awkward on dates, fumbling in the bedroom, not knowing what he was doing. But there was a sweetness to him, even a sadness, that kept her close. Melissa realized now, in hindsight, that she may have pitied him a little bit, saw him as fragile and breakable, like a baby bird she'd picked up off the ground after it fell out of its nest. Something for her to keep and nurse to health.

His secret, meanwhile—the thing that lay behind his quiet eyes and initially drew Melissa to him—Carter revealed slowly, fully divulging only once they were married: a deep-seated insecurity and even self-hatred that she foolishly spent years trying to fix.

An emotionally weak man, she'd come to believe, was among

the world's greatest threats to a woman's well-being. An unhappy woman would usually turn her problems inward and hurt *herself*, emotionally or even physically. But an unhappy man tended to make his unhappiness everyone else's problem, tormented and devoured and sapped the life force of those around him—especially the women in his life.

Melissa was that woman, for Carter. The cause, he seemed to believe, of all his problems—and he had a lot of them. He was awkward, socially isolated; he didn't have many friends; he struggled to make small talk; his coworkers didn't respect him; his boss didn't like him; he couldn't keep a job for more than a few months at a time. Other people, but especially men, made him feel small, weak, less than. His life was a constant barrage of imagined slights, perceived humiliations, overblown affronts to his pride and self-respect. And he took each of those injuries home to Melissa, where he'd make himself feel better by making her—the one person in the world he thought he was better than, the one person he could safely push around—feel worse.

Carter never hit Melissa. Maybe it would have come to that eventually. The hits in their household were emotional, verbal. He'd insult her, subtly: critique her clothes, her hair, her makeup. He'd imply that he'd be happier if he wasn't married, wasn't stuck with Melissa. He'd cry and whine about the terrible circumstances of his life, hold pity parties and demand that Melissa attend, demand that she comfort him—then berate her for doing it wrong.

There were good moments too. Moments when he was, briefly, happy—and when, as a result, Melissa was happy too. But those moments were short-lived. Something would always happen. A thoughtless comment from a coworker. A restaurant server ignoring their table for too long. A man in a truck cutting them off in traffic. Whatever it was, Carter would get quiet, a sour look coming to his face. That look was all Melissa needed to see to know that a fight was brewing. And it was no use avoiding him, letting things blow over. Nothing ever blew over with Carter. Not until he'd spewed whatever venom had collected in his brain onto Melissa. Poisoning her with it.

Melissa sometimes thought she should have left earlier. Ultimately, it was when she had Bradley that she knew she had to get out of the marriage. For a second during the pregnancy she thought, foolishly, that Carter would be different with a child. That becoming a father would change him. But it didn't. She shuddered, still, at the memory of a grown man angry that the baby in his arms was crying, or calling a three-year-old "stupid" for not being able to tie his shoes. She couldn't think about it for long—it was too painful to remember.

Eventually, she left. Divorced the bastard and got custody of Bradley, even though Carter made a play to keep things fifty-fifty. Melissa's divorce lawyer hired a child psychologist to interview Bradley, who then told the truth as only a child can tell it. He was afraid of his dad. His dad thought he was worthless. His dad hated him.

Melissa would be paying the legal debt for years. But she still regarded the money she spent getting away from Carter—and bringing Bradley with her—as the best money she ever spent.

---

Melissa told Thomas all this, and he listened, his head turned sideways on the pillow. At the end, he waited a few seconds. Then he said, softly, "I'm sorry that happened to you."

"Me too," Melissa said. "It hurt me, Thomas, in ways I don't even fully understand. You told me you were broken—well, I'm broken too. And I'm scared, okay?"

"Scared?" Thomas said, his head lifting off the pillow. "Scared of what?"

"I just need to know…" Melissa said, a hitch in her voice. "I need to know if this is real."

Thomas pushed himself up further, propping himself on an elbow. "Real? What part of it?"

"All of it. This thing between us. And *you*."

"What about me?" Thomas asked, his tone grown sharper.

"Are you for real?" Melissa asked. "This whole dreamy doctor, great dad, nice guy thing. Are you…are you actually *good*? Or is it all an act? I need to know, Thomas. I need to know if it's real, or if you're just like the rest of them."

Her uncertainty just then stood in stark contrast to what she had said earlier, in the wine bar—*You're a good man.* But in that moment, she needed assurance. Because she'd made a bad decision when she fell for Carter. Marrying him was a mistake that had cost her years of her life. She couldn't do something like that again.

This time, the wrong decision could cost Melissa her life.

Thomas burst to his feet, walked jerkily across the room. Melissa gasped at the suddenness of his reaction, startled by his movement. He'd put his boxer briefs back on after they'd finished, but otherwise he was still naked. There was something suddenly animal about him, his muscles straining beneath his skin, sinews and tendons popping taut to the surface. Strength coiled within him, and anger. At the wall next to the door, he cocked his fist back behind his head, and though his clenched hand was pointed in the other direction, away from her, Melissa's arms jerked instinctively, protectively upward, toward her face. She braced for the sound of his knuckles against the wall, the cracking and crumbling of plaster, but it never came. Just as his fist was about to make contact with the wall, he stopped himself, pulled up short. His body still pulled taut, he simply placed his hand on the wall, flat. Pressed his weight against it, like he wanted to push it down.

"Goddammit," he whispered.

Then he turned, and Melissa could see his face again. And it was the strangest thing.

The look on his face wasn't angry.

Thomas was crying. His lips pressed together, folded under, a streak of wet down each of his cheeks.

Melissa couldn't believe it, didn't understand. Men were such odd creatures. Their pain always coming out first as anger.

"This again," he said, almost to himself. "I'll never be rid of it."

"Rid of what?"

"The *accusation*," Thomas said, his voice rising, cresting, then growing soft again. "You're afraid of me. After everything we said to each other at the bar. After what we just did *here*. You're still afraid."

His nakedness in the room—the bulk of his thighs, the dimming light playing across the roundedness of his shoulders— underlined for Melissa what he was saying, the vulnerability of what the two of them had just done together. Stripping down to nothing, removing the armor that separated them. *Intimacy.* Yes, Melissa had wanted him, and it was fun. But it was also risk. Risk for Melissa to bare herself to a man she was still getting to know. And maybe, she was realizing, it was a risk for him too. She hadn't imagined it before then, that Thomas with his perfect body and his beautiful face and his physical strength might be nervous, might even be *afraid* to make love to Melissa. But maybe he was.

Maybe he really did adore her. Maybe he really meant it when he said she was beautiful.

Maybe *he* got butterflies in his stomach when he was around her.

And maybe, by doubting him so soon after he'd made himself vulnerable to her, she'd hurt him without intending to.

"I was telling you the truth back there, you know," he went on. "There've been no women, not since Rose. No one at all, until *you*. You talk about me like I'm this desirable thing, like anyone would want me, but—but did you know that the woman who was at the table when you came out of the bathroom, she didn't actually come over to flirt with me? She recognized me. From the news. She asked me how it feels to be a murderer. To have killed my wife and gotten away with it. She said that. To my *face*."

"Oh, Thomas," Melissa said, the ache in her voice matching the pain, the hard lump of sympathy, that had risen in her chest. "How awful. I had no idea."

"*This* is my life," Thomas said bitterly. "People see me, they recognize me from the news, and they approach me. They think I'm guilty, they think I'm innocent. It doesn't matter. Everyone has to comment. And the *women...*" He cut himself off and let out an exasperated puff of air. "I suppose some of them *have* wanted me, actually. *Have* found me attractive. But it's all been tied up with the accusation that I murdered Rose. Half of them think I didn't do it, and they want to comfort me. The others think I did it, but it's some sort of perverse turn-on. Can you believe that? They think I killed Rose, but it doesn't scare them. It *arouses* them."

Melissa bit her lip, feeling guilty. Was Thomas describing her without knowing it? In the past twenty-four hours, she'd been on both sides of the dichotomy he described: gossiping with Lawrence about the case and feeling both repulsed and excited by the danger of it, the danger of *Thomas*—then, in the next moment, imagining him wronged, imagining him innocent, imagining herself as his savior. The woman who could love him back to life.

"Then I finally meet someone I'm actually interested in, someone I really like for a change, someone I might even be capable of falling in love with..."

Melissa let out a gasp at the L-word. *Love.*

"I like her so much, in fact, that I bring her to my house to meet my daughters. I meet her son. We make love—my first time in years. And it's beautiful. Everything I've been waiting for." Thomas's expression soured. "But then here it is again. Rearing its head. The accusation. Ruining it. Making her afraid of me. Because of this thing, this terrible thing that happened to me—I have to be compared to a bad man. A weak man. A man who hurt her. That's who I am, in her eyes. I have to *prove* myself. Even though that's not who *I* am."

Melissa let the covers fall away from her, her breasts baring to the late evening light cutting across the room, and moved to the end of the bed. She clasped Thomas's hand, pulled on it.

"Thomas, stop. It's all right. I shouldn't have said anything."

There was a voice somewhere in the back of her mind, protesting: *But you're right to ask, you're right to be afraid, you're right to want him to explain. There's so much you don't know. So much you still need to know. What about your safety? What about your son? What about the fact that Thomas is changing the subject, refusing to answer your question?*

The voice was soft, though, and small, and it was drowned out by a new fear: the fear that she was about to lose Thomas, and so soon after she'd made him hers.

"You've said it, though," Thomas said. "You can't take it back."

"I know," Melissa said. "I'm sorry. I'm sorry to have doubted you. It was just a moment, okay? A moment of doubt. I'm messed up, remember? My divorce—it messed with my head."

Thomas looked down at her. "Yeah?"

"I need you," Melissa said, and in that moment it felt true. "I need you to help me heal, okay? And maybe you need me too."

She tugged on his hand, and he began to sink once more toward the bed.

"Come back to bed."

"I don't know," Thomas said, but there was no fight in his voice. "Shouldn't we go back to the kids soon? They'll be wondering where we are."

"It's still early. Come on. Make me feel good. *Dr. Danver.*"

She added the last bit as a little improvisation, and Thomas seemed to like it. Suddenly he was on top of her again, his mouth on hers, his tongue darting past her teeth. Then he kissed down her neck to Melissa's chest, her stomach.

She lay back and let him do what he wanted—telling herself that there was nothing wrong with any of this. Nothing dangerous.

Telling herself that because Thomas *felt* good, he must *be* good.

# CHAPTER 7

Thomas's hands were somehow still all over Melissa on the drive back to his house, even with him driving. Darting across the gap from the gearshift, gripping at her thigh as he steered around the lake. She accepted his touch, placed her hand over his and inched it higher, lacing her fingers with his. She was aware of her body, aware of *his*, in a way that was only possible after recently having sex. As a state of being, it felt both hot and embarrassing at the same time. They didn't call it the "walk of shame" for nothing. Melissa felt as though she were still naked, even with all her clothes on, and—glancing over, remembering what he looked like, what his skin felt like against hers—that Thomas was too.

"Do you think they'll know?" Melissa asked.

"Who?" Thomas asked, turning into the cul-de-sac.

"The kids."

"What? That we've—"

"Yeah," Melissa said. "I feel like it's written all over us."

Thomas pulled into the driveway. "They're kids. I don't think they'll have a clue."

Melissa wasn't so sure about that. Bradley might not know—he was only five. But Thomas's girls were grown. Fifteen and seventeen.

Aware of the world, aware of *sex*, in a way that Thomas might not have wanted to think about. Girls had to be, Melissa knew, to protect themselves. It was a matter of survival.

She didn't say any of this, though. He probably wouldn't want to hear it.

They got out of the car and walked toward the house. On the front walk, Thomas caught up to Melissa and grabbed her hand. She yanked it away.

"Not here," she said. "Let's not make it too obvious."

He grabbed it again. "No, let's."

Melissa eyed him, pausing just outside the front door. "You sure? Even if the kids don't know that we—well…"

"Made love?" Thomas offered.

"Sure," Melissa said, smiling in spite of herself. "Even if they can't tell *that*, seeing us holding hands will tip them off about *something*."

"You don't think the fact we went on a date has already tipped them off?"

"Maybe, but—didn't you just tell your girls I was a friend?"

Thomas shook his head. "Nope," he said. "Before you came over, I sat them down and told them I was going out with a woman I liked a lot. Romantically."

"You didn't."

"I did."

"Why?" Melissa asked.

"Because my girls and I are honest with each other," he said. "We respect each other. And that's part of how we show respect. They tell me everything. And in return, I tell them everything too."

"Including when you go on a date?"

"What did I tell you?" Thomas asked. "There's been no one. Until you. This is the first time I've ever told them I met someone I liked."

87

Melissa thought about that, felt the weight of it. No wonder Rhiannon was so quiet, so sullen, when Melissa dropped off Bradley. The girl probably hated her, thought she was trying to replace her dead mother. She might still have been grieving Rose, might not have been ready for a new woman in her dad's life—or in hers.

"But how do you *know*?" Melissa asked, flustered. "Isn't there some part of you that wants to be careful? That wants to hold back?"

Thomas tugged on her hand, pulled her toward him, and suddenly she was in his arms on the front porch, his hands gripping her at the curve of her waist, pulling her close until their hip bones touched.

"People will see," Melissa breathed, but her hands had risen to his neck, the back of his head—she was holding him too. Grabbing him, as though he'd slip away from her if she let go.

"I don't think either of us is holding back," Thomas said. "Do you?"

Melissa pressed her lips together, shook her head.

"And when you know, you know," Thomas continued. "You know?"

"And you *know*, huh?"

He nodded. "I do. I knew as soon as I saw you."

It was such a *line*, the kind of thing that got said in rom-coms and romance novels, but coming from Thomas's lips, it felt to Melissa like the first time in the history of the world that anyone had expressed the idea, the first time two people had ever fallen so hard and so quickly for each other. Then Thomas leaned in, and Melissa gave in to his kiss, pulling at the back of his neck, keeping him from breaking away too soon. She felt lightheaded again, woozy. Thomas said he'd been waiting a long time for *this*, waiting a long time for *her*—and maybe she'd been waiting too. Waiting for a man who'd take care of her the way she deserved. Now she had it, had *him*, and she let the feeling take over, let the thoughts fall away: the neighbors seeing, the kids and what they might think, even Rose and what might have happened to her. It all dissolved in her head until the only thing left was *him*, the taste of his mouth and the feel of her body pressed close to him.

Then the door clicked open, light from the inside of the house falling across their faces.

"Dad?"

Melissa pulled away from Thomas, straightened out her clothes. She ran her hands through her hair.

"Rhiannon!" Thomas said enthusiastically, like there was nothing to be embarrassed about.

He stepped inside and Melissa followed, ears burning at the withering glare Rhiannon was shooting at her.

"How was the evening?" Thomas asked.

"Fine," Rhiannon said.

A sound of pounding footsteps grew louder, and then Bradley came around the corner and threw himself at Melissa's knees.

"Mom!" he shouted. "Can we go home? You were gone a long time."

Guilt pinged in Melissa's stomach. "Didn't you have fun?"

"I did," Bradley answered, but his voice as he said it was dull, exhausted. He'd spent so much of the day in new places, with new people. Melissa shouldn't have left him so long.

"What did you do?"

"Kendall showed me the woods," Bradley said.

Melissa blinked. "The woods?"

Thomas rushed to answer. "The trees behind our house, next to the lake. It's maybe a hundred acres—hardly a forest, but when they were little, the girls liked to traipse through there and pretend they were explorers."

"Kendall said there's a coyote living back there," Bradley said, and then Melissa understood. An older child had played pretend with him, thinking he'd find it fun, but he'd gotten scared.

"Just a bit of adventure," Thomas said as Bradley buried his face against Melissa's leg. "Where is Kendall, anyway?"

"She had homework," Rhiannon said, nodding upstairs. "I sat with him after we came back to the house."

"You walked with them?" Thomas asked, with a surprised smile.

She shrugged. "We didn't go very far."

Bradley looked up at Melissa. She brushed back the hair from his forehead. "Rhiannon made me a snack," he said. "Popcorn, with butter."

"That was nice of you, Rhiannon," Melissa said. She was surprised—from her sullenness when she'd dropped Bradley off, she'd assumed that the older girl would stay in her room the whole evening, leave the babysitting to her sister.

Rhiannon looked away and didn't answer.

"What did you do?" Bradley asked Melissa.

Thomas let loose a nervous laugh. "Oh, you know..."

"Grown-up stuff," Melissa said. "Nothing fun." She had the urge to reach out and give Thomas a furtive squeeze, but she couldn't risk it—not with Rhiannon giving her the death stare.

"Can I come next time?" Bradley asked.

It was the kind of kid question tailor-made for a dismissive answer—*Oh, I don't know...*—but Thomas sank to his haunches and looked Bradley in the eye.

"Would you like that?" he asked. "You know, we've got some really great parks around here. And I never get to go anymore, because Kendall and Rhiannon are too big to do playgrounds." He gave an exaggerated sad face, like Bradley would really be doing him a favor by going with him to a park. Bradley giggled, perked up.

"Can we, Mom? Tomorrow?"

"Yeah, Melissa," Thomas said, looking up at her with a smirk. "Can we?"

She laughed. "Maybe," she said. "If you're good."

"I'll be good," Bradley said.

"Not you. I was talking about Thomas."

"Oh, I'm *always* good," Thomas said, rising again to his full height.

"I know," Melissa said softly, then gave him a smirk. "*Dr. Danver.*"

Thomas's nostrils flared, and Melissa knew that she'd stirred something in him, turned him on again by reminding him of what she called him in her bedroom.

"Text me," he said. "Let me know."

Melissa nodded. "I will."

---

The drive back to Lawrence and Toby's house was short, but Bradley fell asleep in that time, his head lolling to the side in the back seat, mouth hanging open. The sun was beginning to set when she pulled into the driveway, a streak of flaming orange above the interlaced dark silhouettes of the tree branches looming behind the house. Melissa opened Bradley's door and carefully unsnapped the harnesses on his car seat, then leaned over to wrap her arms around his back and transfer his weight onto her body. His chin nested against her shoulder, and as she rose, he turned his head to fold himself closer to Melissa, the heat of him warming her entire body.

"Hmm," he said, half awakened by Melissa's jostling, but sinking back toward sleep in her arms.

"I've got you, buddy," Melissa whispered, rubbing his back as she walked to the house. She took the stone walkway to the back, stepping carefully in the growing dark, then snuck in through the sliding door, which she'd left unlocked.

The main room—kitchen, dining room, living room—was dark, and she stepped through to the hallway without turning on any lights. She smiled to herself as she passed her bedroom, the room where she and Thomas had made love. The warmth of the secret radiated low in her belly. Melissa let herself think about it as she walked into Bradley's room and lowered him toward the bed. She let the memory of their lovemaking grow in her chest as she changed Bradley's clothes, carefully manipulating his limp, sleep-heavied limbs into pajama pants and a soft shirt with a snoozing cartoon T. rex on the front. Then she pulled up a corner of the sheets and gingerly tugged them out from beneath her son's body, pulling them up to his chin.

*Mine*, she let herself think as Bradley snuggled into his covers, turned onto his side. *This is all mine. I'm so lucky.*

This beautiful boy was hers. This place, this refuge—hers. And Thomas Danver—shockingly, inexplicably—hers.

She stood and tiptoed to the door. She left it open a crack and walked away. In the living room, she turned on a lamp and sat in an upholstered chair. She looked out the tall back windows, toward the lake—a mass of black under the dying ember of the evening sky. She stole a hand up toward her neck, let her fingers trail idly back and forth on the stretch of delicate skin beneath her throat and above the cut of her top. She was aware of her body, aware of herself being in a particular place and a particular moment. There was nothing she wanted to change. She felt happy and protected and safe.

And then she glanced away from the window toward the dining room, and it was all gone in a moment. Anxiety iced through her stomach. Her neck pulled tense.

It was nothing, really—nothing but a single object out of

place. Something she didn't recognize. Something that didn't belong.

An envelope, sitting dead center on the dining room table.

Maybe Lawrence had brought it down. Maybe she'd gotten a piece of mail, and he had delivered it to her when she wasn't around.

But somehow she knew that wasn't true. Someone else brought it here. Someone she didn't give permission to enter her home.

She stood and approached the table slowly, as though the envelope were some kind of creature, a scorpion or a poisonous snake, that might lash out and hurt her.

It was unmarked. No writing on the outside. Unsealed too, the folded flap underneath lifting the envelope just a little off the flat of the table.

Melissa picked it up and turned it over. Pulled out the piece of paper inside: a notebook page, lined, the edges jagged and torn where it was pulled from a wire binding.

She gasped when she saw the message, let the paper drop back to the table.

The words were jagged, messy, scribbled—bearing the evidence of haste. Uncapitalized, unpunctuated, written in black ink from a pen. The chaotic shape of the letters seemed to communicate some unsettled state of mind in the person who'd scrawled them. She stepped back, her shoulder blades hitting the wall behind her, but the piece of paper, open on the tabletop, kept sending its threatening message toward her where she stood.

*stay away from him unless you want to die*

# TRANSCRIPT OF RECORDING

**Thomas:** Do you ever think about…us?

**Amelia:** *Us?* What do you mean?

**Thomas:** You know, you and me. Before Rose came along.

[pause]

**Thomas:** Amelia?

**Amelia:** I'm just a little surprised at the question. Your wife is missing. You're a person of interest in the investigation. And you're asking an ex-girlfriend if I still think about when we were together?

**Thomas:** But this is a safe space, isn't it? That's why I came to *you*, not to someone else. I can't admit this kind of stuff to a stranger. They'd just run to the police.

**Amelia:** Admit…what? What is it you want to confess?

[pause]

**Thomas:** I'm ashamed to say it. Even with you.

**Amelia:** You're wishing you'd ended up with me, is that it? You regret marrying Rose?

**Thomas:** Is that terrible? You think I'm a bad person now. My wife is missing, presumed dead, and here I am acting like I'm *glad* she's gone. It's only a part of me, a small part of me, that thinks that way. Ninety-nine percent of me—I'm desperate to get her back, Amelia. Desperate to find her alive. You have to understand that. I'm sorry. I shouldn't have said anything.

**Amelia:** It's all right. I think I understand. Emotions are…they're complicated. Our genuine feelings aren't always what others would recognize as socially appropriate. You're going through a trauma, and your marriage has been difficult at

times—of course some small part of you would be specu-
lating about if you'd made different choices in the past. It's
just...

**Thomas:** What?

**Amelia:** It's nothing. We're here for you, not for me.

**Thomas:** But we're not *really* therapist and patient, remember? Just
two friends, talking during a difficult time. Come on, just tell
me.

**Amelia:** Well, I'm feeling a little annoyed, Thomas. A little angry,
actually. If I'm honest.

**Thomas:** Angry? Why?

**Amelia:** Well, my recollection is that it was *you* who decided to move
on, all those years ago. It's not my fault we didn't end up
together.

**Thomas:** So you *do* think about us.

**Amelia:** [sighs] I suppose I do.

**Thomas:** Okay. Well, first of all—that's not exactly how I remember
it. Yeah, I rebounded with Rose. But you broke up with
*me*, remember? What was I supposed to do? Be alone
forever?

**Amelia:** It wasn't a *breakup*, it was a *break*. We were both in med
school, stressed out of our minds with the workload—I just
needed some space, for a little while. We both did. I didn't
think you'd run out and get yourself another girlfriend so
quickly. Much less marry her.

**Thomas:** You're hurt.

**Amelia:** I *was*. At the time.

**Thomas:** It sounds fresh, though. The way you're talking about it.
You're still hurt.

**Amelia:** Maybe. Maybe I am.

**Thomas:** Well, did it ever occur to you that maybe you hurt me too?
I didn't hear it as a temporary thing—I thought you were

done with me forever. You wanted to split up so you could focus on your work. Your ambitions for yourself.

**Amelia:** What's wrong with that? You were ambitious too.

**Thomas:** Nothing's wrong with it. And you're right. I was also ambitious. It's just, I was second to all the things you wanted to accomplish in your life. I knew that, and I didn't see it changing. So yeah, I went out and found someone else. But it was a mistake, Amelia. That's what I'm telling you. It was a mistake, and now that Rose is gone, I can finally admit that.

**Amelia:** Is that why you tried so hard to keep me close all these years? You knew you'd made a mistake with Rose, so you were keeping me nearby as…what? Your backup plan?

**Thomas:** Come on. You know it was never like that.

**Amelia:** Wasn't it? How did I end up as your next-door neighbor, Thomas?

**Thomas:** That was your choice. Nobody forced you.

**Amelia:** No, but you suggested it. Told me about this perfect house that went for sale next to you, said it would be a great place for me to see patients.

**Thomas:** Okay, and then you moved here. I told you about the house, but you were the one who chose to come. Why? I've confessed to you that I've been thinking about *us*, the way we were together all those years ago, how perfect we were together. Haven't you been thinking the same way? You say I've kept you close—and that's true. But why have you *stayed* close? Is it because some part of you hoped we'd end up together too? Is there a part of you that's glad Rose is gone?

**Amelia:** I'm incredibly concerned for Rose's safety.

**Thomas:** Come on. Just admit it.

**Amelia:** I can't. I won't. Do you have any idea what people would say if they knew we were talking like this? The police, for one?

**Thomas:** Oh, I know. They'd say I killed her.

**Amelia:** No.

**Thomas:** No? Then what would they say?

**Amelia:** That *I* killed her.

# ROSE

*My husband doesn't love me anymore.*

*He used to. I know he did. The way he used to look at me, to speak to me, to touch me. There was no mistaking it. Like I was some rare and precious thing. Like he was the luckiest man in the world, to have someone like me.*

*The way he looked at me when I first saw him. When I opened my eyes and saw him standing there, gazing at me like I was the most beautiful thing he'd ever seen.*

*We were both in graduate school. He was a med student, and I was studying studio art. I was in a bit of a bad place, actually, realizing that I'd gone on to get an MFA in visual art not because I was any good at painting, but because I basically wasn't good at anything else. Because I didn't know what else to do. But that wasn't a good reason to spend thousands of dollars on school, to go into more debt, and I was slowly realizing it. I wasn't going to become a famous painter, probably wasn't even going to get a job as a museum curator or college art professor. I should drop out. But I didn't know what else I was going to do. My life had become all dead ends.*

*I went on a walk to clear my head, and that's when it started snowing: big, fat flakes that tumbled down and settled on my hair and shoulders like dandruff. Under the light of a streetlamp, I raised my face to the sky and felt the cold on my face. The momentary shock of it erased my thoughts for a moment, erased me, until all there was was that moment. Maybe I wanted to be swept away with it, buried in it, the white creeping up from my ankles to my knees, my waist,* my head. *Encased in a snowbank, my body discovered in the spring.*

The thought was scary—scary how much I liked it—and in that moment I heard a voice, saying something about catching my death of cold. My eyes snapped open, and there he was. Thomas. Lit up under the light like a saint, a gold-foiled icon, a stained glass window with light pouring through into darkness. Later, he told me he thought I looked like an angel, but it was he who looked most like an ethereal creature, and anyone who's ever seen Thomas will know what I'm talking about. He's a very handsome man—a perfect smile, gorgeous eyes, wavy hair you want to run your hands through—and in that moment, he appeared to me as a kind of savior. A golden god.

The god reached out to brush the snow from my hair, and I just watched him do it, amazed at this turn of events: from thoughts of dying, of letting myself fade away, to being touched by the most gorgeous man who'd ever deigned to speak to me, in the course of—what? Ten seconds? Then he put a hand to my cheek, skin touching skin, and I swear it was like water in the desert. My body wanted it so badly, a bit of tenderness, and before I knew what I was doing, my hands had darted up to grab his wrist and hold him there. I closed my eyes and pressed into him, and when I finally opened my eyes, he asked me if I wanted to come inside.

I wasn't sure what he meant—inside where?—but I'd have done anything for him just then. If he meant his apartment, I'd have followed him. I didn't even know his name yet, but I'd have let him take me to his bed, if that's what he wanted.

As it turned out, he only wanted me to come into a bar, where he bought me a beer.

*We were from different worlds. His world was the world of science, of labs and figures of the human body, Latin names of muscles and nerves, cadavers to take apart, exams to cram for. Mine was a world of art, of studio time, of figure drawing and clay, of paint daubed on a canvas. And maybe that's why we fit, at first. Because we were so different. For me, he was something steady, when I was the opposite. I was a mess, but he had everything together. I didn't know what I wanted out of life, but he knew exactly what he wanted. He wanted to be a pediatrician. He wanted to help kids.*

*Thomas was something solid in a life that had become unstable. Insubstantial as wind. Thomas anchored me. That's what he was to me.*

*And what was I, to him? An escape, perhaps. Thomas was tied to the earth, bound—as an aspiring doctor—to bodies, bones, flesh. He was tied down by his overwhelming schoolwork, by the grueling medical internships and residencies that were coming for him soon enough. His ambition, the impressive thing he wanted desperately to become, motivated him to work hard, but it was also an unbearable weight on his shoulders. And he wanted to rid himself of that weight. He wanted to fly.*

*Did he think I could help him? Did he think that's what I was doing out there in the snow, my arms outstretched? Flap my wings and lift into the sky?*

*He seemed to, that first time in the bar, and later, as we began seeing each other more. Asking me questions about my studies, about art, like it was a form of magic, of witchcraft. Like I was the practitioner of some mysterious craft. I should have told him the truth right then and there—I wasn't magic,*

*I wasn't mysterious, I couldn't help him defy gravity. But I didn't. Maybe he made me believe it. Believe that I could be his manic pixie dream girl.*

*He learned about me soon enough. Learned about my moods, about my volatility. I'd get depressed, I'd get hopeless, I'd call him crying to come over, begging him to make me stop feeling this way. Panic coming to his eyes as he realized that there were things inside me he didn't understand. That he couldn't see all the way to the bottom of me. That there were things lurking there. Scary things.*

*But here's another thing about Thomas: He really loves the idea of saving people. You see, some doctors go into the profession because they genuinely want to help people. Others practice medicine because they're attached to the idea of helping people. That's a delicate distinction, but an important one. I didn't know which kind Thomas was at the time. But either way, he stuck with me, rolled through my moods, my episodes, learning that they were the price for the things about me that were good.*

*(By the way, in case it isn't clear, Thomas is the second type of doctor. The kind who helps people not because he wants to, because of who it makes him. The protector. The savior.)*

---

*Maybe every marriage is a mistake. Two people, together forever? I'm sorry, but it doesn't work. It's just that some mistakes are bigger than others. Some mistakes aren't fatal. Some mistakes can be managed—those are the "good" marriages. Even good marriages don't work, part of the time. The people in them push through the not-working to the working. They're small mistakes, these marriages. Happy mistakes. The kind where you get to the end of your life and shrug. Maybe it wasn't perfect. Nothing is. But it was more good than bad.*

*Our marriage, Thomas's and mine, was a big mistake. And it was, if I'm honest, my mistake. Not that I was the one to propose—Thomas did that, ever the traditionalist. But I was the one to push our relationship from being fairly casual to something more serious. For once, I was the one who had a plan.*

*It happened around the time that I finally dropped out of school, finally faced up to the fact that it would be nothing more than another dead end. An expensive dead end.*

*Before I made it official, I went to Thomas with...well, with a proposal. We should move in together. I'd worked it all out in my head, you see. We'd get an apartment together. I'd work shit jobs, whatever I could get, to make rent while he worked his way to being a full doctor. I'd wait tables, pull espressos, pour beers into pint glasses. Hustle for tips. I'd support him through school, be his escape. Work hard to be more his manic pixie dream girl than her opposite: depressive harpy nightmare woman. I'd have elaborate dinners ready for him when he came home, surprise parties for his birthday, kooky decorations for Valentine's and Halloween, blow jobs when he crawled into bed after a long rotation.*

*Then, he'd be a full doctor, and I'd be set. My whole life, planned. I'd be flight, he'd be gravity. I'd be wind—he'd be ballast, a rudder, sails. Direction.*

*We did it. Moved in together. Somewhere in the middle of his residency, he moved ahead on the second phase of the plan—I think he knew I expected him to—by asking me to marry him.*

*But it was a mistake. Oh, was it ever a mistake. One of the big ones.*

———————

*I don't know precisely when Thomas started to hate me. I think maybe he always did, even when he loved me. They're more tied up than we think, love and hate—both emotions are a confession that someone matters to us, that they have power over how we feel. Thomas was always puzzled by my dark moods, didn't know what to do about them. They made him feel powerless. But he loved me through them, as well. Adored me still for who I could be, who he thought I was when we first met. The image of me he clung to for far too long.*

*But his hate grew and gradually overtook his love. Dwarfed it. I think his hate for me acquired majority share in the business of his feelings for me when we he realized that nothing he did could make me happy. Not marrying me, or eventually becoming the respected doctor he'd always planned to be—that only made me realize how small I'd become next to him, opening up an emptiness inside me that I could only fill by drinking. And not making me a mother twice over—the girls, Rhiannon and then Kendall, only terrified me with their huge eyes gazing up at me, with their insatiable hungers for food, for attention, for love.*

*It was when the girls came into our lives that the break between Thomas and me became complete. He's still married to me, but only on paper. Only in the eyes of the world. Not in his heart.*

*Whatever love he had for me was transferred to them when they were born. He's a dad now. A good dad. That's*

*what everyone says about him. Throwing it in my face,*
*reminding me how good I have it. Better than I deserve.*
*Such a good dad.*
*Maybe. But a terrible husband.*

# CHAPTER 8

Melissa brought Bradley to day care again the next day and then went straight home. She didn't feel safe in Lawrence's basement anymore—but she didn't feel safe anywhere else either. She felt like she was being watched now, sensed unseen eyes on her as she drove around town, as she held Bradley's hand to the door, as she gave him a hug in the entryway. Back home, she locked all the doors, pulled the curtains. Listened for sounds of movement. For someone trying to break in.

She was supposed to be looking for jobs. That's what she needed—a bookkeeping job so she could pay her rent to Lawrence, fill the fridge with food, pay off the credit card she put the cost of moving on, the legal debt laid on top of her shoulders like a stone.

But she couldn't concentrate.

She was thinking about the note. Still sitting on the dining room table, folded open. She couldn't see the message from where she sat, but she didn't have to. She'd memorized every word, every letter, every jagged swoop.

*stay away from him unless you want to die*

Melissa had so many questions about the note, starting with *how* and *when*. How did someone sneak it into her apartment at all? And when did they do it?

*How* was easy enough. There were three entrances to Melissa's basement apartment. One was through a side door from a garage stall Lawrence and Toby allowed her to use. She usually parked her car inside, closed the garage door behind her, then took some wood steps down to an entry door that put her in a mudroom at the edge of the apartment. Another entrance, obviously, from the top of the stairs. She didn't think anyone could have gotten in through either of those doors. Too many locks and no signs of forced entry.

That left the third option: the back entrance. A sliding glass door to the patio and a view to the lake. Melissa had a tendency to forget about the lock on the sliding door, and often left it unlocked, even overnight. This was a bad idea, she knew, and she was certainly going to lock it from now on. Her intruder almost certainly got in that way.

The next question was *when*. Melissa didn't remember seeing a note on the table when she and Thomas stumbled in from their short date. Then again, they were a little distracted at the time, their hands all over each other as they stumbled to the bedroom. Something could have been there, and neither of them noticed.

Another possibility—that someone snuck in and put the note on the table while Thomas and Melissa were having sex, while she was panting his name the next room over—brought a chill of horror. She couldn't even think about it.

Or the intruder came in while Thomas and Melissa went back to his house to pick up Bradley. Came in through the sliding door, put the note on the table for her to find, and then left before she came back.

The next set of questions, *who* and *why*, were tangled up

together in Melissa's mind. There was a lack of clarity in the note, in its intent: *stay away from him unless you want to die.* Was it a warning? Or a threat? Someone who believed Thomas was a murderer, trying to tell Melissa he was more dangerous than she believed? Or someone who was threatening to hurt her themselves? Maybe it was even—she shuddered again to think of it—the person who really killed Rose. Melissa recalled what Lawrence told her, the night she and Thomas first met. *Rose had a stalker.* What was this, if not stalking?

The first person her mind went to was Amelia. The trace of possessiveness in the way she talked about Thomas, the buzz of attraction Melissa sensed when she came upon them in the coffee shop. They had history. They used to be together, before Rose. And Amelia had opportunity. She lived next door to Thomas, which meant she could have been watching out the window when Melissa went over there to drop Bradley off. Watching again when she came to get him again. Seething inside her house, hating Melissa for stealing Thomas away from her. Stealing him *again*, after already losing him, years before, to Rose. Maybe she was Rose's stalker. Maybe she was the one who killed her.

And maybe Melissa was next.

She shook her head, pushing the thought away. Amelia may have been a little cold, a little aloof, and maybe she *did* still have feelings for Thomas—but none of that made her capable of murder. Besides, if she wanted Thomas enough to kill, wouldn't she have been with him by now, three years after Rose's disappearance?

Just then, Melissa's phone began buzzing. Two vibrations, in quick succession. She glanced at the screen and saw two Facebook notifications. She'd been tagged in a photo. And someone mentioned her in a comment.

Melissa rarely ever used Facebook anymore. Since the divorce, she hadn't wanted to leave too much evidence of herself online, not wanting Carter, her ex, to be able to follow her or see what she was doing. Not even wanting gossip to get back to him, from old friends she left behind in the move. As much as possible, she wanted to have a clean slate.

But Melissa still had a profile. She stood and moved toward the kitchen, where her laptop was on the counter. She pulled out a stool and sat, opened the laptop, and went to Facebook. Clicked on the notification, expecting a photo from the dinner party, maybe—Lawrence tagging a photo of her looking put together and sophisticated, hoping to connect her with even more of his friends in the area.

She should have braced herself for the worst. Because when the photo came up on the screen, she wasn't ready. She practically fell off her stool.

The photo she saw was of her and Thomas kissing. Passionately. She held him by the scruff of his button-down, the fabric straining as she pulled him toward her. Their lips locked together and open, tasting each other. She let out a humiliated groan, and her hands went to her eyes, covering them—but she couldn't unsee the photo. She thought she looked ridiculous, like a drunk club girl throwing herself at a random guy while her friends documented the evidence on their phones.

But how could anyone have gotten a picture of them kissing in the first place? For an irrational second, Melissa imagined the intruder as the photographer, hiding somewhere in the apartment—behind the couch?—as she and Thomas stumbled through the living room. She immediately dismissed the thought. It was impossible; they could have missed a white envelope on the dining room table, but there was no way they'd have missed a whole person, not in this small apartment. Melissa made herself look at the photo again, looking past Thomas and her to the details surrounding them, noticing for the first time the familiar wall decorations, the high-top table, the wineglasses.

Of course. The wine bar. She'd gone to the bathroom, then came back to see Thomas speaking to a woman. And after she left, Melissa had kissed him. Marked her territory, established him as hers. Then asked him back to the apartment. That must have been when someone snapped the photo, put it online.

After the shock of seeing the photo had worn off, Melissa was able to take in the rest of the details. The photo was on the feed of a public Facebook group called *Justice for Rose Danver*, posted there by a user named Kelli Walker. Melissa clicked on Kelli Walker's profile and saw a face she recognized. It was the woman from the wine bar—same blond hair, same tanned, round face. Her profile picture had her posed, smiling, with two husky teenage boys in NASCAR T-shirts and a man with a mesh baseball cap, messy facial hair, and a scowl on his face. Melissa had a feeling she'd dislike Kelli Walker, even aside from the fact that she'd snapped a picture of her and posted it to social media without her permission. Kelli looked like the kind of woman who'd get in a fight with a neighbor over a property line, who'd oppose the construction of a subsidized housing unit in her neighborhood. The kind of woman who was quick to call the cops, to threaten a lawsuit, to ask for a manager.

Back to the Facebook group, and the photo of Melissa and Thomas, where she read what Kelli wrote when she posted it:

Dr. Danger spotted at a wine bar in the north suburbs. Does anyone know this woman? Someone should warn her about who she's locking lips with.

*Dr. Danger?*

Melissa clicked to expand the comments:

Don't recognize her. Is that a name tag I see? Some kind of
    event?
Some sort of singles mixer. I looked, but they both had fake
    names.
Sneaky! What a lying bastard he is.
She's in danger! Help her!
Unless she knows what he is and is into it. If so, this bitch
    deserves what's coming to her.
Hope you're wrong but there are women like that. Lots of
    sick people in this world.
We shouldn't assume.
I think I might recognize this woman. Hard to tell, but this
    looks a little like a woman who moved into my neighbor's
    basement. They're friends of Thomas Danver, people who
    think he's innocent, so it makes total sense that they'd set
    her up with this wife-killer.
God I hate these people. Just look at all the evidence!
    They're setting up another woman to get abused and
    murdered by this evil man. They're as guilty as he is. We
    really need to help her. Can you get her name?
I'll ask around.
Ok I think I found her. **Melissa Burke** is this you?

Below this last comment, Kelli had posted a reply:

Thank you for finding her! I just tagged her in the photo so
hopefully she sees this. **Melissa Burke** please contact us!
You are dating a murderer! Just look at the pinned post for
this group. My DMs are always open.

Kelli's DMs were more than just *open*, apparently, because just as Melissa read her comment, she got a message from her, popping up in the bottom corner of her screen.

Hey! Maybe you've seen the posts on our Justice for Rose group. I'd love to get in touch with you to talk.

Maybe Melissa should have listened to what Kelli had to say, but in the moment, all she could feel was a blind fury. The women in the Justice for Rose Danver group—they all seemed to be women—might have thought they were helping Melissa, but everything she'd seen on the page so far was an invasion of privacy. *Her* privacy. They wanted to convince her that Thomas was a killer, but right then it was Kelli Walker she felt most violated by, Kelli Walker who'd committed what felt like a crime against her. Wasn't it against the law to take someone's picture without their consent, to post it online, to let a group of strangers loose on identifying you? Maybe not, but it should have been. Breaking and entering was certainly illegal, at least—and as she looked at the messages laid out in front of her, the comments on the photo and the direct message, Melissa was seized by the sudden certainty that Kelli Walker was the one who'd snuck into her apartment, who'd left a hastily scrawled message of warning on her dining room table.

Melissa thought of calling the cops on Kelli—but what good would that do? She only had suspicion, no proof. A cop would shrug, ask her to call back when she had more.

Melissa put her cursor in the reply box.

Please stay away from me.

Kelli's response came immediately.

Just look at what we have. The evidence we've gathered.

Melissa shook her head and let out a disbelieving gasp. The gall of this woman.

There are currently no charges against Thomas for anything. You're the one who's breaking the law, by harassing me. Leave me alone or you will be receiving a visit from the police.

The status on the message went to *Read*. Melissa waited, but no additional message came. Finally, Kelli was getting the hint.

Melissa slapped the laptop closed and started walking around the apartment, feeling the need to move. But it was a small apartment; there was nowhere to go. She went to the sliding door and gave it an angry pull, stepped onto the patio, let her feet carry her through the trees to the lake. Melissa was still furious, feeling the violation of privacy on her body, a kind of film lying atop her skin. She was hoping the lake would soothe her, the light lap of the waves carrying these feelings away, but it didn't. She ground the heels of her hands against her eyes, wishing for this angry energy to crest and break. Wishing herself to cry, to let it out. But the tears didn't come, and when she let her hands fall back to her sides, she realized it wasn't just anger at Kelli she was feeling. There was curiosity there too, and dread.

Curiosity at the evidence Kelli and the Justice for Rose Danver Facebook group claimed to have. Dread at what it might be. Whether it would change the way she looked at Thomas.

"Goddammit," she said aloud, resignation in her voice. "Goddamn you."

She turned and walked back to the house. Back to her laptop.

And back to the Facebook group, where she scrolled to the top of the feed. To the long pinned post drafted by—who else?—Kelli Walker.

> Welcome to Justice for Rose Danver. Rose was a close friend of mine, which is why I started this group. I and most of the group members here firmly believe that Rose's husband, Thomas Danver, is responsible for her disappearance. Thomas Danver is a murderer.

We call on the county prosecutor to reinstate the charges against him immediately and bring this dangerous criminal to trial.

Before she disappeared, Rose told me she was afraid of her husband. Thomas tormented her mentally and emotionally. He undermined her, demeaned her, and gaslit her until she could no longer trust her own mind. He sowed paranoia, self-hatred, depression, and substance abuse in her—then used these things to portray her as crazy. He turned her own children against her. And at the end—maybe all along, without my knowing—he was physically violent toward her. I personally sat next to an emergency room bed with Rose, her face lacerated and bruised from what he did to her. I called the police and tried to convince her to press charges against him. But she refused. She was too afraid. Afraid he'd kill her.

I have shared what I know with the police. But still the county prosecutor refuses to bring this case to trial. Why? What does Thomas Danver have on you?

This group has obtained more evidence. The prosecutor's office has tried to withhold it from us, claiming that the investigation into Rose's disappearance and presumed murder is still active. But a source who was involved in the investigation into Thomas Danver has leaked information to us. Here is what we know.

Aside from her murderer, I was the last person to see

Rose Danver. We met for lunch. On that day, she told me that she'd made an important decision, that she was going to leave Thomas, that she was going to the police to take out a restraining order against him. I told her she was making the right decision.

That was the last time anyone saw her alive.

Thomas Danver went on a trip late that night, driving to a remote cabin that he and Rose owned in northern Minnesota. He claims he went there looking for Rose, to see if that was where she'd gone missing.

We also know that an hour before he took this trip, he purchased three items at a nearby hardware store. A tarp, rope, a shovel. Why, Dr. Danver? (Or should I say Dr. DANGER?) Because he was preparing to bury Rose's body.

During this trip, Thomas turned off his phone and his car's GPS. Again, why? So he could not be traced. So the police could not find the place where he buried Rose.

And finally, we know that before he came back to the Twin Cities, Thomas briefly turned his phone back on in the vicinity of his cabin, to email a cleaning service asking for a deep clean of his house, with special focus on the kitchen floor. He specifically asked for bleach to be used. Why? Because when Rose told him of her plans to leave him, he killed her in a fit of rage, hastily cleaned up the evidence, and then hoped that a professional cleaning would remove all traces of blood.

After he returned from his trip, he reported Rose missing. By this time, she had already been dead two days. And by the time the police began to suspect that Rose was dead and began to investigate Thomas, she was already buried in a field somewhere. The house had already been professionally cleaned—though they still found traces of Rose's blood in the kitchen. It's hard to get rid of blood completely.

With the blood, Thomas's hardware store purchases, his delay in reporting Rose missing, and the testimony I provided about Thomas's abuse, they charged him and were preparing to bring the case to trial. But then they dropped the charges.

WHY?

Nausea grew in Melissa's stomach as she read Kelli's post. Lawrence hadn't shared any of this when he told her about Thomas's past— didn't tell her much about the evidence against him except to say that it was weak, circumstantial. This felt like more than that. Maybe it wasn't a slam-dunk case, but it still looked bad for Thomas. Bad for *Melissa*—the woman who was gullible enough, credulous enough, to go on a date with him. To bring him into her bed.

She took deep breaths and tried to remind herself of what she knew. Namely, that Thomas wasn't in jail. He was walking around, a free man. In spite of the evidence against him, he hadn't been convicted of a crime. In fact, as Kelli admitted at the end of her post, the county attorney dropped the charges against him. She claimed not to know why, but Melissa was sure the prosecutor had good reasons for dropping the case. Maybe the evidence was weaker than Kelli Walker presented it. Maybe Thomas had a good explanation for all of it. Who should Melissa trust—Thomas, the man who'd been so kind to her and her son, who she found so attractive, who a dear friend and her own *gut* told her was safe and could never do what he was being accused of? Or Kelli Walker? A woman she didn't even know? A meddlesome, nosy woman who spied on her, took her photo, posted it on social media without her knowing? A woman who might have even broken into her home? The only person Melissa was pretty certain had committed a crime here was *Kelli*.

There was also the fact that Rose had had a stalker. That was the information Thomas and his defense attorney had given to the prosecutors to make them drop the case. Thomas's wife was being threatened by someone, someone who wasn't Thomas, and instead of taking it seriously, the police ignored it.

Kelli Walker hadn't mentioned anything about that, Melissa noted. Shouldn't a group dedicated to justice for a missing and possibly murdered woman have been looking at *all* the suspects?

Melissa expanded the comments on Kelli's pinned post, looking for some mention of other suspects. There was nothing in the comments other than expressions of outrage against Thomas, so she began scrolling through the group feed, looking for other popular posts. She got about three posts deep before she found it:

What about the stalker theory? Has this group looked into that?

The top comment under the post was Kelli's, with dozens of likes on it.

The stalker theory is complete and utter bullshit. It's
something Dr. Danger and his high-priced lawyer cooked
up out of thin air.

Melissa cocked her head, suspicious. Something wasn't right in
how quickly Kelli dismissed the question. Why was she so fixated
on Thomas as the killer, and why wouldn't she consider any other
theories?

Just then, Melissa's phone buzzed on the counter. She glanced
at it to see messages coming in from Thomas.

Hey. Thinking about you today. And about last night.

Melissa felt a flush of warmth spread through her body as she
thought of Thomas in her bed, peeling her clothes away from her
body, putting his hands on her. In spite of herself, in spite of everything she was learning, she wanted him back, wanted him here—
and wanted him now.

I want to see you again.

Melissa sucked in a breath and held it while she typed out a
response.

I don't know. This is going a little fast.

The dots appeared, and the message took a while to come.

I know. And I'm sorry. We can slow it down. As slow as you want.
Just meet me. Now that I've had you, I can't go a day without you. I'm
addicted, Melissa.

Melissa's held breath came out as a laugh, light and airy. She'd
never had a man come on so strong before—never had a man who'd
claimed to be this attracted to her, to want her this badly, to be
*addicted* to her. It was intoxicating.

Maybe she was addicted too.

Meet me at the park, Thomas messaged before Melissa could
think of a response. The playground. I promised Bradley, remember?

You did, she responded.

**So let's do it. After I get off work.**

Melissa paused before responding, thinking it through. She needed to be careful, to look at all the angles. Her body, her gut, were telling her one thing: telling her to trust Thomas, to trust her attraction to him. Telling her that the way she felt about him couldn't be a mistake, couldn't be a lie. But her mind was telling her something else entirely: that Thomas might be dangerous. That she should take the evidence against him seriously, even if it was being presented by a woman she didn't know or trust.

Bringing her son to see a suspected murderer was not something a responsible person—a responsible *mother*—would do.

Then again, a park was a public place. It would be safe.

Maybe, Melissa reasoned, she could do one more meeting with Thomas. One more opportunity to figure out what she really thought of him.

She tapped out a response.

**Okay. Tell me when and where.**

# CHAPTER 9

In the rearview, Melissa saw Bradley's eyes light up when she drove up to the park where Thomas had asked to meet. It was an epic construction, not the standard-issue set of slides and swings and merry-go-rounds Melissa grew up with, but a whole multicolored plastic wonderland full of zip lines and obstacle courses, forts and bridges, climbing walls and rubber lily pads for jumping on. It looked more like an amusement park than a playground. The price of an amazing playground was a big crowd, though, and this place had one—dozens upon dozens of children clambering over every piece of equipment, parents chasing or standing at the edge under shade, fanning themselves against the late-summer heat and craning their necks to keep eyes on their kids.

"This place is *amazing*," Bradley said as Melissa pulled up to the curb, and he was unbuckling himself from his seat and straining against the door as the car whined to a stop. As soon as she got it in park, he opened the back door and tore across the grass to the playground.

"Wait for me!" Melissa shouted as she climbed out of the driver's side, afraid of losing him—but he was long gone, sprinting ahead of her. She followed, the car horn chirping as the doors locked behind her. From the crowd below, a man detached from the scrum of parents and came to intercept Bradley. It was Thomas. He sank to one knee and talked to Bradley for a second, then raised a hand for a high five. Bradley jumped to give it a slap, then ran the rest of the way toward the playground.

Thomas rose from the grass and came toward Melissa. God, would she ever be able to see him without an excited flutter in her chest? In sunglasses and a tight polo that hugged the bulk of his chest and shoulders, he looked like a movie star of the silver fox variety. The evening sun highlighted the gray in his hair, but it made him look distinguished rather than old, and his smile had to be the brightest thing for miles.

"Hey," he said as he came close, then leaned in for what Melissa thought was going to be a friendly peck but then turned out to be a real kiss—just long enough to get her heart rate up, his lips and hers parting only slightly, his hand coming to her hip and sliding down, not so far that he was grabbing her butt in public but far enough to let her know he wanted to.

Melissa felt a little dizzy as they parted, but then she remembered the crowd of parents around and another feeling came in behind the flutteriness: paranoia. Was it her imagination, or were people watching them? Were any of the people there part of the Facebook group? Did they recognize Melissa, know her name? Were they texting each other right now? *Oh my god, he's here, it's Dr. Danger and that woman, he just mauled her right in the middle of the park.* She cringed to imagine it, cringed to think of strangers lurking at the edges, snapping more furtive photos that would end up online.

Melissa took a step back, put a bit of distance between her and Thomas.

"Everything okay?" he asked, a flash of hurt passing across his eyes.

"Fine," Melissa said.

"Push me!" Bradley shouted from a distance. He was sitting on a swing at a dead stop below the bar, kicking his legs uselessly.

Thomas moved toward him, but Melissa walked quickly and got there first.

"I want Thomas to do it!" Bradley whined, but Melissa was already pulling his seat back into the air. She let go and gave him a few pushes until his feet flew high into the air on the upswing.

"Stop!" Bradley yelled as the swing creaked back and forth. "I don't want you to do it!"

Thomas stepped close to her elbow. "Can I?" he asked.

Melissa shook her head. "I got it."

But Bradley kept whining, and after a couple minutes she let him off the swing.

"Why don't you go run and find something else," Thomas suggested. "Your mom and I will watch you, okay?"

Bradley scampered off, and Melissa was alone with Thomas.

"Is something wrong?" he asked. "You seem a little distracted."

"It was a weird day," she said.

"Yeah? Because I'm feeling worried it's something I did. I know in your text you said you felt this was going a little fast, and—well, we can slow things down if you want. Honestly. I just want to keep seeing you."

"I know," Melissa said. "You've made that clear."

Thomas was quiet a beat. Melissa was watching Bradley on the other side of the playground, clambering through a contraption made of webbed rope knotted for climbing. She wasn't looking at Thomas, but she could feel him looking at her.

"Is this about last night?" he asked. "You know, I didn't intend to push you. I honestly thought—it seemed like something you wanted. You kissed me at the wine bar, then asked me back to your place, so I figured... But maybe that was a mistake. If so, I'm—"

"Stop," Melissa said. "It's not that."

"What, then?"

She turned and took a moment to study him. She wondered if she could imagine him doing it—killing Rose. Stabbing her in his kitchen. Then trying to clean up the blood. Putting her body in his trunk, driving north to bury her where no one could find her. At first Melissa thought she *could* imagine it, *could* believe it was true, and something in her recoiled from him, drew back in horror. Then she blinked slow, a split second of black before Thomas appeared again before her eyes, and suddenly it was unimaginable again. Unthinkable that this man standing before her could be a killer.

She sighed and reached for her phone in her pocket. She thumbed it open, tapped her way to Facebook, then showed him the photo. Held the screen out toward him, forcing him to look at it.

"What the fuck?"

"Take it," Melissa said, pushing the phone in his face.

He took it from her hands, holding it gingerly by the sides. "This is us," he said. "But who—oh God. Kelli. That fucking bitch."

Melissa hated that word—*bitch*—but she grinned to hear him use it against Kelli Walker. She'd never met Kelli, never spoken to her in person, but since she'd learned Kelli existed there might not have been a single person in the world she hated more.

"Melissa," Thomas said. "I'm so sorry. This is—it's a total violation of privacy. It's outrageous."

"It gets worse," Melissa said. "I'm pretty sure she broke into my apartment."

Thomas's jaw bulged, and he seemed to struggle for a moment with a wave of anger that tightened his whole body. Then he calmed and suggested they sit down. They found a bench to keep talking. Melissa told him about the note, then about getting tagged in the photo, and what she read on the Facebook page.

"So you read all about—well, I was going to say 'the evidence against me,'" Thomas said. "But it would be generous to call it *evidence*. How about 'what they think they have on me'?"

"You're saying there's nothing to it?" Melissa said, unable to disguise the hopeful note in her voice.

"Melissa, you have to believe me—Kelli Walker is completely nuts."

"She says she was Rose's friend."

Thomas scoffed. "That would be a generous description too. Rose and Kelli met up sometimes. But the friendship, if there was one, was much more on Kelli's side than Rose's. Rose never liked her. Honestly, she thought Kelli was stupid. But Rose was lonely. She hung out with Kelli only to have something to do. She tolerated her. But Kelli was *obsessed* with Rose. I don't know why she got it in her head to hate me so much, but I honestly think she just wanted Rose all to herself. After Rose went missing, I thought *Kelli* might have killed her. Maybe Rose tried to break off the friendship or something, and Kelli snapped."

"Could she have been the stalker?" Melissa asked.

Thomas's eyes sharpened, grew guarded. "You know about that?"

"I've heard some things."

"Rose thought she was being watched," Thomas said. "I never knew what to make of it. She'd sense presences in the house, swear that things were getting moved around in the bedroom or the living room. A chair was warm, like someone had just sat in it. A dead bird on the deck—had it broken its neck on the sliding door, or did someone kill it and put it there? Stuff like that. She had a paranoid streak. She *did* report a stalker to the police about a week before she went missing. That much is true. She never told me about it. I had no idea it had gotten bad enough for her to call it in. But then, later, my lawyer found the police report."

"So you never knew who it might be?" Melissa asked.

"No," Thomas said. "Rose might not have even known. The police report didn't include a name. I did think Kelli might be the stalker—maybe they had a falling out I didn't know about, and she started following Rose, her obsession turning unhealthy. I told the cops they should look into her. But nothing ever came of it. Obviously, the cops didn't arrest Kelli. They couldn't even prove that anybody was stalking Rose at all. Meanwhile, Kelli's got this whole Facebook army of bored housewives with nothing else in their lives but to harass me. And you."

He handed the phone back to Melissa, face down so she wouldn't have to look at the photo again—but she didn't have to see it. She felt as though the image was seared into the back of her eyeballs.

She cleared her throat. "About the evidence," she began. "I'm sorry, I know you don't like talking about this. You told me that last night—having to constantly defend yourself, how furious it makes you. And I get it. But—"

"Melissa, you have to believe me, it's *nothing*," Thomas said. "It's total bullshit. What, I bought a shovel and a tarp? I drove up north and was off the grid for a while? We've got a cabin up near Bemidji—it's nice, I'll take you sometime. I had some brush to clear. A fence post to fix. That's what the tarp and shovel were for. As for not being traceable, I guess my phone went dead for a while. Is that a crime?"

"And the blood in the kitchen? The housecleaning you ordered?"

"Rose cut herself," Thomas said. "Dicing carrots. I know that sounds stupid, but it's true. It was a bad cut too—I had to rush her to the ER, her whole hand wrapped in a dish towel sopping red with blood. A ton ended on the floor. It was a horror show. That was months before she went missing. But blood sticks around, you know."

"And the cleaning?"

Thomas sighed and shook his head, exasperated. "I didn't *order a cleaning*. We had a cleaning service come once a week. I still do. All I did was email them and suggest that they might come by while I happened to be gone, up at the cabin. Asked them to give the kitchen a deep clean with bleach. Seemed like a good time, since no one was going to be around to smell it."

"That's the other thing," Melissa said. "No one was going to be around? Why? You were going to the cabin, but what about Rose and the girls?"

Thomas laughed, but it sounded forced and mirthless. "God, listen to you! You should've been a cop. Look, Rose and I were having problems, okay? It's true, you may as well know it sooner or later. We were having problems, and Rose had told me that she was thinking of taking a break, to think things over. She went missing that Friday, before I left. The girls got home from school that day and couldn't find her. When I got home from work, they told me she was gone. I thought maybe she'd gone up to the cabin for some time alone."

Melissa squinted. Something didn't make sense. "She'd just leave like that? And why'd you head up to the cabin—was it to clear brush or to look for your wife?"

Thomas's jaw tightened again, and Melissa took a sharp breath, realizing she was making him angry with these questions.

"Rose could be rash," Thomas said, his words slow, measured, cold. "She was emotional. It was like her to just pick up and go, leave me behind to take care of things. I couldn't reach her by cell, but that felt like an indication that she'd gone up north—service could be spotty at the cabin. I wasn't worried. Not right away. And I'd been planning on doing some work up there for weeks. So I figured, why not kill two birds with one stone?"

Melissa held back a grimace at Thomas's choice of words.

"My plan was to head up there and find her," Thomas said. "We'd kiss and make up—this was my hope—then I'd spend some time doing the work I'd been planning on, and we'd head back the next day. So I asked Amelia if she could host the girls for a night. I bought the shovel and tarp, then went north."

"When did you decide to get the house cleaned?" Melissa asked. "Before you realized Rose wasn't at the cabin, or after?"

"Before. I had the idea to bring in the cleaners while everyone was gone about halfway. I sent the email from my phone at a gas station, then turned it off. I don't like the distraction while I drive. It was only when I got there that I realized Rose wasn't there after all. But it was too late at night to head back; I was afraid I'd fall asleep at the wheel. So I got a few hours of shut-eye, then came back to the Twin Cities. After checking a few more places, calling a few folks, *then* I finally called the cops and reported her missing."

Melissa was silent a moment, thinking it through. Trying to put herself in Thomas's shoes. The behavior of a husband whose wife has gone missing must always seem illogical and suspicious in retrospect—but in the moment? She could see how Thomas might have liked to believe that nothing was actually wrong, might have been hesitant to call the police for fear of seeming foolish after Rose turned up fine, gone for a completely logical reason. Only the fact that Rose *wasn't* found—that she was eventually presumed dead—cast Thomas's actions in a different light.

"Okay?" Thomas prodded. "Are you happy?"

His explanations made sense—but Melissa wouldn't have said she was happy. Thomas was right the night before: There was something humiliating about having to talk like this. Melissa didn't like interrogating him any more than he liked to be interrogated. It wasn't fair. They'd only just started getting to know each other. This was supposed to be the fun part of the relationship, the part where they obsessed over each other, wanted to see each other every waking moment. The part where they couldn't keep their hands off each other. And that had all been true, the past couple days. But their time together had also been troubled by *this*, these questions, these uncertainties and suspicions.

Thomas had answered all Melissa's questions. And now she felt worse than ever. A sick feeling had taken root in the pit of her stomach. She wondered if simply talking like this—asking questions, demanding explanations—had broken something between them. If this thing was already doomed to fail, when it had only barely started.

Then a cry came to her ears on the breeze, something familiar in the sound. She sat up straight, adrenaline surging in her veins.

"Where's Bradley?"

"He was right there," Thomas said, standing, striding forward.

Still on the bench, Melissa glanced back and forth, trying to remember what Bradley had been wearing. Blue jeans, red shirt. She didn't see him.

Then there was another cry, and her eyes snapped to where it had come from. It was Bradley, in a distant part of the park, a separate structure set atop a small hill, with a stone retaining wall running along the side.

Suddenly Melissa was standing, her feet carrying her forward.

"Bradley!" she said, her voice sharp to cut through the chatter in the air. Melissa willed her son to turn his head toward her. "Bradley!" He still didn't look.

Then she saw that there was a woman kneeling next to him. Blond hair, a ponytail, black leggings, white shirt. She had her hands on Melissa's son, grabbing him by the shoulders. That was why he wasn't turning toward her.

Because he couldn't. Because he was being held, restrained.

Melissa couldn't see the woman's face from where she stood, but somehow she knew it was Kelli Walker.

Now she was running, her feet pounding hard beneath her, her heart roaring in her ears.

"Get away from him!" Melissa shouted. "Get your hands off him!"

The woman looked up, and now Melissa could see clearly that it was Kelli. Melissa recognized her from her Facebook profile photo. She was halfway to Kelli, halfway to Bradley, and at her sides, her fingers hardened into claws, her vision going blurry. It was impossible to know what she'd do when she reached them. Snatch Bradley away? Or attack Kelli?

Kelli stood, let go of Bradley, but he was already leaning away from her, and as she loosened her grip on his body, he lost his balance, stumbled backward toward the retaining wall. It was only a five-foot drop, but the way he was listing, falling head first—

"No!"

Kelli Walker leapt back, drew her hands to her mouth as Bradley fell. Melissa's stomach gave a sickening lurch when his feet left the ground. He fell backward toward the ground below, to some landscaped mulch and rocks, and on the way down he twisted his body, put out his arms to break his fall—

Too late. The ground rushed up to meet him, and he planted right on his face. Melissa thundered across the grass toward him. When she reached him, he wasn't moving.

"Bradley? Bradley!" Melissa sank to her knees next to him, pulled at his shoulders. She felt him squirm, his chest rise and fall— thank God. He was dazed but breathing. But when she got him turned over, his face looked terrible, his forehead bright red with a smear of blood that stopped hers cold in her veins. Bradley's eyes opened, and for a second, he was calm.

"Mama?" he said, confused. "I fell."

"I know, sweetie," Melissa said, blood on her fingers. "Mama's got you."

"Am I going to be okay?" he asked, then started taking big shuddering breaths. "Is that—am I bleeding?"

There was panic in his voice by the time he reached *bleeding*, and his breath broke and became sobbing. Suddenly Melissa was surrounded by people, other parents at her shoulders and heels offering help.

She heard Thomas's voice, calm and loud and confident. "Put some pressure on it," he said. "We have to stop the bleeding."

Melissa felt a tissue being pressed into her hand by one of the other parents nearby—she never saw their face—and she pressed it where it looked like the blood was gushing from, dead center on Bradley's forehead, a little way up from the crook between his eyebrows. Then she looked up.

"Where is she?" Melissa asked. "Where the fuck is she?" She'd heard people joke about mama bears before, but she'd never fully identified with the term until just then. She felt it rising huge within her like a tidal wave: the animal urge to hurt the woman who did this to her boy.

A chorus of voices rose up: "I think she ran off," "I saw her go that way," "It looked like an accident to me." But it was Thomas's voice that Melissa heard most clearly, as he sidled up next to her and spoke directly into her ear, low and direct.

"We have to get him out of here," he said. "We can deal with Kelli later."

Melissa looked up at him, and whatever difficult conversation they were having moments before was completely forgotten. In that moment, the sight of his face brought only relief. His calm, his strength, his knowing exactly what needed to be done.

"Where?" Melissa asked.

"Let me carry him to the car," Thomas said. "I'll show you where to go."

# CHAPTER 10

Melissa drove and Thomas took the back seat, next to Bradley.

"Just keep holding that tissue against your forehead," Thomas said. "You're doing a great job."

"Am I going to be okay?" Bradley asked, his voice shaky. Melissa tried to catch his eyes in the rearview, but she couldn't see his face with the blood-spotted tissue pressed up against it. He'd need a fresh one soon—the one he had was almost soaked through.

"You're going to be fine, bud," Thomas said. "Your mom and I are going to get you fixed up good."

"Where am I going?" Melissa asked.

"Take a right on 96," Thomas said. "And keep going until I tell you to stop."

"ER?" Melissa asked, making sure to use the letters rather than the words *emergency room*, which would only freak Bradley out worse than he already was. She was still new enough to the area that she didn't know where anything was.

"ER would just put us in a waiting room," Thomas said. "We're headed to my clinic. I'll patch him up myself. Hear that, bud? I'm going to be your doctor today. Can you be brave for me?"

"Yes." His voice was so small; Melissa almost cried at the sound of it. *He* was so small. Defenseless against the world.

"Good man," Thomas said.

It was a relief to be with Thomas, to be dealing with this alongside someone strong, and confident—and a doctor to boot. But Melissa was still shaking, all the same. Gripping the steering wheel too hard to steady herself, to anchor herself against something solid. She couldn't get the image out of her head: the image of her son falling, hitting his head on a rock. The image of him being attacked. Of Kelli Walker gripping him hard by the shoulders. Putting her hands on him. Saying something that scared him.

"What did she say to you?" asked Melissa. "That woman."

"She said I was going to die," Bradley said. "That I needed to tell you someone was going to make us both dead."

Anger rose up in her, blotting out the edges of her vision. As usual, a five-year-old's account of events was a little garbled, but Melissa was pretty sure she knew exactly what happened. Kelli Walker told her son that Thomas was going to kill him. And Melissa.

Kelli was obsessed. Unhinged.

"Melissa." It was Thomas's voice. Soft, from the back seat. She glanced in the rearview and saw him looking back at her through the mirror. His eyes gentle, soft, but worried.

"What?"

"You're going a little fast."

Melissa looked to the dash and saw that she was speeding by a good twenty miles per hour, her foot sinking on the accelerator as her anger at Kelli gripped her body. She eased up, went a little slower.

"We're going to be fine," Thomas said. "We can talk about what happened later. Let's just get Bradley patched up for now."

She kept driving for a couple minutes, then Thomas directed

her into a parking lot. There was a nondescript building and a simple sign with no logo, simply the words *Danver Pediatric Associates*. She followed as Thomas got out and carried Bradley to the door, using a key to unlock it. It was after hours, the waiting room and reception desk completely empty.

Bradley's head on his shoulder, Thomas pushed through a door to a hallway, passed an electronic scale, and went into an exam room. He put Bradley gently on the table. Melissa grimaced as she saw the spots of blood on Thomas's light blue polo shirt—Bradley must have bled on him. But if Thomas noticed, he didn't seem to mind.

"All right," he said, "let's get a look at this, shall we?"

Bradley whimpered as Thomas began to pull at the edge of the tissue plastered to his forehead, but he was brave and didn't cry or pull away. When the tissue came off, Melissa saw that his eyes were scrunched closed. The wound looked pretty gnarly to her, a wide gash in the middle of his forehead surrounded by streaks of red, paling to white—bone?—in the middle. But Thomas didn't seem fazed.

"This isn't so bad," he said. "I think this will heal up nicely."

"Will he need stitches?" Melissa asked.

"You know, I think we can do this without stitches. I'm thinking I could pull the skin back together with some butterfly bandages and then seal it up with some skin glue."

"Skin glue?" Melissa asked.

Thomas gave her a warm smile. "It's exactly what it sounds like. It glues wounds closed and then disintegrates as the wound heals. It's less likely to result in a scar than stitches."

"And how about a concussion?"

Thomas's smile didn't waver. "I'll run the protocol after I patch him up. But I doubt there's anything to be worried about. This part of a kid's skull is built for impact. He might have a headache later, but that's about it."

Melissa nodded. Thomas suggested that she get next to Bradley and hold his hand while Thomas bandaged him up. Then, as Thomas worked, she simply watched. He washed the wound with sanitizing wipes, gently blew on it to stop the rest of the bleeding. With gloved hands he applied a few butterfly bandages, then squeezed the skin glue from a single-use plastic vial, blew on it again. Every once in a while, he murmured encouraging words: "You're doing so great, bud. What a brave boy you are. I think someone has earned a treat after this. What do you say, Mom?"

"Oh, definitely," she agreed.

"Ice cream?" Bradley asked.

"Yeah, the biggest ice cream cone you've ever seen," Thomas said.

Bradley smiled. "As big as my head?"

"Bigger! As big as *mine.*" Thomas made his eyes huge, and Bradley dissolved into giggles.

Thomas went into a drawer, came out with a penlight, clicked it on, and had Bradley follow it without moving his head. Checked inside his ears. As he worked, Melissa found herself fixating on Thomas's hands, strong but gentle as he used them to handle her son. On the concentration, the care, that came to his eyes. And the calm with which Bradley responded to him. By the time Thomas was done with the examination, Melissa was practically crying, her eyes brimming with tears. She cleared her throat and blinked them away before he could notice.

"He's fine," Thomas said. "He'll be turning cartwheels by morning."

"And what do I—I mean, how do I…I've never done it this way. Do I owe you anything?"

It was exactly as Thomas had said—disinfectant, bandages, the glue. But doctor's visits, even simple ones, generally cost hundreds of dollars.

Thomas winked. "Friends and family discount." He turned back to Bradley. "What do you say, bud? You ready to get out of here?"

Bradley nodded, and Thomas helped him down with his hands underneath Bradley's armpits. When his feet hit the floor, Bradley fell forward toward Thomas, and at first Melissa gasped, thinking he must have been lightheaded—Thomas was wrong, he had a concussion after all. But then she realized that Bradley wasn't falling. He was hugging Thomas. Wrapping his arms around his waist.

"Thanks, Dad," Bradley said.

*Dad.* Melissa caught Thomas's eye. He smiled, shrugged, as if to say, *What are you gonna do?*

"Oh, honey," Melissa said. "Thomas isn't—"

"It's okay," Thomas said, interrupting her. Melissa was surprised. Did he *want* Bradley to think he was his dad?

"Why don't we head to the waiting room," Thomas said quietly. "There's a little toy area there. He can play while we talk."

They headed back out to the empty waiting room, where Bradley went to a corner to play with some toy cars on a low table. Thomas and Melissa lingered by the reception desk.

"I don't really have anything else I need to tell you," Thomas admitted as they watched Bradley play. "I just wanted to make sure you're okay."

Melissa looked up at him. His eyes were kind, wrinkled at the corners with worry, and this time there was no stopping it—she burst into tears. Then his arms were around her, and it felt so good to be held that the tears came harder. Melissa let them come, knowing he wouldn't let her go.

"I'm sorry," Melissa said through her sobs. "I don't know what's wrong with me."

"You've been through a lot."

He was right about that, and maybe she didn't have to explain—but she wanted to, just to say it. To get it all out.

"It's everything, I think. Losing sight of Bradley for a second, how scary that can be, and then finding him being grabbed by that woman. It's a mom's worst nightmare. Then him getting hurt, and coming here, and—and how sweet you are with him. With *me*. I don't deserve it."

"You do, though," Thomas said gently. He tilted his face down and pressed his lips against the top of her head, spoke into her hair. "You deserve good things. Both of you. Every good thing."

Melissa closed her eyes, overwhelmed with gratitude at this man who'd walked so unexpectedly into her life. Squeezed him tighter, enjoyed the feel of his body against hers. The warmth of it. The comfort.

"He called you *Dad*," she whispered, so Bradley wouldn't hear across the room.

"He did," Thomas said softly. Melissa felt the warmth of his breath on her scalp. "It's okay. Really."

She pulled away without breaking free from his arms, looked up directly into his eyes. "Is it, though?"

Thomas's eyes were sparkling. Could he have been crying too?

"You know, I always wanted a son. A little boy, like Bradley. I love my girls—of course I do. But I always wanted a third. But we decided... well, you know. And I always wondered. What it would be like."

"What are you saying?"

Thomas shook his head. "I don't know what I'm saying. I know I'm not his dad. Not yet. We only just met. I just—I want to be part of your life. Yours and his. I've been clear on that."

Melissa laughed. "You have." *Clear* was one way of putting it. Since she'd met him, Thomas had been *relentless* in making his interest in her known—and she supposed she hadn't exactly been reluctant. She was the first to kiss him. The first to invite him back to her place. She'd wanted him; she couldn't pretend otherwise. And she wanted him now. More than ever.

"Look, I know I'm not the easiest person in the world," Thomas said. "My past is—none of it's my fault, but still. It's a lot to take. A dead wife, two girls. The accusations. The crazy people who are still obsessed with me. Who think I'm guilty. I'm so sorry it's affecting you. But I'm falling in love with you, Melissa. Okay? I'm falling in love with you, and I can't make that feeling go away. This could really *be* something, you know?"

"I know," she said. "I feel that way too."

"And this doesn't happen that often, that two people will feel this way about each other. That something can be this *right*. All the other shit—we can't let it get in the way. Can we?"

She pressed her lips together and shook her head, blinking tears onto her cheeks. "No," she said. "No, I don't think we can."

"So can we try this? Really try it? To hell with Kelli Walker, to hell with the bullshit evidence she thinks she has. To hell with the suspicions, the interrogations, the second thoughts. To hell with all of it. Can I be a part of your life or not?"

Melissa turned to Bradley, who was playing placidly in the corner, pushing a toy car along the arm of one of the waiting room chairs and making engine sounds with his mouth. The bandage on his forehead was a visible reminder of the thing that happened to him—and maybe it was a stand-in for all the terrible things they'd *both* been through, Bradley and Melissa, on the way to right *here*, right *now*. The pain. The hurt. But it was also a reminder of the man standing next to her, still holding her in his arms. The man who'd begun to make it better. The man who bandaged a wound. Who brought healing.

In that moment, there was nowhere she would rather be. No one she'd rather be with.

And nothing else to say.

"Yes."

# TRANSCRIPT OF RECORDING

**Thomas:**  Stop looking at me like that.

**Amelia:**  Like what?

**Thomas:**  Like you think I'm a monster.

**Amelia:**  Thomas, I don't know what you're talking about.

**Thomas:**  You're not looking at me and thinking about what's in the news recently? What *she's* been saying?

**Amelia:**  Okay, I think I understand now. This is about that woman. Rose's friend. Kelli something?

**Thomas:**  Kelli Walker. Yes. Stop playing dumb with me. You've seen her on the news. Talking about me. Spreading her lies.

**Amelia:**  I have to admit. Her recent claims are…troubling.

**Thomas:**  See? I knew you were looking at me different. You think I'm an abuser now? You think this whole time I've been hurting Rose, harming her without your knowing? That I killed her?

[pause]

**Amelia:**  No, I didn't say that.

**Thomas:**  You had to stop and think about it, though.

**Amelia:**  [sighs] She claims to have proof, Thomas. Photos. She says she was at the hospital with Rose a week before she went missing. I've known you for years, and I don't think you're capable of hurting anyone. But still, it's unsettling.

**Thomas:**  I hate this. Here I am, mourning the loss of my wife, hoping she'll be found safe, trying to be there for my girls—and in the midst of it all, I have to be subjected to this? These attacks on my character, my reputation?

**Amelia:**  Your reputation. That's what matters to you right now?

**Thomas:**  It's all I have. I'm a pediatrician, for God's sake—I *heal* people. I don't hurt them. If anyone hurt Rose, it's probably her. Kelli.

**Amelia:** You really think that?

**Thomas:** I do. She's unhinged, Amelia. Rose never even liked her.

**Amelia:** Then why were they friends?

**Thomas:** Rose was lonely. You know that. She needed the company, needed someone to talk to. But Rose always thought she was a little crazy. I think she was afraid of her, actually.

**Amelia:** So what really happened? What's with these pictures Kelli claims to have, of Rose's face all banged up?

**Thomas:** You know what I think? I think Rose was starting to push Kelli away. Maybe she even told her the truth, that she didn't like her very much and didn't want to be friends anymore. And Kelli lost it. Followed Rose—you know she thought she had a stalker, right? And then finally snapped and beat her up. When I saw the cuts later, Rose insisted it was nothing, said she'd tripped and face-planted on the front walk. But I could tell she was hiding something. There was more to it than she let on. Now I know.

**Amelia:** You've gone to the police with this?

**Thomas:** Of course I have! But nobody's listening to me. They've got it in their heads that I killed her, Amelia. I can feel it. I'm about to get framed for something I didn't do.

# ROSE

*I need to talk to someone. With every passing day, my mental health grows worse. I feel like a fraying rope, closer and closer to breaking.*

*I really ought to get back into therapy. Or—I'm drinking more and more, coming to depend on it—rehab. But Thomas won't allow that. Doesn't want me talking to people about what I'm going through. Doesn't want me airing my problems out for strangers, making him look bad.*

*No, I can't talk to a therapist—not without him knowing. And I certainly can't talk to Thomas. Can't be honest with him. He made that abundantly clear. (*There's something wrong with you. You're not right. You're crazy.*)*
*Amelia isn't an option either—like the girls, she's always been more Thomas's than mine, more loyal to him than she'd ever dream of being to me.*

*And I don't have any friends.*

---

*Okay, so that's not exactly true. I have one friend. Kind of. Does a person count as a friend when you don't even like them very much?*

*Because most of the time, I'm not sure if I like Kelli Walker. Sometimes I actively dislike her. And other times, I'm actually a little bit afraid of her.*

*One thing I'm pretty sure of is that she likes me.*

*We met at a school event, a PTA silent auction thing, raising money for something or other. It was a wine and cheese night, which meant a table of sweaty sliced cheddar, crackers, and boxed red and white on a table by the entrance. Then, after you got your plastic cup and paper plate, you walked through the gymnasium, looking at the items and deciding what to bid on. It was the usual—time-shares, free golf lessons, spa packages, baskets of environmentally friendly cleaning products—each prize with a clipboard next to it, for us to write down our bids.*

*I wandered between the tables, then stopped at one. The prize was a collection of paintings by a local woman—a mom at the middle school Kendall attended. I didn't recognize the woman's name. What drew my eye were the paintings, five of them, each propped on a gold-lacquered wooden stand, so they stood upright on the table. At first glance they looked like treacly watercolors of nature scenes: flowers, ponds, long grasses, autumn leaves. The kinds of paintings my classmates and I would have made fun of in art school, dismissed as kitsch. But something about the paintings pulled at me. Particularly one, showing a small frozen lake, brown leafless trees, a path, and a gray sky above. An unfinished quality to the brushstrokes gave the piece the feeling of a dream. And on the path, so small I had to squint to see it, was the hint of a figure I somehow knew to be a woman, the ends of a red scarf blowing out behind her.*

*I looked at her, struggling against the wind under that ugly sky, and thought about the person I'd been before I'd gotten married, before I'd even met Thomas. When I'd been a painter. I hadn't put hand to brush in years, and I felt an overpowering grief at losing who I'd been. I thought that maybe the figure in that painting was her, the me I'd have been if I'd chosen the road not taken. She was cold and alone, struggling against a harsh wind, but I thought she was happy.*

And I was jealous of her—just as I was jealous of the woman, the woman I didn't know, who'd painted these paintings.

I felt a presence next to me, and I turned to see someone standing there. I didn't know her. I only knew that she hadn't painted the paintings in front of me—there was a little photo on a placard on the table, and the faces didn't match.

"What do you think?" asked the woman. There was a sneer in her voice.

"I hate them." I felt bad as soon as I said it—it wasn't true, or at least it wasn't the whole truth. I didn't hate the paintings. I only hated how they made me feel as though I'd died long ago.

But then the woman next to me cackled low and leaned in to press her shoulder conspiratorially against mine. I glanced at her, and her eyes sparkled with cruel glee.

"I know," she said. "It looks like a four-year-old drew them. You should meet the woman who paints them. She's so full of herself. Thinks she's an artiste." The last word she said with a mocking flamboyance, and when I glanced at her, she'd pinched the fingers and thumb of one hand together, as though she was holding an imaginary teacup, or perhaps a cigarette—I didn't know which, and maybe she didn't either.

"You want to get out of here and get a real glass of wine? Something better than this boxed shit?"

---

Here is what I've learned about Kelli Walker in the year and a half since I've known her. She claims to love her family—while having a husband she doesn't seem to care for very much and two unruly sons who treat her with open contempt. She likes to drink, likes to laugh, eats a bit too much, *struggles with her weight, ten pounds she constantly claims to want to lose. She is fun—but her idea of fun usually involves complaining about someone else. She's unhappy but likes it, treats unhappiness as a kind of sport. She has causes: virulently opposes new housing developments in the area, hates her elderly neighbor's yappy dog.*

*She listens to my complaints about Thomas. It is her favorite thing to talk about: the problem with Thomas. This fits with her general negative demeanor, the joy she takes in talking about everything she does not like—but, strangely, the one time she met my husband, she flirted with him openly. I think she might believe that if we were ever to split up, she'd be able to hate-fuck him while also having me entirely to herself.*

*She is fiercely loyal, but God help you if you're one of her enemies. She calls the cops on people for the smallest infractions, maintains deep resentments with a handful of acquaintances and neighbors, and I'm pretty sure she poisoned that dog, the yappy one that lives next door. (I don't know this for sure, but she was a little too joyful when she told me it ate something bad and got sick.)*

*She is also, I believe, obsessed with me. Ever since that first day, the day when we made fun of that poor woman's paintings together and then went out for a glass of wine, she contacts me a few times a week, asking if I can come out for coffee, a drink, dinner—and her favorite activity, shittalking. I don't particularly enjoy her company, and there are days when I wish I'd never gone for that drink with her, but she is the only person I can really talk to, the only person who will receive my darkest, angriest thoughts and not shame me for them.*

*The only thing that scares me is what she'd do if I ever*

*gave her cause to turn on me. If I went from being a person she thinks of as her friend, to someone on her ever-growing list of enemies.*

# CHAPTER 11

The next few weeks passed for Melissa like a dream. The beginning of a relationship was usually a carefree period, and that's what her time with Thomas Danver became after she let her guard down, after she allowed herself to see Thomas without constantly wondering what happened to his wife, if he had anything to do with it, if he was a murderer. The thing that happened at the park—Kelli Walker, Bradley's fall, then Thomas gently bandaging him up—wiped all that away. Their first few days may have been more intense than most new couples got. Mostly because of his past but because of Melissa's too, they'd spent more time than usual excavating their baggage, talking about how their previous marriages ended. Stuff most new couples didn't get to until they were a month or two in, until they'd had some fun together and knew they liked each other. That was where Thomas and Melissa had started.

But after the park, Bradley's injury, and the clinic, they dropped all that. They put the usual relationship rhythm in reverse: hard stuff first, then fun. There were dinners, long hikes through the many parks and nature centers that seemed to dot the Twin Cities' suburbs, flirty midday texts. And sex. Lots of sex. Melissa would sometimes pause, in those heady weeks, to wonder how she and

Thomas were making this work, dating (and having sex) like care-free twentysomethings when Melissa had a kid and Thomas had two, plus a job. But somehow the work of it—the constant logistics, the finding of babysitters and the scheduling of dates and sponta-neous quickies in the midst of everything else they had going on— barely registered in Melissa's mind because of the high, the absolute euphoria, of being so tirelessly pursued by Thomas, by seeing him hunger for her the way he did, every day, every minute.

Thomas owned his own pediatric practice, with younger doc-tors coming on below him to pick up some of the work. As a result, he was able to sometimes get away in the middle of the day to see Melissa, to take her to a lunch that went long and became an early-afternoon happy hour, getting tipsy, groping at each other under the table. Or he'd text her to meet him at one park or another for a hike, where he'd eye her hungrily in the tight black leggings she put on for such outings. His hands always seemed to find their way to the small of her back, the curve of her hips, in places where the trail turned and they found themselves alone in the trees. The bark of a tree trunk rough against Melissa's back, Thomas's mouth on hers, grabbing for her breasts through the down of a puffer vest. No matter what, lunch or hike, they always seemed to end up back at Melissa's place, in the basement apartment, tearing at each oth-er's clothes in the curtained half-dark of her bedroom, devouring each other, needing each other, with a ravenousness that startled Melissa—but that she never wanted to end.

They didn't put their kids together anymore, not after that first date, realizing it probably wasn't a great idea. This was something they *did* talk about, both agreeing that they didn't want to confuse the kids, didn't want to bring any more uncomfortable questions, didn't want to go too fast for them. Not until they were ready. So whenever they went out in the evenings (as opposed to the midday trysts that were their most common way of seeing each other), they got separate babysitters. Often, it was Lawrence and Toby who hung out with Bradley (he loved their landlords, whom he called his "uncles") and Melissa guessed that it was Amelia who checked in on Rhiannon and Kendall, to the extent that the older girls even needed someone to watch them anymore. Melissa knew Thomas still spent time with Amelia, met with her at least once a week for coffee—probably more than that, since they were neighbors. She didn't ask about it.

Summer gradually became fall, and Bradley moved from daycare to school—kindergarten, where Melissa hoped he'd make new friends. Changes came for Melissa as well: specifically, a job, which just happened to be at Thomas's pediatric clinic. He made the job offer one afternoon after they'd just made love, in fact. He'd given some appointments to a colleague so he could sneak off and get a fix—that's what he called it, "a fix," like he was a junkie and Melissa was his drug.

She lay on the bed afterward with no covers on her, which was the way Thomas liked it: he wanted to see her after they had sex, all of her, and she was happy to oblige—happy to be adored. She was on her stomach and he was running his hands down her back to her thighs, her legs, then back up, shivers rippling up her spine as he explored her. Then her phone buzzed. She reached for it and saw an email from a company she'd applied to. They wanted her to come in for an interview.

"I don't know why you're bothering with that," Thomas said after he asked what was so interesting on the phone, and she told him.

"Bothering with a job?" Melissa asked. "You mean making money? Supporting myself and my son?"

"With *looking*," he said. "I'll give you a job. We need an accountant at the clinic."

"You do?"

"We pay a freelance bookkeeper, but we probably need to bring someone on full-time now that the practice is growing."

"Are you being serious right now?" Melissa turned onto her side and looked at him. "Are you really offering me a job?"

He reached for her, pulled her close. "Do you want it?"

Melissa nodded. "Yes."

Then he kissed her, and she gave in to him again. Gave him what he wanted—which happened to be what she wanted too.

―――――

The job was easy—it took Melissa just a little over twenty hours a week, and because the clinic's financial records were all electronic, she mostly didn't even have to leave the apartment. But somehow the job paid six figures, and her first paycheck was more than she'd ever been able to put into her checking account in a single transaction.

On the surface, the job didn't change anything between Thomas and Melissa. The midday visits and the occasional evening dates continued, and they never mentioned the fact that he was technically her employer now. But there was a new charge to it when he came from the clinic to the apartment to make love to her—in spite of herself, Melissa imagined it as two coworkers sneaking away from the office for a tryst, the boss screwing the secretary. There was something just a little bit *wrong* about it now, and maybe that made it more exciting—maybe there was even something wrong and exciting about the two of them all along. Something forbidden. Something secret. The divorceé and the accused murderer.

It became another thing they didn't talk about.

But Melissa would have been lying if she said she didn't think about it.

She did. All the time.

She thought about whether Thomas had showered Rose with love and adoration too, the way he was showering her.

She thought about when things may have gone bad between them.

She thought about whether things would go bad between Thomas and *her*, and whether she'd be able to recognize the signs if they did.

If she'd know when it was time to get out. If she'd even be able to get out. If she was already in too deep.

Sometimes she even thought about how perfectly Thomas had orchestrated things. Made her financially dependent on him. Emotionally dependent. Living on his money, waiting in her basement room for him to come every day and save her all over again. Feeling sad on the days she didn't see him, perking up when he walked through the door. Was it normal to be so dependent on one person for happiness?

This was precisely what she wanted to avoid after she got divorced. Why she didn't want to get in a relationship too soon. Because she wanted to learn how to be happy on her own again. To reconnect with *herself*.

Then she'd tell herself that she was being crazy. That Thomas was the best thing that had happened to her in a long, long time.

---

Sometimes, when she was alone, she'd simply gaze out the tall windows at the back of her house—lake to the left, woods to the right— and wonder at the wildness that existed alongside the everyday of life in this place. The wildness in people. The wildness that lived in her: an animal thing that came out when she looked at Thomas, or when she thought about what she'd do to protect her son. What she was capable of.

People still talked about the coyote. Pets went missing sometimes: a cat one week, a toy poodle the next. The pleas showing up on an online neighborhood group—*Have you seen this dog?*—alongside photos that purported to be of the animal responsible for all this worry. Grainy, distant images captured on trail hikes, reminding Melissa of people who hunted the Yeti or claimed to have seen the Loch Ness Monster.

This creature seemed to be real, though. She'd hear it sometimes at night—at least, she was hearing *something* from those woods, an unearthly yelping that might either be the cries of an animal dying, or the howling of the coyote to its pack—blood calling to blood.

She'd wake up to the sound, sometimes. Listen to it in darkness. Then lie back and try to go back to sleep, thinking of predators and the way they circled just out of sight, waiting for the weak.

———————

What lingering doubts Melissa still had about her all-consuming relationship with Thomas Danver—*Dr. Danger* to his detractors—came calling one Monday morning in mid-autumn, after she dropped Bradley off at school. The weather, which had held on with summer high temperatures well into October, had finally taken a turn for the cold with two weeks until Halloween. The chill in the air bit at Melissa's ankles as she got out of the car to walk Bradley to the school doors, and their breath was visible in puffs of steam that curled from their nostrils with each exhale, then dissipated on the air. Bradley whined at the way the cold pricked at his earlobes—he regretted refusing the stocking cap Melissa had tried to press on him when they left home—and when they got to the doors, he dashed into the school without giving Melissa his usual goodbye hug, eager to get to the warmth.

On the drive back home, Melissa decided to treat herself with something warm: a vanilla latte, a dirty chai, or maybe—it being fall—something with a bit of pumpkin spice in it. She pulled off the road into a strip mall parking lot with a drive-through Starbucks at the corner. Everyone seemed to have had the same idea, and the line snaked all the way from the pickup window to the end of the lot by the grocery store and the franchise sandwich shop. The line inched forward one car length at a time, and Melissa settled in for the wait.

Her mind wandered to the bookkeeping work waiting for her when she got home, which rarely took her more than three or four hours. Mondays were for sending statements of care to insurance companies, Tuesdays were for mailing out bills, Wednesdays were for receivables, Thursdays were for expenses, and Fridays were for anything she'd missed—which was often nothing. The rest of the time was taken up with *Thomas*.

A car horn honked, and Melissa looked up to see that the line had inched forward a few car lengths while she'd been getting lost in thought. More horns sounded behind her, and she fumbled to throw the car into gear, ears burning.

"Sorry, sorry," she mumbled, though no one could hear her.

As she finally began to move forward, there was some movement to her left, and a minivan zoomed from the parking lot into the empty space in the line ahead of her.

"What the hell?"

Now the chorus of honks grew louder, seemingly everyone behind Melissa joining in with their displeasure at the line cutter. Melissa gave her horn a tap to join the chorus, but she knew that, in part, everyone was still mad at *her*—it was her inattention that allowed the jerk in the minivan to jump the line in the first place. For a second, she considered getting out of her car and walking up to talk to them. But she didn't, and neither did any of the other honkers. The people of the state she'd moved to might have been as quick to anger as anyone else in the world—but they were also fundamentally conflict-averse.

Melissa continued inching slowly toward the front of the line until, finally, it was her turn to order. At the pickup window, the barista handed her a white cup, and then shook her head when Melissa tried to hand over her credit card.

"No," she said. "The woman ahead of you paid for it."

The line cutter? "She did?"

"Yup," the worker said. "Threw in a snack too." She handed Melissa a piece of warmed coffee cake in a brown paper sleeve, the smell of cinnamon and brown sugar filling the car.

Melissa glanced ahead, where the gray minivan that darted ahead of her in line had pulled forward but hadn't yet left the parking lot, brake lights lit up red. The driver's door opened, and out stepped—

Kelli Walker.

She stood by her open door and waved.

"Oh, this fucking bitch," Melissa muttered, the words coming out of her involuntarily.

"Excuse me?" the coffee shop worker said.

Kelli stepped toward Melissa, leaving her minivan door open. A long shawl sweater hung almost to her knees, and she gathered the folds of it around her against the cold as she drew close to the window.

"Hey," she said. "Can we talk?"

Melissa felt her jaw harden, the muscles in her cheeks and around her lips growing tight. "I'd rather not."

"Please?" Kelli said. "Just give me two minutes." She tilted her head toward the café, indicating that she wanted to sit down inside.

Melissa glanced at the young barista, her eyes grown large in her smooth face. Two women facing off in the drive-through line wasn't what she had expected when she clocked in to her morning shift, and she clearly didn't know how to handle it. Further back in the line, a chorus of impatient car horns rose up once again.

Melissa sighed. "Fine. Two minutes."

———————

Melissa set her phone on the table when she got inside, a timer on the screen set to two minutes.

"All right," she said. "Go."

Kelli glanced at the screen. "Seriously?"

"You said two minutes. That's what I'm giving you. A minute fifty, now."

"All right," Kelli said. "Well, first of all, I owe you an apology."

"You owe me way more than a measly apology."

"You're right. Which is why I'm offering to pay the medical bill," she offered.

Melissa crossed her arms. "There's no bill. Thomas patched him up for free. A minute and a half."

Kelli's eyes flicked down at the timer. Melissa could tell she was rattling her—and she was glad. "Thomas did that?"

"He did. The man you're so bent on being a murderer. The man whose life and reputation you're trying to destroy. He helped my son. Gave him first aid, for an injury *you* caused. And then, he told me not to call the cops on you. I wanted to press charges for assault, but he said there'd be no point. How's that for rich? *Him* defending *you* from the cops? When you're so desperate to get him arrested and put in jail."

Melissa gave Kelli her hardest glare. Everything she said was true. Thomas *did* try to convince her not to get the police involved—after the experience he'd had with them around Rose's disappearance, he didn't trust them. Melissa couldn't blame him for that. She ended up ignoring him and calling the cops anyway, too furious to let it go. But it was just like he said. They asked her if she thought Kelli had attacked Bradley maliciously, or if it had just been an accident. Melissa had to admit that it was probably just an accident. They said there was nothing they could do. "I could talk to her," the officer on the phone had offered, "ask her to keep her distance from you from now on. Would you like that?" Melissa had just hung up on him.

Kelli looked chastened now, ashamed, like she wanted to disappear under the force of Melissa's fury. "I deserved that," she said.

Melissa wouldn't feel sorry for her. She refused. Kelli had done this to herself.

"You've got one minute," Melissa said.

"Okay, look, I'll just say what I have to say, and if you don't want to talk anymore, you can leave. And what I want to say is, I messed up. I know I messed up. I'm a little nuts, all right? I know it about myself. I get ahold of something, and I can't let go. That's what happened with you and Thomas. I saw you at the wine bar that day—I swear that was random. But I saw you, and suddenly I couldn't let it go. I shouldn't have taken the picture of you, and I shouldn't have posted it. I recognize that now. And then later, when I saw you at the playground—I shouldn't have touched your son. I shouldn't have put my hands on him. That was unforgivable. And what happened after, that was all my fault.

"But I swear, Melissa—everything I did, I did because I honestly, truly believe that you're in danger. I did it because I care about protecting fellow women. Because I care about *you*. Rose was my best friend—my *best. Friend*. Okay? And she told me things about Thomas. Bad things, that made me suspect him when she disappeared. And now I've got a contact in the sheriff's department, someone who was involved with the case—he's telling me the prosecutor should never have dropped the charges."

A contact in the sheriff's department. That must have been where Kelli was getting her evidence from. But who knew if it was accurate or not? Leaking information from an open investigation had to be an ethical violation of some sort. Kelli's contact must have been bitter about how the case against Thomas ended, must have had some kind of a vendetta clouding his judgment. He could have been feeding Kelli overblown or one-sided information.

A voice in Melissa's head interjected: *But you're getting one-sided information too.*

"You've got no reason to listen to me," Kelli continued. "No reason to trust me. I recognize that. I just want you to listen to *yourself.* Trust *yourself.* Is there some small part of you that wants to listen to me? Some small part of you that thinks you might not be safe with Thomas?"

A silence stretched out. Melissa glanced down at her phone screen. The timer counted down: *7...6...5...4...3...*

She sighed. "Fucking hell." She reached out and tapped the *Pause* button. The timer froze with two seconds to go. She picked up the phone and slipped it into her purse.

Kelli looked amazed, like even she didn't believe Melissa would listen to what she was saying. And Melissa could hardly believe it herself. Not with what had happened between the two of them.

"I'm still not forgiving you," Melissa said. "I'm pissed as hell at you."

"I get it," Kelli said. "You should be."

"Maybe I could beat the shit out of one of your kids. Even the score."

"Go for it," Kelli said. "My boys are both assholes anyway."

Melissa burst out laughing, and after a few seconds Kelli laughed too. It felt like a pressure release, letting out something that had been building a long time, and Melissa went on laughing until she was crying, until people at other tables were glancing at her with concern in their eyes. She waved apologetically—*I'm okay, don't mind me*—then turned back to Kelli, wiping tears from her eyes. God help her, she thought she might actually *like* Kelli Walker if she'd gotten the chance to know her under better circumstances.

"So you'll leave him?"

Melissa shook her head. "I didn't say that."

Kelli squinted, confused. "But you believe me."

"I believe you believe what you're saying," Melissa said. "I believe you think you're right."

"But?"

"But…well, you told me to trust myself, right? And you're not wrong—there's a part of me that desperately wants to know what happened to Rose. Part of me that's afraid Thomas might have done it. And there's another part of me too."

"Part of you that wants to believe *him* when he says he's innocent."

"That's right."

Kelli shook her head. "But Melissa, you can't. Don't believe his lies. His whole nice guy, doctor, great dad, perfect abs bullshit—it's an act. Can't you see that?"

"Maybe," Melissa said. "But when I look at the way he looks at me, the way he treats me, the way he is with his girls and with *my son*—I can't ignore that. This might really *be* something, what he and I have. I can't just throw it away. Not after everything I've been through."

Kelli was quiet. Thinking. She didn't ask Melissa to explain herself any further, didn't press her on what *everything I've been through* meant. She was a woman, like Melissa—she could probably guess. Bad boyfriends, bad husbands: bad men. She'd had them in her life too, probably. Women didn't have to explain to each other. They just knew.

"All right," she said. "So what, then? What do we do now?"

"We find out who killed Rose Danver. Who *really* killed her."

Kelli heaved an exasperated sigh. "But I know already."

"You think you know, maybe. But you're not considering all the evidence. And that's what we do, together. We look at everything. I'll consider all the evidence against Thomas. And you'll consider all the evidence in his favor. Take the stalker theory seriously, for instance."

"And then what?"

"Then, at the end of it all, if the most compelling theory of the case is that Thomas killed his wife, I'll leave him. But if the bulk of the evidence points to someone else, then you'll leave him alone. Leave *us* alone. Stop harassing us. Stop trying to prove the man I'm falling in love with is a murderer. Deal?"

Kelli considered it for a moment, then extended her hand across the table. Melissa took it. "Deal."

On the way to the cars in the parking lot, something occurred to Melissa. She stopped Kelli as she walked to her car, put her hand on Kelli's elbow, and pulled her around.

"What?" she asked.

"There was something you didn't talk about," Melissa said. "When you were apologizing for all the bad things you did to me. You didn't say anything about sneaking into my apartment," Melissa said. "About leaving the note."

Kelli reeled back, looking at Melissa with genuine shock—and Melissa realized that Kelli really didn't know what she was talking about. She couldn't be faking it. She wasn't that good.

"Someone broke into your place?" she said.

"You did," Melissa said, hoping that if she stuck with her accusation, Kelli would break.

But there was no change in her expression. She was genuinely confused.

"I have no idea what you're talking about."

Then she got into her car and drove away. Left Melissa behind in the parking lot, reeling. The words coming back to her, burned into her brain.

*stay away from him unless you want to die*

If Kelli didn't leave the note, who did?

# CHAPTER 12

Back home, Melissa spotted Thomas's car in the driveway. She wasn't expecting him this early on a Monday morning, and suddenly she felt afraid about what might have brought him there. She thought of who she was just talking to—Kelli Walker—and wondered if Thomas knew somehow. She knew it was silly of her to think that; there was no way he could have found out so quickly. Except that Kelli *had* made a scene in the drive-through line, drawn attention to herself and Melissa. What if someone had seen them together at the coffee shop? What if they snapped a photo, texted Thomas that the woman he'd been seeing was talking to his worst enemy?

Thomas was waiting for Melissa in the car, and he stepped out as she pulled into the driveway, stood next to the door waiting as her car came to a stop.

"What's going on?" Melissa asked when she got out, unable to mask the nervous shake in her voice.

"We need to talk," Thomas said. "Can we go inside?"

Melissa's hand rose to tuck strands of hair behind her ears—a habit when she was feeling nervous. "Okay," she said.

They went through the garage, taking the steps to the basement in silence. Melissa opened the door to the apartment and let Thomas walk in ahead of her. He went to the center of the living room but didn't sit. Melissa came behind him, lingering a few steps away, hating the awkwardness that had risen between them. Normally they'd be drawn to each other like magnets, Thomas's hands unable to stay away from her body, while she leaned into his touch. But right now, he seemed distracted, agitated—and Melissa realized that she was actually afraid to go to him, hesitant to get any closer.

"What is it?" she asked. "You're scaring me."

"Scaring you?" Thomas said, surprised.

"'We need to talk.' It sounds so serious. Are you breaking up with me? Did I do something wrong?" Melissa didn't mention Kelli Walker—she didn't want him to know about that, if he didn't already.

"Melissa, no." Thomas let out a breath, shook his head as though to dismiss what she was suggesting as ridiculous. "I could never be mad at you."

"What, then?"

"I was wondering," he started, then trailed off. "God, I don't know why this is so hard for me to say."

Now Melissa was confused. If it wasn't something bad, then what was Thomas so nervous about?

"Wondering what?"

"Wondering," Thomas said slowly, cautiously, "if maybe it's time to take this to another level."

Melissa laughed—she couldn't help it. She was just so relieved, and also a little bit amused at how nervous Thomas was, how timid and boyish he'd suddenly become.

Thomas looked a little hurt at her laughter, and she clapped a hand over her mouth. "I'm sorry," she said. "I really am. I just thought it was going to be something bad. You looked so serious."

"I *am* serious," Thomas said.

"I know." She crossed the room to him, took his hands in hers, gave him a kiss that lingered. "I know you're being serious. You're very, *very* serious." She gave him what she hoped was a gentle smile, so he knew she was only teasing.

"Well? What do you say?"

"I guess I'd say—well, what do you mean, *another level*? Are you, like, asking me to go steady? You want to be boyfriend-girlfriend?"

Thomas pulled his hands away. "Stop. You're making fun of me."

She laughed again and moved closer to him, looping her arms around his neck. Reluctantly, Thomas's hands came to Melissa's waist.

"I'm not," Melissa said. "I'm touched, I am. And I want to move forward in this relationship. It's just, well…what other level is there? Things feel pretty serious right now. We've been having sex almost every day. We see each other constantly. You're always sneaking away to come here."

"That's exactly the problem," Thomas said. "*Sneaking*. I feel like you and me, we're this secret thing."

Melissa's fingers moved up, curling in the hair at the back of his head. Pulling him gently toward her. "Isn't it fun, though? Sneaking around. Making love while everyone else is at work."

"Of course it's *fun*. And that doesn't have to stop. I'm just ready for…something more."

She paused, thinking. There was only one thing he could be talking about.

"You want to make it more official with our families. Our kids."

Thomas nodded. "That's right."

"But I thought you liked seeing me this way—sneaking here, keeping me in the basement. Your little secret." She flashed a mischievous grin, but there was a provocation in her words, a test. A part of Melissa was beginning to fear that Thomas was keeping her isolated from the rest of his life on purpose—to make it that much easier to simply cut her out of his life when he grew tired of her.

"No," Thomas said. "You were the one who thought we were going too fast, that we shouldn't bring the kids into this. I let that be the way things were because it was what you seemed to want, and I wanted to see you."

Melissa reddened, her cheeks growing hot. Thomas was right, she realized—*she'd* been the one to want to keep their relationship from their kids, from the world. If anyone had been holding back, it was her.

Thomas, though? He'd been all-in from the beginning. He'd been clear with her about that.

"Your girls," Melissa said. "What do they know?"

"Everything," Thomas answered. "I told them that first night that we were going on a date. Remember? And I've been honest with them since then. They know we're still seeing each other. And that I'm really serious about you."

Melissa spiraled deeper into guilt. Moments ago, she'd thought that Thomas had been getting ready to break up with her, that he'd purposefully been keeping their relationship secret and casual— when all along, this relationship had been exactly what *she* wanted, because of *her* fears, *her* hesitations. Now she understood why Thomas had seemed so nervous. Not because he was about to push her away, but because he wanted more. And he was afraid she'd say no.

"Hey," Melissa said, and put a hand on his forearm. "I'm serious about you too."

Thomas looked at her. "Are you?"

She pressed into him, pulled his hands toward the small of her back. She gazed up at him, linked her fingers again at the back of his neck. "I really am."

Thomas breathed out. "I love you, Melissa."

And there it was. The first time either of them had said it. The first night they made love, Thomas had told Melissa he thought he was capable of loving her, but this was different. This was the first time he'd put those words in that order. *I. Love. You.*

Melissa wanted to say it too, but she held herself back a second or two. Not because she didn't want to, but didn't want it to be a reflex, an instinctive call-and-response. She waited until she knew she could mean it.

She closed her eyes. "I love you too."

Thomas let out a breath. "Whew. Well."

Melissa let a moment stretch out, simply looking at him, at his cool gray-blue eyes, marveling and wondering at the man behind them. The man who loved her.

"Okay," she said. "So what were you thinking? For this whole 'taking things to the next level' thing."

"I want you to meet the girls. Officially. As the woman I'm seeing."

Melissa laughed. "Not the wording I would have chosen. But okay. How are we going to do it? Sit them down and talk to them about it?"

Thomas shook his head. "No. I was thinking dinner. This weekend."

"All five of us?"

"No. Bigger than that. Not just our kids—I want to make this official to our friends too. Come out of the basement, so to speak. You bring Lawrence and Toby. And I'll invite Amelia."

Melissa's jaw tightened, and her arms draped over Thomas's shoulders went taut.

"I know you're not sure what to think about her," Thomas said. "But she's part of my life. I want you to know her too."

Melissa blew out a breath. "Okay. I get it. I do. If she's important to you, she's important to me. I think this is a great idea."

"Do you?"

"I do. I'll talk to Lawrence. You talk to Amelia. And the girls. We'll make it work. Your place?"

Thomas nodded, smiled. "My place." He leaned in and gave Melissa a long kiss. "Thank you for this," he said when their lips parted. "It means a lot to me."

They stood like that for another long moment, just looking in each other's eyes.

"Don't you have to get to work or something?" Melissa asked at last, breaking the silence.

"I do. You've probably got work to do too."

"I do," she said. "My boss has really been riding me."

Thomas let out a low sound from deep in his throat, pulled Melissa's hips close against his. "Don't give me ideas."

"Save it," she said, pushing him away. "Get to work. You've got patients to see."

Thomas sighed. They disentangled, and he walked across the room to the sliding door. He pulled it open, and as he was about to step out the back, Melissa stopped him.

"Hey," she said.

"Yeah?"

"Did you say you loved me earlier? Was that a thing that happened?"

"I did," he said.

Melissa's arms stole around her sides, and she held herself tight, pressed her palms hard against the sides of her ribs. "And did you mean it?"

"I did," he said.

"So say it again."

Thomas took his hand off the door, turned to face her fully. She went on holding herself, as if there was something inside her that she was afraid to let out, for fear of losing it.

"I love you," Thomas said.

Melissa breathed out, and finally her whole body unwound. Relaxed into the safety of it.

"I love you too," she said.

Then he turned away again, and she watched him go, skirting the back of the house to get back to his car. When he slipped out of sight at the corner of the house, Melissa pulled the curtains and just stood there for a while. Felt her breath rushing in and out of her lungs.

The quiet moment was interrupted by her phone, buzzing from inside her purse. She smiled as she walked to it, expecting it to be Thomas—he often texted right after he left her, sending something flirty or even a little naughty.

But it wasn't Thomas.

Hey it's me Kelli

I talked to my contact at the police. The one who gives me info on the case.

He wants to get in touch

Melissa scowled as she opened the phone, entered her passcode. She didn't want to think about the case right now—not after the moment she'd just had with Thomas.

But she had struck a deal with Kelli. If she could prove it wasn't Thomas who killed Rose, she'd leave them alone. And even though she didn't want to be talking to Kelli Walker right then, didn't want to be thinking about the case that made Thomas Danver notorious, she was more invested than ever in proving the man she loved was innocent.

How can I contact him? Melissa asked.

You don't have to, she responded.

He'll find you

# TRANSCRIPT OF RECORDING

**Amelia:** I don't know if we should be doing this anymore.

**Thomas:** What? Talking?

**Amelia:** I mean therapy. I was hesitant about it from the beginning, since we know each other so well. But you were in pain, and I wanted to help you. But now, after what's happened—

**Thomas:** What's happened?

**Amelia:** Thomas. Please don't play dumb with me.

**Thomas:** I just want to hear you say it.

[pause]

**Amelia:** Last night. After dark. You came over here. And we—we...

**Thomas:** Go on.

**Amelia:** You know what happened. We had sex.

**Thomas:** You make it sound so clinical. I'd say what happened last night deserves a different term.

**Amelia:** How would you describe it? We made love?

**Thomas:** There's a level of tenderness implied there that doesn't quite capture what actually happened. Not that I don't feel tenderness toward you. Just that this is the first time we've been together in that way for—God, it must be decades— and I don't know about you, but I thought there was a hunger in it, a desperation even, that requires a different term.

**Amelia:** Fucking. That's what you men like to say, isn't it?

**Thomas:** Is that so wrong? You didn't enjoy yourself, is that it? It wasn't good? You're wishing it hadn't happened?

[pause]

**Amelia:** I didn't say that.

**Thomas:** I'm glad. Because I definitely don't regret it. It's the best thing that's happened to me in a long time.

**Amelia:** Thomas…

**Thomas:** In fact, it made me think that you're the person I should've been with all along. That from the beginning, it should have been you and me. Not Rose and me. I made a mistake, going with her all those years ago. Marrying her. Not waiting for you.

**Amelia:** Thomas, please. This isn't productive.

**Thomas:** Don't you see? We have a chance now, Amelia. What's happened is terrible—but it doesn't have to be terrible for *us*. For our future. We can start over, pretend Rose never happened. You can be a mother to the girls. The kind of wife I've always wanted. We could be a family. A real family.

**Amelia:** Can you hear yourself right now?

**Thomas:** What?

**Amelia:** Thomas, you currently stand accused of murdering your wife. An allegation you vehemently deny. But now, the way you're acting, the way you're talking—I don't know. Even *I'm* starting to believe you did it.

**Thomas:** How could you say that to me? After what happened last night? You don't trust me, after *that*?

**Amelia:** Look, I recognize that you came to me last night out of… of *desperation*, I think. You're going through a tremendous amount of stress. And you wanted to feel something *good*, maybe. And now, today, you're riding high on it, but honestly, your mood today is what I'd describe as manic. Maybe even a bit delusional.

**Thomas:** What do you want?

**Amelia:** I want you to look at this rationally. How other people would look at it, if they knew. Your wife is missing, presumed dead—and you're sneaking into your next-door neighbor's house, having sex with your ex-girlfriend. Worse, talking about *marrying* her. Saying you're glad your wife is gone. Thomas, it makes you look guilty, and it would make *me* look like an accomplice if it got out. We don't even know for certain that Rose is dead.

**Thomas:** I do.

**Amelia:** But *how*?

**Thomas:** I just know. I feel it in my bones. She's gone, Amelia. Forever.

**Amelia:** Maybe so. But for your own good—for the good of your kids, who'll be orphans if you go to jail—shouldn't you at least *pretend* you think your wife is still alive?

# ROSE

*I shouldn't complain so much about Thomas. I'm no picnic. I know that. The issues I've had in my life—the depression, the therapy, the drinking issues, the breakdowns, my inability to hold a job—are no joke. Maybe I should count myself lucky to have a husband at all. Someone who's stood by me through it all.*

*Yes, he's still close friends with his girlfriend from college. But that doesn't mean he's cheating on me. That's probably my own paranoia talking. And no, maybe he doesn't look at me quite like he used to. But what husband does, after twenty years of marriage? I'm not exactly looking at him the same way I did when we first started dating, either. Relationships change over time. That's just what happens.*

*After my last entry, I realized this diary wasn't doing me any good. That putting my negative thoughts on paper wasn't helping me get rid of them—if anything, it was only making them harder to get rid of, entrenching them in my brain, making them look and feel bigger and scarier than ever.*

*So today I'm going to try a different approach.*

*Gratitude.*

*Twenty years, for starters. Thomas and I have been married twenty years. Our marriage isn't perfect, he isn't perfect, and God knows I'm not perfect (most of the time I'm a bit of a mess, actually), but we've stuck it out longer than a lot of people. That's got to count for something.*

*And whatever Thomas's drawbacks as a husband, he's a great dad. The girls adore him, always have. In fact, I've always thought they probably love him a little more than they love me. From the moment they were born, they seemed to respond to him in a way that they never did to me. In my arms they'd squirm and cry and refuse to sleep. When I tried to breastfeed them, they never seemed to latch right, bit and pulled until my nipples were raw and bleeding, and eventually I gave up. Just pumped and let Thomas do half—maybe more than half—of the feedings, from bottles.*

*Some men might have hated this, but Thomas loved it. I suppose he just knew how to handle babies, from being a pediatrician. He had more experience than I did burping them, soothing them, putting them to sleep—even though I was the one who grew them in my body. Mothers are supposed to have a connection with their babies, a love that proceeds from a cellular level. But that was never my experience. I hated pregnancy, felt my babies growing in me like a tumor or a tapeworm, and when they came out, I looked at their faces and saw aliens staring back at me. I didn't understand them, didn't know what they wanted.*

*Thomas did. And as they grew, it was like they grew further away from me and closer to him. I saw it happen first with Rhiannon. She was a daddy's girl from the beginning. When Kendall came, I thought it might be different, that she'd be mine the way Rhiannon was Thomas's, but it only happened again, my youngest drifting away from me. Teams developed: Team Dad and Team Mom. Except that Team Mom only had one person on it—me. Me versus the rest of them. Three against one.*

*Not that they gang up on me or anything. Not on purpose, at least. More that the three of them often seem to be part of some club that I haven't been invited to, speaking a private language that I don't quite understand. Thomas shares a connection with them that I can't replicate, and in turn, they share parts of themselves with him that they'd never dream of sharing with me. He's their safe person, their trusted confidant. And what am I? Their mess of a mother.*

*Often, it's almost as if they're all sharing an inside joke, and I'm the punchline. I know that this is part of their connection, Thomas and Rhiannon and Kendall—they all have to deal with me. With my problems, my ups and downs, my mercurial moods.* Oh, there goes Mom again; it's just Mom being Mom; we have to be nice to Mom, she's having a tough time today. *I suppose I should be grateful for their kindness. But I'm not. I see their father in their pitying smiles, their patronizing indulgence, their eye rolls and impatient sighs.*

*Let's see, do I have an example? A recent one, maybe? It's so hard to come up with an example of something that's a pervasive part of your life.*

*Here's one: I've been feeling a little paranoid lately. Have I written about this before? I'm plagued by the feeling that everyone I meet hates me, that everyone from my family to perfect strangers are plotting against me, that I'm being followed, watched, surveilled even in my private moments. Recently I went on a walk on the trails through the woods near our house, and the whole time I felt as though the trees were spying on me, as though the leaves were made of eyes, that there were cameras embedded in the knots of their trunks. Halfway through the hike, I came upon a dead raccoon on the trail—freshly killed by some predator, flies only just starting to circle. Its belly was split open, guts spilling out onto the asphalt, and its eyes had been plucked out, the sockets bloody, red drying to black. I came upon it and felt certain that whoever or whatever had done this had left it there for me. A kind of warning. A threat.*

*I doubled back, returned to the house, poured myself a glass of water, and gulped it down at the kitchen sink, my hands shaking.*

*"Mom?" Rhiannon's voice came from behind me. "What's wrong?"*

*I turned and saw both girls, Kendall too, looking at me with mouths agape.*

*"There was a dead animal," I said. "On the trail. Someone had taken its eyes out and left it for me to find."*

*At first, both girls looked scared, but then Rhiannon's mouth cracked into a smirk. "Yeah, Mom, like someone would kill an animal and leave it just for you? There's a coyote in those woods, isn't there?"*

*Kendall watched her big sister, her own look of fear replaced by a smile of relief. "Yeah," she said. "The coyote probably got it."*

*"It hadn't been eaten," I said quietly, almost to myself—they'd already walked away and couldn't hear me. I turned back to the sink and looked out the window. It hadn't been eaten. Only cut open, and the eyes taken out. Would a coyote have done that? .*

*Something similar happened even more recently, on a Saturday, when I was certain that a white car parked up the street was the same car I'd seen at the grocery store, and the same car that I'd spotted in my rearview on the way home. Someone inside, a dark shadow behind the windshield, watching.*

*When I mentioned it, Thomas only laughed, and the girls echoed him.*

*"There goes Mom again," he said, not even speaking to me—instead addressing them as though I wasn't even there. "She thinks everybody's watching her. Obsessed with her."*

He turned to me, his eyes sharp, his grin cruel. "It's all about you, right hon?"

I felt a stab of hurt—not only was he minimizing my fear, he was turning it into a taunt. Mocking me in front of my own daughters.

"Yeah, Mom," Kendall said. "Get over yourself."

---

I can't help but think of this as a form of gaslighting. I might be paranoid—but aren't my feelings valid? Couldn't Thomas just say that he's sorry for what I'm going through, that he knows that I feel scared, that he's listening, and that he's here for me? If he did, I know the girls would do the same. They look up to him so much. His opinions become their opinions, and his way of treating me becomes their way of treating me.

If there are teams—me versus them, three against one— it's his fault. That's a dynamic he cultivated, that he created from the ground up from the moment they were born.

Well, would you look at that. I tried to start with gratitude. But I found my way back to negative thoughts eventually.

I wonder, am I the problem? Or is it my life that is making me this way? Am I mad? Or am I being driven mad?

# CHAPTER 13

The week passed strangely for Melissa, a feeling of nervous antici-
pation hovering over every moment.

She and Thomas set the date of their dinner for Friday evening.
Bradley received the news that they'd be eating with Thomas and his
girls with barely a shrug, but her kindergartner's nonresponse only
made Melissa wonder how the news was going over at Thomas's
house. Whether Kendall or Rhiannon (it was Rhiannon she worried about, mostly) were giving him attitude, reacting with sullen
silence or outright resistance. When she prodded him, Thomas
only said that they were excited to have Melissa and Bradley over,
which sounded like a lie to her. Teenage girls were like icebergs,
everything sharp and dangerous about them submerged beneath
the waterline. Melissa wouldn't know what she was facing with
them until she walked into their house on Friday.

Lawrence and Toby promptly said yes to Melissa's invitation
when she texted it upstairs on Tuesday evening—but Lawrence,
insatiable gossip that he was, almost immediately came down to
ask more about what this evening was, and why it was happening.

"Thomas and I have been seeing each other for a few weeks
now," Melissa said. "It's getting a little serious."

Lawrence shot her a withering glance. "*Honey*," he said, "I know. These ceilings aren't exactly soundproof."

Melissa's face flushed hot, and her hands shot up to cover her eyes. Lawrence was a corporate lawyer, part of the in-house counsel team at a medical device company; sometimes he worked at the office, sometimes at home. She supposed she could have been more careful about only bringing Thomas back to the basement apartment on days when she knew Lawrence was gone, but there were times when they wanted each other so badly that they didn't care. They'd been about as discreet as a pair of horny teenagers, stealing moments alone and thinking they were being sneaky while everyone around them rolled their eyes and shared knowing glances.

"Oh *God*, Lawrence," Melissa said. "Please tell me you haven't been listening in on us these past six weeks."

"Melissa, don't be embarrassed. This is why noise canceling headphones were invented. Besides, I'm happy for you. You know that getting you laid was one of my main goals when you got away from that asshole husband and came to live here?"

"No, it wasn't."

"It *was*. The only thing I don't understand is, why do you need me and Toby there on Friday?"

Melissa hesitated before explaining. It all made sense when she and Thomas had made the plan—they were going public, making their relationship official and serious in the eyes of their families and friends. It felt good at the time, hopeful and beautiful. But in the days since then, Melissa's insecurity had reared its head again. Did Thomas really want to declare his love for Melissa to the world? Or did he want Lawrence, Toby, and—worst of all—Amelia there to make the relationship seem *less* than it was? Was he hedging his bets with a bigger crowd at dinner, giving himself an escape route in case his girls didn't take to Melissa as well as he'd hoped?

"You're overthinking," Lawrence told her when she admitted

her misgivings. "Thomas is obviously crazy about you. Who wouldn't be?"

"You're sweet. I think I'm just getting in my head about…" She trailed off, too embarrassed to say it.

"What?"

"Amelia," Melissa said after a pause.

Lawrence waved her worry away. "I don't think you've got anything to worry about there. I mean, they dated back in college. They're, what, both in their mid-forties now? It's ancient history."

"If it's such ancient history, then why is she a part of his life? Why is she his next-door neighbor?"

"They're friends. Close friends."

Melissa huffed an exasperated breath. Lawrence wasn't listening. Melissa had been doing pretty well not thinking about Amelia at all for the past few weeks, but now that she'd brought her up, it was as though she'd pulled all her misgivings to the surface, unable to deny them anymore.

"Is that all, though?" Melissa asked. "She's a beautiful woman, Lawrence. You don't think, in the years since Rose has been gone, that they haven't been tempted, at least once? Her in that big house all by herself? And him a new widower, without a wife to keep him warm at night?"

Lawrence squinted. "I don't think Rose was exactly keeping him warm at night. Not at the end."

"*Lawrence.* You're not helping."

Lawrence put his hand on Melissa's, gave it a squeeze. "Honey. You're spiraling. This is a good thing, okay?"

"What is?"

"You have a man, a good man, who is serious enough about you that he wants to introduce you to his kids."

"We already met."

"*Properly* introduce you, then," Lawrence said. "Introduce you as someone who he wants to be part of his life. Of *their* lives."

Melissa bit her lip. Lawrence was right. She was losing perspective. "And Amelia?"

"Thomas wants to properly introduce you to her too," he said. "She's part of his life. And now, so are you. It makes sense that you'd feel threatened by her—but Melissa, he chose *you*. He had three years to get with Amelia, if that was what he wanted. But he didn't. He waited. And then he saw you at the dinner party we threw, picked you out of all the women in the world, everyone he could've been with. Okay?"

Melissa nodded. "Okay."

Lawrence stood, moved to the stairs. "I'm sorry I was weird about the dinner. I just wanted to gossip a bit. You know me. It's going to be great."

Melissa smiled, feeling better. "It will."

---

But the week kept moving at a crawl. The other thing that hung over it was the deal Melissa had made with Kelli Walker, especially Kelli's promise that her contact in the police department would reach out to Melissa with information about the case against Thomas. A promise that felt like a threat—*He'll find you.*

Days passed, and still nothing. Melissa kept waiting for a voicemail, a text from an unknown number, but it never came—just the usual progression of junk calls, telemarketers, and fundraising scams.

Even Thomas seemed to forget about Melissa that week. He texted her a few times apologizing, claiming he was extra busy at the clinic. But there were no surprise visits, no lunches or happy hours, no stolen midday trysts. The accounting work only kept

Melissa busy for a few hours, and when she finished it each day a little before lunchtime, the afternoons stretched out desolate and depressing, a wasteland of alone time before she had to pick up Bradley from kindergarten. This was what she thought she wanted when she divorced Carter and moved across the country—time to herself, time to reconnect with who she was. But it turned out she was terrible at being alone. Her rush to a relationship with Thomas was proof of that.

In the quiet boredom, Melissa started to feel imprisoned, like a fairy-tale princess locked up in a tower—or, more appropriately, a dungeon. She startled at minor sounds: Lawrence and Toby's clock chiming upstairs, the roar of a lawnmower in the yard next door, the creaks and cracks of the house settling around her. Once, looking up from cleaning a plate in the kitchen, she glanced out the back door and thought she saw someone moving through the trees at the back of the yard, a silhouette that she spotted in one moment and then immediately lost in the tangles of brush and leaves. With a clatter, Melissa dropped the plate back in the sink and went to the sliding door, craning to spot the silhouette again. But she couldn't find it. Maybe she'd imagined it. All the same, she poked her head out the door and called out.

"Hello?" she asked. "Is anyone there?"

In answer, she heard nothing but the wind, the distant sound of cars on the freeway. Instead of easing her fear, the ring of her own voice in her ears brought a shiver. She backed into the house and then whipped around, suddenly feeling eyes on her, not from the trees but from inside the house. But there was no one there. She walked to the table, the place where she'd found a threatening note weeks ago. It was empty. Just her mind playing tricks.

"You're losing it," she said to herself, forcing a laugh. "Time to get out of here."

It was 2:30, still an hour before she had to pick up Bradley. There was a nice park with a trail and a lake close to his school; maybe she could take a walk to clear her head and return to sanity before she got her son. She picked up her keys off the counter and left.

It was a beautiful fall day, cool but bright, an orange autumn sun crisping the few leaves that still clung to their branches. In spite of the cars and highways, subdivisions and strip malls, nature thrived in the gaps, postcard-perfect. Even so, as she drove to the park near the school, Melissa couldn't shake the jittery feeling of being watched. She glanced in the rearview and saw a cop car following close behind her. She wasn't sure where it came from, couldn't remember seeing it behind her until that moment, but suddenly it was on her bumper. Then the lights flashed red, the siren let out a whoop, and she pulled over, hoping the officer merely wanted to get around her to some emergency elsewhere.

But he didn't. He pulled in behind her on the shoulder.

Melissa watched in her rearview as the door opened and the officer stepped out. He hulked toward her, looking abnormally large in the huge vests all cops seemed to wear, armed as if for battle even for a traffic stop. He rapped on the driver's window with a knuckle. Melissa's hand shook as she pressed the button to bring it down.

"I wasn't speeding, was I?"

The cop bent down. Reddish hair, round face, skin slightly red in the sunshine.

"Just want to talk."

"Talk? About what?" A patch on his vest said SPPD—Saint Paul Police Department. But they were in the burbs, not in the city. "You're far from home. Is it even legal for you to pull me over out here?"

The cop just blinked at her, and for a second Melissa thought she'd gone too far—it wasn't a good idea to antagonize a cop. But when he spoke next, it was to say something Melissa didn't expect.

"Kelli sent me," he said. "Kelli Walker."

"Oh," Melissa said, then again, as she put it together: "*Oh.*" Kelli's source on the inside, the one with all the information on the evidence against Thomas.

But something still wasn't adding up. The case against Thomas had been handled by the county. The sheriff's department would have been the agency investigating Rose's disappearance. What business did a Saint Paul cop—a beat cop, at that, not a detective— have with information about a murder investigation conducted in the north suburbs?

"How long have you been following me?" Melissa asked. "Was that you sneaking in the trees about fifteen minutes ago?"

"I wasn't sneaking," the cop said. "I was on official business."

"Uh huh. Outside your jurisdiction."

He sighed and sank lower onto his haunches, steadying himself with a hand on the side mirror, until he and Melissa were eye to eye.

"Maybe we're getting off on a bad foot here," he says. "I scared you, you're mad, I get it. But I'm trying to help you. Can we just talk for a bit? Kelli told me that's what you wanted."

Melissa sniffed. "Might be a little generous to say I *want* it. I agreed to it."

He gritted his teeth, glanced up the road. "Look. There's a café not too far from here. Can we sit down and talk this through?"

Melissa looked ahead, her hands clenched hard on the steering wheel, her vision blurring. She felt sick with fear and anger at the way this man—she still hadn't gotten his name—found her. It felt less like *finding* and more like *stalking*. But he was right about one thing: She had agreed to this, even if she didn't necessarily ask for it. And maybe she even wanted to hear what he had to say.

"Fine," Melissa said. "I'll follow you."

# CHAPTER 14

They ended up at a family restaurant plunked next to a gas station and auto shop at the intersection of two roads. The cop was already sitting at a booth when Melissa came through the door, a bell chiming above her head. Seconds after she sat, a server materialized at her shoulder.

"Coffee," the cop said, then raised an eyebrow at Melissa. "Coffee?"

"A little late in the day for me," she said. "Iced tea."

Then the server was gone, and Melissa and the officer were just looking at each other.

"So, I should probably introduce myself," he said. "My name is Derek Gordon."

Melissa nodded. "I'm guessing you already know my name. Don't you?"

Derek grimaced, like maybe he knew it was a little creepy for him to have this information, to have been invading Melissa's privacy the way he and Kelli Walker had been. But to his credit, he admitted it.

"Melissa Burke," he said. "Yes. I know your name."

"Did you use your cop databases, or whatever, to find that? Run a background check on me? You know my social security number too? My parking tickets?" She didn't actually know what kind of information police officers could gather on people, but she figured they must know *something*.

Derek shook his head. "I didn't do anything like that. I'm part of a Facebook group."

Melissa gave a dark chuckle, shook her head. Of course he was. "Is it called Justice for Rose Danver?"

"It is."

"So you saw the picture of me and Thomas that Kelli posted? The one of us kissing at that restaurant?"

"I did."

"And then you followed me that night. Didn't you?"

Derek blinked. "Huh?"

"You found out where I lived. Followed me to my apartment. Broke in while I was there with Thomas. And left a note on my dining room table."

Derek grew still and quiet. After a moment, he shook his head slowly, a look of wide-eyed confusion on his face. To Melissa, it looked less like he was denying her accusation than he was struggling to process it, marveling at the wildness of its disconnection from reality. If it was an act, it was a good one.

"I have no idea what you're talking about. Do you have any idea how that sounds? Even aside from the part about breaking into your apartment—which I'd *never* do—how the hell would I know where you lived?"

"You found out where I lived eventually," Melissa said. "You found me today. Snuck through my backyard. Followed me, pulled me over."

"What did the note say?"

Melissa sighed, sat back, closed her eyes. She pictured it, the jagged writing, the threatening words.

"'Stay away from him unless you want to die.'"

When Melissa opened her eyes again, Derek Gordon was staring at her with a horrified look on his face, and in that moment, she knew he didn't write the note.

"Someone really wrote that to you?" he asked.

"They did."

"It wasn't me."

Melissa sighed. "I believe you. But it's what you want to tell me, isn't it? That if I stay with Thomas Danver, he'll kill me?"

Just then, the server arrived with the drinks, and both of them were quiet as she put them on the table. When she left, Derek leaned forward and started talking. "I don't know if Thomas Danver is going to kill you. I couldn't possibly predict that. But I do know he's dangerous. And I know this for certain: He killed his wife. There's no doubt in my mind about that."

Melissa figured he'd come to something like this eventually, the bald accusation—but still, it hurt, actually *hurt*, to hear him say it out loud. Melissa had come to trust Thomas, to *love* him; she'd shared moments with him that were as intimate, as vulnerable, as two people could have together. By contrast, she had no reason to trust Derek Gordon, and more than a few reasons to distrust him. Still, there was something about his cop's authority, about his hard certainty, that cracked something in her, brought a sharp, burning pain to the pit of her throat.

"How do you know?" she asked, her voice gone meek.

"Because I investigated him," Derek said. "I questioned him. I sat across a table from him and looked into his eyes. He's a killer, Melissa."

His voice was still hard, certain—but there was something not right about what he was saying. "Hold on a second," Melissa said. "You're a Saint Paul cop, aren't you? But the case against Thomas was a county case. Which means the Saint Paul police weren't involved in the investigation. The Ramsey County Sheriff's Office was. You couldn't have investigated Thomas."

Derek suddenly looked embarrassed, and for a moment, Melissa thought she had him, had caught him in a lie.

"I'm in the Saint Paul PD right now. But I used to be part of the Ramsey County Sheriff's Office. I was an investigator. But then I got..." He trailed off and couldn't meet her eye.

"Got what?" Melissa prodded.

"I was fired," he said.

She sat back, thinking. So the investigator in charge of Thomas's case was fired, then had to get a job in another police department. Not only that, but he got busted back from investigator to beat cop. Must have been pretty bad, whatever got him fired. "What did you do?" Melissa asked.

"It was bullshit."

"Just tell me."

"I was the investigator who caught Rose's stalker complaint before she went missing," he said. "I looked into it but couldn't find anything. Then, after Rose went missing and we brought charges against Thomas, Thomas's lawyer did some digging and found out, made a big stink in the press about how I was incompetent, the case was tainted, all kinds of shit. Really smeared me."

Melissa couldn't hold back a surge of smug satisfaction at the thought, felt it curl in her lips. "Sounds like he may have had a point."

"The stalker theory was bullshit from the beginning," Derek growled. He was hunching over his coffee, barely talking to her anymore—more like he was indulging in an angry internal monologue, nursing a grudge he'd held for a long, long time. "Thomas and his lawyer cooked it up just to create another suspect. But they couldn't even come up with a name."

"Rose *did* report a stalker though, didn't she?"

"Rose had problems," Derek says. "She had a long history of struggling with her mental health, and she'd just recently pulled out of therapy. She was in a bad place when she made the report. I honestly couldn't figure out if someone was really following her, or if it was all in her head. Honestly, if anyone was tormenting Rose, it was *Thomas*. You know there was an allegation that he was physically abusive with her, right?"

Melissa let out a breath almost involuntarily, as though she'd been punched in the stomach. "Rose reported it?"

"No," Derek said. "But you know that's no proof of anything. Plenty of women don't report their abusers. A couple weeks after Rose went missing, it was actually *Kelli* who went public with the allegation that Thomas was violent."

Kelli. Another person Melissa still wasn't sure if she could trust. In her experience, Kelli had been more violent than Thomas had. She was the one who'd hurt Bradley—even if accidentally—while Thomas was the one who mended the wound.

"They were friends," Derek continued. "Kelli was actually *there* when Rose had to go to the ER. Rose was too scared to report what really happened. But Kelli knew."

"Was that what made you start looking at Thomas?" Melissa asked. "It started as a missing persons case, didn't it?"

"It did," Derek said. "And it landed on my desk. We treated it like any other missing persons report, for about a week. We had search parties walking local fields, wooded areas. Calling her name. Beating the brush for bodies. We got her photo on the local news, asked the public for information that could lead to her safe return." He took a sip of coffee, grimaced as he swallowed it down, then kept talking. "With her mental health history, the depression and whatnot, we started off figuring there was a pretty good chance she just had a breakdown and ran off. Or worse, killed herself. But we had a late start because Thomas had waited a while to report her missing. He had an excuse, said he'd had an idea about where she might have been and went to find her before reporting anything."

"The cabin," Melissa said. "Up north."

"Right. It sounded plausible enough, at first." Derek absently moved his coffee cup in small circles on the table, twisting it like a combination lock with his thumb and forefinger on the rim. "But then we got a tip. From a neighbor. Said they'd seen Thomas sneak into his neighbor's house through the back door, past few days. Amelia Harkness. We dig into it, turns out they dated years ago, before Thomas and Rose got married, and then stayed close ever since. Amelia was even watching the girls that weekend, when Thomas was gone and Rose went missing. So I immediately think, affair? That's motive."

Melissa's jaw tightened. Derek was speaking her fears aloud— her fears about the relationship between Amelia and Thomas. She closed her eyes and shook her head, half rejecting what Derek was saying, half trying to push the thoughts out of her own mind, to tamp them back down.

"No," she said. "Amelia is a therapist. He was going to her for support. During a difficult time."

"That's what he said," Derek said. "But it's a perfect cover, isn't it? He makes up an excuse for stepping out on his wife while she's a missing person—pretty shitty behavior, if it becomes public. *And he and Amelia get to claim doctor-patient confidentiality, so none of what gets said between them is admissible in court.*"

Melissa leaned forward. "Did you ever look at Amelia as an accomplice?" she asked. "Or—could she have killed Rose without Thomas's knowledge?" She realized as she said it that she almost hoped it was true. If Amelia killed Rose, if Melissa could prove it, then she could clear Thomas's name *and* get rid of Amelia in a single stroke.

"We looked at a lot of theories," Derek said. "That's one. It *is* strange. I mean, if it was just therapy Thomas was going to her for—well, the neighbor said he was sneaking over there practically every day. Who goes to therapy once a day?"

"Someone who's really going through a terrible time," she said. "Someone whose beloved wife is missing. Someone who's close to a breakdown himself but needs to keep it together for his kids."

"I suppose," Derek said. "But there were other strange things about it. Like the fact that Amelia seeing Thomas as a patient was technically a major breach of ethics. A lot of counselors wouldn't see someone they'd had a prior romantic relationship with. It's a conflict of interest. Oh, they both had their explanations: Thomas was so stressed out by Rose's disappearance that he couldn't handle the stress of finding someone to talk to, Amelia was right there, she was a family friend, their prior relationship was ancient history…"

"It makes sense," Melissa said. "Doesn't it? You could argue it wasn't a good idea. But I understand why Thomas would've pushed for it. And why Amelia would've agreed."

"You could look at it like that," Derek said. "But to me, it looked like two people who had a mutual reason to want Rose Danver gone had figured out a way to be together but not answer questions about it—by calling it *therapy*."

Melissa winced. Derek was right. There were two ways to look at this—one looked good for Thomas, and the other very much didn't.

"And then the tip from Kelli came?"

"Yeah. Though it didn't come as a tip. Kelli made the allegation on social media. Tagged a few local news stations, said it on air."

Melissa frowned. "Isn't that odd? Sounds to me like she wanted the spotlight more than anything."

Derek made a pained face, drew air through clenched teeth. "Yeah. She can be like that. It doesn't mean what she said wasn't true. She had pictures and everything. Rose's face, all bruised up. Cuts on her cheek, on her eyebrow."

Melissa sat back as if pushed, held to the back of the booth by the shoulders. But then her mind kept moving, thinking about all the reasons Kelli Walker might have had photos of a beaten Rose Danver on her phone. Kelli and Melissa had gone through a reconciliation, of sorts, but Melissa still thought Kelli was a little unhinged. And she had no idea what the friendship between Kelli and Rose was really like. Thomas swore that they *weren't* friends, that Kelli was obsessed with Rose, but Rose only tolerated Kelli. Who was to say it wasn't *Kelli* who attacked Rose, maybe after Rose told her what she really thought of her? Then took her to the ER, tried to gaslight her that it was *Thomas* who'd attacked her. And Kelli was, by her own admission, the last to see Rose alive. Could *she* have killed Rose, disposed of the body, then made a public stink about Thomas being abusive, smearing him on the local news, to throw the police off her trail?

"After Kelli's accusation, we started looking at Thomas more seriously," Derek said. "Found out about his purchases, the shovel and the tarp. His long absence up north—enough time to dispose of a body. Him turning off his phone so his movements couldn't be tracked. It was after we found some traces of Rose's blood in their kitchen that we declared Rose presumed dead, then brought charges against Thomas. It was so long after Rose's presumed murder that a lot of the physical evidence was gone or contaminated. Thomas had had the house deep cleaned, the car detailed. We still thought we had enough to get a conviction, though. Until it all went to shit."

"Because Thomas and his lawyer went public with the stalker theory," Melissa said. "And you got fired."

Derek looked down, stared into the mouth of the coffee cup. "I know both of those investigations were as rigorous as they could be—I know because I led them. But it didn't matter. To the public, it looked like incompetence."

"Incompetence that had led to an innocent man being charged with murder."

Derek gave Melissa a sharp glare. "That's how they saw it. But I know he's not innocent."

Melissa sighed. She wasn't sure if this could be a productive discussion. Derek seemed unshakable in his belief that Thomas killed Rose. And part of what he was saying was convincing. But he didn't seem to realize how desperate and untrustworthy his story made him appear, how much he seemed like a person who had something to prove.

"Here's what I see," Melissa said after a moment, speaking slowly, trying to choose her words carefully. "I see a guy who messed up."

Derek's composure cracked, and Melissa could tell she'd hit a nerve. "That's not—"

"Just let me finish," Melissa said, raising a hand. "You messed up. You didn't take Rose's stalker complaint seriously enough. Then, later, when she went missing, you focused on Thomas and never really considered anyone else. You just figured it was the husband."

"That wasn't lazy police work," Derek cut in, his voice rising angrily. "There's a *reason* you look at the husband or boyfriend when a woman goes missing. More than seventy percent of female murder victims are killed by an intimate partner."

Melissa closed her eyes, not wanting to hear it—Thomas was currently *her* intimate partner—and repeated herself. "*You figured it was the husband.* And when new information came out that exposed your sloppy police work—"

"I wasn't sloppy..."

"Your *sloppy* police work," Melissa said again, her voice rising to meet Derek's, "you fixated on the guy who'd made you look like an idiot. And you're still fixated. It's unethical, what you're doing, sharing information on an open case, but you don't care about that, do you? Because you can't let go of the case. Can't let go of Thomas. Can't admit you were wrong."

Derek was silent a few moments, just looking at Melissa. Hearing it laid out like that seemed to have taken something out of him, deflated him of his righteous anger, his defensiveness, his bluster.

"Maybe," he admitted, then lifted a finger. "Or. You're in love with this guy. And you can't see the truth about him. Because you don't want to."

Now Melissa was the one who was quiet, and Derek was the one who'd struck a nerve.

"We're at an impasse," Melissa said. "I don't want to believe Thomas is guilty. And you and Kelli don't want to believe he's not."

"But one of us is right," Derek said. "*Something's* true."

"Yes," Melissa said. "We just have to prove it one way or the other. You really don't think there's anything to the stalker theory? You couldn't have missed anything back when you investigated it?"

Derek shifted in his seat, uncomfortable. "I suppose I could have," he admitted. "Rose reported seeing a white sedan a lot—parked on her street, following her around town. But there's a lot of white sedans out there. She could never come up with a make or model. No license plate. I couldn't do anything with it."

"She never got a look at the guy she thought was following her?"

"Once," Derek said. "White guy, forties, a sort of scraggly beard, and a scar on his chin." Derek made a cutting motion across his face with the side of his hand.

"That's pretty specific."

"Yes, but who knows if this guy was even following her?" Derek said. "Rose was a paranoid woman. She thought the world was out to get her—largely, I think, because Thomas *made* her feel that way.

But this guy? Who's to say he wasn't just driving one of the many hundreds of white sedans on the road, and Rose got a look at him as he passed? Anyway, without more to go on, I couldn't find him."

"Okay," Melissa said. "It's not much, but it's something. A white guy with a scar on his chin who drives a white sedan."

"And what about you?" Derek asked.

"What *about* me?"

"You say I need to consider the stalker theory, to look at it more closely—but what about everything I've told you? That Kelli has told you? Are you taking any of it seriously? What are *you* doing to get to the truth?"

The anger that had been boiling just beneath Melissa's breastbone came once more to the surface, burned the back of her throat, and flamed white-hot at the corner of her vision until it was the only thing she could feel. What did this man know about her? He had his suspicions, his grudges, his need to prove himself. But Melissa had her whole history, her divorce, her hopes and dreams and fears for her son and herself. She also had a man who claimed to love her, a man she was beginning to love in turn—and the misgivings that still prevented her from trusting him fully, because people like Derek and Kelli wouldn't leave her alone, wouldn't stop plaguing her with the things they thought they knew.

And then she thought of the event that was looming in just a day's time: the dinner. Taking things to the next level. A further invitation into Thomas's home, his family—his life.

"I think we're done here," she said to Derek Gordon, then scooted out of the booth and stood. "I'm the one who's actually in this. Me, my son, our future. There's no one who wants to get to the truth more than me."

Then she turned and walked away, not looking back. Close to the door, the server who'd brought them their drinks—Melissa hadn't touched hers—gave her a smile.

"All done?" she asked.

"Yes," Melissa said, then jerked a thumb angrily over her shoulder. "He'll get the check."

# CHAPTER 15

The morning of the dinner, when Melissa was eating breakfast, Thomas texted: Wear something nice tonight. After a second, he added Can't wait to see you! and included some kissy-face emojis— but the first message was the one Melissa fixated on. What did *nice* mean?

She'd finished her work for the week, so she obsessed about it all day Friday while Bradley was at school. After weeks on end of seeing each other almost every day, Thomas hadn't come over at all that week. Not since Monday, when he stopped by to suggest the dinner—and to talk about the idea of moving their relationship to the next level. Since then, there'd been nothing but texts and a few brief phone calls. He claimed he'd been extra busy at work, but Melissa was getting paranoid. What if Thomas was changing his mind about her? What if his daughters—or worse, Amelia—were reacting to the dinner by telling him he was moving too fast? Saying negative things about Melissa, pouring them into Thomas's ear?

Now this: *Wear something nice tonight.* She pored through her closet, thinking of all the people she'd have to look *nice* for tonight, the audiences she had to please. She was afraid she was losing Thomas, so for him she wanted to wear something that blew him away, made him hungry for her again. But for his daughters, and for Amelia, she couldn't look too desperate, too slutty, couldn't show too much skin. Couldn't look like the tart who was trying to steal their dad, their friend and ex, away from them.

After a few hours of laying outfits on the bed, trying things on, and studying herself in the full-length bedroom mirror, Melissa settled on a terra-cotta linen dress with a tasteful brown belt. The dress went past her knees and wasn't exactly *sexy*, but it made her feel pretty, at least, and the neckline, while not showing any cleavage, plunged toward her sternum just enough to pique Thomas's imagination, remind him that she had a body under there—a body he, until recently, seemed to like.

After Melissa got Bradley from school, she dressed him in navy pants, a white shirt, suspenders, a snap-on bow tie. He looked ridiculously cute and handsome in a little-boy way, even if that bow tie wasn't going to last; two minutes after she got him in the outfit, he was tugging at his collar, his face turning red.

"Stop pulling at your clothes," Melissa said. "You look great."

A knock came from up the stairs. Lawrence. Melissa called for him to come down. His footsteps creaked down the stairs, then tapped down the hall. When he came into the bedroom, he took a look at her and whistled.

"Mel, you look gorgeous," he said.

Melissa smiled, accepted the compliment.

"I was just coming down to say we're heading over."

"You don't want to drive together?"

"I thought we should go separately," Lawrence said. "In case you want to stay longer than we do after dinner."

He gave Melissa a mischievous wink, and she rolled her eyes. Gorgeous or not, she didn't think she was getting laid tonight. Not with the kids—*all* the kids—around. This evening was about something else.

Lawrence and Toby left while Melissa got Bradley strapped into the car. They were the last to arrive. When she and her son came through the door, Lawrence and Toby were standing in the living room, talking to Amelia. All three of them had a glass of white wine in their hand. Their eyes turned to her.

"The guest of honor," Amelia said, and stepped toward her. She came close, and before Melissa quite knew what was happening, Amelia was gripping her by the elbow with her free hand, kissing her on one cheek, then the other. "It's good to see you," she said, then flashed what looked to be a genuine smile.

Melissa flushed hot with a feeling of awkwardness—Amelia was so fashionable with her European-style greetings, her effortless self-possession, and Melissa couldn't help but feel foolish in her presence, even if she was being kind. She also noticed that Amelia wasn't troubled by her same hesitation to wear something sexy for this dinner. She was in high-waisted gray slacks that swished loosely around her ankles but hugged the curves of her butt and hips, and a tight black top revealing the inner curve of her breasts, freckles dappling delicate, milky-white skin.

"You've been settling in well?" Amelia asked.

"Settling in?"

"Here in Minnesota. You're still new here. It takes a while."

"Oh," Melissa said, "that. Yes, I'm fine. Thomas has been a big help."

"I'm sure," Amelia said, something knowing and just a little sharp behind her words. "And how about this handsome guy?"

She glanced down at Bradley, who was clinging to Melissa's legs.

"Hi there. I'm Amelia. I'm a friend of your mom's."

Melissa was quiet a beat—they were friends now? Bradley

didn't say anything either, and after a few seconds of silence, Melissa answered for him.

"This is my son, Bradley," she said. Then, quieter: "He's a little shy sometimes."

"I get it," Amelia said. "I feel shy sometimes too."

They passed into a moment when no one seemed quite sure what to say. Melissa glanced from Amelia to Lawrence and Toby, who were usually gregarious, but they wore brittle smiles and had a look of panic in their eyes at the awkwardness of the moment—that moment in a conversation when small talk ends and it seems no one can think of what to say next. Ultimately, it was Thomas who saved them all, breezing in with another glass of wine and a plate of something that smelled amazing.

"Melissa," he said, taking her in, "you look beautiful." He pressed the stem of the wineglass into her hand and gave her a short kiss on the lips—more than a peck, but only barely. Everyone else watched them, even Bradley, and Melissa felt a flush of heat all the way to the top of her scalp.

"What do you have there?" she asked, eager to get out of the moment.

"Grilled flatbreads," Thomas said. "Thought I'd take advantage of the unusually warm weather." He extended the plate and the grown-ups gathered round, peering at what he was offering. "Pear, chèvre, pink Himalayan sea salt, some fresh rosemary, and a light balsamic drizzle."

"Ooh," Toby said, the first to grab for a slice of flatbread. "Thomas is the *best* cook. You knew that, didn't you, Melissa?"

She shook her head. "I had no idea. I'm learning new things about him every day."

Thomas shrugged. "Second best, maybe," he says. "Everyone knows you're the best cook in the neighborhood, Toby."

Thomas offered the plate to Melissa. She grabbed a piece and bit into it as Thomas watched. The perfect blend of flavors washed over her tongue: sweet and salt, herb and acid, a bit of char from the grill. "Wow," she said. "You're full of surprises."

Thomas beamed. "Save some room. Cedar plank salmon for dinner." Then he looked down at Bradley. "How 'bout it, bud? Want to try one of these? Fish later?"

Bradley made a face, and the adults in the room chuckled.

"We'll figure something out," Thomas said. "I probably have some chicken nuggets or mac and cheese around here somewhere."

"You sure that's okay?" Melissa asked.

"My girls were little once," he said. "I know how to deal with picky eaters." He turned to Bradley again. "The girls are around here somewhere. Want to go upstairs and see what Kendall and Rhiannon are up to?"

Bradley shook his head and pressed his face against Melissa's leg, wrinkling the folds of her dress where it fell over her thigh. She tensed, trying to keep her balance as Bradley pushed too hard against her.

"Come on, bud," she said. "You had fun with them the last time."

But Bradley shook his head again. He wouldn't even meet her eyes. "Sorry," Melissa said, giving Thomas an apologetic look. "I don't think it's going to happen."

Thomas assured her it was okay. Soon he breezed back to the kitchen and to his grill on the back deck, leaving Melissa with the others. She sat and tried to enjoy her wine and appetizer, tried to participate in adult conversation—but she couldn't get over her embarrassment at the way Bradley was still clinging to her. Kids were weird, their reactions to situations unpredictable. Last time they were here, Kendall was able to coax him away, but now she was nowhere to be found, and Bradley didn't seem excited about the idea of going to find her. And Melissa wasn't sure why.

She always struggled to know whether her son's reactions to things were random, or if they had a cause she should have been digging into. Sometimes, since starting kindergarten, Bradley would be hesitant to walk into school when she dropped him off in the morning, and each time she wondered—was he just having an off day? Or was there something bad waiting for him in school? Was he being bullied? Was a classmate being mean to him? Sometimes her mind would go all the way to the worst, most paranoid possibility: What if he was being abused? What if something truly terrible was happening in that building? She knew these thoughts probably didn't reflect the truth, but kids could be so bad at talking about what was really going on in their lives. Bradley's silence left so much room for Melissa's imagination to dream up terrible explanations.

She was struggling with a similar thought spiral right now. Last time he was here, Bradley seemed to warm to Kendall and, later, even to Rhiannon. But what if he didn't? What if he was just pretending to like Thomas's daughters because he sensed it was important to Melissa? And what if Kendall and Rhiannon were doing the same, trying to get along with Bradley because they knew it was important to their dad? Rhiannon had been cold, Kendall polite—but they both could have been more hesitant about their dad dating, more hesitant about *Melissa*, than they let on directly. And now, their hesitation might have blossomed into full-on rebellion. How else to explain their absence right now, their refusal to come down and say hello to Melissa and Bradley?

She cast her mind back, tried to remember what Bradley had told her when Kendall and Rhiannon babysat him. They'd played together, taken a walk through the woods at the back of Thomas's yard, then Rhiannon had made him a snack and sat with him while Kendall did some homework. It all seemed innocuous enough at the time—but then Melissa recalled that Bradley had also gotten scared by Kendall telling him that a coyote lived in those woods. An older kid telling a scary story about the legendary neighborhood predator, and Bradley hadn't liked it. Maybe Bradley's hesitance to go find the girls was as simple as that, his remembering that one of them had made him afraid.

That left the girls themselves, and why they weren't coming down to say hello. Thomas's girls had been through real trauma with the loss of their mother. A parent dating someone new was hard enough; add the murder of a loved one to that difficulty, and it was no wonder Rhiannon and Kendall were being distant.

Thomas and Melissa might truly love each other, might have been *in love* with each other—but the rest of it wasn't going to be easy. A single dinner wasn't going to make them one big happy family.

"Melissa?" Lawrence asked.

Melissa blinked. "Yes?"

"You look like you're a million miles away."

"Do I?" She looked around the circle, feeling everyone's eyes on her. Amelia studied her with an inscrutable look. She forced a laugh. "Sorry. Long week. I'm just tired."

Lawrence nodded in a way that said he didn't believe her.

Then Thomas came walking back in, apron off and draped over his forearm, the way a waiter at a fancy restaurant might carry a white cloth napkin.

"Dinner," he said, "is served."

---

The meal was terribly awkward, as Melissa somehow knew it would be. She and Thomas sat next to each other, and occasionally he let his hand rest on her leg, his fingers brushing the bare skin at her knee where the hem of her dress rode up. It was the first he'd touched her in days, but she was too distracted to enjoy it, to imagine Thomas's hands moving higher, pushing her dress up her body. Sitting together with their three kids around them, Melissa felt already like a wife and husband, a mom and a dad, which made Thomas's touch feel chaste, nonsexual.

The kids simply watched them, not talking. Rhiannon's look was a glare, a dark teenage scowl. She picked at her food—the salmon Thomas brought in on a smoking cedar plank, green beans swimming in butter, crisp garlicky roasted potatoes. Her head was mostly down, hair hanging around her ears, but she peered up at Melissa from under her lowered brow in a way that reminded Melissa of the juvenile delinquent from *A Clockwork Orange*, a movie Carter, her ex, made her watch years ago.

Kendall's expression was more pleasant, if a little hard to place. Her smile was dull, but her eyes were sharp and intense on Melissa, and whenever Melissa caught her gaze, she wondered what was behind those eyes—whether the smile was genuine or a mask. Next to Kendall, Bradley simply studied Melissa and Thomas, not smiling but not frowning either. Just thinking. It looked to Melissa like he was putting something together for the first time, and as Melissa met her son's eyes, she felt a pang of guilt at not talking to him before they came over, not explaining to him what this evening was. Not knowing what to say was not an excuse for not saying anything, and she resolved to sit him down as soon as they got home, explain exactly how she felt about Thomas, and what it might mean for them.

The other adults at the table seemed to be picking up on the strained atmosphere. Lawrence and Toby, normally gregarious, didn't seem to have any idea what to say. Even Amelia, normally so put together and sophisticated, seemed completely out of her element when Melissa glanced over at her, wearing the look of poorly concealed social panic people sometimes got when conversation in a group trickled down to silence.

It all felt like a terrible gathering where no one was allowed to talk about the thing that was really going on, but Melissa couldn't think of anything else to talk about either. Five minutes in, they'd burned through small talk about how good the food smelled, how great a cook Thomas was, how he seasoned the fish, and what was that herb on the potatoes? And then there was nothing more to say. Lawrence and Toby tried their best, mentioning a few goings-on around town—a construction project that would have to start moving quickly if it was going to be done before the snow flew, the upcoming city council and school board elections that had everyone putting signs on their lawns, and yet another pet disappearance in the neighborhood—the mythic coyote striking again. Melissa made a few paltry attempts to ask Thomas's girls how school was going, but Kendall only shrugged and said "Okay," and Rhiannon straight-up glared at Melissa with a look so withering she thought she could practically hear the girl snarl.

It was all so terrible that Melissa found herself grabbing for her wineglass over and over again, drinking too much before she'd eaten enough to soak up the alcohol. It went straight to her head, and before she knew it, she was feeling hot and flushed, a little buzzed, and with the beginnings of a headache. At one point she simply closed her eyes and focused on the feel of Thomas's hand, still resting on her leg as he forked his food one-handed. An anchor, a reassurance. His fingertips playing at the soft skin just inches up from her knee, sending tingles up her thigh.

She opened her eyes and looked at him.

"Everything okay?" he asked.

And his face was so beautiful, so kind. The gray flecks in his blue irises, the soft wrinkles spidering from the corners of his eyes. His perfect smile, the way it cracked his face open into something that shone. Melissa recalled that while it might have been a while since they last saw each other, the last time they spoke this man had said he loved her, and she said she loved him back.

"I'm fine," she said, and meant it. "Perfect."

He wiped his mouth, then set his napkin down and stood, addressed the whole table.

"How about a walk?"

---

They went out, leaving the leftover food on the table, the sink full of dishes. The evening was perfect, crisp and cooling, the sunlight cracking into shards over bare branches and falling leaves as it sank toward the horizon. They went out the back door of the house, over the deck and down the wood steps to the yard. The woods lay to the right, still and crackling in the quiet of the evening; a half mile's walk through the tangle of trees and browning underbrush would have brought them to Lawrence's back door and the entrance to Melissa's apartment. But they cut left instead, toward the lake. The sight of it reminded Melissa of the night she met Thomas, his flirty suggestion that they escape the dinner party and go skinny-dipping.

"We never took our dip," Melissa said as they came to the water's edge and an asphalt path that circled the lake—another route to Lawrence and Toby's house, to her basement apartment, albeit by a longer, more circuitous route than the woods. She laced her fingers together with Thomas's, and with her other hand reached across her body to squeeze his forearm through his wool coat, slid her hand up to his bicep.

Thomas grinned. "I'm still game," he said. "It's colder than it was then."

Melissa laughed. She'd put a coat on, and her arms and shoulders were warm—but beneath the hem of her linen dress, she felt the cooling air prick at her calves. She glanced back at everyone following them: Kendall and Bradley walking side by side, Rhiannon behind them, looking sullen, and Amelia, Lawrence, and Toby bringing up the rear.

"Too many eyes right now."

"We've got all the time in the world," Thomas said.

"Oh yeah?"

"Yeah," Thomas said. "I intend for this to last. Don't you?"

"I do," Melissa said. "I'm not sure our kids agree, though. I mean, have you tried to explain anything to them? What have they said?"

"They'll come around."

That wasn't really an answer to Melissa's question—but maybe it answered the more important question of what Thomas wanted. If he still wanted *Melissa*, in spite of this strange week and this awkward dinner.

"All right then," Melissa said. "Skinny-dipping. Next summer when it gets warm again."

"And every summer after that," Thomas suggested. "We'll make it a tradition. On the solstice."

A laugh bubbled out of her, blending with the sunlight and the smell of dried leaves in the air. "Sure. We'll dance naked in the moonlight and make sacrifices to the gods of summer."

Thomas loosed his hand and looped it behind Melissa's back, grabbed her by the hip and pulled her close as they walked. "My sexy pagan mistress."

"Mistress?" Melissa asked. "Is that what we're doing?"

"Oh," Thomas said, with a smile in his voice. "I think you could be a little more than that. If you wanted to."

There were others on the path with them, people they didn't know, out to enjoy the sunshine and lingering warmth before the weather tipped inexorably toward winter. They came toward a park that hugged the shoreline, a couple shelter houses, a parking lot. Some distance from the water, by the road, there was a car with a figure inside it at the wheel that pulled at some recognition in Melissa. Her heart rate spiked. But before she could do anything with the feeling, figure out where she'd seen the car and the figure before, she felt Thomas turning her toward the water.

They'd come to a small wooden dock that jutted out into the lake and then spread out in a T, for fishing or just looking at the scenery.

"Come on," Thomas said, stepping out ahead and walking backward, a playful look on his face as he coaxed Melissa out with him. "Might be our last chance. The park service will close the dock when the lake freezes."

She followed him to the end of the dock, then stopped at the rail and looked across the water with him. On the far side of the lake, the sun was setting below the trees, casting a shadow all the way to where they stood.

"Beautiful," she said.

"You're beautiful," Thomas said next to her—and when she turned, he was on one knee.

"*Thomas,*" she said, suddenly breathless.

"Melissa," he said, and now he was opening a ring box in front of her, revealing a sparkle of platinum and diamonds whose details she couldn't quite make out through the sudden rush of tears in her eyes. "I love you. I can't live without you. Marry me."

Melissa blinked furiously, her eyelids moving open and shut as quickly as a camera shutter, capturing the moment in a burst. "It's so fast. You—you barely know me."

"I knew everything I needed to know the moment I first saw you," Thomas said. "I knew then—*right* then—that you were the person I'd been waiting for, without even realizing it. You fill the empty parts of me, Melissa. You fix everything about me that has been broken since, since…well, you know."

There was a hush on the air, and Melissa glanced to the shore to see that a small crowd had gathered. Around their kids and their small group of friends, strangers out for an evening walk were pausing to watch, surprised smiles on their faces. One of the people by the bonfire had stood up and taken a few steps toward them, and further back, the slim figure of a man wound its way toward the shore from the parking lot, come to see the spectacle. Heat rushed to Melissa's cheeks with the awareness of being watched—but then Thomas's hand tugged on hers, pulled her attention back to him.

"Melissa, I want to spend the rest of my life with you. I want to spend my years making you happy—protecting you. Caring for you. Won't you let me do that?"

Thomas's words washed over her, and she had to close her eyes against the swell of emotion she felt in her chest. She was about to open her eyes and say *yes* when she sensed a small commotion at the shore.

"Daddy?" A small, quavering voice—it took Melissa a split second to recognize it as Bradley's. Her son was afraid, and the warmth in her chest from Thomas's proposal was suddenly replaced by an icy fear as she looked up to see what was happening.

Bradley's face was white. Thomas's girls, Lawrence and Toby, Amelia—they'd all turned to the shore with a mixture of confusion and alarm on their faces. There was some jostling and movement in the small crowd at the entrance to the pier, and then the bodies parted. A gasp darted into Melissa's throat and lodged there as she saw him and recognized him for the first time.

Carter. Her ex-husband.

He'd found her.

"Here she is," Carter said, walking down the pier toward Melissa and Thomas. But he wasn't talking to Melissa. He had his phone held in front of him, taking video, and he seemed to be speaking to an audience on the other end of the recording. "What do you have to say for yourself, Melissa?"

He was live streaming.

Thomas rose from his knee, stood next to Melissa. "You know this guy?"

Melissa couldn't speak.

Carter came closer, pointing the phone at Melissa.

"This is my wife, folks. My ex-wife, Melissa Burke. And there he is." Now he turned the phone on Thomas. "Thomas Danver, accused murderer. I didn't believe it, but here it is, right in front of me. My ex has fallen for a killer. Not only that, I just walked in on him asking her to marry him. What did she say?"

Carter pushed the camera toward Thomas's face. Thomas swiped at his hand, pushed him away. Carter backed off a step but kept his grip on the phone, went on recording. Over the phone, their eyes met—Carter, the man Melissa had escaped, and Thomas, the man she'd fallen in love with. The man who'd just told her that he'd do anything to make her happy. To protect her.

And for a taut moment that seemed to stretch out interminably, Melissa was able to look at both of them at the same time, to appraise them and compare them as they faced off against each other. Thomas, the broadness and the strength of him that she'd grown to love and to feel safe in. A sharpness growing in his eyes, storm clouds gathering, a fierce darkness she'd never seen in him before. Next to Thomas, Carter looked like a boy—lank and wiry, his neck hunched, his shoulders creeping up toward his ears. His cheeks were gaunt, pitted beneath an unshaven spotting of facial hair, his chest almost hollow above the swell of a growing beer gut, somehow fat and skinny at the same time. He never took care of himself, and it looked to Melissa like he'd slid even further since the divorce was finalized. Thomas was stronger than him—but there was danger coiled in Carter's wiry frame, in his look of callow defiance masking fear and deep insecurity. Thomas was a big man; Carter was a small man, trying to puff himself up big.

"Get the fuck away from us," Thomas said. "Go."

Carter's chin jutted out, but he didn't talk back. Instead, he turned from Thomas back to Melissa, phone still held out.

"I want my son back," he said. "I'm going to go for full custody."

"You wouldn't dare," Melissa said, her voice barely above a whisper.

"What do you think the judge will say when he sees this video?" Carter asked. "Marrying a murderer? Bringing your son into that? After all the lies you told about me. Told everyone that I'm a bad father."

"You *are* a bad father!" Melissa screamed, finally finding her voice. "Look at your son right now. Look at how afraid he is of you. Why don't you show that on your little recording?"

On the shore, Bradley was crying, and Melissa ran to him, leaving Thomas and Carter alone on the pier. She scooped her son up, felt him quake in her arms. His tears ran wet and hot against her neck.

"Make it stop, Mama," he whimpered.

"It's okay, baby," Melissa said into his hair. "You're safe. I'm not going to let him take you away from me. Just don't look."

Then Melissa turned and saw Carter following after her from the pier to the shore, the boards creaking under his feet.

"Oh, you're such a good mother, aren't you?" he said, every word dripping with contempt. That was what he was, what he'd always been—a contemptuous person. Full of anger, full of poison. "Taking a boy from his dad and then running off to fuck a criminal, that's what good mothers do? Spreading your legs for a murderer?"

Melissa cowered away from him as he got closer, turned her body to hold Bradley as far from him as she could. Closed her eyes and squeezed her son tighter, as if to fold him into herself, this boy who grew inside her body. And she'd protect him with her body if she had to, put herself between him and danger. Carter would have to break her arms to get to him. To kill her before he pried her boy away.

There was shouting, more footsteps pounding, and then a woman—Amelia?—let loose a scream from somewhere behind Melissa, in the crowd.

"Someone stop him!"

Melissa opened her eyes again. Now Carter was on his back on the pier, still steps away from Melissa and the shore—and Thomas was on top of him. His knees on Carter's elbows, pinning his arms to the wood slats. His hands balled into fists. And a look of absolute fury in his eyes.

"I'm not a murderer, you lying motherfucker," he growled, and punched Carter in the head. Hard.

Melissa looked to Carter's face and realized that Thomas must have already delivered a hit or two while her eyes were closed—his nose was already a bloody pulp, more crooked and damaged than could have been explained by a single punch to the face. Then Thomas went on hitting him—again, again, again, again. With each punch, people in the crowd at Melissa's back let out gasps. She pressed Bradley's face more firmly against her neck, hoping he wasn't seeing any of this, that he'd get to the end of this terrible ordeal not knowing what had happened, not having to remember it for the rest of his life.

Thomas delivered yet another punch, a terrifying blankness in his eyes as his fist smashed down, his jaw clenched and bulging. His knuckles were bright red with blood—his and Carter's. As he lifted his fist back into the air, cocked it, Carter let out a gasp beneath him, a wet wheeze. He was struggling to breathe. Terror iced through Melissa's chest.

"Thomas, stop!" she yelled. "You're killing him!"

She was jostled back and forth as bodies pressed past her to get to the pier, and then Lawrence and Toby rushed toward Thomas and threw themselves at him. Lawrence grabbed Thomas's hand and stopped his punch, but it took both men pulling with all their might to pull Thomas off Carter.

When he came up, rearing back, Thomas's face was red, and there was a terrifying blankness behind his eyes.

Beneath him, on the pier, Carter's face was a bloody mangle.

And he wasn't moving.

# TRANSCRIPT OF RECORDING

**Thomas:** Can I ask you something?

**Amelia:** That's what I'm here for.

**Thomas:** You've done work in abnormal psychology, haven't you?

**Amelia:** You know I have.

**Thomas:** The psychopathy paper you coauthored.

**Amelia:** Yes. Why do you ask?

**Thomas:** It's just that word. *Psychopath.* It's getting thrown around a lot.

**Amelia:** About you.

[pause]

**Amelia:** What, you think I haven't been paying attention?

**Thomas:** No, I know you have. It's just…it's embarrassing. Knowing your friends are hearing all the terrible things that are being said about you.

**Amelia:** I get it. Kelli Walker still seems to be on the news almost every week. She seems to enjoy the spotlight.

**Thomas:** I know. And it's something she calls me.

**Amelia:** *Psychopath.*

**Thomas:** Yes.

**Amelia:** And it bothers you?

**Thomas:** Wouldn't it bother *you*?

**Amelia:** More than the other things she says about you, I mean. She's called you a murderer. A narcissist. An abuser. She's said in no uncertain terms that you killed your wife in cold blood. So out of all the things she's said about you, all the names she's called you, why is it this one word—*psychopath*—that we're focusing on today?

**Thomas:** It all bothers me. All of it. Everything she says.

**Amelia:** Okay. But psychopathy is what you want to talk about. It's what you asked me about.

**Thomas:** I don't even think Kelli Walker knows what a psychopath is. She's not an expert. Not like you.

**Amelia:** Is that what you want to ask me? The definition?

**Thomas:** I figure you know. Better than she does.

[pause]

**Amelia:** There's a generally accepted list of traits. The inability to feel guilt or remorse, a complete lack of empathy, a high degree of impulsivity, and of course a tendency toward violence. Also, superficial charm.

**Thomas:** Charm? How does that fit?

**Amelia:** The psychopath is defined in part by their ability to manipulate others. To make people like them. To hide their true nature, in some respect. Charm is part of this. Charisma. Even attractiveness. The ability to woo or seduce others.

**Thomas:** Because if other people knew what they were really like, deep down...

**Amelia:** They'd be rejected by society. And some psychopaths learn at an early age how to *mask* who they really are.

[pause]

**Thomas:** Do they know?

**Amelia:** Know what?

**Thomas:** That they're psychopaths. Can a person know that about themselves?

**Amelia:** Maybe not consciously. But on some level, they *must* know. The ability to manipulate, to lie, to *appear* to be one thing while really being another—it presumes some level of self-awareness, doesn't it? If a psychopath hides who they are, it must be because they realize, even if only subconsciously, that there is something to hide.

**Thomas:** So how do they hide it?

**Amelia:**  How does anyone hide anything? By pretending to be the exact opposite of who they are deep down. By running as far away from it as possible.

**Thomas:**  For instance?

**Amelia:**  Well, like I said, they tend to be charming. For the high-functioning psychopath, the levels of charm can be extreme. Aggressive, even.

**Thomas:**  Aggressive charm?

**Amelia:**  Yes. The high-functioning psychopath will tend to come on strong when they first meet someone, really try hard to get that person to love them. Merely being liked isn't enough. The high-functioning psychopath isn't content with just that. They have to be *adored*. In new relationships—particularly romantic relationships—they'll love-bomb their target, absolutely shower them with affection, to get that person completely hooked, completely dependent. Eventually they might lose interest, then a partner or friend will report a dark side coming out, that lack of empathy and remorse coming to the surface. But in the initial phase of a relationship, the psychopath is fully engaged with their charm, with their skill of manipulation.

**Thomas:**  How do you know all this?

**Amelia:**  It's in the literature. Psychopaths are *everywhere*, if you really look for them. You'll even see them cropping up sometimes in the helping professions—doctors, church pastors, even teachers or college professors. It's part of the hiding, the masking, of the psychopath's true nature. On some level, they know what they are and they know it's bad. So they go into a profession that could be deemed *altruistic*, even *virtuous*, to create some distance from that part of themselves. How could they be bad, deep down, when they're spending their lives helping people?

**Thomas:** Why am I feeling attacked right now?

**Amelia:** You asked. I'm just telling you what my research surfaced.

**Thomas:** But you went out of your way to say *doctors*.

**Amelia:** I didn't go out of my way. I could've said *psychiatrists* too. You've heard of Hannibal Lecter?

**Thomas:** He's not real.

**Amelia:** No, but the trope exists for a reason. The powerful, respected psychopath, hidden by the veil of respectability afforded by his profession.

**Thomas:** Hmm. And the respected pediatrician who killed his wife, right?

[pause]

**Amelia:** Why would you say that?

**Thomas:** It's what you were thinking.

**Amelia:** It wasn't.

**Thomas:** You think I don't know what you're doing?

[pause]

**Amelia:** Thomas. You're scaring me.

**Thomas:** Scaring you? I'm sorry, I guess I'm just feeling a little defensive to hear my best friend in the whole world call me a psychopath.

**Amelia:** You're projecting. I'm only answering your questions. You're the one who sets the agenda in this room. I go where you lead. Maybe the question you should be asking yourself is, why did you want to talk about this in the first place? Just idle curiosity? Or is it because you're afraid you might—

[loud crash]

**Amelia:** [screams]

**Thomas:** I don't need to be asking myself a fucking thing.

**Amelia:** Go back to your chair, Thomas. Get your hand off my neck and go back to your—

[croaking sound]

**Thomas:** No, you listen to *me* now. You think I'm such a goddamn psychopath? A remorseless manipulator, prone to violence? Well, then you need to ask yourself something. You need to ask yourself why it is that you feel so free to speak disrespectfully to someone you should be afraid of. You need to start asking yourself how you're going to get out of this alive. How you're going to avoid being next. You got that?

[gasping, heavy breaths]

[footsteps]

**Thomas:** This session is over.

[door opens, closes]

[pause]

[sobbing]

**Amelia:** I can't do this.

# ROSE

*It's time for me to be honest about exactly what's been going on. I've been holding back, not telling the whole truth—even here, in this journal, where it's supposed to be safe.*

*But it's time to get it all out now. To put the ugly truth down somewhere. Because I'm scared.*

*Scared that something will happen to me before I can tell the truth.*

---

*It all started weeks ago, after Thomas told me I needed to quit therapy. That it wasn't working. That I needed to try something else—so I wouldn't destroy this family. That's what he told me. That I was destroying my family.*

*I agreed without a fight. I was too beaten down to do anything else. Too afraid.*

*But then, in the days that followed, I had an idea. Maybe, I thought, Thomas was right—therapy wasn't helping. But that was because I wasn't the only one with a problem. Maybe Thomas and I needed to go to someone together. Couples therapy. Or even family therapy, with the girls. Thomas liked to think that I was the crazy one, the messed-up one, the broken one. But what if Thomas was wrong? What if they all were wrong? What if my problems were* our *problems, and we could fix them together?*

*Thinking about it, I began to feel hope—real hope—for the first time since I could remember. For a whole day, I felt my depression dissipating. There was a light at the end of the tunnel. I was going to fix my family, my marriage, myself. I could do this.*

———————

*I brought up the topic with Thomas the next night, after the girls were in bed. I was in bed too, sitting propped against pillows under the light of my reading lamp, waiting for Thomas to brush his teeth in the master bath. When he finally came in and crawled beneath the sheets, I put my hand on his arm.*

*He gave me a strange look, a surprised smile on his lips. Maybe he thought I wanted to have sex—it had been months, and I knew that I ought to give that to him, that it'd be good for our feeling of connection to each other. I knew he'd be disappointed when he found out what I really wanted, and I resolved that after he said yes to what I was going to ask, we'd have sex that night, as a sort of reward. The start of something new between us.*

*But that's not what happened.*

*"You were right to suggest that therapy wasn't helping me," I started, coming right out with it. "But that's because our problems are about more than just me. They're about us. We all need help. And we need to seek it together."*

*Thomas's smile dimmed.*

*"Rose," he said, with the tone of a father speaking patiently to an irrational child, "it sounds to me like you're being defensive. Blaming me for your problems, instead of confronting your own issues."*

*I let out a frustrated breath, put my chin down so Thomas couldn't see my face. This wasn't going at all the way I had planned.*

*"Thomas," I said. "I need you to hear me. I want to go*

to someone else. And I want you to come with me. It's time to get honest about what's wrong with us. With you and me, and with this family."

Thomas glowered, his eyebrows moving down into a hard line. "What does that mean, time to get honest? Are you threatening me?"

"Threatening? Thomas, no. What could be threatening about—"

"Because if you want to talk about what's wrong with this family—well, Rose, I think you've always been the problem here. Since the beginning."

Hurt stabbed through me, and I flinched. "You don't mean that."

His face had transformed into a mask of cruelty. I found myself wondering which was my husband's true face—the kind one he'd worn when he came to bed, or the one he showed me now, of a man who knew he was hurting me, and liked it.

"It's really unfair, putting your issues on us like that," Thomas said. "There's nothing wrong with me and the girls. Nothing. Just because you're too lazy to do the work on yourself, to try to get better—you can't put that on us. It isn't our fault."

Tears came hot, pricked at the corners of my eyes. "There are reasons for the way I am," I protested, my voice breaking. "There are reasons. I wasn't always this way."

"But you were," Thomas said. "You were messed up before we ever met. You just hid it from me. I never should have married you. I know that now. I think about it every day."

"Stop it," I whispered. "Stop saying these things."

But he couldn't be stopped now. "And for you to refuse

to get better—not only to refuse, but to actually say that we're the problem? To threaten to drag us through the mud with you?"

"I'm not threatening anything," I protested, practically sobbing now. "Just to talk about it, to tell the whole truth for once—"

"Don't you dare!" Thomas screamed, his face suddenly inches from mine. I cowered back, pressed myself into the headboard of the bed.

"It's my job to protect this family," Thomas said. "God knows you won't do it. So I have to. And if it has to be you I protect this family from, I'll do it. I'll do whatever it takes, Rose. The girls, this life, everything I've built—I'd kill to protect that, do you hear me?"

I gasped. In all our years of marriage, Thomas had never yelled at me like this, never intimidated me physically, never threatened violence. But here we were. He hadn't come right out and said what he'd do if I kept pushing him—but I thought he was making himself clear.

If I didn't do as he said, Thomas would kill me.

And I believed him.

# CHAPTER 16

Someone in the crowd must have called the police, because soon after Lawrence and Toby pulled Thomas off Carter's limp body, sirens filled the air. An ambulance arrived first, paramedics running out to help Carter—and then the cops arrived. Two cruisers, then a third, their red and blue lights spinning, lighting up the trees, the leaf-covered grass, the glassy surface of the lake in the encroaching dark.

"You know these men?" an officer asked Melissa.

"My ex-husband," she said. "And my…my—"

She wasn't sure what to call Thomas. Her boyfriend? Fiancé? She hadn't gotten around to saying yes to his proposal.

"Your boyfriend beat up your ex-husband, do I have that right?"

She nodded. Bradley still clung to her, his head against her shoulder.

"Is Daddy going to die?"

"No, sweetheart," Melissa whispered, although she couldn't say that for sure. She was the one who yelled *You're killing him!* when Thomas was delivering blow after blow to Carter's face. And Carter still hadn't moved. She craned to see around the cop's legs, get a view of his body. The paramedics were putting him on a stretcher, the kind that held the head and kept a patient from moving their neck. Would they have been bothering with that if he was dead?

She looked back up at the cop questioning her. "Is he…is he going to be—"

"He's conscious," the cop said. "And he answered their questions. Knows his name, the president, the year. He's hazy. But responsive."

Melissa breathed out. Carter was a terrible husband, a terrible father, and she was furious with him for following her. Stalking her. But he didn't deserve to die.

More importantly, though, she didn't want Thomas to be guilty of manslaughter for killing him. She'd done so much work reconciling herself to Thomas's past, the accusations that were made against him for his wife's disappearance and death. So much work convincing herself that he wasn't a murderer. After all that, after she came a split second away from agreeing to marry him—he couldn't become a real murderer now.

Melissa scanned around, trying to find him in the growing dark of evening, then spotted him by the trees at the water's edge, with one of the other police officers. Thomas had his back turned to the officer, and cuffs were going on his wrists.

"You're arresting him?" she asked the cop by her.

"This is a pretty serious assault, miss," he said. "*Felony* assault. We'll have to take him to county, for processing."

"County?"

"Ramsey County Correctional Facility."

Melissa was numb. She couldn't believe this was happening.

"Can he get bailed out?"

"After he's arraigned," the cop said. "A judge has to set the bail amount. It being the weekend, might be a day or two. He'll probably spend the weekend in jail, at least."

A cry rang out on the air. At the trees, the cop was walking Thomas to the cruiser. Thomas's head hung down, shamed. Nearby, Rhiannon's face was crumpled up in tears—it must have been her who let out the loud sob, breaking down inside to see her father taken away. Close to her, Kendall looked completely numb, her eyes wide and blank, gnawing on a bent knuckle like an anxious little girl. Something swelled in Melissa, and she nearly burst into tears herself, thinking of these poor girls and everything they'd been through. First, they lost their mother. Now this.

And it was all Melissa's fault. If she hadn't come into their lives, into their father's life, none of this would have happened.

Amelia came toward Melissa through the dark. "We have to leave," she said. "We need to get the kids out of here."

Melissa nodded, pulled herself together.

"I still need to finish taking your statement," the cop said. He looked to Amelia. "Yours too."

Amelia pulled Melissa by the elbow. "You have her address," Amelia said to the cop. "You can finish your report later."

She gathered the girls, and Lawrence and Toby, and together they walked back to the house in darkness, not talking. Back at the house, the leftover food was still on the table.

"God," Melissa said, seeing it. "This is depressing."

"Come on," Amelia said to her. "We can do this."

Melissa found a TV and set up Bradley in front of it. Kendall and Rhiannon disappeared to their rooms upstairs, and Lawrence and Toby started clearing the table. Amelia and Melissa stationed themselves in the kitchen, scraping food into the garbage, putting some dishes in the dishwasher, washing others in the sink, working wordlessly side by side.

"Can I ask you something?" Melissa asked when they were almost done.

"Sure," Amelia said.

"What's the story between you and Thomas?"

"The story?"

"Please don't be coy with me," Melissa said. "I can't take it tonight. There was something between the two of you."

Amelia sighed, gazing out the window into the dark as she dried a platter.

"We dated ages ago. I think you know that."

"Yes."

"But then we stopped, and then suddenly—there was Rose. And that was that."

Melissa tried to read the emotion in her voice. Regret? Resignation? Relief?

"But you stayed close."

"We did," Amelia said. "That was mostly Thomas's doing, in hindsight. He was the one who kept our friendship going. Seeking me out, calling me. Flirting with me."

"Flirting? Even when he was married to Rose?"

Amelia glanced at Melissa. "I don't even know if he knew he was doing it. Thomas pursues people. He woos them. He makes them love him. It's what he does. He doesn't know any other way to be."

Melissa thought about the way he had pursued her. She thought it was because she was special, but maybe not. Maybe Thomas was that way with everyone. Doing whatever it took to make them love him, for some reason of his own.

"And you never thought about getting back together? After Rose disappeared?"

Amelia opened a cupboard, set the platter inside.

"There was one night," Amelia said. "One night after, where… well. We found each other."

Melissa held her breath. Was Amelia really saying what she thought she was saying? Confessing that she and Thomas had slept together, when Rose's disappearance—her presumed death—was still fresh?

"But it was a mistake," Amelia went on. "I knew it right away. And then Thomas and I had a falling out."

"A falling out? Over what?"

Amelia shook her head. "I'm afraid I can't say."

"Can't? Or don't want to?"

Amelia bared her teeth in a pained grimace. "It was a hard time, with Rose being gone, and the accusations against Thomas. He wasn't himself. And I realized that I'd gotten too close to him. Let him *keep* me too close. Closer than I wanted to be."

"But you're still close today. In spite of your falling out."

Amelia squinted. "Are we?"

Melissa scoffed in disbelief at Amelia's confusion. Was she pretending not to know what Melissa was talking about? Or was she being genuine?

"You're neighbors," she said. "You have coffee every week. His girls call you 'Aunt Amelia.'"

"I thought about moving away," Amelia said. "Getting some distance from all this. But something kept me here. Even after our falling out, even when we weren't really talking. I cared about him. I still do. And his girls too. But also…"

"What?" Melissa prodded.

"There's something about Thomas that I've never quite understood," Amelia said. "A hidden part of him I've never solved. I know him so well—but also, he's a mystery to me. Maybe that's what keeps relationships going for so many years. Even complicated ones. Messy ones. Another person presents us with a mystery. And the people we keep closest are the ones who stay mysterious."

They entered into a long silence. Melissa thought about Thomas's proposal at the pier. Did he ask her to marry him because she was a mystery he wanted to solve? And did she fall for him because *he* was a mystery? His outburst of violence against Carter wasn't exactly something she expected, wasn't something she knew he had inside him. Did she want to see the rest? Did she want to discover everything he'd hidden away in the secret parts of himself?

"I'm no threat to you, Melissa," Amelia continued. "Is that what you really want to know? I'm not going to steal Thomas from you. There was a time when I wanted him. Maybe I even wanted to take him from Rose. But that time has passed. Thomas is all yours. You can have him. And I hope you're happy together. I do. You deserve that. Both of you."

Melissa sighed, suddenly feeling a huge weight on her shoulders—the burden of the decisions she'd have to navigate in the days ahead. Thomas's arrest and arraignment, but also Carter and his threat to sue her for full custody of Bradley. She was sure everything that had happened would help Carter's case against her, his claim that she was marrying someone who would pose a danger to their son. Melissa wanted happiness more than anything—but she wasn't sure if it was going to be possible for any of them. If this story would have a happy ending.

Lawrence came in from the dining room. "Everything's cleaned up. We're heading home. Will you be coming too?"

Melissa glanced at Amelia. "Who's going to stay with Rhiannon and Kendall?"

"I've got it," Amelia said. "Aunt Amelia to the rescue. You go. Try to get some rest tonight."

Melissa left and walked upstairs to get Bradley from the den where she'd put him down in front of the TV. On the way there, she passed Rhiannon's room, the door open a crack. She paused, lingered, heard voices. Kendall was inside, the two sisters whispering to each other. Melissa was sure they were terrified for their dad, unsure what would happen next, and as she stood there, she wondered if she should walk in, try to say something to comfort them. But then she heard Rhiannon's voice, clear on the still air in spite of her whispering.

"She's not Mom..."

They were talking about *her*. She backed away from the door, then walked the rest of the way to get Bradley, who'd fallen asleep on the couch, an episode of *Bluey* playing at low volume on the TV, his face lit up in intermittent flashes of colored light. Then she stole out the front door of the house with him hot in her arms, put him into the car. She thought about what she'd heard all the way back home, Rhiannon's one-sentence rejection of her, finding her wanting, lacking—the cause of everything that had gone wrong.

*She's not Mom.*

---

Back home, Melissa laid Bradley in his bed still sleeping, manipulated his limbs to get him out of his dress-up clothes and into pajamas. Back in the living room, she kicked off her shoes and fell on the couch. She was exhausted too. She grabbed for her purse with her phone inside—she'd left it at Thomas's house when they went on their walk, and then didn't look at it while she and Amelia cleaned up in the kitchen. Now she found the phone lit up with dozens of notifications, social media tags, and mentions in comments.

She sat up straight, her body suddenly taut with dread. Her fingers quivered badly enough that she had to put in her passcode twice before the phone lit up.

It didn't take her long to find the source of all the notifications blowing up her phone. Somehow Carter had gotten the video on Facebook. Melissa doubted he uploaded it from the hospital— Thomas had knocked him out, and Carter might not even have been conscious yet. No, he must have been streaming when he took the video, like Melissa suspected, and after the stream was cut short, it uploaded automatically, as live streams on social media always did. She watched the video through her fingers. It was somehow worse than experiencing it the first time around, maybe because she knew how it was going to end. Carter coming upon them with Thomas on one knee and her hands up by her face in shock, about to say *yes*. Then Carter's taunts, accusing her of spreading her legs for a murderer. It was all completely nauseating. Then, suddenly, the picture jostled, the phone dropped on the dock, and all she could see anymore was the sky. From there to the end of the video it was only sound: the gasps of the crowd, the wet thudding of Thomas's fists against Carter's face, and then Melissa's scream at the end: "You're killing him!"

The video had hundreds of comments on it, and it was a second before Melissa realized Carter had streamed it not to his main feed but to the Justice for Rose Danver group.

A circuit closed in her mind, and fury lit up inside her like an electrical current, practically crackling from the tips of her fingers. *Kelli Walker.* She was responsible for this. Pretending to be on Melissa's side, acting like she was only concerned for her safety—when all the while she was bringing Carter back into her life, hurting her and Bradley and putting them in more danger than she knew. Melissa scrolled back in the Facebook group's timeline, looking for evidence of what she already knew in her gut.

And there it was. A comment on the photo of her and Thomas kissing, the one that started this whole mess.

I know this woman. She's my ex-wife. But who's the guy?
And who is Rose Danver?

Carter must have found the group when Kelli Walker tagged her in the photo. Melissa saw Kelli's reply to his comment, explaining who Thomas was, the accusations against him, the reasons the group had for believing him guilty.

Carter had commented in reply.

This is disturbing. Melissa is an adult, and she can make her own choices. But she has my son. I'm worried about his safety with a man like this.

Dozens of women chimed in with their support.

I'd be worried too if it was my son with this psycho!

I'm so sorry Carter. Praying for you.

If she wants to date a killer she should at least give up custody to you!

The prejudice against dads is insane. You're obviously a fitter parent than she is! Why is she the one who gets to raise your son?

And then, there was Kelli again.

Here to support you, Carter. My DMs are open.

Melissa was so furious, it was all she could do to resist throwing the phone across the room, to hurl it through the glass of the sliding door into the backyard. In that moment, she was certain that Kelli helped Carter find her. Told him exactly where to look.

Melissa tapped out a text to Kelli.

You fucking bitch. Do you know what you did? Carter is a toxic asshole. I moved here to get away from him, to get Bradley away from him. And you sent him right to us. You are evil.

She smiled at the last bit, thinking of how it would wound Kelli. Moral superiority and being a crusader was her whole thing; the notion that she could be bad, that she could be evil, would hurt her feelings, which was exactly what Melissa wanted to do in that moment.

Almost right after she sent the text, she saw the three dots indicating Kelli was composing a text in response. Melissa gritted her teeth, settled in for a nasty text fight. But the message that came only said: We need to talk.

I don't want to talk to you, Melissa tapped out. I want you to go to hell.

I'm coming to you.

Melissa almost screamed out loud. Are you not listening? Don't come here. I don't want to see you.

But now there was no response, and somehow, Melissa knew Kelli was on her way, no matter what she said.

---

Kelli showed up at the back door five minutes later, materializing like an apparition in the darkness, illuminated by the floodlights shining down on the back deck. She tapped on the glass and waved, timid. In spite of Kelli's chastened look, Melissa was as mad as ever at the sight of her. She rushed over to the sliding door, pulled it wide, and pushed past her, not letting her come in.

"Do you want to talk inside?" Kelli asked, glancing at the pajama bottoms and sweatshirt Melissa had changed into. "It's a little cold."

Melissa set her jaw and shook her head. "My son is sleeping in there. I don't want you anywhere near him right now."

Kelli bit her lip. "I understand. And I'm sorry."

"You know Carter's going to try to get him back, right? He's going to try to get full custody. Take my son away from me. You can't see it on the video, but Bradley was *terrified* to see him. He's afraid of his dad. Because he's a bad person. And it's your fault he's in our lives."

"I know," Kelli said. "I want you to know that I didn't tell him where to find you. Okay? I swear."

"You sure? Because I saw you offered to DM with him. You sure you never gave him an address?"

"I didn't," Kelli insisted. "In fact, I told him he shouldn't come here, that that would make things worse."

Melissa crossed her arms over her chest, trying to suppress a shiver at the sharpness of the night air. "Uh huh."

"Look, Melissa—there's something else you should know. I'm sorry about what happened with your ex-husband. But that's not what I came to talk to you about. There's been a break in the case."

Melissa blinked. "The case?"

"Rose's disappearance. Her death."

Just then, more footsteps crunched in the darkness beyond the reach of the floodlights. Kelli turned, and Derek Gordon stepped into the light. He was in civilian clothes, not his cop uniform.

"What are you doing here?" Melissa asked.

Derek glanced at Kelli. "Did you tell her yet?"

"I was just about to."

Melissa looked between the two of them, wishing they'd just come out with it already.

"What?"

Kelli was the one to say it.

"Rose's body has been found."

---

"The online group helped find the body," Kelli said. "One of our members showed Thomas's photo around to some friends and family, and one of them recognized him. Her elderly father. He lives on an acreage up north, and he remembers seeing Thomas late one night. Parked on the side of the road, poking around some woods, a creek. Looked like he was looking for a place to dump something."

Melissa turned her face away so Kelli couldn't see her reaction. They'd moved inside, out of the cold, and now Kelli and Derek sat together on Melissa's couch, explaining what had been found. They'd only just started, but already Melissa found herself wanting to argue with their evidence.

"He remembers this from three years ago?" she asked. "Come on, Kelli. Maybe he saw someone—but how can we be sure it was Thomas? What if he looked at the photo and wrote his face onto a memory of seeing someone else?"

"Fair point," Kelli said. "And that's possible. But Melissa, the place where he thinks he remembers seeing Thomas poking around—the local police dug there, and they found the body. It's Rose. DNA evidence proves it. It's quite a coincidence, isn't it? For him to be sighted in the place where her body is found?"

"It still could've been someone other than Thomas," Melissa said. "The stalker, for instance."

Derek spoke next. "I'm sorry, I know you think he's innocent. And I know he just asked you to marry him."

Melissa let out a sound of disgust. Neither of these people should have known anything about her and her personal life—the only reason they knew Thomas proposed that night was that they watched Carter's video. One of the worst days of her life was public knowledge. She felt exposed, dissected, her insides spread out for everyone to examine.

"There's more you should know," Derek said. "Rose's body was wrapped in a tarp. The same kind of tarp Thomas purchased the day Rose went missing. There's no way to prove it's the exact same one, but it's the right color, the right brand. And Rose's body has fibers on it that match the upholstery in the back of Thomas's car."

"I'm sure she drove it too," Melissa said. "Put things in the back. Groceries. There's plenty of reasons why she might have those fibers on her body."

She was saying these things—but more and more, with each passing second, she didn't believe them. It was hard to keep her faith in Thomas's innocence in the face of this onslaught of evidence.

By their faces, Kelli and Derek seemed to know that she barely believed what she was saying. Kelli shrugged indulgently, the way you might with a petulant child, and Derek gave a considered nod, the corners of his mouth turned down ponderously.

"Possibly," Derek said. "I suppose that could introduce some reasonable doubt. I'm sure these are all things that will be considered, when the case goes in front of a jury."

Melissa drew in a breath. "They're bringing the charges back?"

Derek nodded. "I've been up there where the body was discovered most of the morning—not in any official capacity; I just had a day off and headed up there since I have an interest in the case. I was able to speak to some of the officers there, and I also called some old friends at the Ramsey County Sheriff's Office, to see how the coordination was going. From what I hear, they think they've got what they need to bring the charges back, and actually bring the case to trial this time."

Melissa's first thought at hearing all this was of Thomas, sitting in a cell somewhere for beating Carter to within an inch of his life. Not knowing what was about to hit him. He'd be charged with assaulting Carter, of course—that seemed like a pretty open-and-shut case. And by the sound of it, the charges for murdering Rose would drop on him soon too. By the time he was arraigned on Monday, his bail was likely to be in the hundreds of thousands. If they granted him bail at all.

"What the hell am I going to do?" Melissa said out loud, even though she was half talking to herself.

"I don't know," Derek said. "That's up to you. I know you're involved with this man. But if I were you, I'd turn my attention to my son."

Melissa gave him a sharp look—who was he to tell her what to do with her son? But then she realized he was right. Guilty or not, this was a mess Thomas and Melissa's relationship wasn't likely to survive. He was slipping away from her—if he, the real Thomas, was ever truly hers to begin with. She couldn't lose Bradley too.

"Melissa," Kelli said, "think about this. Carter has said he's going to go after custody of your son. He has Thomas on video beating him half to death. And now Thomas is about to go on trial for the murder of his wife. Don't you think it would be a good idea to split with him? And to make it public?"

It *would* make sense—there was no denying the wisdom in what Kelli was saying. She just wasn't ready to admit it to these two people.

More than that, Melissa wasn't ready to let go of what she had just a few hours before. The perfect moment on the pier, when Thomas sank to one knee and told her he wanted to love her forever. The moment when she saw her future stretch out perfect and golden all the way to the horizon.

Before everything fell apart.

# TRANSCRIPT OF RECORDING

**Thomas:** I owe you an apology.

[pause]

**Thomas:** Are you going to say anything?

**Amelia:** I'm listening.

**Thomas:** I got a little carried away at our last session. And I'm sorry.

[pause]

**Thomas:** Well?

**Amelia:** I don't know what to say.

**Thomas:** You can say anything with me. You know that.

**Amelia:** Can I? I'm afraid of you, Thomas.

**Thomas:** You don't have to be. It will never happen again.

**Amelia:** Won't it? You sound like an abusive husband. You're apologetic, you say it won't happen again, until—what? Until I make you mad again?

**Thomas:** Now you're hurting my feelings.

**Amelia:** Why? Because of what Kelli Walker is saying about you?

**Thomas:** As if I could ever hurt Rose.

**Amelia:** She has pictures, Thomas.

[pause]

**Thomas:** So you believe it now? That I hurt her? That I killed her? Because you saw some pictures of Rose's face all beaten up?

[pause]

**Amelia:** Thomas, the last time I saw you, you flipped my glass coffee table. Shattered it. And then you choked me. You put your hands around my neck and squeezed. And I couldn't breathe.

**Thomas:** I was angry. I wasn't thinking straight.

**Amelia:** Men and their anger. You seem to think it's a blanket excuse. "I was angry," so—what? So you can do whatever you want?

**Thomas:** Come on. You know I'm not like that.

**Amelia:** I'm beginning to question what I know.

**Thomas:** I'm going through the most stressful experience of my life. I've lost my wife. My kids are depressed and traumatized. I'm being publicly accused of things I didn't do. And I'm paying a lawyer a small fortune to build a defense, so I don't have to go to jail. I'm not myself, Amelia.

[pause]

**Amelia:** Be that as it may—there's something I need you to know.

[pause]

**Thomas:** Yes?

**Amelia:** I've been recording these sessions.

[pause]

**Thomas:** What? Amelia, at our first session, I *asked* you, and you told me…

**Amelia:** Yes. And now I'm telling you the truth. I've been recording from the beginning.

**Thomas:** But why? Don't you trust me? After all we've been through?

**Amelia:** I don't know what I know, Thomas. Not anymore. And that's why I've been recording. Because I wasn't sure if I could trust what I thought I knew.

**Thomas:** Amelia, please. This is a betrayal. You have to delete them.

**Amelia:** No. Not after what happened last session. I've saved all the recordings on the cloud. And I've set it up so that if anything happens to me—if I die—an email will be sent with a download link to those recordings. Sent to the police and to the press. Including the recording in which you attacked me.

[pause]

**Amelia:** I've listened to it. The sound quality is very clear. I believe anyone listening would understand exactly what is going on.

**Thomas:** Why are you doing this?

**Amelia:** I needed to do that, and I needed to tell you about it, to feel safe in here with you. Unless I log into my email, unless I enter a password only I know and prevent the email from being sent each day—the police and the press will receive the recordings. And I imagine they'll be very interested in them.

**Thomas:** Doesn't that go against your professional ethics? Privilege, confidentiality?

**Amelia:** I'd say we're well past that, aren't we? You already pushed me to go against my professional ethics when you demanded that I be the one to treat you—in spite of knowing you, in spite of *telling you* I was uncomfortable with it. You forced me to do this.

**Thomas:** So you figure you'll just break everything now? Broadcast to the world things I've said in here in confidence?

**Amelia:** I'm not required to keep confidentiality in all cases. For instance, if I believe there's imminent threat of a crime being committed, of a threat against a person's life. In this case, I believe that person to be me.

**Thomas:** You really think I'd...that I'd kill you?

**Amelia:** It doesn't matter what I believe. All that matters is that you know. If anything happens to me—if I die, or become incapacitated, the world will know everything that has been said in here.

**Thomas:** You've made your point. So what now?

**Amelia:** Now I have some questions of my own.

# CHAPTER 17

Melissa woke the next morning from an uneasy sleep, pursued by a threatening dream whose details skittered like cockroaches to the deep recesses of her mind as soon as her eyes opened. She groaned and put a hand to her head, recalling not the dream—that was long gone—but the events of the prior day and night. Carter, the fight, Thomas in jail, Rose's body discovered, the charges of murder coming back.

Reality was nightmare enough.

She rose and checked on Bradley. He was still fast asleep, exhausted. In the kitchen, she busied herself making breakfast. After the coffee was poured, she stood for a moment at the back window.

"What am I going to do?" she asked the woods.

The bare trees didn't answer.

Her phone buzzed with a number she didn't recognize. She let it go to voicemail as she sat with her yogurt and coffee, then checked the transcription of the message.

Hello, Mrs. Danv—excuse me, Ms. Burke. I'm Jonathan Klein, Thomas Danver's lawyer. I'm here at the Ramsey County Correctional Facility, coordinating with my client on a few details, and he's requesting a meeting with you. Today if possible. I wonder if you could give me a call back at—

Melissa left the message and immediately called the number back.

"He'd like to speak to you as soon as possible," Thomas's lawyer said when she got him on the line. "There are some complicated developments here, and—well, I know you're not his legal partner, but it's my understanding that—"

"I'll come," Melissa said, cutting him off. She didn't want to talk about the proposal, didn't want to ponder the question of who she was to Thomas with this man, a stranger. She did want to see Thomas, though, even if she couldn't say why. Maybe she wanted to give him the chance to win her back one more time, convince her yet again that he wasn't a murderer. Or maybe she only wanted closure, before she never saw him again. A goodbye.

"Normally there's a process for scheduling a visit," the lawyer said. "But I'll pull some strings and get you on the list. Can you be here around noon?"

She agreed, then ended the call and started planning. She couldn't take Bradley to the county jail with her. She'd have to get Lawrence to watch him while she was gone. It was still a long way to noon, which gave her plenty of time to get Bradley up, fed, and dressed, and to explain things to Lawrence.

The phone buzzed again, and this time she answered without even looking at the screen, thinking it must be Thomas's lawyer again, calling with some important detail he forgot.

But it was a woman's voice on the other end of the line.

"Melissa, it's Amelia."

"Amelia? How did you get this number?"

"It was on Thomas's phone. I have his passcode, for emergencies."

She felt a surge of annoyance at Amelia and Thomas's

closeness—even Melissa didn't yet know Thomas's phone pass-code. Until she remembered what was going on, the fact that she was supposed to be done with Thomas. After everything that had happened, Amelia could have him.

"I need your help."

"What is it?"

"Rhiannon and Kendall. They're missing."

————————

Melissa was at Thomas's house thirty minutes later. She had to wake up Bradley earlier than she wanted to, rush him through break-fast, and wrestle his sleepy limbs into a shirt and pants. Then she packed him upstairs to Lawrence and Toby, who were still waking up themselves, fumbling through apologies to all three of them as she went out the door.

Now Amelia was opening the front door, a look of feverish panic on her face.

"You slept here last night?" Melissa asked, imagining her in Thomas's bed—a bed she'd still not been in herself. Then she shook her head. She needed to stop this. There were more import-ant things happening than her jealousy of Amelia and Thomas's relationship.

"I was on the couch," Amelia told her. "I know I'm only next door, but it didn't feel right leaving them alone in the house. I was up at seven, and they didn't come down. I figured that wasn't a problem—they're teenagers, they sleep in. But then they still weren't down by nine-thirty, then ten, and I went to check on them. That's when I saw that their beds were empty."

"Where could they have gone?"

"Anywhere," Amelia said.

"That can't be true."

"It is. Thomas's car is gone. Rhiannon's seventeen; she has her driver's license."

Melissa walked inside the house and glanced at the clock on the wall. It was quarter to eleven. "Did you hear anything last night? Engine starting, garage door opening and closing? If we know when they left, then we could figure out how far they might have gotten."

"I didn't hear anything," Amelia says. "I slept like the dead last night."

"And when did you go to bed?"

"I don't know," Amelia said, lifting her fingers to her temples in a jerky motion. "Ten-thirty, maybe?"

More than twelve hours ago. They could have been in a different state by now.

Amelia looked genuinely worried, jittery and stricken, her lips pulling away from her teeth as she breathed through her mouth, heavy and panicked. Melissa felt a pang of sympathy as she realized how long Amelia had known Thomas's girls—since they were babies. She must have felt like a surrogate mother to them, as much a part of their lives as Rose, and far more than Melissa was right then. Probably more than she'd ever be. On a sudden urge, Melissa grabbed for Amelia's hand, gave it a squeeze, watched as the other woman's eyes came to hers, wrinkled with anxiety.

"Hey," Melissa said. "They'll turn up. Okay? They're going to be all right."

Amelia breathed out. "You think so?"

Melissa nodded. "They probably just want to get away from all this for a while. Right? I mean, it's pretty stressful. I don't really want to be dealing with any of this right now. Do you?"

Amelia gave a hesitant laugh. "No," she admitted. "No, I don't."

"They're probably just… I don't know, where do teenagers go when they want to be alone? The mall? A friend's house? Have you thought about calling the police?"

Amelia gave her a grim look. "I did think about it. But…have you seen the news this morning?"

Melissa hadn't—but she didn't even need to ask. She knew what Amelia was going to say before she said it.

"They've discovered Rose's body," Amelia said. "Up north. And now the Ramsey County Attorney says he's bringing back the charges against Thomas. With all that—I thought maybe it would be best not to get the police involved. If we can find them ourselves…"

"I get it." Melissa glanced again at the clock. "Look, Thomas has asked me to come meet him at the jail."

"At the jail? Why?"

"I don't know. But I'm going to go. I need to be there in a couple hours. But maybe before I go, I could check at some parks, parking lots, maybe take a quick walk through Rosedale Mall."

Amelia nodded. "Go. I'll drive around and look for them too."

"Shouldn't someone stay here, in case they decide to come home?"

Amelia shook her head. "I can't stand it here. I need to do something. Besides, I'm afraid the press is going to be here soon. Set up camp outside the house in case Thomas makes bail, harass the neighbors with questions about whether they think he's guilty. I don't want to be here when they come."

Melissa nodded—it made sense. Now that Amelia mentioned it, she'd like to get out of there too. She thought local reporters would love to get a shot of the woman Thomas Danver had been seen with around town. The woman he'd been captured on video proposing to, then beating the pulp out of her ex-husband.

The woman who screamed, begging him not to kill anyone.

---

Amelia and Melissa left separately. Melissa did what she said she was going to do: She looped the neighborhood, driving past some local parks and other places where two teenagers might hang out, then took a quick walk through Rosedale, the closest shopping mall. She didn't see any sign of them—in fact the mall had only just recently opened its doors, stores still rolling up their metal cages and letting the day's first customers in. She needed to leave soon if she was going to make it to the jail in time for her meeting with Thomas.

She went back to her car and set her phone's GPS for the Ramsey County Correctional Facility—not a trip she ever imagined taking. The directions took her to a squat, forbidding stone-and-brick building at St. Paul's eastern edge, plopped in the center of a broad, desolate field. She followed the signs for visitors, then went inside and followed a female guard's terse instructions for signing in and passing through security checkpoints. She half expected to be taken to one of those rooms with webbed glass and a telephone, like in the movies, but the guard led her to a private room instead: square, with white cinder block walls. There, Thomas and a man in a suit sat waiting.

"Ms. Burke," the well-dressed man said, rising from his chair and offering his hand. "We spoke on the phone."

"Jon, could you see if we can get a cup of coffee or at least some water to drink?" Thomas asked. He was wearing the expected orange prison jumpsuit, which sat loose on his frame. He looked diminished, smaller somehow than he did just a day before, something timid and childlike in the way he sat at the metal table, his hands folded in his lap. Melissa could hardly recognize him—and, looking at him, she realized that she barely knew him at all.

The lawyer left without saying another word, and then they were alone. Melissa sat, and Thomas reached for her hands across the table. She snatched them away before he could touch her.

Thomas's back slumped against his chair with a thud, a look of surprise and hurt on his face. "You're mad at me, then?"

Melissa breathed hard through her nose, realizing in that moment just how angry she really was. Where to even begin?

"Why don't you just tell me why you wanted to talk to me," she suggested.

"I asked you a question last night," Thomas said. "Before we were...interrupted."

Melissa's mouth fell open. "That's what you want to talk about? Now? After everything that's happened?"

"I need an answer," Thomas said. His eyes glistened.

She felt herself taken back to that perfect, fragile moment on the pier—Thomas on his knee with a ring in his hands, the waves lapping gently around them, the ambering evening light glowing at her shoulders, the air crisp and clean. There was no getting back to there from where they were, no turning back the clock to make it play out differently. Now her answer to Thomas's question had to come *here*, in a cinder block room in the county jail.

"I can't give you an answer," she said. "Not here. Not like this."

"Why not?" Thomas pleaded, his voice breaking with emotion. "I need your support now more than ever, Melissa. Things are happening, bad things, and I need to know that you still...that you love me."

*Of course I love you.* The words were on her lips, and she was so tempted to just blurt them out. But something stopped her. *Did* she still love him? She was certain that she did as recently as yesterday—but *yesterday* felt like a very long time ago.

"Melissa, you're going to start hearing things," Thomas said, dropping his gaze with shame. "It's about more than this assault, now. The charges of murder—they're coming back."

"I know," she said.

Thomas's eyes snapped up to her. "You know?"

This wasn't the time to admit that she'd been talking to Kelli Walker and Derek Gordon—Thomas's enemies. "It's already on the news," she said instead.

"Then you know why this is so important," Thomas said. "Melissa, I'm on video proposing to you. People know that we're together. For you to leave me now, to turn down my proposal—it would make me look guilty. But if there was a woman standing by me, sitting behind me in that courtroom, supporting me..."

She gasped and rose to her feet, her chair clattering to the floor behind her. She turned and walked to the door, her hands rising to the sides of her face. She swept them through her hair in a rapid movement, then turned back to Thomas, suddenly furious.

"Is that what this is about? Optics for your goddamn murder trial?"

Thomas's face twisted in agony. "Don't make it like that. I want you standing by me because I'm about to face the challenge of my lifetime—staying out of prison, protecting my reputation, being there for my daughters. I need the woman I love beside me while I face it."

"And what about what *I'm* facing?" Melissa said, so mad she could barely see, blotches of color flashing in front of her eyes. "My ex-husband is going to try to get full custody of my son. My *son*, Thomas. He's going to haul me into a courtroom and tell a judge that I'm a bad mother, that I'm putting my son in danger. And because of you, he's got a case. Because of what you did."

*Because of what you did.* The words dropped from her lips and fell on the table between them. A silence descended in which Thomas looked like he was wondering what she meant by *what you did*—and maybe Melissa was wondering too. Was she only referring to Thomas's attacking Carter, sending him to the hospital? Or did she also mean killing his wife? Had she gone from being one of Thomas's defenders to believing he was guilty?

She wasn't sure, and she also wasn't sure if it mattered. Something had been broken between them, and it would take time to put it back together, if it could even be repaired. In the meantime, Thomas had a trial to face—and Melissa had her own problems to deal with.

"I need to focus on my son right now," she said.

Thomas breathed out, seeming to deflate. "So that's it. This is over."

"Maybe. Maybe once the dust settles, we can get back together, see if there's anything still here."

Even as she said it, Melissa knew what she was saying would never happen. It sounded absurd in her own ears. A perfunctory reassurance, an empty promise of a possibility that could never be. She was sure Thomas could hear it too.

"Goodbye, Thomas," she said. "Good luck to you."

He didn't answer, and she left the room under the shroud of his hurt, angry silence.

Her vision blurred on her way to the exit, the hard lines of the cinder block and the metal bars at the checkpoints warping and floating, like the swirl of one shade of paint mixing into another. Only when the cool air of the outside hit her cheeks did she realize she was crying.

# CHAPTER 18

As Melissa drove out of the parking lot, she spotted something up the street. Across a two-lane road with a narrow strip of gravel shoulder on either side, a residential neighborhood sat opposite the jail. On an intersecting street a couple hundred feet down the road from her, a car was parked. It looked like Thomas's, but of course he couldn't have been driving it. It was the car that went missing from his garage that morning. Melissa squinted and spotted some movement behind the windows.

Rhiannon and Kendall? They'd either followed her to the county jail, or they'd come by themselves, keeping watch—wanting to be close to their dad.

Melissa had intended to turn the other way down the road, but instead, she cranked the wheel in their direction and sped toward the car with a staccato squeal of tire rubber. When she reached the street the car was parked on, she made a sharp turn and then screeched to a stop on a diagonal just ahead of the car's front bumper, blocking escape. Then she got out of the car and walked toward it.

When she reached the driver's side door and craned down to look in, Melissa only saw Rhiannon, looking sheepish with her hands on the wheel. Kendall was nowhere to be found. Melissa signaled for Rhiannon to roll down the window.

"Where's Kendall?"

Rhiannon shook her head. "I don't know where she is. I was looking for her."

"She's not with you?"

"I woke up in the middle of the night, and she wasn't in her room. Her bike was gone." A quaver in Rhiannon's voice told Melissa just how worried she was about her younger sister. Melissa couldn't blame her. She was a fifteen-year-old girl wandering the city, apparently with nothing but her bicycle. Reeling from her dad's arrest. Confused, not thinking straight.

And maybe Rhiannon wasn't thinking straight either. She was older than Kendall, and she affected a worldly aloofness in the way that only seventeen-year-old girls could—but beneath that exterior, she was still a girl in most of the ways that mattered. She was scared and confused too, and unlike Melissa, she didn't have the luxury of walking away from Thomas. It was her last living parent locked up across the road, facing down the prospect of life in prison. Rhiannon was at serious risk of becoming an effective orphan, and the brokenness behind her eyes told Melissa that on some level she knew it.

"Are you okay?" Melissa asked.

Rhiannon folded her top lip over the bottom and looked forward. She closed her eyes, and the movement of her eyelids scraped tears onto her cheeks.

"This is your fault," Rhiannon said. "Before you came, everything was fine. We were happy."

Melissa felt an urge to argue, to defend herself. She didn't choose any of this, after all. Thomas pursued *her*. But it felt more important in that moment to empathize with Rhiannon, to meet her where she was at, rather than argue with her.

"I know," Melissa said. "I know it must feel like all these terrible things started happening when I came into your dad's life. And I'm sorry. I am."

"Why were you talking to those people?"

Melissa blinked, not sure what Rhiannon was talking about. She thought Rhiannon was angry at her for what had happened between her dad and Carter—she was right that he'd never have gone to jail for assault if it wasn't for Melissa. But now it seemed like there was something else on her mind.

"What people?" Melissa asked.

"That woman who hates Dad so much. And that…that *man*."

Melissa suddenly realized—she was talking about Kelli and Derek. But how could she have known that Melissa had been talking to them?

"Do you mean Kelli Walker?" Melissa asked. "And the detective who investigated your dad three years ago?"

"He investigated Dad?"

"He did. I know it must be confusing to know that I've been talking to them. But…" Melissa trailed off, not sure how to explain it. She couldn't tell Rhiannon that she'd actually started to believe what they'd been telling her, that in the face of all the evidence piling up against Thomas, she no longer believed he was innocent. She couldn't tell this poor girl that she actually believed her father killed her mother. So instead, she went with the truth as it stood just twenty-four hours ago. "I'm working with them to figure out who really killed your mom."

"To prove Dad's innocent?"

Melissa nodded. It *was* true at first, even if it wasn't the case anymore.

Then Melissa realized something. Something Rhiannon asked only seconds ago, about Derek. *He investigated Dad?*

"Wait a second," Melissa said. "The man I've been talking to.

You didn't know that he was in charge of the investigation into your mom's disappearance?"

She shook her head. "Dad shielded us from most of that. Always had us go over to Aunt Amelia's whenever the police came over."

"But nobody questioned you? Took a statement?"

"They had someone else talk to us," Rhiannon said. "Some woman. A social worker."

This made sense, Melissa supposed. You don't want to traumatize two girls who've lost their mother, don't want to interrogate them the way you'd interrogate a witness or a suspect. So Derek got someone who worked with kids to take their statement. But then...

"So how do you know Derek?"

"That's his name?" Rhiannon asked. "I only know what he looks like."

Melissa breathed out with impatience. "Yes, but from *where*?"

Rhiannon swallowed hard. "Mom...cheated on Dad. He didn't tell you that?"

Melissa clamped a hand on the side mirror, suddenly dizzy. "Wait, you're telling me...with Derek?"

Rhiannon nodded. "I saw them together. Not, you know, like *that*. But the way they were together. And Mom's face when she saw that I saw. I knew. And then she admitted it. It turned into a huge fight at home, between Mom and Dad. But I was the only one who ever saw his face."

Melissa's mind raced. No wonder Thomas had never told her—an affair gave him a motive to have murdered Rose. Or...

"What happened after your mom admitted the affair?"

"She broke it off," Rhiannon said. "But then he kept coming around."

"Derek did?"

"Like I said, I didn't know his name. But yeah. I saw him parked in a car down the street from our house a couple times. Spying on us or something. And once, when I was out with Mom at the store, he came up to her. Grabbed her by the arm, said they needed to talk. I thought probably they had started up again. But…"

"But what?"

"She was afraid of him. Mom was. Pulled away and told him to leave her alone. There were red marks on her arm afterward. From his fingers."

Melissa backed away from the car door, literally reeling. In that moment, her body needed to move, to keep up with her racing thoughts. She looped away from Rhiannon's window, then turned and saw the prison once more, looming across the road like an accusation. She'd made a terrible mistake. Part of her wanted to rush back over there, take back everything she'd said to Thomas—of course she'd marry him, of course she knew—*knew*—he was innocent.

Derek. The Ramsey County Sheriff's Office may have fired him, but he must still have had friends there—friends who'd given him access to the evidence from the old case, the fibers collected from the back of Thomas's car. And he coordinated with the police department where Rose's body was found, by his own admission. He could have planted evidence. Could have framed Thomas.

She needed to tell someone. She fished her phone from her pocket and dialed the first number she could think of.

"Kelli," Melissa said when she answered. "Where is Derek?"

"I haven't seen him yet today," Kelli said. "But he's coming over to the house in a few minutes. He was going to give me an update on the case."

Melissa's heart sped up in her chest. "Are you in the house alone?"

"I am," Kelli said. "My husband and the boys like to get out of town and go hunting most Saturdays in the fall. It's deer season. They just left."

Melissa glanced back at Rhiannon, who was watching her, listening to everything she said. She heard Melissa say Kelli's name when she answered the phone, knew who she was talking to. The girl's eyes sharpened, and she started the car, threw it into reverse. Melissa ran toward her, but it was too late—she'd backed down the street. Then she put the car in drive and turned around Melissa's car, rocketed onto the two-lane road without even looking for oncoming traffic.

"What's going on over there?" Kelli asked.

"It's nothing," Melissa said. "Look, you have to get out of the house."

"What? Why?"

"It's Derek. Kelli, you can't trust him."

"Derek? I've been working with him on this for years."

"No," Melissa said. "He's been lying to you. This whole time. He's been lying to everybody. From the beginning, he's been trying to frame Thomas."

Kelli sighed. "Melissa, I thought you were finally coming around on this. Thomas is guilty."

"Kelli, you have to listen to me," Melissa said. "Derek and Rose had an affair. They got caught. And when she broke it off, he didn't like it. He kept following her."

Kelli was silent on the other side of the line, slow to understand. "Rose hinted there might be someone. Once. But I don't see—"

"It's the stalker theory," Melissa said. "Remember I said we should be taking it seriously? Derek didn't get fired because he failed to find the stalker. He *was* the stalker."

# ROSE

*What happened next was terrible. And it was my fault. I know that.*

*I cheated on Thomas. Before I even started writing in this journal, I betrayed him. Betrayed our marriage. Betrayed our family.*

*I should've started with that, but I couldn't bring myself to admit it, even to myself. Couldn't bring myself to write it.*

*I feel terrible. I hate myself more than I've ever hated myself before.*

*But is it really all my fault? Cheating is always blamed on the cheater—but infidelity happens for a reason. If I shattered our marriage, brought it all crashing down, it's because Thomas has been chipping away at its foundations for years. Neglecting me. Treating me with contempt. Turning our daughters against me. And refusing to listen to me when I tell him that something's seriously wrong.*

*The world wouldn't see it that way, I know. But I know the truth. Thomas shares some of the blame for this.*

---

*It all started the morning after our fight—the one where Thomas refused to go to a new therapist with me, accused me of endangering the family and his reputation, and then threatened me. After the fight, Thomas left and slept in the guest room, too angry to share a bed with me.*

*When I woke the next morning, I felt as though a heavy weight was pinning me to the bed, sitting on my chest,* keeping me from breathing. My depression was a physical thing, a thick, rancid sludge spreading through my veins. I heard voices through the door—Thomas and the girls murmuring to each other as they got ready for work and school, whispering to each other to leave me alone, Mom's having another one of her bad mornings.

As though my despair didn't have a reason. As though it was something that just happened to me. As though it didn't have a cause that Thomas refused to name, refused to admit.

When they left, doors closing and car engines droning away to nothing in the distance, I lay and listened to the sounds of the house. Sometime after ten I finally pulled myself out of bed and went downstairs. Maybe some coffee would help snap me out of this funk. But when I opened the cupboard and looked at the half-empty bag of grounds, I realized that it wasn't coffee I needed.

I went to the other cupboard and found a bottle of white wine. Poured myself a glass, unchilled. The taste didn't matter to me—I wanted the buzz, the feeling of floating and sinking at once, the light oblivion that came with being just a little drunk.

Soon I had finished the bottle, and I still wasn't out of my pajamas. Shame washed over me as I tried to pour another glass and saw a few last drops trickle from the mouth of the bottle. I didn't feel better. I felt worse, my head feeling loose and jangly, like an old failing house whose joists and floorboards creak with every footstep, every gust of wind.

I went back to bed and stared at the ceiling as the room spun around me. I closed my eyes but didn't sleep. Somehow the day passed away, minute by excruciating minute ticking by on the digital clock that sat by my bedside, and suddenly it was two o'clock in the afternoon.

My phone buzzed, and I looked at it.

Hey lady! Want to meet up for an afternoon drink before the kids get home from school?

It was Kelli. I didn't want to see her, and the last thing I needed was an afternoon drink, after how much I'd already had—but in my shame, I thought that if I managed to get myself out of bed, if I showered and put real clothes on, then the day wouldn't be a total waste. That if I could claw myself to this one pitiful piece of normal functioning, there was hope for me to get all the way back to the way I'd felt the night before, when I thought I could see all the way from this hell I was living in to the bearable life I wanted.

I skipped the shower but managed to get some nice clothes on, ran my fingers through my hair, then got into the car. Behind the wheel, I realized I was still a little drunk—not as bad as I'd been a couple hours before but probably still too drunk to drive. But I backed the car out of the driveway anyway and then headed off down the road, concentrating hard to keep from drifting.

I'd barely made it a quarter mile when I saw the black car driving up tight at my back bumper, the police lights flashing on the dashboard. I panicked and almost swerved right off the road, hit my brakes too hard, but somehow managed to pull to the shoulder.

The man who climbed out of the car was in plainclothes, blue jeans and a navy polo. The car was unmarked.

"You had something to drink today, ma'am?"

I looked up at him, his face of angry authority wearing all the disapproval and contempt I felt for myself. Reflecting it back to me.

*And I burst into tears.*

*I swear they were genuine. I wasn't trying to manipulate my way out of a DUI. It was all just too much—Thomas's hatred toward me, my hatred toward myself. The cop's reflexive judgment against me: a lawbreaker, a drunk driver. And imagining everything that would happen next. Would I go to a holding cell? Would Thomas have to bail me out? Would there be a mug shot, a court appearance? I was only sitting in a parked car on the side of a quiet suburban road, but I felt as though the eyes of the whole world were turning to me in judgment.*

*I went on crying for a few minutes, looking at my lap, then glanced up again at the cop and saw his face transformed from disapproval to sympathy. There even seemed to be some guilt there, for being the one to make me cry.*

*"You don't have to do that," he said.*

*"I'm sorry," I sobbed. "I know this is bad—I fucked up. I'm a fuckup."*

*"Hey," the cop said, his voice quiet now. He reached his hand through the window and set it on my shoulder. "You don't have to say things like that about yourself. You made a mistake."*

*"My whole life is one big mistake," I said.*

*The cop squinted, looked up and down the road.*

*"Where are you coming from?" he asked.*

*I told him my address.*

*"Tell you what," he said. "Why don't you just turn around and go home. I'll follow you to make sure you get there safe. And we can both forget this happened."*

*I'd be standing Kelli up, but it was better than going to jail.*

*"Really?" I said.*

"Sure," he said. "I'm not really a traffic cop anyway. I'm an investigator."

"An investigator?"

"A detective," he said. "I was out taking some witness statements on a domestic disturbance when I saw you pass by. I don't want to give you a DUI. I just want to make sure you don't hurt yourself."

I smiled. "Thank you, officer," I said, my gratitude real, not feigned. I found myself noticing how handsome he was, the kindness in his eyes. Not like Thomas, whose superficial kindness masked contempt.

I drove home, and the cop followed me, just as he said. I put the car in the garage and then went into the house. I heard a knock on the door. It was the cop again.

"You change your mind about giving me that DUI?"

He shook his head. "No harm, no foul. I just wanted to ask—well, I'm not sure what I wanted to ask."

He let out a little laugh and looked at his shoes. Butterflies fluttered in my stomach as I realized that I was making him flustered. I wondered if he might be attracted to me. It had been so long since anyone had found me beautiful, I'd forgotten what it was like, no longer knew the signs.

"Are you okay, I guess is what I wanted to ask."

I shook my head, smiled. "No. Is anyone?"

He made a pained look. "I suppose we all have our struggles. But something in the way you were talking back there..." He trailed off, then cocked his head to the side, looked past me into the house. "Are you home alone?"

"I am."

"And do you...do you feel safe? At home?"

I laughed. Of course I didn't feel safe at home. Home, I

*wanted to tell him, was the place where the people lived who could hurt you the most.*

*"My family hates me," I said. "And half the time I agree with them."*

*"You have a husband?"*

*"Oh, he hates me the most."*

*"I'm sorry," he said. "You don't deserve that."*

*I studied him, struggling to understand what he was trying to do by being so nice to me.*

*"You don't know anything about what I deserve."*

*"I know more than most," he said. "I see a lot of things in this job. I know a good person when I see one."*

*I was so overcome with gratitude that I couldn't speak.*

*Still standing on the stoop, he glanced around, like he thought someone might be watching. "Look," he said, reaching in his pocket, "I don't normally do this, but I'm going to give you my card. In case you ever need to talk. Okay?"*

*He handed it over to me, and I took it from him, and in the instant that my hand touched the card, his finger darted forward and brushed against mine. His face flushed red at his own brazenness, and his gaze dropped to his shoes again. My cheeks grew hot too. He was cute when he was bashful. I glanced at the card. Derek Gordon.*

*I was still a little drunk and dazed at this man's kindness toward me, the interest he was showing. But what happened next was my decision, all the same. It was something I wanted, something I made happen. On this, I have no excuse.*

*I reached across the threshold and grabbed for him. Pulled him toward me by the fabric of that tight polo.*

*And then we were kissing. I must have tasted terrible, the warm white wine stale on my tongue, but still, Derek*

Gordon opened his mouth, darted his tongue past my teeth. And then we were stumbling up the stairs and ripping at each other's clothes.

I sat on the bed and pulled down his boxers, took him in my mouth. Above me he moaned, and I looked up to meet his eyes.

"Lie back," he said, his voice rough. "I want to be inside you."

I did as he said. "Be gentle with me," I said. "It's been so long since..." I trailed off, let the sentence go unfinished as he pulled my pants and underwear off, arranged my legs the way he liked. When he pushed himself inside me, I burst into tears.

"Do you want me to stop?" he asked.

"Keep going," I said, and this, more than anything, is the detail that makes me feel guiltiest when I remember it.

I could have told him to stop. But I asked him to keep going.

---

Afterward, we lay together for a while, then put our clothes back on in silence.

"Can I see you again?" he asked as we crept down the stairs, walking softly even though we were the only ones in the house.

"I don't know if that's a good idea."

"I need to see you again," he said, amending his prior question.

"I have your card."

At the door he stole one more kiss—gentle, affectionate.

I pulled away and pressed my fingers to my lips as I saw

*her coming up the front walk, her feet scratching to a halt on the flagstones, her face ashen.*

*It was Rhiannon.*

*She knew.*

# CHAPTER 19

"I'm going to confront him."

"Kelli, are you nuts?"

Melissa was driving, speeding on the interstate to get to Kelli's house as quickly as she could. The phone was on speaker.

"I can't believe Derek lied to me all this time." She sounded angry, offended—not as scared as Melissa thought she should be.

"Kelli, do *not* tell Derek that you know what I just told you. Who knows what he would do when he's cornered?"

There was a pause. "He's at the door. I'm going to say something, Melissa. I have to."

The call ended, and Melissa loosed a scream into the close air of the car. Kelli Walker could be such a fool. Overconfident that she could find Rose's killer, she couldn't let go of her moral crusader nature even when it put her in danger. She needed to get out of her meeting with Derek, not let on that she knew anything. Then, when she was safe, Melissa and Kelli could make a plan to tell what they knew to the police, to the county prosecutor—to convince them it was Derek and not Thomas who killed Rose.

It took Melissa fifteen more minutes to get into Kelli's neighborhood. She slid off the freeway, then drove to the address Kelli gave her. She pulled up in the driveway. Before she even got out of the car, she could sense that something was wrong.

The front door to Kelli's house was wide open. It drifted on its hinges, giving the impression that someone had just come bursting out, but then Melissa realized—it was only the wind. Whoever ran out the front door and left it open was gone now.

Melissa's heart pounded so hard she could hear it, a thrumming static roar in her ears. She paused outside her car, afraid to go in, steadying herself on the side mirror. And then she forced herself to walk forward, to take the steps up to the front stoop.

"Kelli?" Melissa called at the door. In answer, there was only silence.

Melissa walked inside, past a front entryway, skirting along a small, white-carpeted living room, and moved into the kitchen with its gleaming granite countertops and a broad center island with stools pressed up against the overhang.

It was Kelli's feet Melissa saw first, jutting out past the island. One foot was wearing a leather house shoe, but the other had only a gray sock, the shoe missing somewhere. Then Melissa noticed the blood, a bulging pool of it, shiny and so dark red it verged into black. Melissa drew her hands toward her mouth, a guttural sound emerging from deep in her throat.

She inched further around the island to see all of Kelli, keeping close to the wall. A sob ripped from Melissa into the air when the rest of her came into view. Sprawled out on her stomach, her neck turned to the side so her cheek lay on the blood-streaked tile, her eyes glassy, dead. One hand lay daintily at her waist, palm up. The other arm bent at the elbow and reaching past the crown of her head, as though grabbing for something.

"Oh my God."

The voice came from behind Melissa. She whirled around and saw him standing in the doorway. Derek.

"What the hell happened here?" He stepped into the kitchen. Dread swelled in Melissa's chest, and her eyes darted to the counter, to a butcher block. She seized the biggest handle and drew out the knife, brandished it flashing in the air in front of her.

"Stay away."

Derek's hands came up, like Melissa was a skittish animal. "Melissa, what do you think you're doing? Put that down."

She backed away from him. Her heel slipped in the slick of Kelli's blood, but she kept her balance. "Stay back!" she yelled. "Don't come another step."

"Okay," he said. "Okay. I can tell you're scared. But Melissa, you're not thinking clearly right now."

Anger rose up in Melissa's throat like bile. She was so sick of people telling her what she thought and didn't think, what she knew and didn't know. "That's not true," she spat. "I'm thinking clearly for the first time. I know exactly what happened here. *You* killed her."

Derek's eyes bulged in a look of shock so genuine-seeming Melissa had to remind herself how good a liar, how good a pretender, this man was. "Melissa, I just got here."

"I know that's not true," Melissa said. "I was on the phone with Kelli when you knocked on the door."

"It had to have been someone else," Derek said.

"Who?"

He shook his head, his eyes seeming to go out of focus. He was panicking, Melissa was pretty sure, realizing he was caught—realizing Melissa had him trapped.

"I don't know," he admitted. "It's true, I was supposed to meet her fifteen minutes ago. She might have assumed it was me at the door. But I was running late."

"You're a liar," Melissa said. "You've been lying from the beginning. I know. I know about you and Rose. I know you had sex with her. And that after you got caught and she tried to break it off, you stalked her."

Derek started moving into the kitchen again, slowly closing the distance between them. His hand held out, trying to calm Melissa.

"We did have sex. Once. Only once. And I did follow her after that. But I wasn't stalking her. I was *worried* about her. I could tell there was something not right at her home. I thought Thomas might be abusing her somehow. That she was in danger. And Melissa, I was *right*. Don't you see? With all the evidence against him?"

"Then why did your bosses fire you?" Melissa asked. "Why did they drop the charges and then treat you like something they had to hide?"

Derek kept inching closer. He'd come around the end of the island now. Melissa had backed away from him so far that her shoulders were pressed against the far wall. There was nowhere for her to run.

"Rose did report a stalker," Derek said. "She reported *me*. I panicked, got into the reports and altered them so my name wasn't on them, went to Rose and told her not to do that again. I threatened her, scared her. And I'm ashamed of that. But I didn't kill her. And when she went missing, and I caught the case—Thomas didn't recognize me. Didn't know my name or my face. He didn't know it was me who Rose had cheated on him with. One of his daughters had seen me, but I always assigned someone else to talk to them."

"You hid the truth," Melissa said. "On purpose."

He shook his head. "I wanted to run a clean case. To find Rose—or find the person who killed her. And I did. We brought charges against Thomas, and they were solid. But then his lawyer went digging, found the stalker police report. When my bosses looked, they could tell it had been doctored, and they figured out that I'd done it. They only fired me to avoid the embarrassment."

"They should have investigated *you*," Melissa said. "*You're* the one who should be in prison right now."

"You don't think they tried?" Derek says. "For a while after they dropped the charges against Thomas, I was their prime suspect. But they couldn't find anything to prove I killed Rose. Because I didn't do it, Melissa. Thomas did."

"No," Melissa said, trying to sound more certain than she was. "Because you destroyed evidence. Covered your tracks. Framed Thomas."

Derek had been inching ever closer as he spoke. He made a loop around Kelli's body—careful, Melissa noticed, to keep the soles of his shoes out of her blood—and now he was inching toward her, looming larger with each step.

"Stop there," she demanded. "I'll cut you if you get any closer, you hear? I'll do it."

Derek shook his head, gave a thin smile that chilled Melissa to her marrow. "I don't think you will. I don't think you have the guts."

The knife still held out, Melissa reached in her pocket for her phone, took it out, and tried to open the emergency keypad one-handed—but she fumbled it, and it clattered to the tile.

Both Derek and Melissa dove for the phone at the same time. In the scramble, Melissa caught one of Derek's elbows in her face, and her vision went white for a split second, a dizzy explosion of stars. Blinded, she slashed out with the knife and heard Derek yell out.

"Fuck! You fucking bitch!"

Melissa blinked, her vision coming back, and she saw Derek scrabbling away. Blood was oozing from his cheek, from one of his hands. Melissa grabbed for the phone and finished dialing—*911*.

"911 what is your—"

"I'm being attacked!" she shouted out. "A man killed my friend and now he's trying to kill me. His name is Derek Gordon." Melissa gave the address, staring hard at Derek while she spoke, watching his eyes grow panicked. There was no escaping now, no covering up what he'd done.

"Is your attacker in the room with you right now?" the voice on the other end of the line asked.

Derek stood and walked a few steps away, then began running. He was gone. Melissa was safe.

"Just send someone," Melissa said. "Send someone right away."

"Units are on their way, ma'am. Just stay with me."

She leaned back against the wall, rested her temple against it. Everything in her went loose, all the tension of the confrontation with Derek seeming to exit her body at once. The fear she felt and had been holding back. It washed over her all at once, then broke, like a wave against a rocky shore.

Her shoulders began to quake. She let sobs wrack her body as the sound of sirens filled the air.

# ROSE

*Somehow everything has gotten even worse since I last wrote in this diary. I write this with a head aching from a concussion, squinting at the page through eyes nearly swollen shut, a cut on my lip, another on my cheek. I probably shouldn't even be writing—the doctor at the ER told me I should rest when he discharged me. But I need to get this down.*

*I need to bear witness to what happened to me.*

---

*Where can I even begin? I suppose I might as well start where I left off last time—with Rhiannon coming up the front walk as I said goodbye to Derek Gordon, the man I had just slept with.*

*I spent the rest of the afternoon begging her not to tell Thomas when he came home. I swore to her that nothing happened—and then, contradicting myself, revealing myself a liar, that it would never happen again. She agreed.*

*When Thomas came home that evening, I was so terrified. Sitting through dinner with Thomas and the girls, I kept my eyes on Rhiannon the whole time. Watching her sullen expression for some sign that she was about to blurt out what she'd seen.*

*She kept quiet. Thank God.*

*But my problems weren't over.*

---

*The next day, after Thomas and the girls left, I called Derek Gordon, using the number on the card he'd given me.*

*"We can never do that again," I said. "I have a family."*

*"I can't accept that," he said. "I don't want to."*

*"Well, you'll have to," I said, then hung up the phone.*

*But he didn't listen. That same day, I went out to get the mail from the mailbox at the road and saw his car—the same black car that had pulled me over the day before—parked down the street. His silhouette visible behind the windshield. Watching.*

*And he was there the next day. And the next. The next. Just sitting and watching for hours at a time. In fact, he's been following me for weeks now—followed me through the writing of this journal, a presence at the edges of my life I couldn't bring myself to acknowledge.*

*Thomas thought I was being paranoid—but I couldn't tell him the truth. Because convincing him I was being stalked would have required me to admit to what I'd done. Admit to cheating on him.*

———

*One day not long ago, Derek was watching at the curb when Rhiannon came home from school—and right when she came in the front door, I knew she'd seen him. The look on her face said it all.*

*Last weekend, I saw him again when I went grocery shopping. The girls were with me. Though it's not enough to say that I merely saw him—he actually came up to us. He's getting bolder.*

*"I need to talk to you," he said, in the middle of the frozen foods aisle. He grabbed my forearm, tried to pull me*

close. Rhiannon's eyes lit up fierce and scared, while Kendall watched with worried confusion at this stranger putting his hands on her mother.

I pulled my arm away. "We don't have anything to talk about."

"I'm worried about you," he said, his voice going low, so others couldn't hear. "Is he doing something to you?"

"The only person bothering me right now is you," I said. "Stay away from me. I never want to see you again."

———————

As I unpacked the groceries back at home, I realized that Derek wouldn't stop following me just because I asked him to. This had become something more for him. Whether it was the sex or the feeling of being a knight in shining armor—a hero saving me from a terrible marriage—I couldn't say. Probably, it was both.

Either way, this wasn't going to stop unless I did something extreme.

I put the milk away in the fridge, then called the police and told them that there was a man stalking me. I even gave them his name.

"Derek Gordon. You probably know him. Can you please tell him to leave me alone?"

I thought that would put an end to it.

How foolish I was.

———————

I was home with the girls the next day—yesterday, the day before I'm writing this. Thomas had gone into the office *for something or other. It was a lazy Sunday afternoon, with nothing in particular to do. I was thinking about a glass of wine when a loud knock came at the door. I went to answer it.*

*I'd only opened it a crack when it came flying back toward me, pushed by some incredible force. The edge of it caught me on the forehead and I staggered back. As the door flew open, Derek Gordon came rushing in, huge and red-faced with fury.*

*"Don't you ever do that again," he said. "Don't you dare call my work and report me."*

*"I asked you to leave me alone," I said. My voice sounded quavery and fearful in my own ears, and I hated it—hated my weakness. "You weren't listening. I had to do something." I put my hand against my head where the door had hit me. It came away wet and bloody.*

*"I was trying to help you, you understand that?" Derek yelled, his voice growing, ballooning.*

*"Keep your voice down," I pleaded. The girls were in the house somewhere, and I knew they were listening. Hearing everything.*

*"If you don't want my help, then you can fucking die in this house for all I care," Derek said. "But don't you dare try to make me out to be the bad guy here. I had to beg the person who took your report to take my name off it. I could get in a lot of trouble for that if anyone found out. Don't do it again. Or I'll kill you."*

*Then he turned and left, leaving the door wide open, still swinging on its hinges.*

---

*I knew I was in trouble as soon as Thomas got home. He went upstairs, and right away I heard the girls' footsteps, coming out of their rooms to intercept him. Muffled voices through the floor.*

*Then Thomas came down, met me in the kitchen, where I was sitting with a glass of wine. Trying to calm my nerves. There was a bandage on my forehead—the wound from the door hadn't turned out to be big, and the bleeding had stopped.*

*"The girls tell me a man came by today," Thomas said. "They say he shouted at you. Is that true?"*

*"It is," I said, bracing myself for what I knew was coming.*

*"Rhiannon said it's not the first time she saw him. She said he talked to you at the grocery store last weekend."*

*"He did."*

*"And that she also saw him coming out of our house a week before that. She said she saw him kiss you. Is that right?"*

*"It is."*

*"Did you have sex with him?"*

*Something broke in me then. I felt a fullness at the back of my throat as I spoke. "I'm so sorry, Thomas. But I did."*

*"In our bed?"*

*I dropped my gaze as I nodded, too ashamed to meet his eyes.*

*He was quiet for a long time after that, long enough that the silence was hard to bear, that I almost begged him to say something, yell at me—anything. But I kept my tongue and simply listened to him breathe, the air rushing in and out of his nostrils.*

*Finally, he spoke.*

*"I don't think I've ever felt so betrayed by you before. So*

hurt. *So angry with you. And I don't think I've ever hated you more than I do in this exact moment."*

*The calmness with which he said it hurt more than anything. I'd have preferred it if he raised his voice, if he screamed at me, if he grabbed a plate from the cupboard and smashed it against the wall.*

*"I know," I said. "I know I messed up."*

*"I need..." he began, then trailed off and let out a breath. "I don't know. I need to leave the house for a bit. I need to not be in the same room as you. Before I do something I regret."*

*I nodded. "I understand."*

*He walked away in silence. I winced as the door slammed behind him, as the car squealed away on a cloud of tire rubber.*

---

*Sometime after Thomas had left—I had no idea where he was—a knock came at the door again. I clenched when I heard it, thinking Derek had come back to finish what he started. To really hurt me this time. I went to the living room and peered out the window at who was standing there.*

*It was only Kelli. The sight of her brought annoyance rather than fear—I muttered, "Oh, for fuck's sake, what is it now?"*

*I yanked the door open. "What is it?"*

*Kelli looked offended, her head snapping back atop her neck, skin wrinkling up under her chin. "Well, hello to you too."*

*"Sorry, it's been a terrible day."*

*"What happened to your forehead?"*

*"I don't want to talk about it."*

*Her eyes narrowed. "Did Thomas do that?"*

*I sighed. "No. Christ. What is your obsession with him?"*

*"I don't have an obsession."*

*I rolled my eyes. It felt good to be mad at someone—with everyone else in my life mad at me.*

*"Come on," she said. "Let's go out. I feel like it's been forever since I've seen you."*

*"Kelli, just leave. Thomas and I are going through some problems, and—I just can't right now, okay?"*

*She shook her head. "I don't know why you don't just divorce him."*

*I glared at Kelli, hating her. She was so smug, so certain in her judgments of the world. So confident that she knew exactly what everyone else should do. I wanted to reach across the doorframe and slap her where she stood.*

*"Kelli," I said, starting slowly, calmly. "You're a busybody and an emotional vampire. The only reason you're so obsessed with my life is because yours is boring and pathetic. You're a profoundly unhappy person who loves it when other people are miserable, and I've never liked you. Okay? Now get away from my house and my family before I come out there and remove you physically."*

*Kelli's face reddened. As I spoke, there were parts of what I said that felt good—this was the strength I needed with Derek, and with Thomas. But after I was done, I only felt bad. I felt the urge to apologize, to take it all back immediately. But I'd said what I'd said.*

*"You made an enemy today," Kelli said, then turned and walked back to her car.*

---

*Inside, I walked back to the kitchen and stood at the sink for a while, looking outside. The sun was poking through the trees at the edge of our property, flaring in my vision, blinding me. A part of me enjoyed the loss of sensation, the feeling of some part of me being blotted out. I closed my eyes and felt the warmth of the sun as it poured through the glass, and I thought about the day. The mess I'd made of everything.*

*Then there was a creak of footsteps on the floor behind me, and I turned. I caught a flash of some object heading toward me—a fist? a bat? a piece of wood?—and then pain flashed red through my skull. Something solid thudded against the back of my head, and it took me a moment to realize it was the floor. I'd fallen. By some primal instinct, my body knew to curl up, make itself small as more blows rained down on me—some hard thing hitting against my stomach, my back, my legs. My face. Bruising bone, splitting skin.*

*And then, as quickly as it had started, it stopped. Footsteps receded as quickly as they'd come.*

*I lay there, drifting in and out of consciousness. Then there was another knock at the door—timid, light. The door opening. More footsteps.*

*"Oh my God!"*

*Kelli again. I suppose I should be glad that she's the kind of person it's impossible to get rid of.*

*"I came back to say sorry, and—what happened? Can you move?"*

*I sat up straight, wincing, each microscopic movement bringing a lightning bolt of pain. "I need to go to the hospital."*

*"I'll take you."*

*In the car on the way to the emergency room, Kelli asked*

271

*me if it was Thomas who'd done this to me. I looked out the window and said I didn't know.*

*But that was a lie.*

*I know exactly who attacked me.*

# TRANSCRIPT OF RECORDING

**Amelia:** Why did you really insist on seeing me for therapy, Thomas?

**Thomas** We've been over this.

**Amelia:** We have. And you've had answers. You trust me, I'm good, it's convenient. But I don't think I believe you. Not anymore.

**Thomas:** Well, I still don't have any other answers to give you.

**Amelia:** Have I ever told you my diagnosis of Rose? My opinion on why she struggled so much in the years you were married?

**Thomas:** You never treated her.

**Amelia:** That's true. But I've been your neighbor for years. I've observed things.

**Thomas:** I always figured Rose's issue was just some sort of chemical thing.

**Amelia:** And you did try medication during some portions of her treatment, didn't you? And that helped. But that wasn't the whole of it. Because there was a deeper root to her depression. A reason for it. More than just brain chemistry.

**Thomas:** What's that?

**Amelia:** There was some basic fact of her life that she couldn't bring herself to acknowledge. I sensed it every time I interacted with her. Some horrible thing that she couldn't allow herself to say, couldn't allow herself to admit. To me. To you. To anybody. Even to herself.

[pause]

**Thomas:** What was it?

**Amelia:** You'd know that better than me. She never said anything to me. You know that.

**Thomas:** You think I know? I have no clue, Amelia. I wish I did. I wish I knew what was wrong with Rose.

**Amelia:**   Be that as it may. This kind of a situation—where there is some fundamental fact that the mind feels it has to repress, for whatever reason—it fractures a person's psyche. Divides it from itself, alienates a person from their own reality.

[pause]

**Amelia:**   Thomas, I believe that you know what this fundamental fact is. This thing that your wife could not allow herself to say. And I think that you pulled her out of therapy before she went missing because you feared she was going to say it. Am I close?

[pause]

**Amelia:**   That brings us to the second question. Why you insisted that I should be *your* therapist, over my repeated objections. And I think that you, too, have a basic fact of your life that you can't admit to anyone. Something that has split your own psyche in two, divided you against yourself. Threatened your conception of yourself as a good person. A good man. A good husband. A good father. A protector and healer of children. And I think this reality, this repressed and denied thing—I think it has something to do with Rose's disappearance. With her murder.

[pause]

**Amelia:**   And I think you want desperately to admit it to someone. To finally say it out loud. Which is why you insisted on coming to me. Because you think that if you can say it to anyone, you could say it to me. To your old friend. Your old girlfriend. You even seduced me, slept with me, to bring us even closer together. To make me even more the person that you can admit this thing to, a person who will keep your secret. This shameful secret, whatever it is.

[pause]

**Amelia:**   What is it, Thomas? It can't really be that bad, can it?

**Thomas:** I...

**Amelia:** Wouldn't it feel good to say it? Finally?

[pause]

**Thomas:** [crying] I'm sorry. I can't.

# CHAPTER 20

Melissa started to feel a little fuzzy while she waited for the police to arrive. She knew she should have gotten up and walked out the door, waved them in, told them where to find the body—anything but stay there, paralyzed on the floor, staring at Kelli's body as her dead eyes gazed back glassily at her. But that's exactly what she did. For some reason, she couldn't make herself move. Her limbs had gone cold and distant. Soon, red and blue lights flashed on the walls through the windows, and the sound of footsteps and voices came to her, muffled as though traveling through layers of water to get to her ears. Then strong hands grabbed hold of her, pulled her to her feet and walked her out the door—but even then, it was like it was happening to someone else. Melissa felt like a marionette, someone else pulling the strings.

Somehow, she found herself leaning up against the fender of a police cruiser. A gray, scratchy blanket clung loosely to her shoulders; someone must have wrapped it around her. Gradually she came back to herself, looking around to see four police cars in total and a handful of uniformed officers walking around the lawn, in and out the front door of Kelli's house, crisscrossing the street as they talked to neighbors who'd come out of their houses to gawk.

There was an officer close to Melissa too, a man, trying to ask her something. Trying to get her to respond.

"What did you say?" Melissa asked.

"I asked if you knew her," the man said. He had a mustache and a kindly face wrinkled with concern. "The woman in the house."

"I did," Melissa said. "Not very well. I'm a little new in the area."

*What a silly thing to say*, she thought. As if he cared about how long she'd lived there.

"Did you see who…" he began, then trailed off before regrouping and trying again. "Did you see who did that to her?"

Melissa was about to answer when another officer came up. "Neighbors say we're looking for a white female, fairly young, maybe teens or early twenties, brown hair, driving a—"

The wrongness of what he was saying brought her back to herself, snapped her body and her mind back into alignment. Suddenly she was completely alert, coming up off the hard frame of the police cruiser.

"That's not right," she said. "A woman didn't do that. I told the person on the phone, didn't I? The 911 dispatcher?"

"What did you tell her?" asked the first officer, the one with the mustache and the calming voice.

"It was a man," Melissa said. "Derek Gordon."

The two men exchanged a look, then the other officer—the one who came up saying they should be looking for a young woman—was the next to speak. "Did you see him attack her, ma'am?"

"No," Melissa said. "But I know it was him."

The guy with the mustache looked at the other officer, who had a round face and pockmarked cheeks. "You know the name?"

"Used to be with the sheriff's department," the round-faced officer said. "He got fired a few years ago, something connected with that murder case—you remember the one, the one that was in the news so much. Doctor killed his wife. Derek botched the investigation somehow, but he couldn't have done this. I knew the guy."

"Isn't that case back in the news?" the mustached officer said. He scratched his cheek, then snapped his fingers. "Yeah, I heard it on the radio this morning. They're bringing the charges back."

"That's exactly what this is about," Melissa said. "The woman in there, Kelli Walker—she was involved in a group that was trying to solve that old case. So was Derek. But…" She paused, realizing that what she was about to say was going to sound completely crazy. "But he was the killer."

"The killer of the woman in the house."

"No," Melissa said, her frustration rising. Then she caught herself, shook her head, closed her eyes. This wasn't coming out right. "I mean, *yes*, he killed Kelli. But he also killed Rose Danver, three years ago. He tried to frame her husband for it. But Kelli and I found out, and Derek killed her."

The two officers were looking at her as though she'd lost it, mouths slightly open.

"You have proof of this?"

Melissa breathed out exasperation. "No, but—"

"And you admit that you didn't see Derek Gordon kill Kelli Walker."

"When I got here, she was already dead. But then Derek was here."

"*After* you? You're trying to tell me he killed Kelli Walker, fled the scene, and then came back?"

Melissa didn't answer. She paused, turned her body away slightly. He was right, it didn't make sense.

"Meanwhile I've got two neighbors across the street saying they saw a teenage girl come to this house before you. She went in the front door, then came running out later. You see anything like that?"

Melissa shook her head, thinking. There was only one teenage girl she could think of in that moment: Rhiannon. She'd been listening when Melissa was talking to Kelli on the phone. "What kind of car was she driving?"

The officer looked down at his notepad, then read out a description.

It sounded like Thomas's car. The one Rhiannon was driving. "I don't—I don't understand."

He looked away, already writing Melissa off. The officer with the mustache kept looking at her, but there was a pained look on his face, like he was embarrassed for her, or worried about her. Like he thought she was just a crazy woman who'd been through a shock. Someone who was not thinking straight. Someone who didn't have any information—someone who couldn't help.

"Look," he said. "We're going to need your contact information, to take your statement on all this later. But we're going to be a while here. Can you get yourself home? Is there anyone you could call to come and get you?"

Melissa's mind drifted back to Bradley, who'd been all day without her at Lawrence and Toby's house. Safe, but probably wondering where she was. Meanwhile, she hadn't had a bite to eat since breakfast. She gave the officer her contact information, then went to her car. There she found her phone on the center console, screen lit up with messages she missed when she ran in the house to find Kelli dead. Each message was from Amelia.

Where are you

You have to get back to Thomas's house

It's Rhiannon

I know who killed Rose

Where are you? Are you okay? Please tell me you're getting these.

---

There was a crowd outside Thomas's house. Three news vans, reporters, cameramen, and a crowd come to gawk. Some held signs: *Murderer, Justice for Rose.* Instead of turning in, Melissa drove past the cul-de-sac, parked on the street. Then she snuck across a few backyards, crossing Amelia's before coming to Thomas's house and entering by the back way.

She found them in the living room. Rhiannon on the couch, her face red with crying, Amelia pacing, hands to her forehead. Her arms dropped when she saw Melissa, and she let out a breath.

"There you are."

Melissa stared at Rhiannon, who seemed to shrink under her gaze. "It was you," Melissa said. "You killed her. Both of them. Kelli and Rose."

The girl's face crumpled, turned inward on itself. She didn't say anything.

"Melissa, no," Amelia said, and took a step toward Melissa. "You're not thinking straight."

Melissa's eyes snapped to Amelia. "What are you talking about? She was just spotted at a murder scene."

"It wasn't me!" Rhiannon shouted from the couch. "I only found her. I was too late. Just like you."

"Then who?"

Amelia walked to the coffee table, picked up a leather bound book, navy blue, with a ribbon tucked between its pages halfway through. She handed it to Melissa.

"What's this?"

"Rose's diary," Amelia said.

"She kept a diary?" Melissa asked. "Why didn't the police find it?"

"Rhiannon had it." Amelia looked at her with an expression that mingled accusation and admiration. "She was hiding it."

"What does it say?" Melissa held it out in front of her, just looking at it. There was an elastic clasp looped around it. She was almost afraid to undo it and open the pages.

"Just read the last entry. It wasn't Rhiannon."

Amelia reached out and pushed the diary closer to Melissa's body.

"It was Kendall."

# ROSE

*It's time for the whole truth.*

*There's no escaping it anymore. Not after the attack. I'll never be safe—my whole family will never be safe—until we can acknowledge the truth.*

*Thomas might not want to talk about it. He'd prefer to deny it, repress it, cover it up.*

*But that doesn't mean that I have to.*

---

*I love my girls. Love them as much as Thomas does. More, even. I'm tired of agreeing to his definitions of things—his definition of love, his definition of what it means to be a good parent. Love doesn't mean ignoring what's wrong, insisting over and over again that your children are perfect when you know they're not. Rhiannon and Kendall have always preferred Thomas because he's the one who coddles them, who gives them what they want, who is always fun—never a disciplinarian. He's managed to distort that, turn it into this idea that he's a better parent than I am. That he loves them more. Even they have come to believe it.*

*But it's not true.*

*The days when my daughters were born were the two best days of my life. I can see that now, own it in my own way. I loved the girls—love them—and they loved me too, before Thomas turned them against me.*

*Yes, I was afraid of my babies at first. What mother isn't, a little? Maybe it was my love for them that scared me, the fierceness of it, the feeling of all my cells, my DNA, reorienting themselves toward these creatures that had been laid in my arms. The hormones flooding my body, bonding me to them. I'd do anything to protect them, even if what I had to protect them from was me and Thomas, from the brokenness we carried with us. Determined that whatever was wrong with the two of us, I could not allow to be passed down to them.*

*Rhiannon was my quiet one, my shy one—so beautiful, so sensitive, so vulnerable to every wound and slight the world had ready to deal her. I saw myself in her as she grew, saw myself in the way she would bring her pain inward, internalizing every bump, every bruise, every careless word from a mean boy on the playground. The realization blossoming dark and sad behind her eyes:* So this is the way the world is. *I saw it in her even in the early days, from her first halting steps, from the falls she took as she learned to walk and then run. Each new hurt brought an equal hurt in me, and I found myself wanting to draw her to me, to love the pain away, to reassure her that everything would be all right—even when it was a lie.*

*Kendall was something different. Bright and outgoing where Rhiannon was shy, she reminded me more of Thomas: aggressively charming even from an early age, with some spark inside her that drew people to her. From the day I brought her home from the hospital, I had people commenting on what a beautiful child she was. Seeing a new face, her own face would brighten, smiling from her eyes, laughing, dimples coming to her cheeks. I loved her. I did. I write this now and know it's true. I loved my second daughter.*

*But there was something unnerving about her as well. The world was charmed by Kendall, drawn in by her* charisma. But I saw something else when I looked at her eyes—or rather, behind her eyes. There was an emptiness there. A lack of feeling that terrified me.

This, too, reminded me of my husband. I realized it about Thomas after we got married—too late. He'd charmed me when we were dating, pursued me like I was the only thing in the world he wanted, showered me with love and affection. It was only after the hunt was over and he began to lose interest in me that I realized there was a yawning emptiness at the core of him. A black hole that sucked up everything that got too close. Thomas's charm masked something dark and dangerous. He'd learned over time to conceal it from the world—but a wife knows her husband better than anyone. And I could see through him.

A mother knows too. And I knew there was something wrong with my Kendall. It reared its head soon enough. My first memory of having my fears about her confirmed came when she was four. It was summer, one of those languid days when the air conditioning struggles to keep up, the kids running in and out of the house constantly, faces flushed and slick with sweat, bare feet browning with dirt. Sometime in the afternoon, Kendall appeared at the front door with something dead cradled in her arms. A squirrel.

"Look!" she said, red-faced with excitement.

I completely lost it. My first thought was of the diseases that corpse must be crawling with, and I rushed at her with a mix of panic and disgust that rose as bile at the back of my throat. Unable to hide my aversion, I shouted at her to put it down right away, then packed her into the bath. Only later, as I scrubbed her skin raw with rubber gloves on my own hands, did I realize the entirety of what I'd seen. The animal was not just dead but mutilated, its tail cut off, its eyes gouged out of its sockets.

"Kendall?" I asked. "Did you notice how the animal you found was all cut up? Did you find it like that?"

But she wasn't about to tell me anything. I'd terrified her with my reaction, and now she was whimpering in the bath, her shoulders shuddering with the aftershocks of the sobs that had wracked her body after I'd yelled at her. Kendall was capable of shame, of understanding that things she did could bring people to reject her—though not, as I later came to believe, capable of remorse, or empathy with the suffering of living creatures.

I told Thomas about it when he came home, but he swore it was nothing. The first of his many, many denials.

"She's a kid," he said. "How does a kid even catch a squirrel?"

Perhaps. But I felt certain that somehow, our child had, for the simple experience of torturing another living thing.

---

Kendall's unsettling behavior escalated as she grew—older, bigger, stronger, more difficult to contain. Alone with me, she'd sometimes become suddenly, irrationally angry and throw a heavy object at me, or fly across the room at me, a screeching whirlwind of fists and feet. I'd have to physically restrain her, hold her wrists and wrap her in a straitjacket hug until she calmed down. Small though she was, I couldn't always subdue her in time, and as I scrambled to grab at her flailing limbs, I'd receive a tiny fist to the face and see stars. Once, as I held both wrists, she actually snarled at me like an animal, strings of spittle flying from her lips, then lunged forward and bit me on the cheek, drawing blood.

Thomas insisted it was nothing. "Kids get dysregulated,"

he said. "They have tantrums. It's your job to help her learn how to manage her emotions."

My job. Like this was all my fault.

I knew the problem with Kendall was something more than her getting dysregulated. Rhiannon had her moments of anger too, her fits, her tantrums—but this was different. Yes, sometimes Kendall would go on the attack because she was angry, but other times, her outbursts of violence seemed to come from nowhere, to have no cause. One minute she'd be calm, even sweet—that charm she inherited from her father—the next, murderous.

She went after Rhiannon too. I know she did. Sometimes I saw it, put myself between them, sacrificing myself to protect my daughter. Other times, I'm pretty sure it happened without my knowing. I found bruises on Rhiannon's body sometimes, freshly scabbed cuts, the surrounding skin still angry and red. When I asked her where they came from, she'd just shrug and say she couldn't remember. Taking her pain inside, still, internalizing it. Thinking she deserved it.

Most terrifying of all was when Kendall began coming to my bedside to watch me sleep. Sometimes I'd wake up and see her standing next to me. Once, she held a hammer. Another time, a knife. Her eyes glowing white in the darkness, looking at me with such icy calm.

I knew, then, that she wanted to kill me.

_____

Or maybe it was only someone she wanted to kill, to know what it felt like. The way she'd once mutilated an animal. Some murderous curiosity inside her, desperate to be satiated.

*And then, one day, it happened. We were on vacation at the time, escaping the doldrums of winter at a resort in Cancun. Kendall's violent behavior had abated somewhat, giving fuel to Thomas's claims: She was a kid. She was growing out of it.*

*How wrong he was. I knew—Kendall wasn't better. She was merely learning how to hide her violent tendencies better. To suppress them. But they weren't gone. Only waiting.*

*At the resort, Thomas swam in the pool, explored the beach, started drinking cocktails at noon, as soon as the bar opened. Rhiannon stared at her phone, curled in a beach chair with headphones in, and didn't talk.*

*Kendall, meanwhile, found a friend. A boy her age who'd come with a different family.*

*And I watched her.*

*They began by playing in the pool together, Kendall and the boy. He splashed, did cannonballs, puffed up his chest and acted big, even though he was a couple inches shorter than her. Kendall watched him, put her chin down, giggled. At the beach, they made sandcastles, threw rocks in the water, stood looking out into the ocean while the waves washed around their knees. Once, I even saw them briefly holding hands.*

*Anyone looking at them might have thought it was a case of puppy love. Two kids playacting at flirting, copying the teenagers in the TV shows they liked to watch.*

*But I knew. This was trouble.*

*It happened toward the end of our vacation, when we went on an excursion to some oceanside cliffs, arranged by the resort. We piled on a shuttle bus, sunscreen slathered on our faces and water bottles at our sides. Then we saw the other family get on—the parents of the boy Kendall had befriended.*

*Thomas talked to them the whole way to the cliffs. Asked where they were from, what they did, how they were enjoying their vacation so far. They beamed at him as he turned to their son, asked about how he liked school, called him "young man." I kept quiet, angry and anxious for reasons I couldn't quite name.*

*When we arrived at the cliffs, the vacationers scattered, finding the perfect spots for selfies, exploring the rocks, shielding their eyes with their hands held flat at their brows as they looked to the horizon. At a certain point, I realized I'd lost track of Kendall, then glanced off and found her walking with the boy, close to the edge of the cliff. His gaze was down, looking over the edge, and behind him my daughter was glancing around her, as though to see if anyone was watching.*

*Suddenly, my heart was at the back of my throat, and I began to walk toward them.*

*Then she gave the boy a shove.*

---

*I play the next moments back in my head all the time. They come to me in my nightmares, frames of a movie I can't stop replaying.*

*Falling to my knees, my ears filled by an icy scream that might be mine.*

*Thomas running to Kendall, yanking her away from the cliff edge by the shoulders.*

*The boy's parents at the edge, looking hundreds of feet down at their son's broken body on the rocks. The mother on all fours, keening wildly. The father on his feet, pulling her back, choking back sobs.*

When I reached Thomas, still holding Kendall by the shoulders, I said, low in his ear, "I saw what happened."

"I did too," he said. "He tripped."

That's not right. *The words lodged in my throat like a pin bone, jagged and painful.* That's not what happened.

---

*There was an investigation. An inquiry. The local authorities conducted one, and then the resort held their own, wanting to avoid liability and a PR nightmare.*

*Thomas hissed at me that night in our room, furious but keeping his voice down. A quiet roar, low but full of venom.*

"I know what I saw," I said.

"He tripped," *Thomas insisted.* "He tripped on a loose rock and went over the edge. It was an accident, you hear? An accident."

"That's not right."

"I can't believe you would do this to your own daughter," *Thomas said.* "There's something wrong with you. You're not right. You're crazy."

"I'm not."

"You are," *Thomas said.* "You're not thinking straight. But I am. I'm protecting this family. From you."

*I cowered under his glare. Turned away as tears came hot and stinging to my eyes.*

"When they question you, you're going to say what I tell you to say," *he said.* "Then, when we get home, I'm pulling you out of therapy. I can't risk you telling someone else this insane delusion about our daughter. This* *has to stop. We can't be victims of your mental problems anymore."*

------------

*I tried, Thomas. I really did. I tried doing things your way. I tried getting "better." I tried denying the truth about Kendall. I tried pretending that the only problem with our family was me.*

*It drove me deeper into depression. It drove me to drink. It drove me to a personal hell deeper than any I've ever known.*

*But I can't deny the truth anymore. Kendall's attack against me makes it clear. There's no denying our way through this mess. She's killed before. And I believe she'll do it again.*

*I know I won't get support from you. So I'll have to do it myself.*

*I'm confronting her today. Telling her she has a problem. Asking her to get help with me. Asking her to confront the truth together.*

*I've never been so afraid.*

# CHAPTER 21

"I can't believe it," Melissa said as she came to the end of the diary entry. Rose's last written words—before she died. Killed, by her own daughter. "Kendall's always been so sweet."

"It's all an act," Rhiannon said bitterly.

"No," Amelia said. "Not an act. That part of Kendall is real enough, in its way. The part she created to protect her from the reality of who she really is."

"But how could she have actually killed Rose?" Melissa asked. "She was, what, twelve when Rose was killed?"

"Maybe she surprised Rose," Amelia said. "Stabbed her a couple times before she even knew what was happening. After that, with the blood lost, she could have been too weak to fight back. To call for help."

Melissa glanced at Rhiannon, whose face was so white it looked like she'd lost some blood herself.

"Did you see it happen?" Melissa asked.

She shook her head. "No. I found them after it was over." She drew in a shuddering breath, then broke down again. Melissa could tell it was something she'd been holding in for a long time. "There was so much blood. And Kendall was—she was digging at Mom's eyes. Saying something about how she wanted Mom to stop looking at her." Rhiannon let out an animal wail, the sound seeming to possess her body. Her hands came up to the sides of her head, her fingers hooked, her nails clawing into her skin.

*Digging at Mom's eyes.* Melissa's stomach lurched, burning, to the back of her throat. She clapped a hand over her mouth.

Amelia rushed to Rhiannon, sank to her knees in front of the couch, grabbed at Rhiannon's hands. She pulled them away and held them against Rhiannon's lap, where she couldn't hurt herself with them. Then Amelia leaned forward until her forehead was resting against Rhiannon's.

"It's okay," Amelia said softly. "You're safe now. And it's not your fault. Okay?"

"Dad told me I could never tell," Rhiannon said. "He told me I had to keep it a secret."

Amelia put a hand behind the girl's neck, angled her head until they were looking eye to eye. "He shouldn't have done that. People aren't supposed to live with things like this without telling anyone."

Rhiannon looked at Amelia for a long moment, then closed her eyes, folded her lips together, and gave a little nod. Melissa let them be. It was their moment. It had nothing to do with her.

"You didn't know?" Melissa asked softly after a few seconds passed.

Amelia turned to her, shook her head. "No. Thomas came to me that day and asked me to take the girls. He said Rose was missing, he needed to go up north to look for her at their cabin. Kendall was calm, but Rhiannon..." She looked back to Rhiannon, squeezed her hand. "Rhiannon had obviously been crying. I thought she was scared for her mom, but now I know she was in shock. Honey, I'm so sorry."

Rhiannon only shook her head, her face contorting with a blend of emotions Melissa could only guess at. There was sadness there. Perhaps forgiveness, for Amelia. And maybe a touch of relief.

Amelia turned back to Melissa. "But I had a sense that something was badly wrong, long before that day. It started when they came back from that trip and Thomas pulled Rose out of therapy, even though she clearly needed it. And then after she went missing, when he insisted on coming to me for therapy. He can be very persuasive."

Melissa thought of how he pursued her, how he won her over in spite of her hesitations. "He certainly can."

"Rose was hiding something," Amelia said. "All along. There was something she wanted desperately to talk about, but she couldn't. Then, after she went missing, and Thomas insisted that I should see *him*, it was the same thing. It was almost like he wanted to admit it all to me. He was subconsciously creating the conditions for a full confession. But then he couldn't bring himself to do it."

"Why did you stay? Why didn't you move, if you knew something was wrong?"

"I cared about him," Amelia said. "God help me, I cared about Thomas. Still do. And the girls. I think I had the sense that I had to stay close. That something terrible would happen if I left. And now—"

She glanced back to Rhiannon, who'd gone limp on the couch, her eyes glassy.

"When I saw that woman's body," Rhiannon said softly, as though she was talking to herself, "it was like it was happening all over again. Like I was finding Mom's body again."

"You were following me today, weren't you?" Melissa asked.

"I was."

"To protect me from Kendall?"

"She was so angry after Dad proposed to you, and that thing that happened," Rhiannon said. "The big fight, and Dad getting arrested. She's protective of Dad. I think he's the only person in the world she really loves. She thought you were bad for him. And she was going to do something bad to you, I know she was. I tried to talk her out of it."

Melissa thought of the conversation she'd overheard between the two sisters the night before. "*She's not Mom.* That's what you told her. You were defending me."

"She wouldn't listen. She snuck out that night, went through the woods to your house. I followed her. That's how we saw you talking to Kelli. And that man. Derek. Dad's enemies. We were hiding in the trees and heard everything you said before you went inside. Kendall was going to kill you that night, but I talked her out of it. Told her she'd get caught. But then later that night, she left again. I woke up early and found her bed empty."

"So you took the car and went to find her." Melissa ached all over, thinking of it—Rhiannon, just a girl herself, taking on the responsibility of keeping everyone else safe, of being a human shield between her dangerous younger sister and the rest of the world. "You staked out the house in case she came back to get me. Then followed me to the jail. And went to Kelli's house after you realized she was the one in danger."

"Kendall's panicking, I think," Rhiannon said. "Now that Mom's body has been discovered, she thinks she's going to get caught. She's going after anyone who's trying to get to the truth of how Mom really died."

"Okay," Melissa said. "So where is Kendall now?"

Amelia stood. "Who's a threat? That's who she'll go after."

"Derek Gordon? But he ran off after I accused him of killing Kelli. She can't possibly know where he is. And I don't see how she could overpower him. Even if she did take him by surprise."

"That leaves…" Amelia trailed off, winced. "You, Melissa. The woman who's trying to steal her father away from her. The one who's responsible for the assault that landed him in jail. Bad things didn't start happening until you came into their lives. It's not fair, but it's how she sees it. She'll come looking for you next."

"Me? But she doesn't know where I am eith—" Melissa stopped short, a sudden panic washing ice-cold over the surface of her skin. Lawrence and Toby's house was the only place Kendall would think to look for her. She wasn't there.

But Bradley was.

Melissa fumbled for her phone and called Lawrence. She rose as the call rang through, clutching her keys, ready to run to the car if she didn't get him. He answered.

"Melissa?"

"Lawrence. I'm about to come back home. Just—if Kendall Danver comes by, don't let her in, okay? Don't even answer the door. In fact, you should lock up until I get there."

"Melissa, what are you talking about?"

"I'll explain when I'm there," Melissa said, her hand on the doorknob, getting ready to run.

"But Kendall is already here."

Her hand stopped on the knob. Instead of turning it, Melissa braced herself against it as a wave of dizziness passed over her.

"Lawrence, I need you to tell me exactly where she is."

"She's in the backyard with Bradley. She said you asked her to come keep him company until you got home. Bradley was happy to see her."

"I need you to go get him right now," Melissa said. "Get him away from her."

"Away from Kendall? Honey, you're scaring me. What's going on?"

"Just do it!" Melissa shouted.

She heard rustling on the end of the line as Lawrence moved through the house to the back. The sound of a sliding door opening.

"Lawrence?" Melissa asked, willing him to answer. To tell her Bradley was safe.

"They're not here," Lawrence said. "I'm so sorry, Melissa, I don't know where they could have—"

Melissa ended the call. Spun around to face Amelia and Rhiannon.

"She has him," she said, her voice pitching up, growing loud and shrill with panic. "She has my son. She's going to kill him. She's going to…"

Melissa couldn't breathe. Amelia advanced toward her, hands out. She met her in the center of the room, grabbed onto her arms just above the elbows. Melissa fell halfway against her, let her shoulder some of the crushing fear that had come down on her shoulders—but there was little relief in it, in leaning against someone else. Melissa was still imagining her boy out there somewhere with Kendall. Or dead already, the life bleeding out of him in a ditch. Too late to save.

"We'll find him," Amelia said. "It's going to be okay."

"How?" Melissa demanded. "Where?"

"I know," another voice came. The two of them, Melissa and Amelia, turned together. Rhiannon had risen from the couch, whatever brokenness that had been in her face gone and replaced by something else, something hard as stone. Certainty. Grim determination.

"She took him into the woods."

# CHAPTER 22

Amelia called 911 and told the police to hurry, told the dispatcher that a boy had been kidnapped and his life was at stake—but Melissa couldn't wait. Minutes could be the difference between saving her son and finding him already dead.

"I want you to take me," she said to Rhiannon. "Right now."

"But that's what *she* wants," Rhiannon answered. "Kendall knows the place better than you do. Better than I do too. She wants you to come. She's luring you. So she can kill you."

Melissa nodded. "I know. And I don't care." She'd never felt so certain of something in her life. She wasn't afraid for herself. She'd do anything to protect Bradley. Even if it meant dying herself. If her last sight was of her son safe and sound, she could die happy.

Rhiannon nodded and walked to get her coat.

Amelia's gaze followed Rhiannon, then snapped back to Melissa, her eyes fierce and frenzied. "I'm coming too."

Melissa shook her head. "No. You have to be here when the police come. You have to tell them where to find us." The cops would have to run a gauntlet to get to them—pushing through the press and the crowds to even get to the house. If, after that, they found the house empty, there was a risk they'd just leave, and Kendall would get away. Or worse.

Amelia's mouth thinned, and she let out a breath through her teeth. But then she nodded.

"Come on," Rhiannon said. "Let's go."

Melissa zipped up her coat, then felt a squeeze on her elbow. She looked back up and met Amelia's eyes.

"Be careful."

Melissa nodded, and then she and Rhiannon left out the back without another word.

---

The din of the press and the crowd at the street was muted in the backyard, blunted by the hulk of the house. If Melissa didn't know better, she might have thought there was a flock of birds milling about on the front lawn. A phalanx of noisy geese, pausing on their way south for winter.

She followed Rhiannon to the edge of the grass. The girl lifted her feet to step over some knee-high undergrowth and into the trees. Melissa followed, low-hanging branches pulling at her coat, her socks already clumping with burrs.

"Where are we going?"

"Kendall has a place she likes to go," Rhiannon said. "In the middle of the woods."

"What does she do there?"

Rhiannon was quiet, walking, and at first Melissa thought she didn't hear her question. But then she answered.

"You'll see."

They walked for what seemed like a long time—though when Melissa slipped her phone from her pocket to light the screen and peek at the time, she saw it had only been a few minutes since they'd left the house, her fear for Bradley making the seconds stretch out long, dripping slowly like snowmelt from a tree limb. Still, the woods felt vast, larger than she'd realized driving the winding road that bordered them to the south, the one connecting Thomas's cul-de-sac to Lawrence and Toby's dead-end street. The speed of cars tended to compress spaces in the mind, while the slowness of walking expanded them. Melissa let her head fall, trying to recall how long the trip took in the car, how big the woods must have been. A square mile?

"Do other people walk through here?"

"Some," Rhiannon said. "There aren't official trails or anything. Just little cuts, worn-down spots on the ground made by people's shoes."

"But nobody's ever found Kendall's spot?"

"I don't think so," Rhiannon said. "She found a place that's pretty secluded."

She spoke so softly, Melissa could barely hear her above the crunch of their footsteps, the tired creaking of the trees as a cold breeze passed through them. Melissa was speaking quietly too, she realized, watching where she stepped, avoiding dried twigs that could snap loudly underfoot and announce her presence. Everything seemed to have a sharpness to it; she was hyperaware of sounds, of the hard-edged cool of the air on her cheeks, every hint of movement in the undergrowth. Adrenaline surged through her veins, turning her animal, alert—and for a moment she wondered what she was, predator or prey. Hunting or being hunted.

They reached a deep and sudden cut where the ground sloped sharply downward into a hollow. Coming to the edge of it, a foul smell hit Melissa's nostrils, and her hand shot up to cover her mouth and nose.

"What is that?" she asked, her voice suddenly too loud.

"We're almost there," Rhiannon said, glancing back. "Follow me."

As if she had any choice.

Melissa stepped down into the cut, making her way carefully into the hollow. She followed a few steps behind, the rot on the air getting worse, fouler. Ahead, two jagged trees leaned together, their branches intertwined until they seemed to become one organism. Rhiannon passed beneath the branches.

Melissa bent down to do the same and then felt something catch in her hair as she stood straight on the other side of the hanging branches. She ran her fingers through her hair, expecting some leaves or sticks, but her fingers caught on something wet and soft instead. Revulsion seized her, pulled all her muscles taut and then twanged them in a shudder that rippled through her, head to toe. She swiped at her hair, panicked, desperate to get this thing—she didn't know what it was, but she knew she didn't want it on her—away from her body. Finally, it came free, but it didn't fall to the ground, only swung away from her, suspended from the branches above by some sort of string. Something circular, so blackened and desiccated with rot that it took her a moment to recognize it, to see the hint of a vein zigzagging across its surface like the line of a river on a map. Then the iris, then the pupil.

It was an eye.

Melissa opened her mouth to let out a scream, but Rhiannon's hand clamped hard on her lips, and then her face came into view, her eyes wide and pleading, communicating a warning. The scream lodged in Melissa's throat. She nodded, swallowed it back, then looked around.

They were standing in what could only be described as—what? A torture chamber? A slaughterhouse? An abattoir? It was full of animal corpses in various states of decay, some reduced to skeletons, others fresh and rotting. Melissa spotted a raccoon, a house cat, a dog with pet tags still around its neck. Animals slit open, guts spilling out; animals rotting on the ground, their soft parts writhing with maggots; animals hoisted into the air, the sharp ends of branches serving as hooks, a rack to pin them on.

And everywhere, eyes like the one that got stuck in Melissa's hair. Dangling from pieces of twine or speared onto twigs like morbid little berries, some fresh and only starting to yellow, others old and blackened, desiccated, like rotten grapes.

"Oh my God," Melissa whispered, unable to keep silent. "The coyote. It was her all along."

"Maybe the coyote's real," Rhiannon said. "But Kendall has killed more animals than it has."

"I had help," came a voice from above, and both Melissa and Rhiannon looked at the same time.

It was Kendall, perched on the lip of the hollow. Melissa's heart spasmed in her chest when she saw Bradley standing beside her. He was crying, his face streaked with tears and dirt, as though he'd fallen on the ground and then wiped his eyes with muddy hands. But he looked unhurt. Kendall held him by his shirt collar with one hand. In the other, she held a knife.

"You can't blame it all on me, Rhiannon," Kendall said. "You brought some of those animals to me."

"Yeah, to keep you from going after *people*." Rhiannon looked scared, but she set her jaw, appearing to find her anger. "I'm done with that now, Kendall. *You're* done."

Kendall pulled Bradley close, moved the knife toward his neck. "I'll decide when I'm done."

Melissa's gut plunged as the blade moved toward her son's skin. "Let him go!"

Bradley wailed, his face breaking past fear to absolute terror. "Mama!"

"It's okay, baby," Melissa said, forcing a calm she didn't feel. "It's going to be okay."

Kendall's face glowed electric with a wild smile. "Is it, though? Parents are such terrible liars, aren't they, Bradley?"

"What do you want, Kendall? I'll give you anything you want. Just let him go."

"I told you what I wanted months ago," she said. "I told you to stay away from my dad."

*Stay away from him,* Melissa remembered, the jagged scrawl passing through her mind. *Stay away from him unless you want to die.*

"I'm listening now," Melissa said. "I'm listening, Kendall. And I'll do what you want. I'll stay away from him from now on. From your family. *Just let him go.*"

Above her, Kendall shook her head, pressed the knife a little closer to Bradley's neck, the sharp point denting his skin but not yet breaking it.

"It's too late for that," she said. "You've already ruined everything. Brought poison into our lives. Dad's in jail. Those *friends* of yours found Mom's body. Dad's going to go to prison for killing her—or I am."

"No," Melissa said. "It doesn't have to be that way. I told the police that Derek Gordon did it—that's the detective who investigated your dad three years ago. We can make it stick to him. We can. You just have to stop killing people."

She was lying, of course—Melissa had no intention of framing Derek Gordon for what Kendall and Thomas did. But she needed Kendall to see a way out of this, to believe that she could get away with it—if she let everyone go, unhurt.

"No," Kendall said, and Melissa's stomach dropped. "You're full of shit. You did this—now someone has to die for it."

"Let it be me, then. Please, Kendall. Let him go. And kill me."

Kendall was quiet, breathing in and out like a frenzied animal. Her hot breath puffing in the air, steam rising from a sheen of sweat at her neck. A few taut seconds passed, and she took the knife away from Bradley's neck. Without letting go of the knife, she reached in her coat pocket, then threw a couple of small objects down onto the ground in front of Melissa and Rhiannon.

White plastic zip ties.

Fear spread icy-hot over the surface of Melissa's skin when she saw them, and in that moment, she realized just how much trouble they all were in, how far gone Kendall really was. They were just a couple pieces of plastic, something anyone could buy online, the instruments of horror and violence just a few clicks away. You didn't have zip ties in your possession unless you were planning on doing something with them—unless you thought about killing every day, yearned for it. Melissa understood something about Kendall then: understood that her first two kills might have been accidents, of a kind, but that it had become more serious since then. Maybe she'd pushed the boy off the cliff out of a sense of curiosity, a desire to find out what would happen; maybe she'd stabbed her mother to death in anger over the revelation that she'd cheated on Thomas. But she'd grown a taste for killing then—and now, it was hard to imagine that they'd get out of this situation without *someone* dying.

Kendall nodded to the zip ties. "Put those on. I'm not stupid. I'm not going to let you get up here and attack me."

"Okay," Melissa said. "Okay. I'm doing it."

She held out her hands to Rhiannon, wrists together. "Come on. Put it on."

She knelt, grabbed a zip tie, looped it around Melissa's wrists. The latch snapped as it zipped snug.

"Tighter," Kendall said.

Rhiannon winced. "Sorry," she whispered, then pulled the tie tighter, until the plastic cut against Melissa's skin.

"You too, Rhiannon," Kendall said.

Melissa helped with the tips of her fingers as Rhiannon looped a tie around her own wrist, then used her teeth to pull it tight.

"There," she called up. "You happy?"

"Melissa, you come up," Kendall said. "Rhiannon, you stay down there."

Melissa turned and walked up the way she'd come. Without the use of her hands for balance, she stumbled and nearly fell on her way up the steep grade but managed to keep her feet beneath her. At the top, she circled the lip of the hollow toward Kendall and Bradley.

"Send him here," Melissa called. "Then you can have me."

Kendall grinned. "You really think I'm stupid, don't you? You're not getting him back. Just a closer look when I kill him."

She tugged at Bradley's collar, pulling him close. Brought the knife around. Agony gripped Melissa's body, and her legs went weak. She dropped to her knees.

"No!" she screamed.

And then Kendall's hand stopped.

"What are you doing here?" Kendall asked.

Melissa turned and saw Amelia coming through the trees. Then she looked back at Kendall, whose face had taken on a strange pallor, Amelia's presence affecting her in some unexpected way.

"Kendall, please. You don't want to do this. I know you don't. Somewhere deep inside you, you know this is wrong. Don't you?"

The last sentence was phrased like a real question, not rhetorical—Amelia really didn't know whether Kendall knew the difference between right and wrong anymore. Wasn't sure how far Kendall had fallen, how evil she'd become. The slightest hint of a flinch in Kendall's face was an answer: She wasn't completely gone. There was something in her, still, that wanted to stop.

"You don't know anything about me," she said, but the

conviction had left her voice. She sounded like a little girl—the child that she was.

"I do," Amelia said, taking a few steps forward, arms held out. "I've studied people like you, Kendall. And I can help you."

Kendall shook her head. Her eyes crinkled in a way that looked like crying, even though no tears came. "Nobody can help me."

"That's not true," Amelia said. She wetted her lips with a dart of her tongue. "Tell me, Kendall—why do you take their eyes?"

Kendall's chin jutted out. Next to her, still collared, Bradley's legs shook. A dark trickle started at the crotch of his pants and ran down his leg to his socks.

"It's okay, baby," Melissa whispered, urging strength across the distance that separated them, mother and son. "It's almost over."

Kendall's eyes darted to Melissa, then back to Amelia. "I take their eyes," she said slowly, "because…I don't know why. Because I want to."

"I don't think that's true," Amelia said. "I think you do it because you don't want them to see you. These creatures, these victims, who've come to know you. The real you. You take their eyes because you're ashamed. Because you want to hide."

Kendall didn't answer, didn't argue—only breathed hard through her nostrils, twin plumes of steam.

"But you don't have to hide *here*, do you?" Amelia looked down into the hollow where Rhiannon still stood, hands bound. Looked down at the dead eyes dangling from tree branches. "This is a place where you can be seen. Seen for who you truly are."

Amelia's gaze stayed on the hollow for a few seconds, long enough that Kendall looked too, as though seeing the place—*her* place, her secret place—for the first time.

"Everyone will see it soon," Amelia said then, and Kendall's gaze came back to her, fiery and off-kilter. Amelia stretched out her hand. She held a phone, the screen lit up. Somewhere in the distance, a siren wailed.

"They're coming, Kendall," Amelia said. "I followed Melissa and Rhiannon into the woods before they got to the house—but I've been talking to them this whole time, telling them where to find us. Telling them exactly what's happening. There's nothing you can do about it now. You could kill all four of us if you wanted to, but the world is still going to see you. See you for exactly who you are. And that's what you're afraid of, isn't it? That's what he taught you to be afraid of most."

*He.* Melissa knew she was talking about Thomas. That he was there with them in the woods, responsible in his way for the people who'd died and the danger they were in—even if he never picked up the knife, never spilled blood, never killed a soul.

The mention of him seemed to break something in Kendall. Melissa watched it in her, something new coming over the girl, starting in her eyes then bleeding downward, shifting the substance of her in a different direction.

"Everyone will see," Amelia said. "They'll see that you're a monster."

Kendall's hold on Bradley loosened, and she began to lean away from him. Began to orient herself toward Amelia instead. She gathered her energy, her rage, and then launched herself at Amelia with an unearthly shriek, the knife held out in front of her.

Wrists still bound, Melissa balled her hands into fists and punched at the ground, rocks and dirt digging into her knuckles as she pushed herself to her feet. She rushed to Bradley as he fell to the ground, his legs going limp with relief. She looped her arms around him, pulled him to herself.

"I've got you, baby," she whispered into his hair as she felt his weight against her arms. The heat of his body. Even the smell of the urine he'd let out, his bladder loosened with terror—Melissa was glad for all of it, every bit of evidence of the physical reality of him, because it meant he was alive, it meant he was safe, it meant he was still hers.

She turned around and saw Kendall on top of Amelia. Amelia had her hands on Kendall's wrists, holding the girl back as she tried to push the tip of the knife into Amelia's chest. The point of it was inches from her, Kendall seeming to have a superhuman strength in her rage. Her face red, her neck ropy with muscles and sinews. Teeth bared, spittle flying in Amelia's face.

Melissa heard a rustle, and suddenly Rhiannon was next to her. "We have to help her."

Somewhere in the distance, the sirens grew louder. In the encroaching dark, flashlights bounced in the distance, past the tangle of the undergrowth. Men's voices shouting indistinctly, coming closer.

Melissa grabbed Bradley's face between her bound hands, cradled his cheeks in her palms. "Look at me," she said. "You have to run. You have to go with Rhiannon. Go toward the light and the voices. Shout for them."

He shook his head. "I can't."

"You can. You have to be brave. Now go."

Rhiannon and Bradley ran away, disappearing through the trees. Melissa breathed a sigh of relief, but it was short-lived. Amelia and Kendall still struggled on the ground, and Amelia was starting to lose her strength. She screamed as the tip of the knife got closer, as it began to pierce the down of her jacket and press against her skin, against her rib cage. A guttural sound that started low and then broke high.

Melissa tugged her wrists apart, but the zip tie wouldn't break. She couldn't free her hands. And Amelia was running out of time.

Melissa moved fast, outrunning her ability to think or plan. She darted behind Kendall and looped her wrists around her neck, pulling her back. She didn't want to choke the girl, only get her off Amelia. First Kendall resisted, but then her weight lifted beneath Melissa. She shifted her momentum and then wasn't just coming up but actually launching herself backward, kicking her head back. Melissa saw a flash of white as Kendall's skull knocked against her forehead. Then Kendall's whole back caught Melissa's chest like a battering ram, and they were flying together.

They landed in a heap on the ground. Melissa's spine lit up with pain, and all the air went out of her. She wheezed as Kendall rolled off her, struggling to take a breath—and then Kendall was launching through the air, her face a picture of snarling rage.

By some instinct Melissa rolled to the side and got to her knees, oxygen finally filling her lungs. Kendall scrabbled up and stabbed out with the knife, making a straight line with her arm directly toward Melissa's torso.

Melissa didn't think, just moved—twisted her body, her arms, quicker and more gracefully than she thought possible. Kendall's arm shot into the loop made by her arms and her bound wrists, slicing the air all the way past her shoulder. Melissa was a needle, Kendall's arm the thread. And when Kendall was tangled all the way into her, about to withdraw her arm and stab again, Melissa pulled her wrists back with all her might. She caught Kendall's forearm in the crook made by her wrists and the zip tie, pulled it hard against her shoulder.

She heard a crack. Kendall screamed. The knife fell. Melissa let go.

"You bitch!" Kendall yelled, staggering back, cradling her wrist. "You broke my fucking arm!"

"I'm sorry," Melissa said—and she really was. She didn't want to hurt anyone.

Kendall kept on staggering backward until her back hit a tree trunk, and then she sank to the ground, sobbing.

"Oh, God!" she yelled. The bobbing flashlights were getting closer now. The shouts.

"I didn't mean to." Her voice was hoarse, weak, and looking at her, Melissa almost felt sorry for her. Almost believed her, that this was all a big mistake. "I didn't want any of this! I can't help the way I am. Oh my God, these things I've done. I didn't know how to stop, don't you see? Why didn't anyone help me?"

Amelia walked to her, sank to her haunches, put a hand on Kendall's shoulder. "It's okay," she said. "It's going to be okay."

Kendall leaned toward her, and Amelia caught her in a hug.

"I'm sorry," the girl sobbed into her shoulder. "I'm so sorry, Mom. Mom, I'm so sorry..."

Kendall's mother wasn't there to forgive her. The dead don't speak. But Amelia didn't correct her. "I know, sweetie. I know you're sorry. Just hush now. Help is coming. You hear? We're going to help you. You won't be able to hurt anyone anymore."

Melissa fell to her knees, sat back on her heels, exhausted down to her bones.

And they stayed like that, a tableau in the middle of the woods—Kendall crying, Amelia comforting her.

After a moment, Melissa stood and moved into the darkness of the trees—stumbling through the undergrowth. Pressing toward light, toward hope. Toward her son, the boy she'd die to protect.

# TRANSCRIPT OF RECORDING

**Thomas:** I can't believe you came.

**Amelia:** I'm a little surprised myself.

**Thomas:** Nobody visits me.

**Amelia:** Can you blame them?

**Thomas:** Will Rhiannon be coming anytime soon?

**Amelia:** I don't think so, Thomas. She's still pretty shaken up. Pretty angry. It might be a while. If ever.

**Thomas:** I'm certainly not going to see Kendall.

**Amelia:** No. There's no way. Two inmates from different institutions? Impossible. Only if you ever get out. I suppose that's up to the parole board.

[pause]

**Thomas:** Accessory after the fact. What a joke. Who'd have thought they'd give so many years for "accessory after the fact"?

**Amelia:** It's as bad as the actual murder, in the eyes of the law.

**Thomas:** Why are you here, anyway? You come to finish our therapy? Finally cure me? You've got your recorder and everything.

**Amelia:** No. This is for me.

**Thomas:** For you, huh?

[pause]

**Amelia:** Unfinished business. There was something I wanted to see about. To ask you, I mean.

**Thomas:** So ask.

**Amelia:** Back three years ago, when I saw you as a therapist—when you *forced* me to see you in therapy, to go through that ridiculous charade—we had a fight during one session. You remember. You attacked me, put your hands around my neck. I thought you were going to kill me.

**Thomas:** I remember.

**Amelia:** Do you remember what we were talking about, that made you so mad?

[pause]

**Amelia:** Thomas?

**Thomas:** [sighs] The definition of a psychopath.

**Amelia:** What were you really asking about that day? Were you trying to figure out if Kendall was a psychopath? Or were you worried that *you* were the psychopath?

**Thomas:** I was worried about Kendall, obviously. Even though I couldn't tell you at the time. I wanted to—God, how I wanted to. I was dying to come clean about all of it. But I couldn't, in the end. I had to protect her secret.

**Amelia:** That's what I thought you'd say. But it doesn't explain how angry you got that day. Here's what I think. I think you were afraid of Kendall after she killed Rose, wondering just how dangerous your daughter really was. But I think you were also afraid because what you saw in her—the darkness, the anger, the violence—was something you saw in *yourself.*

**Thomas:** I've never killed anyone. I've never done half the things Kendall did.

**Amelia:** Maybe not. But it was in you, I think. And maybe somewhere along the way you learned how to control it better than Kendall. To hide that part of yourself. To create your persona, the mask you put between yourself and the world. Good father, good husband, good doctor. Good *man.*

**Thomas:** It wasn't a mask. That's who I was. Who I *am.* I don't deserve any of this.

**Amelia:** But I don't think that's true, Thomas. You came to therapy for my reassurance—you came hoping I'd tell you that you were still a good person. Because you were beginning to doubt it yourself. Doubt your mask. Doubt the lie you'd been telling to the world and to yourself for years. And you needed me—needed a woman—to give you that reassurance. But we discovered something in that room together, didn't we? Something real. You may not be a full-fledged psychopath yourself. But you bear some of the signs. The aggressive charm, the manipulation, the way you pursue people. Hunt them. Make them adore you. Then turn on them. You did it with Rose. And you were going to do it with Melissa too.

**Thomas:** I loved Melissa. I did. I'd never have hurt her.

**Amelia:** No? You loved Rose too.

**Thomas:** I didn't kill her, Amelia. Everybody talks like I killed her, but I didn't.

**Amelia:** No. But there are more ways to hurt a person than just physically. And when someone *did* commit violence against her, you hid the body. You covered up what happened.

**Thomas:** I protected my daughter. Protected my family. That's who I am, Amelia. It's what I've dedicated my life to. I'm not a killer. I'm a protector.

**Amelia:** Maybe so. And you did protect Kendall. Protected yourself. But you didn't protect *Rose*, did you? You didn't protect Rhiannon—she spent the next three years afraid of her own sister, taking on the responsibility of keeping her at bay, trying to keep her from hurting others. And you certainly didn't protect Melissa or Bradley. Why did you even pursue Melissa? Why did you try so hard to make her fall for you?

**Thomas:** I didn't know Kendall was going to do it *again*, did I? She had her reasons for killing Rose—she cheated on me, for one. But I had no idea Kendall would go after Melissa too. Or her son.

**Amelia:** Rhiannon knew.

**Thomas:** But I didn't know about that either. Rhiannon didn't tell me what she was doing to keep Kendall at bay.

**Amelia:** You knew. You did. You were just in denial.

**Thomas:** None of this is my fault.

**Amelia:** But it *is* your fault, Thomas. You bear your share of the responsibility. You're an accomplice—not just to Rose's death, but to all of it. Everything that happened. And the worst part is, you made *me* complicit too. Pulling me into it. Inching up to the truth, then dancing away from it. Trying to convince me that you were good. Trying to convince *yourself*. Begging for absolution. I stayed close to you for far too long. I cared about you—still, after everything. Because there was a mystery there. Something I couldn't quite solve. But I've solved it now. There's no more mystery to you. I know who you are now, Thomas. I know everything. And I'm done.

**Thomas:** Is that why you came? To say goodbye?

**Amelia:** Maybe it is.

**Thomas:** So we're done here?

[pause]

**Amelia:** Yes, I think we are.

[rustling, chair scraping]

**Thomas:** Amelia, wait.

**Amelia:** What is it?

[pause]

[muffled crying]

**Amelia:** Thomas?

**Thomas:** Can you talk to Melissa for me? Ask her to visit? I need to see her, Amelia. To explain—this isn't my fault. I never intended for any of this.

**Amelia:** I don't think that's going to happen.

**Thomas:** But I need to know that she still loves me. That she still thinks

I'm a good man. Please, Amelia. I'll never make it in here without that. Without *her*.

[pause]

**Amelia:** Goodbye, Thomas.

—End of Recording—

# EPILOGUE

Melissa spotted Amelia sitting on a bench at the edge of the lake, with an asphalt trail sitting between her and the water's edge. It took her a moment more to find Rhiannon, wandering through some tall grasses at the place where the waves lapped at the dirt, head bowed, hands laid together and drawn up to her waist as though she held an invisible bouquet of flowers.

"I see them," Melissa whispered to Bradley as she let him out of the car, then, as he craned his neck from the parking lot, pointed them out through the trees. He darted off, and Melissa followed at a slow walk, smiling.

"Amelia!" Bradley called as he reached the park bench. Melissa smiled as Amelia made a show of being startled, jumping where she sat, putting a hand to her chest.

"Bradley!" she said breathlessly. "You little rascal. You scared me!"

Bradley giggled, and Melissa shared a smirk with Amelia as she came through the trees to the trail. She loved how her son had taken to Amelia, and she struggled, now, to imagine that she'd ever thought of the other woman as a rival, an enemy.

It had been six months since that terrible night in the woods, winter come and gone again, and so much had happened since then. The biggest things—Thomas and Kendall in prison, the media firestorm following the revelations of Rose's journal and Amelia's recordings, combined with the inescapable physical evidence against father and daughter—seemed minor in retrospect, next to the small thing that had become more important than Melissa could have ever imagined: the friendship that had grown between her and Amelia in the wake of their trauma, and the little found family that had grown between the four survivors. Melissa and Bradley, Amelia and Rhiannon. They'd saved each other's lives in turn, helped each other excavate the truths they'd feared, suspected, and known but couldn't bring themselves to say. And now they were bound together, forever.

Rhiannon was living with Amelia now—and together, both had moved from the north to the south suburbs of the Twin Cities, wanting to get away from the house and the neighborhood where Rhiannon's traumas had occurred. The girl was a legal adult now, didn't require a guardian as a matter of the law, but all the same, Amelia was talking of adopting her, making Rhiannon her daughter.

Melissa, meanwhile, had moved too, gotten a new apartment, a new accounting job. Anything to get away from the woods where she and her son had nearly died, the sight of which still gave Bradley fits of breathless panic. With Amelia's help and referrals, she'd also found a good child therapist to assist Bradley in processing everything that had happened—and another for Melissa too, a kind-eyed younger woman who'd spent the past few months gently guiding Melissa through why she'd been so drawn to Thomas in spite of her misgivings, while assuring her at every step that none of this was her fault.

Melissa and Amelia also met once a week themselves, with Bradley and Rhiannon, who'd developed their own sweet relationship: Rhiannon protecting Bradley while Bradley practically worshipped Rhiannon, almost like siblings.

"Where's Rhiannon?" Bradley asked Amelia. She pointed toward the lake, and Bradley scampered off to meet her, Rhiannon's gaze rising and a gentle smile breaking across her face. Melissa watched as Bradley ran into the arms of the girl, eighteen now, warmth spreading through her chest, even against the still-crisp April air. The winter had been long and grueling, but spring was breaking through, light streaming from above as life pressed up through the ground, turning brown to green.

Melissa basked in the moment, then turned to Amelia. "Hey," she said.

Amelia nodded. "Hey."

The two women moved toward each other, shared a brief hug. Melissa closed her eyes and accepted Amelia's kiss on one cheek, then the other—a greeting that had embarrassed Melissa months earlier, but that had come to comfort her now, a sign of Amelia's fundamental warmth and kindness beneath her sharp, intellectual exterior. There were surfaces and depths to people, Melissa had learned. Sometimes a kind exterior hid something dangerous under the surface—but it could also be the other way around, the person who seemed intimidating or aloof turning out to be the one who saved your life.

"It's good to see you," Amelia said, something fierce and urgent in her voice. Melissa understood. They had a lot to talk about.

Bradley and Rhiannon's footsteps rustled in the underbrush, and then they came onto the path, walking hand in hand toward a small playground a couple hundred yards distant.

"Shall we follow?" Melissa asked.

Amelia came next to her and looped her arm through Melissa's. Leaned against her, the warmth of their two bodies combining even through their coats.

"Slowly," Amelia said.

They walked a few steps as, ahead, the kids reached the playground, Bradley running to a set of swings, Rhiannon slowing behind him. A wind came off the small lake, chilling Melissa, then died down.

"So," she began after a silence. "You saw him."

Amelia sucked in a breath and seemed to steel herself, her arm going taut in Melissa's.

"I did."

"And?"

Amelia turned to face her. "Do you really want to know?"

"I don't know," Melissa admitted. Then, after thinking about it: "Yes."

Amelia sighed and was quiet for a few steps. Melissa knew she was thinking.

"He wanted me to tell him he was a good man," Amelia said at last. "And I think…"

She trailed off, and Melissa waited. "What?" she prodded, when the end to her friend's thought was slow to come.

"I think that's what he wanted all along," Amelia said. "When he first came to me, after Rose went missing. And again later, when he saw you at that party."

Melissa looked ahead, thinking of that moment—the moment when she'd seen him across the room, the moment when their eyes had met, the moment when she'd thought herself plucked out of all the women in the world. Chosen to be pursued, to be desired, to be loved. Knowing everything she knew now, what could that moment have possibly meant to *him*? To Thomas? What could he have been thinking?

"I still don't understand it."

"I know," Amelia said, then raised her eyes to the sky, squinted into the sun. "But I've been thinking about it. And I think that there was something inside of Thomas—something dark and cruel that he didn't like to talk about. Something he hid away deep inside and built a whole persona against. A mask, to hide this part of him. He even fooled himself, I think. But then Kendall came along, and it was a part of her too, and seeing it—it destroyed him. He needed to hide it, needed to hide *Kendall*, because it was what he'd learned to do. Conceal. Deny. And protect. Protect his family. Protect himself—his vision of himself, the false self he'd built to fool the world. That's why Rose died. And that's why he came after me next. And you."

They kept walking like that, arm in arm. Melissa felt sad in a way she couldn't quite name. The trees, bare of branches, looked harsh and jagged as they poked at the sky, and for a moment she was afraid.

"I can't believe I didn't see it," Melissa said. "I feel so stupid. To have been sucked in by him. To have put my son in danger."

"But it's not your fault, Melissa," Amelia said. She stopped, unlooped her arm from Melissa's, then grabbed her by both shoulders, turned her so they were face-to-face. Melissa resisted at first, but then looked directly into Amelia's eyes. "Listen to me. It wasn't your fault—and it wasn't even about you. Okay? It was about Thomas, all along. He wanted you and your love for his own reasons. Wanted to use you as armor, don't you see? Armor against what he really was. Armor against the terrible things he'd allowed to happen. To Rose. To Rhiannon. Even to Kendall—she's a victim here too. Because she didn't get the help she needed, when it would have done her some good."

Melissa was quiet, letting it settle in her. *None of it had been about her.* Her mind drifted, then, not to Thomas, but to Derek Gordon—another man disgraced following the revelations of Rose's journal, a cop who'd abused his position of authority to take advantage of a troubled and vulnerable woman. He'd quit the force entirely under public pressure, would never serve as a police officer again. No doubt he'd told himself that he was trying to help Rose, that he was trying to save her—later, that he was trying to get to the truth of her murder. But he was just another man using a woman to fill some part in his own story. To absolve himself of the things he'd done.

Melissa still wasn't sure what to think about Thomas, though. She didn't tell Amelia that there were times when she felt sorry for him, wondered what she'd have done in his place. Ultimately, he was only protecting his child, trying not to lose her, preserving what was left of his family after Kendall killed Rose. Melissa knew what it felt like to love a child so much you thought you'd do anything to protect them, sacrifice your own well-being to save them, even from the consequences of their own actions. If it had been her, would Melissa have sacrificed the rest of the world too? Endangered others to hide a child's crime?

She still wasn't sure—but between her uncertainty and Amelia's conviction, one thing was clear: It was time for her, for all of them, to move on.

Melissa pressed her lips together and made a little nod. Amelia squeezed her by the arms.

Gradually, Melissa became aware that they were not alone on the path; some dozens of paces ahead, a man walked with a dog, a square-jawed gray boxer nosing through the grass. The man looked at them as he passed, and something in the man's eyes made it clear that he wanted to talk to them—that he was interested in Melissa or Amelia, or both. He was handsome, but also a stranger, and Melissa felt a chill, imagining what might be behind his eyes. What this man she'd never met might be thinking of as he watched her and Amelia embracing on the path.

"Don't," Amelia said, and Melissa's eyes came back to her friend. Amelia gave her head a small shake. "Let him stare. We've got other things to think about."

Melissa nodded. She understood. Her eyes drifted past Amelia's face, over her shoulder and to the playground, where Rhiannon pushed Bradley on the swings—higher, higher, his toes pointing to the sky.

"Let's go," she said.

And together they turned and crossed the grass, went toward the young ones it had fallen to them to protect with their lives.

SHE THOUGHT SHE KNEW HER
HUSBAND. SHE WAS WRONG.

READ ON FOR AN EXCERPT OF ANDREW
DEYOUNG'S THRILLING NOVEL
*THE DAY HE NEVER CAME HOME*

# CHAPTER 1

The day before he went missing, Regan's husband bought her a lake house. A surprise, for her birthday.

She was annoyed at first. Regan had planned the day painstakingly—booked a babysitter months in advance, reserved a table for brunch at her favorite restaurant, a couples' massage at a little spa in the mall after that. Small pleasures, but Regan was looking forward to each of them in turn. She'd been so busy with the kids lately, frenzied even. Etta was four, Philip one and a half, and they both needed her so much, stretching the limits of her ability to give. The two of them had devoured every single moment of her free time, every ounce of her energy. John worked long hours, barely helped with the kids, and Regan hadn't done anything for herself in ages.

So yeah, she was a little irritated when, kid-free for the first time in what seemed like forever, John took a wrong turn, away from the brunch place, and pointed the car toward Lake Minnetonka.

"John," she said as he navigated the car down a twisting road, lakeside mansions rising up on one side of them, a grove of trees huddled thick on the other. "What the fuck?"

"Just a little detour," he said. "You'll like it. I promise."

She crossed her arms, sighing as the car reached the end of the winding lane and the Edina Realty sign came into view. This was something she and John used to do together, in the early days of their marriage—they'd go to an open house in a rich part of town, walk around some huge home pretending like they had a chance in hell of owning it, and dream together about what might be someday. But times had changed. She wasn't interested in reliving their old days. Wasn't interested in dreaming. They were in their thirties now, their *late* thirties. They had little kids. She hadn't had an uninterrupted night's sleep in months. She didn't want to waste time walking through a house they couldn't afford. She wanted French toast, a mimosa. She wanted to close her eyes and lie face down on a table while someone put their hands on her body and made her feel good.

But then, as they walked up to the house, the front door opened and a real estate agent stood inside. She knew John's name, and he knew hers: Diane. And inside there was nothing. No other people. Not even furniture.

"This isn't an open house," Regan said, looking between John and the agent, her annoyance morphing through confusion to a kind of free-falling giddiness. "What's happening?"

John's lips were pressed together. He looked like a little boy, one who had a secret he wanted to share. Bursting with it. Then his face cracked open in a smile, and God, he was beautiful when he smiled. Regan had almost forgotten. They'd both been so busy, him with work, her with the kids, that sometimes they went days, weeks even, without really noticing each other. She couldn't remember the last time she'd looked at his face. Really looked at it, and saw him looking back at her with adoration in his eyes, as he was now.

"It's ours," he said.

Regan felt dizzy. She put a hand to her chest, reached the other behind her to brace against a wall. John went to her, but she waved him away; she was fine. He stepped back, the smile gone, replaced by a look of concern.

"Do you want it?"

Regan let out an airy laugh. "Maybe I should look around a little."

They raced together from room to room, the agent making herself scarce, giving them privacy. The house was huge, three stories, built into a hill sloping down to the lake. A broad deck past the kitchen and dining room on the main floor, and a walkout from the bottom level to the dock and an empty boat lift at the water's edge.

"But how?" Regan asked, once she'd seen it all.

"I started looking a couple months ago," John said. "I wanted it to be a surprise, for your birthday. Wanted to time it just right. I did everything—made the offer, set up the financing, scheduled the appraisal and the inspection. We close in an hour."

"No, not that, I mean—*how?* How could we, I mean… You know, can we really—"

"We can," John said. "It's been a good year, Regan. A great year. I didn't want to say anything at first, in case things went bad, but they haven't—it's been two really good quarters now, and it doesn't look like it's a fluke. I've doubled my client base, doubled my revenue. I've been making some good picks recently, and a lot of people want in. Everything I invest in goes up."

Benevolence flooded Regan's body. All the late nights, the dinnertimes he'd spent on the phone, ignoring her while she struggled with the kids, sleeping obliviously through Philip's midnight wakings, missing playdates, working weekends. At the time these things had enraged her, made her feel abandoned, but it was all forgiven, now—now that she knew what it had been for. She loved him, at this moment, for working so hard, for being so good at his job. He'd made a future for them.

John looked down, swallowed hard, pulled at the back of his

neck. "I just thought, you know, you've been so busy. With the kids. I know you don't think I notice, but I do. I notice. I see everything you do. How hard it all is on you. But you're so good, Regan. You're such a good mom, and a good wife, and you deserve this. It'll be your name on the deed, not mine, because I'm thinking of it as *your* house, *your* place—a place you can go when you need to get away. Leave the kids with me, or your folks, and just…relax."

His voice was full with emotion, and now Regan was crying. She threw her arms around John's neck. He laughed into her hair and clutched her to him—and here was something else she'd forgotten. The feel of his body against hers, his breath blowing hot in the crook of her neck.

At the closing Regan was still too stunned to follow all the details of the documents that passed on the table before her. But still she signed every time the closer asked her to, a flurry of signatures and dates and initials, her handwriting becoming wilder, more shaking and swooping, on every dotted line. And then she was done, the house was hers, and they were driving back, walking through the rooms once more, running their hands over the walls. In a closet they found a left-behind duvet with its cover still on, and like a couple of horny teenagers they brought it to the living room, stripped down to nothing, pulled the duvet over their naked bodies, and made love right there on the carpet.

Afterward, Regan rolled off John and walked out onto the deck, the duvet draped around her shoulders. The cold fall air pricked at her calves, tugged goose bumps to the surface of her skin. She looked out at the lake, listened to the waves lapping lightly at the shore, reflecting on the fact that this, too, was hers now: this view, these sounds. This was something that could be bought. This happiness. This peace of mind. Her stomach rumbled—they'd never gone to brunch—but she didn't care. In every way that mattered, she was full.

John padded up beside her a few seconds later, in his boxer briefs and a T-shirt.

"Think the neighbors can see us?"

Regan looked to the right and the left. They were shielded on each side by trees.

"I don't think so," she said. "We could fuck out here if you wanted to go again."

John laughed. "What's come over you?" he said, then grabbed at her through the duvet, put his hand on her hip, and pulled her close. "I like it."

She leaned into him. "I like my present is all," she said. "Thank you."

He draped an arm around her, and they stood like that for a while. Regan's eyes wandered down to the dock, where the sellers had left something else behind: a little wooden boat lashed to a post, bobbing on the waves. The back-and-forth motion soothed her, and she simply watched it for a while, setting her cheek against her husband's chest. He was a good man, all things considered. Not perfect by any means, and they'd been through their share of storms—the early money troubles, the issues with her family, the strain of caring for the kids. But they'd weathered them all, went on bobbing on the surface through every swell, like that little boat at the dock. Somehow they'd found their way, together, to a safe harbor.

It was a nice thought, a perfect crystalline moment. Then John spoke, and almost ruined it.

"I have to head into the office tonight," he said. "I might be home late. I hope that's not a problem."

Regan struggled for a moment with a surge of annoyance. He was always doing this, springing things on her, using work as a blanket excuse to leave her with Etta and Philip. John at the office meant that she'd have to feed and put both kids to bed that evening, that she'd have to do it alone, that she'd go to bed stressed and exhausted and be woken up by John hours later, when he crawled into bed sometime after midnight. *I hope that's not a problem*, he'd always say, seeming not to know or perhaps not to care that his sudden absences *were* a problem, every time. She felt herself about to snap at him, felt it rising up inside her like a reflex, until she remembered where she was standing, what had happened today, and her anger sank down as quickly as it had risen, like a pot of boiling water removed from a flame.

"It's fine," she said placidly.

"Is it really? Or does *fine* mean you're angry?"

"It's really fine," she said again, and was surprised to realize that she meant it. John's work took him away from her and the kids too often, left her with far more than her fair share of the parenting—but also, John's work had made *this* possible, had brought in enough money that this house now belonged to them, to *her*. Maybe this was the trade-off, and maybe it was even a payment of sorts, a reward: in exchange for everything she'd done for their family, for giving up her own career to parent two small humans, for all the times she'd agreed to look the other way—a house.

Regan closed her eyes and set her cheek once more on John's solid chest, felt it rise and fall with his breathing. At that moment, she felt no regret, no resentment, as she thought about the choices and compromises that had led her to this.

It had all been worth it.

# ACKNOWLEDGMENTS

Thank you to my editor, Deb Werksman, who was an integral part of the development of this book from the moment I first got the idea for it and who was extremely patient with me as I felt my way through the story. As ever, I also received a ton of support from the whole Poisoned Pen crew, including Jocelyn Travis, Emily Engwall, and Mandy Chahal.

Thank you also to my agent, Kate Garrick, for all the ways you advocate for me and for the wisdom and calm you bring to every situation!

I'm incredibly grateful for my growing community of fellow crime writers, especially the Minnesota contingent—you know who you are!

I owe some sort of acknowledgment to my neighbors in the northern suburbs of the Twin Cities, where I've set this book. What I've called "Lake Julia" here is actually a fictional amalgam of Lake Johanna and Lake Josephine, and the wooded area behind Melissa's home is a stand-in for any number of regional parks and wild areas we enjoy up here. This part of Minnesota is just as beautiful as it is in the book—though quite a bit less treacherous in reality. I appreciate the indulgence of my community in allowing me to use our neighborhoods as a setting for my imagination to run wild.

And thank you, finally and most importantly, to my family—my parents, my siblings, my children, but especially my wife, Sarah, who is kinder, more patient, and more supportive than I could have possibly asked for. I'm so lucky to have you.

# ABOUT THE AUTHOR

Andrew DeYoung is the author of *The Day He Never Came Home*, his first domestic thriller, and *The Temps*, a speculative novel about the end of the world. He works as an editor at a children's book publishing company, and he lives with his wife and two children in the Twin Cities area in Minnesota.